END OF DAYS –

A NEW CURTAIN OPENS

By Richard P. Matthews

Revitalizing Ministries
Hill, New Hampshire

PUBLISHED BY REVITALIZING MINISTRIES
Copyright © 2013 by Richard P. Matthews

This book is a work of fiction. Names, characters, businesses, organizations, places, events, and incidents either are the product of the author's imagination or are used fictitiously. Any resemblance to actual persons, living or dead, or events, is entirely coincidental.

Most Bible translations quoted here are taken from THE MESSAGE, Copyright, 2002, and used by permission of NavPress Publishing Group. All others are translations of the author.

Published in the United States by Revitalizing Ministries, Hill, New Hampshire.
www.RevitalizingMinistries.com
The portrayal of the embossed leaf with Revitalizing Ministries is a registered trademark of Revitalizing Ministries.

Library of Congress Control Number: 2007932585
Cataloging Data.
Matthews, Richard P.
A New Curtain Opens/Richard P. Matthews.—1st ed.
p. cm.
1. A New Curtain Opens—Fiction. 2. Inspirational 3. Body-mind-spirit-earth 4. Conservation. 5. Poaching. 6. Meditation. 7. Spirituality
I. Title. II. Matthews, Richard P.

ISBN 978-0-9798106-4-0

PRINTED IN THE UNITED STATES OF AMERICA

1 0   8   6   4   2   1   3   5   7   9

First Edition

Acclaim

Finally, what most animal lovers are already aware of is now in print. In *A New Curtain Opens*, the animals are connected to the presence of the 'Great I Am' within them. Now, He is going to protect them, while we continue to destroy the planet and ourselves. Hayah, the superhero in this story, is helping the animals to awaken us. As in all species, wild and domestic, we see elephants rejoice in His presence; we see mountain gorillas heal themselves; we watch Rhinos find peace in the midst of a conflict; and we witness the tigers finding harmony with the new Ranger team. Because of the animals, there is still Hope. Read this book and discover it for yourself. (Mariann Andersson, The Swedish Animal Whisperer)

A New Curtain Opens is a book intended to help the reader connect to the 'Great I Am' at the center of one's being, instead of a more intellectual idea of enlightenment. The main focus of the book, told through allegory, is how we can learn from the animals, who are more connected spiritually than we are. I found it a very interesting read! Bekah J, motherhood-moment.blogspot.com

A New Curtain Opens discusses enlightenment and advocates an intriguing concept: that animals are connected and protected, and are trying to help humans connect to that enlightened state. Chapters discuss the end of an old path and a completely new way of living, revealing how individuals can connect to the greatness already within them. It's about visions and end days, new beginnings, and the notion that enlightenment possibilities exist within everyone - even (perhaps especially) creatures that walk among us. Accounts of journeys both physical and spiritual in search of these paths makes for an intriguing blend of new age, travelogue, and spiritual reflection that will appeal to any interested in new age thought. "California Bookwatch"

CONTENTS

CHAPTER 1
The City

I am going to reveal to you the most carefully guarded secret since the beginning of time. How can you connect to the 'Great I Am' within you?

A new curtain is opening to you. Forget mythology and theology. Abandon your search of the cosmic heavens for some Divine power. Awaken to the fact that there is no higher intellectual power. Shut down your chattering mind and swollen ego. Stop, and listen to the silence within you. Listen, for in that silence you will find the 'Great I Am' within you. That is step one!

My name is Hoss Proxetter. I am just another nobody trying to live off the grid, a family tradition since 1399. That said, my father was from Wales and a descendent from the House of Plantagenet and my Great-grandfather (many removed) became a highwayman to pester the crown and noble houses, a kind of fifteenth century "Robin Hood." I don't have any of those leanings, but the qualities of honesty, fairness and equality seem to be in my blood. Add to this, that on my mother's side, my Great-Grandmother (many removed) was a full-blooded Massachusett Indian and you have a very interesting gene pool. All the members of my family are dead now, so you might say that my line stops here. I have no desire to be wealthy. I have all I need, and I don't want more. Fame is a joke to me. By today's worldly standards, all the people we call famous, we will forget in the next two decades, except maybe Marilyn Monroe. The point is if you try to Google Hoss Proxetter you won't have any hits, and I like it that way.

This is a story about the past, the eternal present

(where the past and future come together) and things yet to come. In the present moment, we are all we have been and all we will be. We cannot change our past, and we cannot become anything we aren't right now.

I pause, thinking how deep that is, maybe too deep. Then I hear the voice of the 'Great I Am' within me, "It's fine. You write what I give you!" I think better about arguing the point. However, you will discover that is not always the case.

This morning I had a vision. I was taken to a magical place and saw wondrous things. I sense it is about things to come in some future time, an evolution from now.

I am in another world or another dimension of this world. It is technologically much more advanced. The first things I notice are the vehicles. They are of every design imaginable and no two are alike. Some are sleek and racy. Some are round or bulbous. Some are cubed and angular. It is as if aerodynamics doesn't matter. They glide quickly and smoothly on their wheels that look more like gyroscopes than tiers. Then I stop abruptly, frozen in my footsteps. Something is so different it is haunting me. I question what it is. Slowly all my senses becomes extremely acute. I search for the difference. What can it be? It is like a visual meditation. I close my eyes and bathe in the silence. Suddenly it hits me; the people are driving vehicles that make no sound. I open my eyes and clap my hands to make sure I haven't gone deaf. The sound is so loud it makes me flinch and a driver pulls over to ask if I need help.

"I'm fine," I say. "But tell me what kind of motor do you have in that thing?"

"Motor?" the driver, a caring woman, asks.

"You know; the thing that makes your vehicle go," I say with a condescending tone.

"I know what a motor is; I used to build them. But we don't use those anymore."

I try to recover, "Please excuse my rudeness. I'm in a state of shock, because the vehicles make no sound. What makes them go?"

She laughs, "I do, silly!"

I can't imagine what the expression is on my face, because I'm feeling confusion, stupidity, embarrassment and totally out of my element all rolled together. Here is a kind woman sizing me up and who knows what bizarre conclusions she is experiencing. I stand there dumfounded.

She must be able to read my dilemma, because she takes pity on me. She opens the door and says, "Thank you for thinking I'm a kind woman... In this city, we can propel our selves using the energy of our inner spirit. Those outside the city still have to use motors."

The inside of her vehicle is simple but elegant. The dashboard has several digital instruments and sensor readouts. There is still a steering wheel even though the front gyro-wheels do not seem to turn. I imagine that its purpose is to tilt the gyros to change directions. Then I notice that there is still a pedal on the floor. I find that odd, so I ask, "What's the pedal for?"

"That's the brake pedal. It's still easier and safer to stop the vehicle with brakes than reverse the power in your center. Besides, the negative power doesn't feel that good, although, some use it just for the rush. They say it makes the positive power feel even stronger."

I stand there in amazement, watch her close her door and drive away smiling. I recover enough to wave goodbye.

The next thing I know, I'm watching a flock of bicycles go by. They are almost as fast as the vehicles.

Their wheels are also like gyroscopes, and the handlebars don't turn, but tilt the gyro and turn the bike. What a marvelous invention. Then I realize the riders are not pedaling. In fact, there are no pedals, only foot rests. As I watch the bicycles fly by, I begin to put one of these bikes on my wish list along with the ability to harness my inner power. Just as my imagination is about to carry me away; a herd of skateboards zooms past me on my other side.

I jump from their extreme motion and the whirling wake of air they leave behind. The kids riding them are bobbing and weaving while playing with each other. Their laughter and joy shatter the silence and bring smiles to the faces of the bike riders as they sail by them. The skateboards have no wheels and literally skate on the air. One skater flies past being chased by another kid. The skater goes faster and faster, but the kid chasing him is closing the gap. Suddenly the skater shoots up in the air and does a loop-de-loop, coming down behind the other kid. The kid looks back and the two collide. The two skateboards crash to the ground and the kids fly head over heels up in the air both screaming and laughing.

I cringe, hold my breath and wait for their bodies to hit the ground.

They come down fast tumbling and turning. About half a meter before they hit, they level out and stop in midair. They stretch out their hands and feet, stand up, pick up their skateboards, flip them onto the air, step on and fly away laughing.

I stand there in total amazement. When I look around at the expressions on everyone else's face, I see joy and tranquility, as if nothing can harm these children. What a gift; a place where children are truly safe. In fact, I begin to sense a feeling of harmony in everything I am seeing.

I continue to walk and find myself on a walking path. I set my usual brisk pace of about seven kilometers an hour. After a few minutes, an older man buzzes past me walking faster than I can run. Then a woman passes me at even a greater pace. I watch them carefully. They are definitely walking. Their stride is quick and even and appears to be effortless and casual. Then three more people pass me at even a brisker pace. I begin to wonder what speeds they can reach if they are running. Is this due to their level of fitness or is there something else at work here? Can the energy of their inner spirit be maximizing the efficiency of their muscles, blood flow and breathing as well? Where am I? Suddenly, I realize that all my questions answer themselves. Again, the feeling of wonder fills me.

As I continue down the walking path, I begin to notice people's clothes. The most prominent garment, I will save until last. Everyone wears a close fitting garment that moves like a second skin. It is slightly shiny and appears to be silken. There are many solid colors and many multi-colors. Over this, they decorate their bodies in many ways. There is no sense that there is any dominant design element. Each garment appears to be an expression of the individual wearing it. These outer layers are everything from fishnet tunics, to flowing gossamer-like bands of fabric that flap behind them like wings, to a simple wrap of a heavy fabric about the waist, to elaborate wraps of rich fabric with many tucks and ties, and everything in between. The foot covering is unlike anything I've ever seen, while functional and fashionable at the same time. It too seems to be an expression of each individual. Finally, I must tell you about the hats. Most everyone wears some kind of hat. Each hat is an expression of the wearer's mood, and it changes as their mood changes. If they are meditating or quiet, the hat is more simple and subdued. If they are having a heated discussion, each hat animates the wearer's point of view. If they are playing and laughing, the hat becomes electric and flashy. If they are connected to the 'Great I Am' within them, the hat becomes majestic, sometimes displaying many crowns, sometimes spires of light, or even an aura. This seems to be a regular state, because everybody is wearing the majestic hat at one time or another. I have never seen anything like it.

Moments later, I'm standing on a hill overlooking the walking path. The glistening tall buildings look like spires of crystal growing out of the landscape. They are so clear you can make out every detail of the people working or living there. The foundations are gold and set with every precious gem imaginable. The color of the gold and gems radiates up through the crystal giving it an ever-changing hue. The whole city is shimmering with light, but the source of the light is not the sun or moon. The light is emanating from within the city, from within the people. The closer I look and examine the buildings in every detail; I begin to realize human hands are not building them. After a while, I begin to sense that something is missing. For the life of me, I can't see what it is. For this city has everything that one can humanly need. Then it hits me, there is no place of worship, no temple, church, synagogue, mosque, shrine or any other place of worship. I can see people meditating at their places of work, in the schools, in their homes, in parks, on the street and everywhere else you can imagine. It becomes obvious to me that they are the temples for the 'Great I Am' is within each one of them.

Even the birds and animals share in this magnificent place. The strange thing is that they seem to be more natural and at home than do the humans. Most of their behavior is normal. The crows still play their game, "One crow too many in a tree," where the tree is full of crows, each with a perch, except for one. The one flies to the top of the tree and forces the one perching there to move down. Thus, they all squawk and crow while changing perches and moving down like dominos. Finally, there is one crow without a perch and it starts all over again. The dogs still chase the cats, but with a little more play on the part of the dog and a lot more mischief on the part of the cat. They still have all the food they need. The exceptions from the norm are few. They have absolutely no fear of humans or each other. Humans can finally understand the animal languages and enjoy listening to what they have to say. Most importantly, the lion learns to eat grass and graze with the lamb and gazelle.

CHAPTER 2
Their Lives

Still in my vision, my eye shifts away from the city and animals when I see two riders on horseback. The horses are magnificent. One is a Palomino Quarter Horse. The other is a gray Andalusian. The riders are using working Western saddles and training the horses in five gaits: walk, trot, canter, gallop and pace. It is beautiful to watch, with both rider and horse performing in perfect harmony. Each gait is clean and natural. However, there is something very strange. The riders are dressed in traditional western work clothes, unlike all the other people. Their clothes are western in every detail from the hat to the boots, and one of them even has an oiled slicker great coat. All of this underscores the freedom of spirit with which these people live. As they ride up a country lane, my attention shifts to farmers working their fields.

The tractor is bigger than anything I've ever seen. Yet, like the vehicles, it has no engine and there is no engine housing in the front of the tractor. It takes the internal energy of three people to power this machine. The cab is wide enough to accommodate three people comfortably. The center person drives the tractor. The other two control the different functions of the machine. The wheels of the tractor look like normal tractor wheels. However, there is a huge gyroscope above and behind the cab, with many smaller gyroscopes at different locations on the machine. The tractor is pulling three sections: a twenty-blade plow, a three-stage harrow and a seed-sowing device. Inside the cab, the driver uses a standard steering wheel, a few controls on a light panel and a brake pedal. The operators on either side have a complex light-panel with touch controls. Their hands are moving constantly over the lights of the panels and their touch is so delicate the operation looks very magical. After a few minutes, I can feel that they are functioning as a well-coordinated team. All three team members work in perfect harmony with each other. Like the vehicles earlier, there is very little sound. I can only hear a faint rhythmic hum of the many moving parts.

Obviously, the machine that does the harvesting also plows the field with deep furrows. This machine moves quickly across those furrows plowing for a second time; the harrow then breaks up the clods, coarsely raking, leveling and fine raking; finally, it plants the seeds. The machine does this in one pass. In ten minutes, the team can plant a half acre of land. I can only stand in wonder and remember my own labor and hardships of working on a farm as a boy.

Outside the city, I can see a complex of large geometric domes. These fascinate me. I decide to move in that direction. I do a couple of yoga stretches to prepare for the trek. As I straighten up and breathe out, I find that I'm already standing in the middle of the dome complex. To my surprise, they are not manmade either. Like the crystal buildings of the city, they seem to be growing out of the earth. They are made of hexagonal shapes that look like giant translucent fish scales growing together to form the dome. I open a door and go inside one of the domes. The light is soft but bright, a perfect light to work in, and strangely it is all natural light emanating from the hexagon scales.

To my surprise, the domes are factories. This one is building the vehicles like the ones I saw earlier. The whole factory is a center of bustling activity. All the people are working in teams at specialized workstations. It is a very different kind of assembly line. There is one person moving each vehicle from station to station and participating in the work at each station. I learn that this person is the eventual owner of the vehicle. Yes, you actually design and build your own vehicle and that is why they are all different.

At each station, the owner shares the design with the team, and they all go to work to create their part of the vehicle. There is no machinery involved in doing this. The vehicle is put on a special stand. Then at a series of light-top workbenches, the team and owner create each of the parts for that station. Their hands move rhythmically and together in a coordinated pattern, with fingers gently touching or stroking the lighted panel on the workbench. The part magically takes shape under their hands, and they carry it to the next workbench. When they all finish the parts for that station, the owner and team carry them over to the vehicle and set them in place. Then they all place their hands on the vehicle, and in a flash of light they fasten as a permanent part of the vehicle. Once they finish, the owner moves the vehicle on to the next station.

When I look ahead, I see the gyroscope wheel station. When I first arrived in the city, I had a feeling that the gyroscope wheels were the biggest secret of these vehicles. "Oh, I have to see that," I say, and instantly there I am overlooking the gyroscope station. The owner and team go through a similar routine to create all the parts and assemble them. There is an outer wheel made of a rubberlike substance that seems to be growing organically on its rim. Inside this wheel are suspended seven other wheels each within the other. They build four of these to fit this vehicle. When they are complete, they assemble them in place on the vehicle. To make them fast, they use the same laying on of hands and a flash of light.

Now, the owner steps forward and closes her eyes. After a moment, I can see beams of light dancing on her head. She opens her eyes, walks to each wheel and touches it with her index finger. The inner wheels spring into motion, and I see the vehicle stand up and come to life.

As I walk out of the dome, I truly believe that these people can do anything. While passing a grocery store, I become curious and decide to go in and check it out. I expect to see the shelves full of organic products, but there are no signs indicating such. I expect to see a limited amount of processed food, but that section is as vast as any supermarket I've seen. I expect to see a small international section, but each culture has everything to offer. Not being a junk food addict, I want to see on which junk food these people are hooked. All I can find are some corn nachos in the Mexican section. There are no potato chips or snack food of any kind. Checking out all the isles, I find practically every food a person can need. The only things missing are all the brands. When I reach the produce section, I stop in my tracks and my mouth falls open. It takes up almost half the store, and this is where most of the people are shopping. That's when I hear a voice behind me.

"Hoss, you should walk through the produce and check it out."

I turn to see the woman from earlier. "Hi, but I'm afraid you have me at a disadvantage. I don't know your name. How do you know my name?"

She holds out her hand, "I'm Alice. Everyone here knows who you are. We all knew about your visit."

"That's strange. I didn't know I was coming until I arrived." We both laugh.

We walk slowly through the produce section, smelling this and testing that. Everything is at its peak of perfection. Alice takes a bunch of sorrel. I ask, "What's that. How do you use it?"

"It is a sour grass. I put it in my black bean soup. It gives it real character."

I comment, "It surprises me that none of the food here is marked organic."

"That's because it's all organic," Alice clarifies.

As we pass the strawberries, I pick up a half liter to smell them.

Alice encourages me, "Taste one. They expect it."

With a big grin on my face, I take one and sink my teeth into it. The taste sensation is out of this world. It is juicy and sweet with a strong strawberry flavor. "Oh, my, this is the best strawberry ever!"

"Take a liter for your journey," Alice says.

She doesn't have to ask twice. Although I begin to wonder how I'm going to pay for them.

As we approach the checkout, I see a man loading his groceries into four cloth shopping bags. When he finishes, he walks out without paying.

"Look at that," I say to Alice, while pointing at the man. "He is walking out without paying!"

Alice begins to laugh, but I can't see the humor in it. She says, "We don't have to pay for things. There is no need for money here. We all work and do what we love to do, and we all share equally with everything we need from the bounty the 'Great I Am' gives us."

"You're kidding!"

"Do you need anything else for your journey?"

"This will be perfect," I say holding up the strawberries. "Thank you very much."

"Don't thank me. You know who to thank."

"Yes I do," I say putting my hand over my heart.

As we walk out the door, Alice leads me to a park with many people milling about. I see a woman leading a yoga class, but many in the class look ill. Without my asking, Alice says, "She is one of our doctors here. She uses yoga to help unblock the natural healing power of the body. Can you say how old the woman is on the far side over there?"

The woman looks to have prematurely white hair. Her body is shapely and well trained. Her face glows as she does the routine. "She is in her late forties early fifties, but that is probably too high."

"She's one of the oldest pupils. She is eighty-seven. Most of the others will soon look like that too."

"Much of what I see here borders on miraculous."

"I know, but that's the way it is here."

I look up and see another teacher coming down the path toward us, with a flock of students around him. Alice and I step out of their way. I can hear that they are deeply engrossed in a discussion as they pass. I ask, "What are they discussing, philosophy?"

"Oh no, the human species is no longer preoccupied with rational thought; we are now connecting with the creative experiences in our right brain and can utilize our brains to their fullest capacity. That professor is teaching his pupils how to problem solve."

"So he is teaching them math?"

"In some ways yes, but not the way you think. If you write on a surface the abstract number 2 with the plus sign and another 2 followed by an equal sign the abstract solution is 4. However, that is not the correct solution in reality."

I'm quick to respond, "I know it is five."

Alice comes back, "Try six. If you have two real

objects on your right and two real objects on your left, how many objects are present? Since you are present, that makes five. But since the 'Great I Am' is within you, that makes six. And believe me the 'Great I Am' prefers to be called an object than to be left out of the equation."

I laugh, "Actually He finds it kind of fun!"

Alice joins me in laughter, "Yes She does! But that is just one of the problems the professor is solving. For example, How do we learn to listen to what a person is saying, really listen without reacting or judging, listening until we understand exactly what they say and what they mean? How do we become tolerant of each other's experiences and perceptions, learning from the differences and embracing the similarities? Look at the two men over there on the park stools. Their discussion is passionate without anger and division."

The two men are sitting on the park stools facing each other, with their knees less than twenty centimeters apart. Their gestures are highly animated. Their voices are loud and passionate, without shouting. The energy flowing from them is extremely powerful. Alice and I step closer to listen to their conversation. After a few minutes, I catch the gist of their discussion. They are talking about the 'Great I Am' within them. One man describes his discovery as part of his observer mind. As he embraces the vastness of the space within him, he sees the 'Great I Am' moving and working within that space. The other man describes his encounter as part of his meditation. As he shuts down his mind and ego by focusing on his breathing, he reaches a level of absolute nothingness and peaceful darkness. Then out of the nothingness comes a powerful Light, which fills the darkness with absolutely everything and a dynamic Love. That Light and Love fill him and speak to him. Each man listens carefully, often repeating back what the other says to clarify it. They are each experiencing the 'Great I Am' in two very different ways. It is the same 'Great I Am' they are embracing, and by learning from each other, they have a more holistic view of the 'Great I Am'. It is so powerful; I want to learn how to do this.

Alice breaks the silence between us, "No Hoss, you cannot take the class. You are on your journey."

"OK, Alice, but I have one last question before I continue my journey. I notice that the sun shines most of the time here, and almost everyone seems to enjoy it. So why does that man walking over there have a dark cloud over his head, which rains on him every now and then?"

"Some people enjoy rain more than the rest of us. So why shouldn't they have what they want?"

"Fair enough Alice. Thank you for all your help."

We hug as if we have known each other for an eternity.

Alice whispers in my ear, "Only you can do this Hoss!"

I don't have a clue as to what she means by that, or why she is in my vision.

CHAPTER 3
The Journey

I head into the wilderness and begin to feel more energized as I eat the strawberries and move quickly up the path between the large trees. It seems that with each step, I grow stronger and faster. The forest becomes tighter and the trees older. All the creatures are communicating with me and keeping me on track. Every tree and bush is assisting me. The energy of the city is far behind me now, and my focus on the journey intensifies. Soon I'm flying through the trees from branch to branch. I feel like Tarzan, and his call rings inside my head. The forest canopy is my playground. My body seems to know the way. I'm going up, higher and higher. Suddenly the forest canopy peters out, and I find myself back on the ground fighting my way through scrub and scree. Then just as quickly as the scrub and scree field starts, it ends. A cliff and a rounded domed mountain loom over me. I begin to look for a way up or around the cliff.

Upon closer examination of the cliff and mountain, I see that it is nothing more than a pile of junk. There are large blocks of compacted trash, made up of old bicycles, metal sinks, bathtubs and baby carriages; all stacked neatly to form the cliff wall. The huge scree field is bits of porcelain sinks and toilets, floating on a bed of Styrofoam cups, boxes and packing materials. No matter which direction I look in, that is all I can see. The debris left behind by some lost civilization or on the edge of a great-civilized world. I can't tell which.

What am I doing here? There must be some purpose! I stop and listen to the stillness. My mind is racing a mile a minute. It is telling me, "Examine the trash more closely. One civilization's trash is an archeologist's treasure. There is no end to the information you can learn from a broken bit of toilet porcelain." That is it! My mind is full of .... All my knowledge doesn't amount to a speck of crap on a bit of toilet porcelain. Then my ego starts in, "You're too good for this. Go back to the forest and enjoy your life. There is nothing here for you." I know I have to shut these voices down.

I start to focus on my breathing. It takes several minutes to stop the chatter in my head. Finally, the stillness and silence engulfs me. My body relaxes. I embrace the space within me and the space around me. None of this is real. The only reality is my inner peace, my rhythmic breathing. Then in the darkness of my mind, I see a constellation of stars form and shine brightly. Out of the constellation, I hear a voice.

"You must try to become the first ape to be human. You must find the way. My purpose for you is to become human." The constellation begins to fade.

I shout after it, "How am I going to find it?"

The voice is distant now, "You must find the way." The constellation is dim, but it stays within me.

I open my eyes and see other apes standing around me, watching me. They all have numbers pinned to their clothes. I look down at my shirt and see the number "84 Nobody" pinned to it.

Close to where I sit, there stands a large gray haired ape, who is looking me over closely. When our eyes meet, he looks away and begins to pick lice out of the hair of his mate and eat them. His tag reads, "33 Professor of Knowledge and Wisdom Literature."

His mate keeps staring at me as if she wants to stare me down. Her tag reads, "34 Doctor of Medical Science."

I smile and she looks at the ground.

To my left stands a tall thin ape, who keeps playing with his fingers. For some reason, he cannot look at me. His eyes are fixed on a nearly broken off toilet handle. His tag reads, "61 Technological Leader." Next to him stands the fattest ape I have ever seen.

She also has the strangest tic I have ever seen. She taps the top of her head three times with her middle finger. Next, she pulls her right earlobe twice. Finally, she puts the tip of her thumb in her mouth with her palm down. After a few seconds, she repeats the routine. Her tag reads, "57 Communications Guru." She never looks at me.

I stand up and turn to walk away. There, several meters away, are a group of male and female apes each walking in their own little circle and mumbling while they read from a little book. Their costumes range from pretentiously ornate to extremely plain. They pay no attention to each other or anyone else. I can see that their tags range from 77 to 83 and read simply, "Cleric."

Between all these apes, not one speaks to me. I look down at my number 84, the last in the line of those sent over the last ten thousand years. I realize the failure of all these apes. Why are they failing? What can I do that they can't? All I know is that I have to get out of this dump.

I climb to the top of the porcelain scree field and make my way along the base of the cliff wall of trash cubes. It seems to go on forever, but finally I begin to see thicker and greener scrub. I can't express my elation when I come to a real rock wall and real soil on the ground. I kneel down just to smell the soil.

I continue. The scrub is a rich healthy green now. After another hundred meters, I come to a large setback in the rock face about ten meters wide and five meters deep.

In the back wall of the setback, there is a narrow crevice about a meter wide at the bottom and growing slightly wider at the top. On the right side of the crevice, an overhang goes deep into the rock and looks to be about eight meters wide and one high. Between the overhang and the stone slab below, there is an old metal structure with large nuts and bolts as big as my body. I study the rock face above and can see old stress cracks, with some minor new stress cracks shooting off the ends in different directions. When I study the metal structure and tap it with a stone, I can hear that it is weakening. No way is it safe to climb this chimney with the rock in such a weakened state. If this structure gives way the whole face will give way, and I can fall to my death. Maybe I can test the structure.

I look around for a large stone to throw at the metal structure. There are many stones. I pick up the largest I can lift and walk over to the first metal pillar. I remember the woman making her own vehicle when she reached inside herself and focused all her inner energy on setting the gyro wheels in motion. I need to do that now. As I focus on my inner energy, I begin to see an image of the gap between the overhang and the stone slab full of stones. I drop the stone.

That is the best idea yet. If I fill the gap and then test the structure, it is a win-win scenario. If the structure collapses, it has nowhere to go. I go to work to fill the gap. By the time I finish, I use every stone nearby, plus I find a large steel rod with which I can test the structure. This often happens to me, and I simply say, "Thank you," and continue.

I pick up one end of the heavy steel rod and stand in front of the pillar. I center myself and reach for all the inner energy He can give me. Suddenly, I pluck the rod off the ground, swing it around my head and down against the first pillar. The rod sticks to the pillar with a flash of light. The pillar becomes liquid with a white light running through it and with intense heat. The rocks next to it turn to liquid. And so on, until all the pillars and rocks liquefy. When the white light fades, everything is one solid mass, metal and rocks together. As the light comes back into the tip of my rod, it falls from the side of the new wall. I let go of the rod and it rolls down the hill. Still looking at the massive formation, I say, "Now that should confound the archeologists, not to mention that magical rod." I turn and look down the hill, "Oops! I hope the apes don't find that."

From deep within me, I hear His voice, "Don't worry, the magic is not in the rod! But you will never convince them of that."

All I have to do now is climb the chimney. "All?" I say as I look up, "You're kidding!" This is one tall chimney. It disappears into a cloud far above. I have no idea how high it is or what the size of the crevice is at the top. It will be like climbing into an abyss without protection. I sense that my mind and ego are about to do a number on me, so I focus on what needs to be done. I step into the chimney and stand in position to start chimneying. I find myself saying, "OK, You're my protection." I put my back against one wall and one foot on the opposite wall and push. My other foot is now free to move, and I bring it up under my butt. I put the palm of one hand on the wall next to my hip and the other hand on the opposite wall about the same height. Pushing up with my arms and pushing up with my legs, I slide my butt up the wall about twenty centimeters. Alternately, I put one arm straight out from the shoulder and let the forearm and hand dangle at right angles with my palm against the wall. The other hand I put on the opposite wall about shoulder height. Now I can put the lower foot on the opposite wall and move the upper foot up a few centimeters. Then by putting my lower foot back under my butt, I can pull up with my arms and push up with my legs. By repeating this routine, I'm off the ground about a meter in the first minute. To rest, I put both feet on the opposite wall to keep my body in a jam position in the chimney. When I do rest, it is only about two minutes so my muscles cannot cool down. It takes many hours before I reach the cloud.

In the cloud, I can only see about a meter up or down. I can barely see the wall where I'm at that moment. Soon time or distance, be it vertical or horizontal, both becomes irrelevant. I'm fulfilling the purpose the 'Great I Am' has for me in each move that I make. Suddenly, all eternity is right here in the present moment. I feel an incredible energy in my body. There seems to be a ball of light around me. From that point, I have no idea how long I'm climbing or how high. I just keep chimneying. Whenever, whatever, however, the top finally appears and becomes part of my present.

I keep climbing until my lower back is above the rim. I put both feet on the wall opposite jamming my pelvis into the other wall. Now I can put the palms of both hands on the edge of the rim and push up. Slowly, I'm able to slide my butt up onto the rim and lie back.

It feels like I'm lying in the palm of a great hand. Then it feels like my heart is in the hand of the 'Great I Am'. I cross into this world, and I'm safe. I can still not see more than a meter in any direction. I roll away from the crevice and build a campfire. As the fire grows stronger, I can see a light coming up behind the cloud.

I wake up and look at the clock. It is 05:00 exactly. I say, "Well Abba what does that mean." There is no response. I begin to wonder if I'm some kind of a missing link. I start to laugh. I can see the news flash, "Missing link found, Hoss Proxetter, lying in bed contemplating his navel."

CHAPTER 4
First Encounter

Why does the 'Great I Am' always choose the odd ball, the insecure weakling? It happens all throughout history in every culture, in every social class, in every religion and in every spiritual community. The list is endless. Some say that He has a profound fondness for the odd ball, the underdog, which may be true. Being one of the oddball weaklings, I want that to be true. But the 'Great I Am' tells me, "I choose the oddball and weakling because their visions of My family are all-inclusive; they show everyone how anyone can find me within their inner being."

This is how He comes to me, and for the life of me, I can't understand why. I'm the most mischievous and insecure kid you can imagine in my community, and I'm only twelve. I go to almost any length to create the ultimate prank. The fact that I love science and have a mechanical aptitude helps me some. But it never completely compensates for my insecurity. However, I have one strength; I follow a very strict code of ethics. Each prank has to produce a maximum annoyance to the subject, without causing bodily injury or damage to property.

Just to give you an idea as to how these principles work, I'll give you a few examples.

At age ten, I had a very nasty teacher named Miss Roach. And believe me; she was nasty to everybody, putting everybody down, not just me. I can't remember one thing from her classes, except how small she made me feel and my delicious pranks. And I am sure that everyone remembers them vividly to this moment. Every slate blackboard had a narrow tray at the bottom to hold the chalk and eraser. I took an eraser and tied a light weight monofilament line to it and ran the line down the chalk tray, down to the baseboard, (using thumbtacks to change directions) to the corner of the room, down the wall to my row, and down behind my row, to my seat. During class, Miss Roach was writing on the blackboard and without looking reached for the eraser. Just before her hand reached it, I pulled the eraser a couple of lengths down the tray. The whole class took a deep breath in surprise. Miss Roach looked at the eraser and reached for it again. Just before her hand connected, the eraser moved again. The class started to giggle. She turned to look at the expressions on our faces. Miss Roach turned back to the eraser and reached for it again with extreme focus of intention. The eraser moved before her hand could grab it. She grabbed again. The eraser moved. The class was laughing. Now Miss Roach stalked it like some naughty student, screaming and grabbing repeatedly, but the eraser kept moving. The class was hysterical. Suddenly, she sank her claws into it, and I yanked hard. The line broke, and I rolled up and had the excess line in my pocket before she noticed the small bit of line on the eraser. The uproarious laughter of the class died instantly under her ferocious gaze.

By the end of that school year and after witnessing Miss Roach not spare the rod on two classmates, I wanted to see justice prevail. But lacking the strength and courage to confront her, I came up with another way. I discovered a book the same size as my textbook in a garage sale and bought it for ten cents. A plan instantly came to me. I went down to the auto parts store and bought a replacement starter solenoid for my dad's car. I then took the fully charged solenoid out of my dad's car and replaced it with the new one. Taking the book, I hollowed out a compartment inside the book to hold the solenoid; I drilled two tiny holes, front and back, for wires; and I glued two thin sheets of copper foil on the front and back of the book. Next, I soldered two fine wires to the front copper foil and back copper foil and ran the wires inside to the compartment. I then very carefully connected the wires to the solenoid making sure that I did not touch both plates at the same time. I took the cover off my textbook and punched 100 pinholes, over the copper foil area, in the front and back. It was now ready! The next day, holding it only by the edges, I put the book on the teacher's desk and put hers in the desk drawer. When class began, I waited. The whole morning passed and Miss Roach did not use the book. We were half way through the afternoon before she needed it. She picked it up to smash one of the girls, who was passing a note. She lifted it over her head preparing to bring it down, when she made contact with the plates. The book bit her with an electrical jolt. She screamed and the book flew back through the air and hit the blackboard. In the next instant she treated the class to the first, swear words we ever heard in the classroom, and we all laughed joyfully. Miss Roach kept screaming at the class, "Who did that?" The class became very still. Finally, the preacher's kid in the back of the room said loudly, "I think God is striking you for what you were about to do!" Miss Roach sank into her desk chair white as a sheet. Even though the Principal found the real evidence, the popular theory stuck, "God doesn't like child abuse."

After I turned twelve on the following All Hallows eve, I chose the police chief as my target. He was a good man and a very good police chief. He had a great sense of humor and cut us kids a great deal of slack. However, I once overheard him tell his men that no one ever got the

best of him on Halloween. To me this was a bully
comment; I was the butt of many bullies in my life; so this
was a challenge to exceed all challenges. I couldn't resist.

Like all weaklings, secrecy gave me strength. I
gathered the things I needed for the prank: a small metal
washer painted black, some lightweight fishing line, a
thumbtack, two croquet hoops, a short stick and a fish
head. I barrowed my dad's binoculars, and filled my
canteen with water. I dressed in a night camouflage outfit
complete with a mesh hood. On this night it looked just
like another Halloween costume, and to aid the deception, I
carried all my stuff in a trick-or-treat bag. After dark, I
struggled through the woods along the back of the police
chief's house.

While the police chief's wife was taking care of
trick-or-treaters, I slipped into their backyard. This was the
riskiest part of the plan. I knew that the police chief kept
his extension ladder hanging on the tool shed. I took the
ladder and put it up over a second floor window. Then I
tied the washer to the end of the fishing line and climbed
the ladder. I tied a loop about four inches above the washer
and secured it to the corner of the window frame with the
thumbtack. The washer just touched the corner of the
window. I cut the fishing line at the thumbtack and tied
the end to the washer. I climbed down quickly and put the
ladder back in its place.

I threw the spool of fishing line through a tree on
the edge of the backyard and ran the line about twenty
yards into the woods. There in a small clearing I pushed the
first croquet hoop into the ground and passed the fishing
line through it. I then tied the short stick to the line and
pushed the second hoop into the ground over the line about
eight inches from the first one. When I pulled on the line,

it moved back and forth about eight inches, and the washer tapped against the window. Finally, I cut the line and tied the fish head to the end.

Everything was ready. I climbed the hill behind the house and found a place where I could see everything through my binoculars. I waited for over an hour and nothing happened. I thought of a dozen things that could be wrong, like maybe the line hung up some place. After another half-hour, I decided to sneak down and check it out. I stowed all my gear and climbed over the edge. That was when I heard it, "Tap, tap... Tap, tap, tap." The police chief's cat finally found the fish head.

I climbed back into my hiding place. Things really started to happen. Every light in the house went on. The police chief's wife started to go from room to room to find the sound, but she couldn't find it. She peered out in to the dark backyard, but she couldn't see anything. The sound continued, "Tap, tap, tap." Minutes later the police chief pulled up with his bubble flashing.

The chief went from room to room. It was so hysterical that I was rolling on the ground with silent laughter. The chief peered through the different windows, but there was nothing. Finally, he found the right window and quickly opened it. The tapping stopped. He looked all around and shined his flashlight over every inch of the backyard. There was nothing. He closed the window and started out of the room. Just as he reached the door, it started again, "Tap, tap, tap." He turned and stood there. His face was red with anger. The sound continued, "Tap, tap... Tap, tap." He turned and ran out of the room.

A few seconds later, the chief ran into the backyard. The sound stopped. He searched everywhere, with his powerful light. He looked into the bushes along the back of the yard. There was nothing. He was frantic, talking to himself and screaming into his walkie-talkie. Then the whole scene became even funnier.

Every squad car in town pulled up in front of the house. Soon it was like a keystone cop movie. The cops were everywhere. They checked every bush a hundred times. At one point, the chief drew his weapon and threatened the trashcan. He screamed, "Whoever is in there, come out!" Within seconds, the whole police force had their guns trained on the trashcan. The chief kicked over the trashcan. The trash went everywhere.

One of the officers asked the chief, "Should I arrest the empty beer bottles?" Everyone laughed and the chief looked humiliated. They all went inside.

It took ten minutes for everyone to relax. Then it started again, "Tap, tap, tap." The house looked like a nest of blue hornets flying in a panic. They threw open windows and the tapping stopped. They closed windows and the tapping started again. They peeked around corners and the tapping stopped. They went back in the house and the tapping started up again. They were going crazy. By this time, my sides were aching from laughing, and I slipped over the hill and went trick-or-treating. I made the best haul ever and couldn't stop laughing the whole night. The image of the police chief was so vivid; it stuck in my head. When I came home, I stashed my goodies and went to bed with my costume on.

Just before daybreak, I went back to collect all my things. The chief was asleep in a lawn chair in the backyard. From the little clearing, with one firm pull, the thumbtack popped loose. I rolled up the line and took everything but the fish head. The police chief's snoring made more noise than I did.

But that is not how the night ends for me. As I walk back to the house, a tall thin black man with graying hair is suddenly walking beside me. I nearly jump out of my skin. If I stop, he stops and looks at me. If I continue walking, he walks with me. The strange thing is I don't feel any danger. We walk toward home.

Finally, he speaks to me in a very deep voice, "Well Hoss are you happy with yourself?"

Insecure, but with a laughing lilt in my voice, I say, "Yep, I nailed the police chief. He'll never be able to brag about it again."

"Well, you nailed him all right, and he will never really know what happened here. And every Halloween the story will be told many times and with many theories. Some will believe that the chief's house is haunted. Some will literally think he has bats in his belfry. Some will think it is a woodpecker. However, every year for many years the police chief will sit in his lawn chair in the backyard on Halloween night hoping that the ghost will come back."

I sheepish say, "But I won't."

"No, you will be working for me."

I look up at him. His smile penetrates deep inside me, and I can feel a joy and laughter in my heart. In a very innocent tone, I ask, "And who are you?"

"When Moses asked that question, I answered, 'I am Hasher I am,' although many people call me many names to suit their own purposes. Some try to use my name to have power over others. But that is not Who I am or What I am! I am not a name. I am not a label. I am not an idea or object to study, like so many do. I am an experience, your experience. I am your dynamic essence. I am the essence of being in all people and all things. I am within you and everyone. I want everyone to connect with me inside them.

Simply put, 'I Am'. That is how I want people to know me. I'm counting on you, Hoss, to make that clear."

Oddly enough, I understand everything He says in spite of my age. Here He is standing right beside me, but at the same time, I can feel him inside me, in my heart, in my head, in my body, everywhere. I ask Him confidently, "Then can we call you the 'Great I Am'?"

"That's perfect. I knew you were the right one for the job."

That's when I became uncertain, "What's this job? I thought you just needed help with this title business."

"You're my chosen one. You will become my spiritual spokesperson. You will stop the negative spiral the world is…"

"Wait just a minute!" I interrupt. "That's a huge leap from helping you with a title. I'm not spiritual!"

"You're my chosen…"

"I don't care. I'm the weakest kid in the village, a social reject, an odd ball, a do nothing nobody! Find somebody else. You see what I'm capable of with the police chief. I am no goody two shoes!"

"What makes you think that you pulled off the prank on the police chief all by yourself? The cat won't find that fish head until tomorrow. What makes you think you were working alone to stop Miss Roach? If you think you are some punkster genius, then we have an ego problem to work on. With me inside you, you are the strongest kid in the room or on the playground."

"That's nice, thank you, but…" I'm embarrassed to say it, but I blurt it out, "Look, I'm trying to tell you I am not religious, never have been, never will be."

"The last thing I need is another religious nut. I've enough of those to straighten out already. I have chosen you, because you can do the job."

"What job is that?" I timidly think the least I can do is to listen to His pitch.

"This is it; I want you to stop the negative spiral the world is in. We are going to take some drastic measures."

"You are aware; I'm only twelve years old?"

"I know; you have a lot to learn; and we have to prepare you and prepare the world."

"What drastic measures do you have in mind? Do I have to build a boat?"

He laughs, "No. I'll let you know when you're ready and the time is right."

"Come on, give me a little hint. I need something to satisfy my insecurity, if I'm going to do this." I start bargaining with Him, "I haven't agreed to do this yet."

"OK, I'll tell you what it is not. It is not something people are expecting. I am not wrathful, nor will I be wrathful. I will not destroy my creation. Humans are doing a better job at that than I can. On the positive side, my Love will be steadfast."

We walk in silence as I consider; no one has ever had this kind of confidence in me before; maybe He can make something out of me; after all He made everything else out of nothing, "All right, I'll do it."

We end up at my house. I turn to ask, "You will help me with this; won't you?" But He is not there.

"Of course I will. I'm right here inside you, always have been, always will be."

There you have it. The 'Great I Am' picks another odd ball, another looser. It is the end of my punkster career and the beginning of my spiritual journey.

CHAPTER 5
A Secret Life

Every day, as I grow into manhood, is full of conversations with the 'Great I Am'. As positive as this is, I soon learn that it has to be a complete secret. Not because the 'Great I Am' or I want it so, but because the world is not ready for it. People who speak to a Supreme Being are one thing. A person, who hears a Supreme Being speak to him or her, or any such voice, is delusional in this age of reason. The science of Psychology says so. As insecure as this makes me, I soon learn that the world has a crippling view of knowledge and a false perception of religious faith. The "age of reason" advances false hypothesis like "the mind is our higher nature and the body is our bestial nature," or Descartes', "I think, therefore I am," which blocks the true development of the human mind and our essence of being. We are lead to understand that knowledge is the greatest and only real treasure and Divine Love a bunch of sentimental-clap-trap.

Oh, I learn. I go from a poor and sometimes failing student to an excellent student, and not by myself. Everything the teachers impart to me, He enhances. However, I can never reveal that He is helping me.

For example when I'm only fifteen, my Principal calls me into his office and confronts me with a paper I have written. As I sit down, he stands up and shakes the paper in my face, "Did you write this? No way, I say!"

Fear and intimidation fill my mind; then He stands me up and makes me look him in the eye; and the words come out of my mouth, "But it IS my work! What's your problem?" He backs off and sits down. I remain standing.

My Principal opens the paper and reads a phrase,

"'When Zarathustra comes off the mountain he learns that fate is not absolutely unalterable.' How can you know that?! It's a preposterous idea. Fate cannot be altered!"

"I value your opinion sir, but apparently you haven't read the AVESTA"

He says screaming, "What's that? You quote it here, 'AVESTA, Vispered VIII, v. 15; only Ahura-Mazda can alter its course.' You can't just invent things like this. Do you think we're stupid?" His anger is boiling over.

With my knees knocking I reply, "No, sir, because only a stupid man will not be willing to learn. The AVESTA is the ancient sacred book of the Persian people."

He sits there in silence for a few moments looking at the paper. Then he looks up and asks, "Did you actually read that or find the quote somewhere?"

"I'm actually reading it, sir."

"Who's this Ahura-Mazda?" He asks.

Now I'm receiving all kinds of cautions from the 'Great I Am' who can see a trap lying ahead. (Once you connect with the 'Great I Am' within you, the whole concept of Him being all knowing becomes more understandable. Since He is in the other person, He knows what that person is thinking before he or she speaks. If you're listening to the 'Great I Am' in you, He can tip you off.) He helps me choose my words carefully. "She-He is their essence of being."

He grins like a fox, "You mean God, don't you?"

"No, sir, I mean essence of being. You know I'm not allowed to use the 'G' word in a public school. This is a 'G' free zone. I congratulate you on your courage to use it."

He dismisses me. As I reach the door, he calls my name. I turn, and he gestures by touching the side of his eyes and then pointing at me to let me know that he will be keeping an eye on me. I in turn gesture to him forming a large circle in the air starting at my heart, up to my eyes, head and then to him. I'm sure that he misinterprets my gesture, but what I'm actually signing is that the 'Great I Am' is watching him. I step out the door, side step out of his sight and lean back against the wall to stop shaking.

The following year, there is a similar problem with my shop teacher, Max Oar. He assigns the class a term project, which we can work on in class and at home. I design a jewelry box for my Mom and order the materials. I decide to make it out of walnut with an inlay of her name in the top. The top edge of the lid will have a cherry-maple herringbone bead. The base is to be a scroll cut molding with a roman-ogee profile shape. It will also have an inside compartmentalized tray. I use the school machinery in the shop to do all the rough cutting, milling and sanding. I cut the dovetail corner joints by hand at home. I cut and mill the roman-ogee molding, rabbet the inside top edge, miter the corners and sand it in the shop. I assemble the box at home without the base. I power sand it, cut off the lid and do the finish sanding in the shop. I add the maple cock-bead around the lid opening, install the lock, catch and assemble the tray at home. I do the extra fine sanding in the shop. At home, I do the inlay of my mother's name, Marsha, lay in the herringbone trim and French polish the whole box. I then line the inside with blue velvet. I sign it, "In the Love of the 'Great I Am'," and turn in the project.

When Mr. Oar returns the jewelry box, I discover that he has given me a failing grade. Shock overcomes me. Below the grade he has written, "You did not do this work. You are a cheat and a fraud! Max Oar." My insecurity takes over.

Even though I want to hate him, the 'Great I Am'

will not let me. He helps me see inside Max, and I see a tormented little man with marginal skills, a huge inferiority complex (I can identify with this.) and a ton of jealousy. The 'Great I Am' tells me, "Take this to your father. He will know what to do."

I show the jewelry box to my father. He oohs and aahs running his hand over the surface and turning it to see every detail. After several minutes, he opens the box; his mouth falls open; his eyes grow wider, and he lifts the tray examining it. He sets aside the paper in side. He finally says, "Hoss, this is the finest work I have ever seen." (My father is in the finishing trade.) He looks at the paper and asks, "Is this a note to your Mom?"

"No, it's my grade."

He picks up the paper, opens it and reads it. In a flash, he goes ballistic. He starts flying about the room in huge strides. (As a young man, my father flew biplanes in combat. He was an Ace pilot.) He looks like he is stalking the enemy and shooting him down. He looks cool but ferocious. His eyes are flashing. His jaw is set. He breaths in and out slowly and deliberately, making an audible breathing sound. This is a first for me to see him like this. It takes almost an hour before I can calm him down and have him take out his worry stone.

Finally, I say, "I know what you want to do about this, but what can we really do about it?"

He thinks for a moment rubbing his worry stone. Then he stands up, walks over to his desk and picks up the telephone. He takes a deep breath and dials a number. "John, this is Harold. I need to talk to you about a school problem. ... Yes, it's serious, extremely serious if you ask me. It involves one of your teachers. ... Max Oar. Can I come over right away? ... I'll see you in five."

I ask, "Was that the School Board Chairman?"

"Yep. Can I borrow your jewelry box and note for a half hour?"

"Sure, but wrap it up first, so Mom can't see it."

He wraps it in an old baby blanket and is out the door before I can ask to go along.

When my father comes home, he hands me the jewelry box wrapped in the blanket and tells me, "Hide it someplace safe." Before a holiday, my Mom always searches in every nook and cranny under the pretence of cleaning to have a peak at her gifts before I wrap them. I always have a couple of places she doesn't know about.

I'm feeling very insecure. I ask my father, "Is he going to do anything?"

"There will be a meeting in a couple of days, which you and I will attend. John thinks this might be the tip of an iceberg. Keep this to yourself and don't let on that anything is happening."

Over the next two days, there are members of the School Board poking around the school offices and asking many questions of some of the teachers. I try to be cool and pretend not to notice. My mind is beating me up; I should keep my mouth shut; now I'm really in trouble!

On the third day, I come home from school and find my father waiting. He says, "We have our meeting tonight. It will be an emergency meeting of the whole School Board. I hope this doesn't become political. We have to sit down and make a list of the work at home and the work in your shop class concerning your project."

"No problem, it's all written down in my journal."

"Good, fetch your journal and we'll make a list."

CHAPTER 6
Turning Lives Around

After we finish, I skip dinner and try to meditate before the meeting. It is not easy to be in control of my chattering mind, but in about twenty minutes, I settle into my peaceful place. I'm not alone. The 'Great I Am' assures me that I'm on track, and He will be with me. My only danger is to slip off track and become vindictive. Then He says, "Remember, I am in everyone else there too, and trying to guide all those who are listening. Unfortunately, some of those who will be there are blocking me completely. Perhaps you will be able to help me reach them."

"This is not about a jewelry box; is it?"

"No, it is about turning some lives around. I want this meeting, and they need this meeting. But it has been a long time in coming. An institution, organization or government has no essence of being, even though some people like to think it does. They call it their 'super-ego', which it is. But the fact is that only the people, who are part of the institution, can connect to me. Keep the line open, and I'll guide you through it."

At the meeting, I sit in silence and listen carefully to their discussion. They all start by examining the jewelry box. A positive reaction is all I need; for the grade no longer matters to me. Since my ego is not controlling me, I'm able to watch people's reactions to each other. Max watches the people as they touch and caress the box. He is very insecure and nervous, but he is masking it with an air of self-righteousness. When people examine Max's grade and comments and then look up at him, he cannot hold their gaze, looking down at the floor. One of the board members reads the comments and nods in approval.

Another board member sits with knitting in her lap, and the needles are going a mile a minute. She only stops to examine the box and read the note. Otherwise, the needles are clicking constantly. The Principal barely even looks at the box, as if he knows it by heart, and doesn't bother to read the comments. His face is smug; he is projecting a haughty air of self-confidence, as if he already knows the outcome of this meeting. The Chairman then passes out copies of my work list from a spirit duplicator. The board member who nodded approval suddenly begins to worry. The Principal barely glances at his copy and then does a double take, now reading it more carefully. As he reads, his left eye begins to twitch, beads of perspiration form on his upper lip, and his pencil breaks in his hand. Max reads his copy and starts scratching his head. His nervousness increases; his self-righteous air begins to crack.

The Chairman begins, "The work list that you have with dates were taken from the boy's journal. I saw these entries myself." I look at my father in disapproval, and he shrugs. The Chairman must have seen this exchange, because he looks at me and adds, "I assure you Hoss that I saw only these entries, because there was a mask over all the others." I breathe a sigh of relief, and he turns to Max. "Mr. Oar, will you explain your evaluation of this boy's work?"

Max clears his throat, "That's just it Mr. Chairman. It's not his work. It is too perfect. That is the work of a master craftsman, with many years of experience, not the work of some sixteen year old kid who is in love with himself, if you read the inscription carved in the bottom."

I'm about to object and explain the inscription when the 'Great I Am' says, "Not important! And this is not the right time or venue for that argument. Let it be our secret for now." I sit back and smile.

The Chairman asks, "Mr. Oar, how do you account for the work in your class?"

Max begins to sweat, "He substituted this box for the one he was working on."

"Aren't you supervising the class?"

"Of course I'm!"

"Did you see the boy sanding the assembled box?"

"Yes, but…"

"How are these dovetails different from the ones on the box he was sanding?"

"I don't know. I didn't look that close."

"How about the molding for the base?"

"Yes, but…"

"How was that base different from this base?"

"Look I just know the boy is a cheater and a fraud."

"And how do you know that?"

"Principal Purvis showed me his file, and asked me to keep an eye out for cheaters."

All eyes shift to Principal Purvis. The twitch over his eye grows stronger and his left knee start bouncing up and down. His haughty air evaporates and a feeling of panic engulfs him.

The Chairman smiles and says politely, "Thank you Mr. Oar. Now we come to the main purpose of our meeting. Dr. Purvis, you said at a faculty meeting two years ago, and I quote, 'I will not tolerate cheating in my school. I want you all to be on the lookout for cheaters. I will reward those that find them. Those that don't will be put under extreme scrutiny.'"

"I never…," starts Dr. Purvis, but the Chairman interrupts him.

"Before you answer Dr., I want you to know I have

the minutes of that meeting right here in front of me."

"Yes, I abide by that policy."

"And what reward did you agree to give Mr. Oar for his cooperation?"

Principal Purvis looks at Max, and Max looks like a man about to confess everything, "A four percent salary increase for next year."

The Chairman picks up my file and asks, "Dr. Purvis, I note that there is a red dot sticking to the tab of Hoss' file, red flagging him as an alleged cheater. How many others have you red-flagged?"

"I don't know, maybe a couple."

"Try 328 Dr. Purvis! Do you have any real evidence to support any of the clams you have written in these files?"

"Just what the teachers gave me."

"But all those are vague and based on innuendo. You have involved 23 teachers in this scandal. How much have your rewards cost us over the last two years?"

"I don't know. I'm not an accountant." He laughs, but the Board members are at a full boil.

"Dr. Purvis, I agree with the popular observation, 'Show me a man pointing the finger at someone and I can show you three fingers pointing toward himself. As you know yourself, you know others.' Therefore, Dr. Purvis, have you done this before?"

"Don't be absurd!" says Dr. Purvis. He looks away and holds down his left leg so it won't bounce so noticeably.

The Chairman takes out a file from his briefcase, "I have here your file, Dr. Purvis, which now contains a copy of your dismissal from the last three schools where you worked. I also have a letter from the person who supposedly was the author of your letter of recommendation." Holding up a letter, he asks, "Did you write this letter of recommendation, forge the signature and send it to us?"

"I think I should have my lawyer present before I answer any more of your questions."

The Principal's face is as red as a beet and he is vigorously wiping the perspiration off his face and neck.

The Chairman is cool and firm, "Dr. Purvis, this is not a legal proceeding, but after our deliberation and your notification it may be wise for you to acquire legal representation." Addressing the Board, "Does anyone have any other questions for Dr. Purvis and Mr. Oar?" The room is dead silent. You can hear and feel a feather falling. "Hearing none, Dr. Purvis and Mr. Oar, you are dismissed so we may deliberate."

The two men file out of the room. The Principal is trying to mask his defeat with an air of defiance and indignity. Max is humbled and worried. He turns back as though to say something apologetic, but shakes his head, turns and leaves.

My father stands up and motions to me. I start to stand up when the Chairman ask my father, "Harold, can you and Hoss stay for the deliberation. The Board feels that the boy should hear the outcome of all this since he is a victim." My father sits back down, shots me a smile and a thumbs-up.

The Chairman stands up, closes the door and then returns to perch on the front of the desk. He is much more informal now, "OK, we are off the record now. Let's have it all out there so we can figure out what to do."

The discussion begins with an apology from the board member who appeared to agree with Max, "I must apologize, because I feel a little guilty for being the one who recruited Max for the job. I thought I knew the man and never would have believed him capable of this." The discussion that follows is very heated and full of anger. Gradually the tension in the room grows more and more hostile; until everyone is ready to lynch the guilty parties. They want blood for blood. I search inside myself to find a place of calm.

Finally, one of the board members jumps up and shouts, "Mr. Chairman, I move that we start legal proceedings against both Dr. Purvis and Mr. Oar and immediately dismiss both of them." Another board member shouts, "I second the motion!"

The Chairman raises both his hands to quiet the group, but it takes almost a minute for the group to settle down. He then walks around the desk and stands behind it. He speaks calmly, "I guess we are back on the record." He gestures to the recording secretary, "Will you please record the motion and second. The motion is open for debate."

I raise my hand. The Chairman recognizes me and I ask, "Mr. Chairman, may I have permission to address the Board?"

"Are there any objections?" The Chairman asks. There is none. The Chairman nods to me and says, "You have the floor Hoss."

I walk to the front of the room and calmly turn to face everybody. I can feel He is with me. I begin to speak softly but with strength and clarity, "I know that what these men were doing was wrong, and you probably have a very good case against them, but there must be a way to change their attitudes without destroying their lives. Max Oar is a very good teacher and a good man, and his idea gave me the opportunity to build that box. For that, I am eternally grateful. Because of his own insecurity, he was easy prey for a negatively zealous leader who made him forget all the help he gave me. If you give him a second chance, I will gladly accept whatever grade he wishes to give me.

"As for Principal Purvis, he needs to see the error of his actions and be willing to change his attitude. A lawsuit will not do that. It will only drive him deeper into his distorted perceptions. Not only will a lawsuit cost you a lot of money; it will not resolve any of the problems or damage that this situation has caused. You have 328 corrupt files with false information. Why not require Principal Purvis to rewrite, not amend, but rewrite each file and give an apology to the teachers and request an unbiased grade. You can then instead of a lawsuit accept his resignation with a signed agreement that he will never seek employment in education again, thus allowing the man to start a new life without a blemish.

"As to the 23 teachers, they all need to right their wrongs. They need to reevaluate students and give them a fair and honest grade for the record. Then instead of dismissal, they must willingly accept a ten percent cut in pay for one year, thus recovering the lost bribe money.

"Finally, all the good teachers who rose above the temptation should have a reward with an extra two percent salary increase for next year.

"All these actions will produce a positive outcome and promote a healing atmosphere in the school community. Thank you for hearing me out." When I finish there is a deep silence.

During my speech, the board member, who was knitting, sets down her work to listens intently. She now stands in silence and waits to be recognized.

The Chairman takes over a full minute to stand up and recognize her, "Eleanor, you have the floor."

"John and all of you, I am deeply moved. This

young boy has addressed us with more compassion and wisdom than all of us combined. He is truly a very gifted boy." She is holding back tears. "I want to make a motion that we adopt his proposal in its entirety."

The Chairman reminds her, "Eleanor, we have a motion on the floor."

The seconding board member calls out, "I withdraw my second."

The board member, making the original motion, calls out, "I withdraw my motion and second Eleanor's motion."

The Chairman turn to the secretary, "Can you read us the content of Hoss' recommendations as separate items?"

The secretary reads out each of my suggestions summarizing them into salient points. As I listen, I hear His voice in each one. I am amazed and feel unworthy of this gift. For the life of me, I can't understand. Why me? (That is a feeling that stays with me my whole life.) By the time she finishes there is a transformation in the atmosphere of the room, and it fills with light.

The Chairman turn to me, "Is that an accurate summery Hoss?"

"Yes, Sir."

"Eleanor is that your intended motion?"

"Yes it is."

"The motion is on the table. Is there any debate?" The Chairman scans the room. There are no hands. "Is there anyone opposed to the motion?" There is no one. "Hearing none, I declare the motion carried by acclimation! This meeting is adjourned."

After the meeting, the woman with the knitting approaches me. She says, "You are a very gifted boy, you know."

I humbly respond, "And I'm very grateful to the one who gave me the gift!"

Suddenly, I realize that I'm learning how to keep the secret without letting people peg me as hallucinogenic or delusional. However, for the next forty years I will have to keep the secret from my family, friends, classmates, roommates and all my social contacts. When I become a teacher, the 'Great I Am' is part of my secret privet life. But I find ways to introduce Him through "Voice and Movement" by helping students find their centers or through "Meditation" by helping others to find the Light within. It is like talking in code. Slowly, I become aware that what everyone considers reality in this world is not reality at all. The 'Great I Am' is my only reality and He has a mission for me.

CHAPTER 7
Not Yet

While most people are searching for some purpose or meaning to their lives, I embrace the purpose the 'Great I Am' has for me. I put myself in His hands. This fills my every moment with joy, the joy of living, the joy of learning, the joy of doing and mostly the joy of being in Him and Him being in me. I have a smile on my face that is there in every passing moment. There is no need for a goal. I just know I'm going somewhere, but I don't know where. It is like boarding a train and letting it take me wherever it is going. Thus, I can remain in the present, while filling my journey with the enthusiasm of going. That means that my going never produces frustration.

When the Vietnam War begins, I want to do something about it. I will not pervert the truth by calling it a cold war. There is nothing cold about it except the hearts of those who fuelled it in the name of "US national security."

I beg the 'Great I Am', "Let's do something! This is not right! Let's stop the killing!"

His answer is an empathetic, "Not yet."

"Aren't we going to stop the negative spiral the world is in?"

"Yes, but **Not Yet!**"

He says this with such force I know it is not open for debate.

In the early fall of 1958, the State of Michigan selects me to explore the possibility of forming an Intercollegiate Model United Nations for the state of

Michigan. They send me to a one-week seminar in Washington, DC and New York City along with representatives from each state in the US. In DC, we hear lectures from Vice President Richard Nixon and Senator Hubert Humphrey of Minnesota. In NYC, we hear Dag Hammarskjöld, Secretary General of the UN and Mrs. Eleanor Roosevelt. To say that this week is profoundly electrifying is a gross understatement. I'm so enthusiastic when I return to Michigan that I organize the first Intercollegiate Model UN in six weeks and schedule it for April in 1959. Dag Hammarskjöld is to be the keynote speaker.

At last, I feel that the 'Great I Am' is preparing me for something big. We are on the move. In the spring, I meet Dag Hammarskjöld's plane, and we go over his itinerary for the next three days. Dag is to welcome each delegation from each country (chosen by lottery by each participating college or university) and do the opening speech on the first day. Each day is packed with full sessions of the UN debating the hot current topics. In the evening of each day, Dag will close with comments and suggestions. Throughout the Model UN, I perform the normal functions of the Secretary General. At the end of the final day, Dag is to give a closing speech.

The event runs smoothly with only minor snags. Behind the scenes, there are several teams: sound, lighting, hospitality and a steno pool with several runners. The largest of these is the steno pool. For every event there is a stenographer writing down everything in shorthand and handing it off to a runner. These notes then go to a typing pool, are typed onto a mimeograph stencil and given to a runner. From there the stencils go to the mimeograph room where ten mimeograph machines are printing and assembling everything. The runners then deliver the compiled booklet back to the sessions within twenty minutes after the session closes. This is a major feat and surprises everyone and especially Dag Hammarskjöld.

On the final day after Dag's inspirational speech, the two of us make a final check of the building to make sure that everything is in order. Everything is perfect until we come to the steno pool. This huge room is a total disaster. The owners of the typewriters and mimeograph machines have taken their equipment, but there are drinking cups, paper plates, empty boxes, bits of paper and stencils everywhere. The tables and chairs are still up and in disarray. But there is not one member of the team in sight. I turn to Dag, apologize for the mess and ask if he can wait there for a couple of minutes while I track down the team. I search everywhere and find no one. Finally, I give it up and decide to go back to the room and tell Dag I need to make some phone calls. On my way, I look at my watch only to discover that a little over a half-hour has passed. I expect to find my very important person angry and pacing the floor. When I walk in, I stop and stare with my mouth open. The tables and chairs are down and on their carts. All the boxes are full of trash, and Dag is emptying the last dustpan of dirt into a box. My heart sinks and I feel awful. I walk over to Dag to apologize. But he senses my frame of mind and holds up a hand to stop me.

He says, "Let's go grab our coats."

"But I…" I start, but he cut me off.

"Hoss, it's nothing. But I will share with you a lesson I learned when I was your age. The King of Sweden told me under similar circumstances, 'Sometimes a leader needs to roll up his sleeves to get the job done.' I'm sure you will have the opportunity to pass that on one day."

Deep inside me, I hear and feel His rolling laughter. When I'm alone again, the 'Great I Am' says to me, "Well Hoss are you ready to tackle the world?"

I can feel the jovial nature that fills this question. But I sheepishly respond, "Not yet."

In September of 1959, I have a call that makes me feel that the 'Great I Am' is about to make His move. As the President of the Young Republicans at Western Michigan University, Gerald Ford asks me if I can set up a Republican Rally in the new field house for Vice-President Richard Nixon to announce his candidacy for the upcoming Presidential campaign. I tell Gerald I will check out the possibility and call him back later that day or early tomorrow.

I call and schedule a meeting with the University President for that afternoon. Since the President is a Democrat, I'm less than doubtful that I can pull this off. In the meeting, the President starts talking about the success of the Model UN and what a great experience for him to meet Dag Hammarskjöld at one of the 'Meet and greet' gatherings. He goes on and on about what events like this mean for the University. My ego is taking such a stroking that the warning bells start going off in my inner center. Finally, we get around to the reason for meeting. I present the idea of the Republican Rally with Gerald Ford and Vice-President Nixon. All the enthusiasm is sucked out of the room for a moment. The President leans back in his chair and swivels to look out the window. We sit in silence. My rational mind goes into over drive and comes up with a dozen reasons I can throw at him as to why he should do this, for example, this is a state school, Ford's assistance in raising the money for the field house and how often do you have a Vice-President visit the University. I shut down my chattering mind and ego and just try to read the President's energy. I can see that he is struggling with a decision.

Finally, he turns to me, and asks, "Hoss, what do you think I should do?"

"Sir, you are a fair man. Only you know what is best for the University." And I mean it. I'm willing to accept whatever he decides without argument.

"Hoss, I don't know how you knew the one word I need to hear, 'fair', but that was exactly what I needed to hear. I'm sitting here wondering about what I'm going to say to the Democrats when they become upset with me for hosting a Republican event. I'll simply tell them that the Democrats are welcome here too. Can I tell them that you will coordinate their event?"

I answer without giving it a thought, "Of course I will. I will be happy to." My ego starts in on me, and I have to shut it down fast. The 'Great I Am' agrees that it is the right thing to do.

The President makes a phone call and gives me two dates that are open in late October.

On the day of the event, Gerald picks me up in a limo to go to the airport and pick up Vice-President Nixon. On the way back to the field house, Nixon pumps me for all kinds of information. Such as who won last week's football game? Who is the star player and how many yards does he gain? How many foreign exchange students are in the school? How many students are in the University? Is education still the largest department? All of this, he asks in a very friendly and personal way without taking notes.

During his speech, every one of these details became part of the content. Not only does this make him appear to be interested and knowledgeable about the University, but also his warmth and sincere tone make him appear to be our champion. The people love him and are ready to pledge their support right there on the spot.

A reception follows the rally at the Student Union Reception Hall. The Vice-President and Gerald work the room, but I choose to lay back and keep track of all the details. When it is time for the Vice-President to leave, Gerald finds me and says that the Vice-President wants me to join them on the way to the airport. He wants to discuss an important matter with me.

In the limo, the Vice-President is overly thankful and flattering about the success of the event and my role in it. It is quite deep when he says, "Hoss, you have a real future with the Republican Party. Bright men like you are what this country needs."

My ego goes into overdrive. It takes every ounce of self-control to keep it in check. I try to focus and be positive, waiting to see if the 'Great I Am' has a plan in all this.

Suddenly, the Vice President's tone changes completely. It is a different voice, a different look on his face and you might say a very different personality. "I want you to look this over." He hands me a manila envelope, and I open it and begin to read as he talks. "I want you to discreetly circulate these so no one knows where they came from. You know, in the school newspaper mailbox, accidently left in the faculty lounge, a doctor's office, a dentist office, on a bus, on a reporter's desk, use your imagination. Can you do this for me?"

What I'm reading is shocking. There is personal information on John F. Kennedy, Hubert Humphrey, Wayne Morse, and Lyndon B. Johnson which appears to be factual and incriminating and involving every scandal imaginable. I look up at Nixon (I have just lost all my respect for the man.) and say, "None of this is true. You do know that?"

"Of course I know that, boy, of course." He is leaning into me now.

"That would make it unethical," I state factually.

"What, what, what do you mean unethical? There is no politics in ethics; I mean there is no ethics in politics. All that matters here is that I get the power!" He can't look me in the eye. But I can see a fire burning behind his eyes and tightness in his eyebrows.

My inner energy takes hold of me and gives me enormous strength and courage. I say, "You really don't think that people are going to believe this, do you?"

"Look boy. I'm going to tell you something. John Q public is dumber than a doorknob. They'll believe it, because they want to believe it. They love gossip. And not only will they believe it, within five days they'll think it's the greatest revelation since the resurrection of Jesus Christ." He laughs a maniacal laugh.

Sensing the danger, I sit in silence focusing all my energy to keep an expressionless face.

As we pull into the airport, he says, "Just do this for me boy and don't get all wound up about it." He pats me on the knee as the Secret Service opens the door for him.

I make a move to stand up, but Gerald catches my eye and shakes his head no.

When the door is closed, he says, "Just protocol." I nod that I understand.

Gerald and I sit in silence most of the way back to the campus. I finally reassemble all the papers and put them back in the envelope.

Gerald says, "For what it's worth, you can do what

you want with those and I won't think any the less of you either way. Just don't tell him." I nod that I understand.

I want to tell Gerald that my expectations of him are at ground zero; my disappointment that he can noncommittally agree with Nixon's "dirty tricks"; but my inner voice is telling me to say nothing. I no longer have the slightest notion of going into politics.

The next morning I drive down to Chicago and meet with Bobby Kennedy at the JFK campaign headquarters. I tell him the story and hand him the envelope. That day I became an Independent and resigned as President of the Young Republicans.

The conversation I have with the 'Great I Am', when I'm back in my room, lasts for three days. The high points are these. He is still finding it difficult to have people realize that he is right there inside them. Many of the people who do connect with Him are not taking the time to listen, which makes it impossible to reach them. Many people like Nixon have minor demons controlling their unconscious mind (rational mind and ego). There is no reason to have any concern for people like Nixon, because the demon will ultimately be his undoing. Unfortunately, it is another "Not yet." Knowing all this, I can see why. My only satisfaction is that JF Kennedy wins the election in 1960.

CHAPTER 8
Still Not Yet

The next ten years are the most difficult. The downward spiral of the world picks up speed. I'm ready and willing to step in whenever He asks.

On 18 December 1961, my friend and mentor Dag Hammarskjöld dies in a plane crash under suspicious circumstances. I say to the 'Great I Am', "We have to stop this insanity."

His response is, "You have no idea how hard it is to just hold things together. Name three people you can tell your story to, who won't take action to have you committed as a lunatic."

I think hard, "I can only name two now that Dag is dead, John Kennedy and Martin Luther King, Jr."

His concern is obvious, "It's a full time job just protecting you, so **not yet**."

On 5 August 1962, Nelson Mandela is arrested for his militant anti-apartheid activity. I say to Him, "Don't tell me we are losing another one."

"That's right! There are so few people listening."

I add, "OK, not yet." But I don't stop there. I organize an anti-apartheid demonstration before the trustees of Drew University, who are investing heavily in South African companies. It takes almost a year, but finally they sell off their financial holdings in those companies. It is a drop in the bucket, but at least it is something. This pleases the 'Great I Am', "Who knows it may spread. And thank you for doing it without drawing attention to yourself."

On 22 November 1963, President John F. Kennedy

is assassinated. The 'Great I Am' and I mourn together with the Nation and the world. I ask Him, "Is it that we will lose the war if we act now? Is that why you're waiting?"

"No, but the loss of souls will be far greater than I can bear, so I have to say **not yet**. By the way, I don't like the word war in any of its forms. Hatred fuels all wars and no good outcome has ever come from war or has a war produced a resolution to any issue. And I don't care what the Ego Literature may tell you."

"What is Ego Literature?"

"The Historical Fantasies that one person wants you to believe really happened. The list is endless. And not one of them has any merit unless you like living in a world of conflict, intrigue, and lies. And that is not the world of My creation."

On 4 April 1968, the American pastor and leader of the civil right movement Martin Luther King, Jr. is assassinated. The prophets are dropping like flies in a closed up summer house with no one home. I ask Him, "Are we even close to the end of this insanity? I loved that man and his mission. I was proud to be a white face on his marches. I feel like a man standing in the middle of a stream; the water's been somewhere, and the water's going somewhere; but I'm a fly-fisherman trying to catch a fish that might pass by; in the end I'm just a man standing in the middle of the stream."

The 'Great I Am' adds to my sentiments, "I love Martin too. We are connected. He likes to call me his 'Mountain'. Now maybe you'll understand why I worry for you. As for your little parable about a fly-fisherman, I like it. It is a perfect description of eternity in the present moment. You are the present moment. I am the stream.

Because I am in you, a connection exists between you and every place the stream comes from and every place the stream is going. The fish that will give itself to you is my love for you, everyone and all things. And I want as many as possible to catch the fish. Therefore, the answer to your question is **not yet**. We're not even close by your standards."

To end this decade of insanity, the prophecy of the 'Great I Am' is born out. On 20 January 1969, Richard M. Nixon becomes President of the United States of America, with Spiro Agnew as Vice-President. Thus, the seeds are sown for the economic unraveling of the US and World; plus the politics of fear and paranoia are born.

The 'Great I Am' says, "Before you ask, no, I am not helping him to do this. He has had no connection with me since he was eight. His rational mind and EGO are in total control. To coin a phrase, 'God help America'. Unfortunately, not even that is possible now."

"OK," I say. "I'll ask another question. How long is he going to be able to fool all the people? You are all knowing, aren't you?"

"I am all knowing, but not as you imply. I know what everybody is doing because I am right there with them, whether they're connected or not. However, because of 'free will' I don't know what they're going to do until they make the choice and in some cases not until they do it. I used to be a little better with nature until humans started messing up the balance of things. As for Richard and Spiro, they will be caught eventually, maybe not in the first term; but if they manage to win a second term, I'll be surprised if they make it past the second year. You have no idea the things that Spiro has been up to."

This is a reversal. I'm feeling very compassionate for the 'Great I Am', "You don't have it easy! Do you? I'll be a good lad and accept that in this discussion there is a '**Not Yet**' some place."

The next year is clearly an extension of the insanity of the last decade. The Financial/Industrial Technocracy is cranking out greedy millionaires who want more and more. Nixon escalates the war in Vietnam and expands it into Cambodia. Protecting the "National Interest" becomes the buzzword that justifies any atrocity. Protest demonstrations break out everywhere, and the House Un-American Activities Committee (HUAC) is taking names and making a list.

Then on 4 May 1970, the Ohio National Guard kills four students and wounds nine others on the campus of Kent State University.

As a university Professor, I'm outraged and find it very difficult to keep a lid on my anger. The 'Great I Am' and His mantra '**Not Yet**' is the only thing keeping both of us from losing it on several occasions. To mention just a few:

Sweden emerges as the strongest social democracy in the world under the strong leadership of Olof Palme, the leader of the Social Democratic Party from 1969 to 1986. This is the golden age of Sweden. Then on 28 February 1986, he is assassinated.

On the positive side, the 'Great I Am' begins to see a changing of the tide when the Moral Majority (The Christian Right) collapses in June 1989. Their fundamentalist control of the minds of their people is blocking His connection with the people just as much as the Islamic fundamentalists are doing.

Another sign of the changing tide is the release of Mandela on 11 February 1990, and his election as the President of South Africa on 10 May 1994.

In 1999, the 'Great I Am' alerts me that we are close. He is about to test the Spiritual energy of the world and see how many people are ready to connect. For two years, I increase my Yoga exercises and strengthen my meditation. Slowly I find that I'm living in the Light of the 'Great I Am' for most of every day. I will be ready. I will not let Him down.

Then our hopes and optimism are smashed in one day. At 04:33, I wake up with the 'Great I Am' screaming inside me, "No! No! No! You will undo everything!"

"What have I done?" I call back. There is no answer.

I start meditating. When I reach my inner space and move through the black peacefulness toward the Light, I feel a churning energy unlike anything before. The Light is swirling and pulsing. It keeps changing in color. I watch it intently. I'm like a small child watching a parent franticly doing something. I need to wait until He is done. I need to be patient. But the action of the Light is so extreme I cannot calm myself.

Finally, at 8:30 the 'Great I Am' speaks to me, "Hoss, I can't stop them. I am struggling to reach them, but no one is listening. All I can do is to delay some people from arriving at work." For the first time, I see the 'Great I Am' weep and moan.

Tears are rising under my eyes, "Can I help. Tell me what to do. I'm ready."

"It's too late. Hatred is breeding more hatred. This day will unleash the greatest hatred and rage the world has ever known. She shall not; she will not win. You shall bring her home."

The day is 9/11 2001.

By 7 October, the US is at war with Afghanistan. Terrorism becomes the new bogeyman for the world. The politics of fear and paranoia will live unhappily ever after.

CHAPTER 9
Before Creation

I say, "I need to ask a question."

"I know your question. The answer is **Not Yet**. I have to figure out a way around this mess and put us back on track."

"Well that's a first. That is not my question. My question is why don't you destroy evil? You have the power."

"Yes, I do. I can, but I won't."

"I don't understand."

The 'Great I Am' places his hand over my heart. "I need to show you the beginning. Close your eyes and start to do your meditation. Tell me what you see."

I close my eyes. After a moment, "There is only darkness and an empty space. It feels peaceful with a profound silence. There is nothing. Now I see a glowing blue sphere flowing through the space. You are the sphere. There is an energy swirling within the blue sphere. That energy is your mind. You have an image of everything you want to create. You know it in every detail, every cell, every atom and every electron particle. But it is trapped in your mind and cannot emerge. Now I feel your longing to bring it all into being. Oh my, your longing is so great. It is almost too great to bear. Now I see the blue sphere moving off through the vast empty space.

"Now I see another glowing red sphere floating through the darkness. It has a regular pulsing rhythm within it, like a beating heart. It too has an energy that is flowing out from its center. I feel it faintly as it comes closer. Now I feel it all around me and within me. It is the most powerful Love that I have ever felt. But I am not the one; She does not feel my presence as She floats on into empty space. Now I feel Her longing as She floats off to find the right One. Her longing feels even greater than yours does, and I realize that you are Her One. How will you ever find each other in the vastness of this space?

"Now after time without number or quicker than the present moment passes into the next present moment, I see the two spheres moving toward each other. They flow and float. They float and flow ever closer. Slowly and slower, they come together until they are all but touching. Their longing fades away as they look deeply into each other.

"The red sphere surrounds the blue sphere with Her Love. She looks within the blue sphere and sees all the images waiting to come into being. She sees the crystal city in its splendor.

"The blue sphere releases the energy of its mind and engulfs the red sphere. He looks within the red sphere and sees Her beating heart pumping life through countless veins. He sees within them the red fluid, in which She is pumping all Her life giving power.

"The love of the red sphere penetrates the blue sphere and surrounds every image in the mind of the 'Great I Am'.

"The energy of the 'Great I Am's mind penetrates the red sphere and charges the blood within Her heart and veins.

"Now they touch. Now they press closer together distorting the outer shape of their spheres."

Suddenly, I realize and cry out, "She is the Divine Mother!" As I say those words, "I see a brilliant flash of **LIGHT** and hear a voice say the Word 'light. Then, I hear an enormous **BANG,** as the two spheres become ONE,

swirling and pulsing together. All this is happening in the
same present moment. The ONE brilliant white sphere is
spinning so fast that specs of light are cast in all directions.
Out of the ONE brilliant white light emerges a transparent
female human form. She is beautiful with long flowing
hair. As the voice Words all things into being, the Divine
Mother fills them with Love. Slowly, everything takes shape
behind Her. The stars, the planets, our world takes shape
and comes into being. Now quicker than the present
moment passes into the next present moment or after time
without number, all the images that are in the mind of the
'Great I Am' are worded into being and are given love by
the Divine Mother. Through the Mind, Word, and Love
They make all things, and all things come into life.

"I can feel the combined energy of the Three
flowing out through the universe. That feeling is unity,
harmony, oneness, peace and joy. From the voices of
everything in creation, I can hear a choir singing the praises
of the creator Three."

I turn and look at the 'Great I Am' as though He is
done. He says, with His hand still on my heart, "Keep
meditating. You need to know the rest."

I go back into my meditation, "I see that the
newness is gone. The earth is buzzing with life. The Divine
Mother is talking to the 'Great I Am' who has a transparent
male human form. His facial features are African and his
body muscular. As they speak stars of many different shapes
come out of their mouths. I cannot understand their star
language. Their Son does not have human form. He is like
a ribbon of mist and light that is flowing and floating
around, between and through His Mother and Father.
Whenever He speaks, I can see His face in the mist and
light. He translates everything for me that you are saying. I

can feel a tension that was not there before.

"The Divine Mother says to you, 'I want you to give me the power to create on my own.'

"You reply, 'I cannot do that.'

"'Why not? You gave that power to Eve.'

"'That was different. Besides, she can only create from the seed of Adam.'

"The Divine Mother is growing angry, 'How is that different?'

"'They are not creating out of nothing.'

"'I demand that you give me the power. Why should you keep the power all to yourself?'

"'I am not keeping it to myself. Creation is from the three of us.'

"She is becoming furious, 'I don't believe you! Give me the power!'

"You are patient and gentle, 'How can I give you what I do not have?'

"She is in a full rage now, 'You are hiding it from me! Give it to me!'

"'I am not hiding anything. When we met, I was wandering through the darkness of space. All my images were locked inside me. It was you and our Son, who unlocked them. He worded them into being, your Love filled them and I breathed life into them. We can only create as three together.'

"She is not listening to any of this. In a flash, Her love flips into hate, 'Then let me go down to earth, and give me dominion over everything. At least I can have power over that creation! Do not refuse me!'

"'Go then,' you say. 'But you shall not destroy our creation, and you shall not destroy those who connect with me.'

"'I agree! Do you agree?'

"You sigh and say, 'I agree. The Love you brought to me and taught me shall always be here for you.'

"Now I see a new image emerge from under the Divine Mother's feet. It is like smoke from a fire. As she laughs a hideous laugh, it curls up around her and takes shape behind her. It is the image of a dragon. Slowly she becomes a red dragon with powerful wings. She can change her shape at will. As she flies up and circles us, she screeches back at you and your Son, 'You are both fools! With very little encouragement from me, your precious puny humans will destroy your creation and each other! Hssssss, hssssss, Hssssss!' she hisses as she flies down to Earth. I cannot see the place."

I look up into the face of the 'Great I Am'. There are tears running down His cheeks. I ask, "You still love her, don't you?"

"Yes. Can you understand why I can't destroy her?"

"Of course." Then I add hesitantly, "But I should tell you that I have seen the Dragon Lady many times in my meditation. We have done battle each time; until I figured out that it was Love that made her run away."

"I know. But what you don't know is that if enough people can reflect the Love back on her, she may come home. And then creation can continue. The Love has to come from the enlightened spirit within the people, not from me. That was why I chose you."

"Thanks a bunch!" I laugh, "It is close, isn't it?"

"Yes it is. I have a plan."

"Finally!" I am ready.

CHAPTER 10
The Quest Begins

My readers should take notice here; my life is rather long. My body is healthy and fit. I still work out every day, do yoga and meditate. But my body strength is no longer that of a thirty five year old. It has all the scars from surgery, illnesses and wounds. It has all the aches and pains from growing old. I can no longer power my way through a project or normal work, but now I have to work smarter doing the same activities with less effort. I'm no longer fast, but I always finish.

I wonder what plan the 'Great I Am' has in mind. One thing is for certain, I can't read his mind as He can read mine. I'll just do whatever he wants me to do. That's what I have always done and always will do. I guess I am as ready as I'll ever be.

I begin my morning meditation and quickly quiet my chattering mind. That's strange. My ego must still be sleeping and that's not like my ego. Suddenly, I'm so cold. I slowly breathe into my mantra to relax; it feels like something is sucking all the heat from the room. I have warm up pants on. I have layers on the top, a wool shirt and a sweatshirt. Yet I still feel ice-cold. My hands and feet are like ice. This makes no sense; my body is always so warm. What is happening to me? I breathe deeply into my mantra to quiet all this chatter and focus on the light.

The eye of the Dragon Lady comes into my head. It is a fiery circle with a black pupil. The fire swirls about the black pupil in violent torrents. Now her other eye comes into my head; it is the same. I'm inside my head clinging to the Light, as the darkness of the Dragon Lady swirls beneath me. The fire of her eyes gives off no light, only dull red whirlpools that suck everything into the black pupils of her eyes. Now her eyes move to where my eyes are and I feel trapped in my head. I confront the Dragon Lady with the light that is in me, as weak as it is, and call her out. Her eyes are burning at the portholes of my skull. I summon up all the love that is in me. She burns on. I see the hate in her eyes and ask, "Why is love so far from you? Remember, your Love and the Love of the 'Great I Am' are One. From your love, a Son, a new light, was born. The great Love from all three of you created everything. Creation is a beautiful expression of the Love that you were. The Love I know from Him was your Love. The power of your Love runs through my veins. There is no greater power in creation, than the power of creation you have together. If you take all the Love that is in me, it will just fill up again, because it is your Love. Take it all and return to the 'Great I Am'." I cross my arms over my chest and bring up all the Love that is within me. It glows with a warm red-yellow light. I stretch out my arms to her and pour out all of it. Before she can move, the love is sucked into the whirlpools of her black pupils. In a nanosecond, she vanishes.

I cross my arms over my chest again and new Love floats in. It is her Love; only she has forgotten it. There needs to be more of us, and maybe she'll remember.

"That was well done, Hoss." The 'Great I Am' is standing next to me, instead of talking to me while I'm in my meditation. I feel 12 years old again and remember His first appearance to me. "You do understand that you can do this better than I can. When you pour out your love to Her, you are revealing Her presence in creation. Believe me, that is a powerful revelation coming from a human. Ultimately, humankind has the love power to bring Her back to me. You have just shown me that it is possible.

Now let's get down to business."

"To what do I owe this honor? I am not used to your external presence," I ask.

"We have some very important things to discuss, and I feel that it will mean more to you if we do it face to face. I have a plan that you will like."

"Before you start, I need to ask you something. Am I going to be able to do this? I'm not a young sprout anymore. I am eager to do this and ready to do this. But my age is a real factor."

"Your age is irrelevant. You took care of your body and overcame every weakness without giving up. You're more than able to do this. Now to the point, as you rightly notice, the one you call the Dragon Lady (a name we can use, but not one that reflects my Love for Her) is manipulating the rational minds and egos of most people. Thus, She blocks our every attempt to bring forward those who connect to me (the ones enlightened or conscious). But She is overlooking a huge section of the population of this planet, all the non-human creatures.

"The connection of most of these creatures goes back for many millenniums, and humans are wiping them out indiscriminately with no regard for the role they play in the delicate balance of each ecosystem. So you are going to save a few of them to capture the attention of the masses and help the people find me again. That is your mission. People need to find me within themselves and not simply feel my presence. I want them to listen and hear my voice. I want them to be one with me, so I can be one with them. I have a plan and purpose for everyone if only we can become one again. However, the one thing that made humans higher than all other creatures in creation, the thinking rational mind, is now making them lower than all other creatures. Because the Dragon Lady is corrupting the rational mind and fostering an ego that is totally out of control, the animals are now going to teach humans.

"There are four species that I want you to help: elephants, silverback gorillas, rhinoceros and Bengal tigers. You will be going to Chad, Rwanda and Kenya in Africa as well as a very sacred place in India. The animals all know that you are coming and will be waiting for you. Humans are hunting them to extinction, and you are going to stop the carnage and protect them forever."

"Wait just a minute; you want me to do battle all by myself?" His enthusiasm is incredible. But I have this image of me standing in front of a bunch of animals with a sword and shield or a Moses staff. "Don't you mean that I am going to bang my staff down on the ground, and you are going to open the earth to swallow up the bad guys?"

"I know that's the way the religions of the world think it will happen, with an angry God full of hatred and vengeance wiping out evil, but they miss the mark. First, that is totally out of character for me. That is not who I am! Yet I know that humans think that way. Secondly, if I do that, there will be "no more nothing left.""

"What you are going to do is redefine the term 'battle'. It will no longer mean, 'two opposing forces trying to kill each other,' but instead it will mean, 'one force choosing between killing itself or living in peace with me'. I will always remain the loving and forgiving Father. But make no mistake; there will be an apocalypse of Biblical proportions as evil destroys itself. You, Hoss, are about to turn the world upside down, or should I say you, Ja Hayah Im, are going to set the world right side up again."

"Who's that?" My confusion is growing.

"In your new persona you need a new name. The

name I've chosen is Ja Hayah Im. You can call yourself Hayah for short. This name represents our oneness. I will always be in you. We will be doing everything as one."

"OK, but I don't understand the new persona bit."

"When you are doing my work, no one will see you as Hoss, as you are now. They'll see you as Ja Hayah Im."

"Is this some kind of Zorro mask or disguise? I like Zorro, the fox; it's a great image. Uh-oh, I don't think I will look good in tights any longer!"

"I don't do tights, masks or disguises. You will become a new person."

"Woo, that's pretty far out there! And, how is that going to happen? Do I need to go into some secret telephone booth?" I wasn't taking Him seriously. But I can see He isn't laughing as he usually does. "I'm just joking." He doesn't even crack a smile. "I'm sure glad we are doing this face to face. Otherwise, I will be in deep trouble. Now, I'll shut up and listen."

Now He smiles, "You are so much fun; I like the idea of having this much fun with everyone on this planet, maybe one day…" Now there is a look of worry on His face. "I want this to be as natural for you as taking a breath." He pauses again.

What does He want me to do? The pause becomes longer. Does He want me to say something? So I say the words, "Here I am! Tell me what to do."

"Can you take five steps?" He smiles broadly.

"Of course, I can take five steps." I take five steps and turn back toward Him. "Wow! What is happening? The arthritis in my knees is gone. I have feeling in my feet. I feel straighter and stronger, as in my prime. This is fantastic!" I start jumping up and down. I run around the room. Again, I say, "This feels fantastic! I can run again."

I leap over the ottoman like a gazelle. "This brings back memories from forty years ago." Now the 'Great I Am' is laughing. I fly past the mirror, catching a glimpse as I pass. "WHAT!!?" I come to a screeching halt causing the rug to wrinkle like an accordion. I even do this, without losing my balance. I slowly walk back toward the mirror.

I'm not one to look in the mirror much. Once, after living in a place for a year, I finally had company. The next morning my friend asks me where the mirror is. I think for a second and realize that the only mirror I have in the whole place is in the bathroom. As a result, I bought this huge mirror at a garage sale.

Cautiously, I step in front of the mirror. I'm speechless. My gray stubble beard is now full length and a rich red/brown again. My gray hair is now long with its original dark blond color and curls. My glasses are gone as are the bags under my eyes. My body is back to its prime condition, a well-trained swimmer's body. I look like I'm 35 again. I slowly turn toward the 'Great I Am', but I can't help looking over my shoulder into the mirror. "Now that is a miracle!"

"Hardly," the 'Great I Am' looks me over, head to toe. "That will do quite nicely, Hayah. Now, you can take five steps in the other direction and turn back into Hoss."

"What if I don't want to?"

"You have no say in the matter. When you need to be Hayah, I will make the change for you. When you don't need to be Hayah, I'll change you back. The only help I need from you is to maintain your connection with me and not make the change so obvious to other people. Try sitting down in your chair."

I start to sit in my chair. By the time I'm three quarters of the way down, I can feel my old body again, and

my butt falls into the chair with a kaboom. That is when I
notice something is still the same. My lightness of being is
the same now as it is when I'm Hayah. I ask, "Why does
my lightness of being never change?"

"I am your lightness of being. It is your connection
with me. That is the same since the day you were born.
Thank you for noticing that, Hoss. I think you are ready."

I stand up and turn to look in the mirror. "When
do I leave?"

"There is a lot you have to do before you leave. Sit
down at your computer. I'm going to dictate some very
important messages, which you will send out."

I sit down and boot-up my computer. My hands
are poised on the keyboard. I look into the face of the
'Great I Am'. He is deep in thought. It is a marvel to see
Him this way. I always assume that His pauses are due to
taking care of so many people at one time. Or maybe he is
shifting from one language to another. But now, I can see
on His face that His incredible mind is cooking up
something special. I wait in silence.

"Hoss, I am one hundred percent connected to
everyone and everything. I can carry on over a trillion
conversations at the same time with people, creatures and
plants. Although right now there are very few people
connecting with me, but not for my lack of trying. Imagine
listening to a man praying for two and a half hours, and not
being able get a word in edge wise. He doesn't know that
I'm here. He is talking to me, but he is only thinking of
himself and his problems. His ego has him so pumped up;
he is blind to my presence. When he finishes, he is up and
out of there so fast it even make my head spin."

CHAPTER 11
The Letters

The face of the 'Great I Am' changes from minor annoyance to determination. "Now, let's get down to business. Take this down:

Dear (whomever),

Over the next few weeks, you will be noticing an unusual migrating pattern of the animals in your area. They are being called together for a specific purpose. Please do not hinder their movement, but make every effort to protect them during this migration. Please distribute and post the following "WARNING" to all troublemakers and poachers who may try to do them harm.

WARNING: From this day forward, all endangered species shall be under the protection of the 'Great I Am'. Any hostile or violent actions taken against these creatures will **"boomerang"** back onto the perpetrators in equal proportion to their intended action. Heed this warning or directly suffer the consequences for your own actions.

I will be visiting your area soon and will contact you with the exact date.

Thank you,

Ja Hayah Im.

The 'Great I Am' nods His head, "Yes! That should do it, no more rules, no more laws just consequences. What you give out; you shall receive back. If you give love, you will receive love. If you try to kill, you will only be killing yourself. Hatred stops here! As a leader in one of my ancient American tribes once said, 'Hatred is the poison a brave takes in hopes that his enemy will die.' Now it's all about consequences."

"OK, Hoss, what's your reaction?"

My heart is pounding in my chest. Is this what He means by redefining the meaning of battle, "one force choosing between killing itself, or living in peace with me."

I understand the words; they sound very good. But I can't see how He is going to protect the animals and me. I focus on my inner peace and shut down my screaming rational mind and ego. That's all right. I can live with it. Every moment of every day, I am prepared to give my life for Him. My life is His anyway. Now, He is asking me to risk it for a very good reason. Without another thought, my lips say the words, "Yes, I'm here; send me."

"Right now, you are going to do the sending. I want you to mail this letter to the following:

Peter Fearnhead, the CEO of African Parks

Lee White, head of Gabon's national park system

Matt Lewis, senior programmer, World Wildlife Fund

Diane Skinner, program officer for IUCN

George Wittemyer, science director for Save the Elephants

Kenya's President Uhuru Kenyatta

Ian Craig co-founded Kenya's Northern Rangelands Trust

Bellim Wijnstekers, CITES secretary-general

Tom Milliken, director of ETIS

Idriss Deby, Chad's president

Rian Labuschagne, manager of Zakouma

National Park in southern Chad

Mike Cranfield, executive director of the Mountain Gorilla Veterinary Project,

Craig R. Sholley, African Wildlife Foundation

Veronica Vecellio, gorilla program coordinator Dian Fossey Gorilla Fund's Karisoke Research Center

Game Rangers Association of Africa

Kenya Wildlife Service Rangers

Omer Hassan al-Bashir, Khartoum, Sudan, Africa

Damien Mander, International Anti Poaching Foundation

Nagarjunsagar-Srisailam Tiger Reserve of Andhra Pradesh in India

National Tiger Conservation Authority of India

"That should start the pot boiling. Now, we have one more letter to write. Take this down:

Dear (name),

Be advised! The trafficking of body parts of any endangered species, taken by poaching, must stop. All those in possession of such body parts or any object or potions made from them must destroy them by fire within 30 days of this letter. Any attempt to dispose of your tainted possession by any other means will constitute an instant failure to comply. This includes all body parts taken in the past or present regardless of international treaties, local allowances or any other allowances. Failure to comply will result in a severe illness and death equal to the suffering of the slaughtered animal. Any person who is not aware of this letter until after they have contracted the illness will have 3 days to destroy their tainted possessions by fire and have the illness reversed. THIS IS NOT A HOAX!

Please share this letter with all those in the trade and with the local press and media.

I will be visiting your area soon and will be happy to meet with you.

Thank you,

Ja Hayah Im

"That's it." The 'Great I Am' looks out the window. His face is very stern. I can feel that He doesn't like having to do this. "What a waste of life, all those poor slaughtered animals die to feed human greed and vanity."

"Are you sure you're not a lawyer?" I know it is a bad joke as soon as I say it.

"Don't remind me that I'm the one who created the law." He shakes His head. "Give a human a law at sun rise and he or she will breed more interpretations by sun set than a gnat can breed in a lifetime. I hope we do better with consequences."

I start laughing so hard at His comment that He can't help but smile.

The 'Great I Am' reflects with His eyes closed. Finally, He says, "It sounds very harsh. Is there any way it can be softened?"

This is a first; He asks me for my advice. I read over the letter several times. There are no loopholes. In actuality, the first letter is harsher, because there is no way to escape the immediate consequences. This letter is harsh, but fair. In fact, it is outright generous compared to what is happening to the animals. I respond, "It is perfect just the way it is. It has to be strong enough to stop the carnage and end the greed that profits from it. It simply includes everyone from the smuggler to the profiteer to the carvers and medicine maker to the people buying the stuff. The only people excluded are those that put the people up to this in the first place."

"I considered that group, but decided the thing that will hurt them the most will be to take the profit out of the venture. I may have to change that later, but let's go with this for now. Here are the places I want you to send this letter.

"Monsignor Cristobal Garcia, in the Philippines

Mr. Thi Phayuha Khiri's head ivory dealer

The Elephant Monk in Kruba Dharmamuni

Steve Galster, director of the Freeland Foundation, in Bangkok

Xue Ping, Li Chunke, China

Gary Zeng of Guangzhou

Meng Xianlin, executive director general of China's CITES

TRAFFIC, the global wildlife-trade monitoring group

Manila, Ivory carvers

The Prime Minister, of Zanzibar, the Islamic island off the coast of Tanzania

All the ivory carvers in Phayuha Khiri and Surin in Thailand

Bangkok's amulet market

China's Beijing Ivory Carving Factory

Guangzhou's Daxin Ivory Carving Factory, in China

Beijing Arts and Crafts Emporium

The Pope, in Rome
All Buddhist monasteries
All international press outlets
CNN and all international media broadcasters
"And anyone else you think can get the word out globally. There, *'Alea iacta est'* (the die is cast) and the new plan is set in motion." He is still staring out the window, with a pensive look on his face. Slowly, He walks over and sits down on the ottoman. He leans forward and holds His head in His hands, with His elbows on His knees.

I watch silently and don't move a muscle. Suddenly, I feel a profound sadness fill the room. It is His sadness. My heart aches and I feel a heavy weight on my chest. I feel this sadness many times in my life, but He is always there to lift the burden from me. How can I possible lift this burden from Him? I can say nothing!

CHAPTER 12
The New Time Begins

As I watch, the 'Great I Am' begins to weep and weep and weep. He sobs for several minutes. I put my arm around His shoulders and cry with Him. His grief is shaking every fiber and cell of my being. My heart seems to sense what is causing it. I have no idea how long this goes on, but then time doesn't matter.

Finally, He begins to speak through His tears. "I want everyone to return and be with me. I want everyone to share in the building of Paradise, which is not a fantasy place or utopia, but a real life with me. Now so many people will die!" A deep moan comes from within Him as though He feels the loss of each soul personally.

"Why are humans so blockheaded? I tell them the same thing repeatedly, and they just don't connect. I sent messenger after messenger and they always heard something else and made the same mistakes. I sent my Son, and they still didn't listen. In fact, they walked away.

"The human mind is denser than the hardest stone in the galaxy. For so many millenniums, I kept trying to reach them, and it was always the same. They always needed to do it their way and have everything their own way. The Dragon Lady can twist them around her little toe in six-tenths of a second and they're happy for it. They search for some magical fix or quick fix, but never fix anything. Without giving it one gram of concern, they can upset the balance of an entire ecosystem, and their only response is, 'Oops, that will take billions of years to reverse itself.' Then, they can turn around the next minute and do it all over again with something else. They don't grasp the fact that they will 'Oops' themselves right out of existence.

"All I hear is 'Master, you are our God. Master listen to us! Master, forgive us! Master, look at us and do something! Master, don't put us off!' And on and on they go telling me to do this and do that. Yet only a few stop to listen to me or connect with me inside them. What they don't realize is that if they make that connection, I will sort things out in a flash.

"As I told my Prophet, 'the desecrator will march into the Sanctuary and citadel, banish worship and prayers and set up an obscene sacrilege in its place.' I thought that was clear at the time, but clear is not possible when it comes to humans. They over think their own mindset, so what do the people hear? The desecrator is some fanatical enemy they can hate. Any bogeyman will do. The Sanctuary and the citadels are their precious churches of brick and mortar, their houses of god, their holy of holies. What they don't realize is that they are building new idols with their own hands (just like the no-god idols of old), thinking I will have a place to live. The worship and prayers are their showy rituals, tedious messages and gim'me prayers from the book of gimme prayers. Then there is their doctrine and dogma, their hundreds of rules telling them what to believe and not believe. Finally, they destroy what is good calling it an obscene sacrilege, like any kind of joyful celebration of My Love, any Devine connection that doesn't fit their formula and any New Age idea that is totally out of the box. With this view of my prophecy, every religion can hate every other religion and that seems to suit them just fine.

"My real and true meaning is simple and clear. The desecrator is humanity's stupid intelligence. I'm their Sanctuary and citadel within them, and they banish their connection with me for pseudo-knowledge of good and evil. Their constant and endless formation of religious

institutions is their obscene sacrilege. Finally, only when
those who return to me within themselves will the
destruction of their pseudo-intelligence and ego be
complete. Only then will they be free.

"In the City of Paradise, there is no temple. For I
and the Lamb are the Temple within everyone there. The
City doesn't even need a sun and moon for light. I am their
eternal light. They will bathe in splendor and their sun
shall never go down. Now you watch, 'Human intelligence'
will turn that into something else. They will say, 'He says
we will no longer need a sun and moon. We can take down
our streetlights, headlights, lamps and candles.' Then when
night comes, they will scream and holler, 'See He doesn't
deliver! There was no miracle. We still have night and day!'
They prefer to live the rest of their lives in the darkness
within them, praising their ignorance, than to connect with
me and live in my Light and Love.

"But all those who discover me within themselves
will rise to heights higher than the highest mountain. I will
turn on their Lights and show them my ways. They'll see
the whole picture and feel how right it is. They will all
experience an incredible lightness of being. And our Light
will be a beacon to the rest of the world. All people will
stream to it saying, 'Let's climb the mountain so we too can
bask in the Light.' However, if they are not connected to
me and hatred is any part of their lives, they will just be
climbing another hill.

"My Son also told them the same message over and
over again; 'the kingdom life is within you; a fire is within
you; the Holy Spirit is within you; I am within you; you are
in me; He will change your life from the inside out.' He
could not have made it more clear when He said to His
disciples, "Let me lead. The 'Great I Am' is in the driver's

seat. Self-sacrifice is the way, my way, to finding yourself, your true self.' Yet their 'pseudo-intelligence' and egos will always foster an 'I-know-better-than-you mentality again and again, playing a holier-than-thou part instead of connecting with me.' They think they can use my words in their Bible studies, meaningless rituals and blah-blah theology, but never have to connect with me in the center of their being. Joshua said to them, 'The Light is inside you. If you nurture it so the Light inside you is not darkened by your chattering mind, ego and materialism; if the whole body shines with Light, with no dark corners; then you will surely live in its radiance.' My favorite is the flesh and blood analogy, 'My blood is in you; your flesh and my flesh are one.' Yet they turned their backs on Him and walked away."

The 'Great I Am' stops weeping while He is talking about His son. I sit down on the floor and look up at him like a child.

He looks deep into my eyes. "The last time I cried like that was while I watched my Son suffering. The greatest problem is, He never stops suffering. The way the so-called-churches twist His message to manipulate and gain power over the people. They create atrocities in His name. They create mountains of greed, ego, self-aggrandizement, cults of personality and an endless list of twisted judgments and rationalizations all supposedly serving Him. Well no more! For the last two thousand years I have been comforting Him and promising that I will come up with a plan to end the hatred and madness." He can see what I'm thinking and says, "Go ahead ask your question."

He holds my gaze, "Will I have to suffer like that?"

"I know you gladly will if I say yes, but you will not have to bear such horrific physical torture. As for the emotional suffering, we will both be going through more than Him. And unlike the events leading up to His death, our endgame is completely unpredictable. Freewill shall take its course. I may know what someone's choices may be and which way they may be leaning, but what they choose will come upon us without warning."

"Let it come!" My words sound a lot braver than I feel. My heart is pounding and the blood is racing through my veins faster than a salt flats race car.

"Well, the new time has begun. Now there will be consequences.

"You mail the letters out and book your flights: 1. To N'Djamena in Chad, Africa. To go from N'Djamena to Zakouma National Park contact my people at MAF (Mission Aviation Fellowship). They will be expecting your call, and Dan and Nan will take you to all your locations in Africa. 2. Then you will need to book a flight from Addis Ababa, Ethiopia to Hyderabad, Andhra Pradesh, India. From there you need to go to Nagarjunsagar-Srisailam Tiger Reserve by bus. 3. The next leg will take you from Hyderabad to Manila, Philippines. 4. From there, you will go to Bangkok, Thailand. 5. The first leg of your return will be from Bangkok to Jerusalem, Israel. Allow two days travel for each leg and three days in each location, except for Africa, where you will need ten days. India may also require five days. You should book changeable tickets just in case there are some unexpected delays."

"Wow, that's quite a journey!" I'm a bit overwhelmed. I know this is not going to be a vacation or easy by any stretch of the imagination. You don't go from the proclamation, "The new time has begun" to "Have a nice trip." I'm still trying to grasp what this new time actually is. Not to mention, how are we going to pull it off?

I can feel His confidence in me, which is very real. But am I really up for the task? That question is not coming out of self-doubts or insecurity, but it is coming from not really knowing or understanding what we are going to do. Add to that, that it often feels like He doesn't know where it is going either. However, I remain positive and ready to serve, "Let's do it! It will only take a couple of days to be ready."

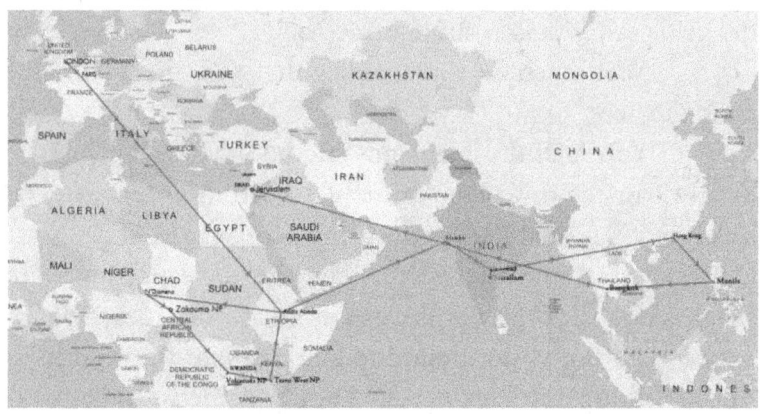

He is in a much happier and determined mood now, "I'll start the animals on the move. Our connection is so strong that they will respond without question. They also need to be ready to meet you. In recent years, their trust in humans is down. But I think they are going to like you. They will see me in you and you in me, just as you will see me in them. You and I will rebuild their trust in humans. What we are about to do is going to turn all that around.

"The animals will lead them! I want the people to see what the animals can do and realize that they can do it as well. The animals have no hate in them. People need to lose their hatred, which comes from an unconscious ego. The animals are all connected to me and will do what I ask unquestioningly. People need to find me within themselves and become part of my will once again. The animals have unconditional love for each other and me. People need to learn the true meaning of Love apart from their sexual passions. They need to be one with my unconditional Love. The animals have a trust and respect for the balance of every ecosystem. The people must stop their blind destruction of the planet for greedy exploitation and become a harmonious part of the world in which they live.

"We have a lot to do Hoss. As you say, 'Let's do it!'" The 'Great I Am' begins to glow brighter and brighter. When the Light reaches its full intensity, it becomes smaller but equal in intensity until it is the size of a tennis ball. The light moves toward me and enters my chest.

I close my eyes and sigh, "Ah, I feel whole again!" He laughs.

CHAPTER 13
The News Is Out

N. al-Egsiro is walking through the open market in Khartoum, Sudan. He is wearing a plain off-white tunic and a stark-white turban with the end of the wrap draping luxuriously around his neck and shoulders. He appears to be a man of confidence and power, as he should, since he is the President of Sudan. He carefully examines some produce.

A few meters way, his number two wife, Diwad, is chatting with another man and his wife. She is an attractive woman with a bright and cheery appearance. She has a plain-blue shawl over her head and around her shoulders. An elegantly rich red-print fabric wraps tightly over her left shoulder and around her body. The man and woman she is talking with are laughing at something she says.

Al-Egsiro picks up a vegetable and sniffs it. Unsatisfied, he sets it back down. He looks up and sees Diwad. He watches her for a moment; a look of disgust comes into his face. He throws his head and shoulders back in a haughty masculine gesture and strides over to where she is standing. In a voice of vibrato, he tells her, "Cover your face woman!" He then nods politely to the other couple.

The other man's wife quickly covers the lower part of her face with her shawl.

Diwad slowly takes the edge of her shawl and holds it tightly over her nose and mouth. Though her eyes are on fire, she nods obediently to al-Egsiro.

Al-Egsiro takes her by the arm and forcibly leads her away from the other couple. "Woman, focus on what we are here for and stop making a spectacle of yourself!"

There is no fear in Diwad's eyes, but she nods

obediently to al-Egsiro.

Al-Egsiro picks up a vegetable, and Diwad shakes her head no and points to another table a little further along. Al-Egsiro walks to the other table and examines the vegetables. He selects three and turns to Diwad. She nods yes. Al-Egsiro turns to the vendor and asks how much.

"For you Mr. President, 70 Pounds."

"That's outrageous!" barks al-Egsiro, "50 Pounds not a pound more!"

The vendor bows his head and reluctantly nods yes.

As al-Egsiro takes out the money and starts to hand it to the vendor, Diwad reaches out and removes two coins from his hand. The vendor is about to object when he locks eyes with Diwad. Suddenly the vendor becomes very nervous and covers it by laughing. He takes the remaining coins in al-Egsiro's hand.

Bowing his head, he says, "thank you, thank you, thank you."

As al-Egsiro and Diwad turn to walk away, she hands the two coins to al-Egsiro. Al-Egsiro smiles and rolls his shoulders back, looking very victorious and every bit the general that he is. They finish their shopping and walk home with silence between them. On the way al-Egsiro greets people and plays the President; inflating his ego with every contact.

When they reach their stately villa, Diwad flies in the door first ripping off her wraps and shawl and throwing them to a servant girl, who runs out of the room. Diwad spins around and is in al-Egsiro's face before he makes three steps inside the door.

She shouts in a low intense screech, which is almost a hiss, "Don't ever humiliate me like that again! I know you have to keep up appearances in public, and I allow you that.

I even allow you an occasional show of dominance for your precious public image. But don't ever try a stunt like that again. Get it?!"

A flash of rage swells up in al-Egsiro, and he starts a swing to slap Diwad.

Before his arm can move fifty centimeter, Diwad has a hold of his thumb and his momentum bends it backward. With her other hand, she karate thumb strikes him in the Adam's apple. In less than a second, al-Egsiro is gasping for breath and trying to scream; which comes out as a squeak. He struggles to free himself, but Diwad is right with him and controlling him all the way increasing the pressure on his thumb. Finally, she maneuvers him into his overstuffed chair and grabs him by the testicles, clamping down hard. He squeaks out a scream.

Diwad's hiss is more guttural now, "Listen, you pathetic excuse for a man, you play by my rules or I'll give you a real reason to be infertile!"

Al-Egsiro goes limp in his chair and begins to moan and whimper. As Diwad lets go of his thumb and testicles, he grabs his throat with one hand and his scrotum with the other and massages gently.

Diwad crosses the room and turns on the TV for him. She turns back to him and says in a genuinely kind and sweet voice, "There, you can watch yourself on the news." She then calmly leaves the room as though nothing happened.

Al-Egsiro sits quietly watching himself on the government TV channel. Occasionally, he tests his voice after watching one of his speeches, "La, la, la." He clears his throat and does it again, "La, la, la. La, la, la." Each program inflates his ego and pumps new swagger back into his masculinity.

Suddenly a special bulletin interrupts one of his favorite conference clips. The newscaster says with excitement, "This is just in. There seems to be a mass migration of most of the African elephant population. They are heading for Sothern Chad. Here we see an entire herd of elephants crossing the Nile River about 30 kilometers North of Abri in Northern Sudan. Authorities expect that they will cross the desert tonight. Their course is direct and their only detours are to go around small villages and camps...."

Al-Egsiro is on the edge of his seat. He calls out, "Hey, Sugar, come and see this!"

"Some of the tribes see this as a Holy event. You can see them bowing and kneeling. While others are doing ancient dances...."

Diwad strolls in, but does a double take on the TV. She can't take her eyes off the picture. "What the hell is this?!" Slowly she sidesteps into the room and sits on the front edge of the sofa.

"Here we have one of the tribal leaders. Can you tell us why the tribe believes that this is an event to celebrate?"

"There are ancient legends that predict a time when the animals will lead us."

"Where will they lead us?"

"They will lead us into the new time."

"What does that mean?"

"The new time has begun! The elephants are telling us that...."

Al-Egsiro's face fills with worry, "It's just like that letter I showed you. Apparently, it is not a hoax."

Diwad asks, while her eyes stare at the TV, "What

did you do with the letter?"

"I threw it in the trash. How am I supposed to know it's important? I remember you said, 'Don't give it a second thought.'"

There is an excitement building in Diwad's body, "Switch to CNN."

Al-Egsiro quickly punches buttons on the remote.

CNN is already in the middle of the live news report, "...from Ethiopia, South Sudan, Central African Republic, Cameroon, Nigeria. An elephant migration of this magnitude has never been seen before. There must be several thousand. Ten years ago, before the slaughter of so much of the herd, that number can have been a hundred times..."

Diwad jumps to her feet, "Hit the mute button!"

Al-Egsiro complies immediately.

Diwad can hardly contain herself, "What do you see, Big E?"

"A shit load of elephants, Sugar."

"I see a shit load of ivory! It's harvest time!"

Al-Egsiro is feeding off her excitement, "That will be the biggest haul of ivory in history."

"Forget about history. That haul of ivory will give us a corner on the market for the next fifty years. Can you do it Big E?"

"It's a piece of cake. From my new airfield in Kurmuk, I can deploy 6 Mi-17 choppers, 180 troops, and 2 of those white flatbed trucks to haul out the ivory. We can paint UN on the front of the trucks, and it will look like we are hauling aid supplies. I'll come up with a place to hide the stash, so we don't flood the market."

Diwad straddles al-Egsiro in his chair and gives him a passionate kiss. "I love the way your mind works. When can you start?"

"The elephants are probably going to Zakouma National Park in Chad. Been there done that. It will take them about eight days to get there. I can have the trucks rolling on the morning of the fifth day, which will put them in place when the elephants arrive and give us on the ground reconnaissance. That means we harvest the ivory at daybreak nine days from now."

"Woo wee! I can't wait! I love it." She is smothering him in kisses, "I love it," grinding in his lap, "I love it."

I wake up in a cold sweat. It is 04:23 in the morning. "What's this? A nightmare? How can anyone have so much sex without a speck of love? These people not only have an obsession with wealth, they have an obsession with power and destruction," I tell myself. I go to the bathroom. The images haunt me. I begin to sense that this was more than an erotic dream. I remember those names from some place. I sit down and start to meditate. In less than a minute, I see his light within me. "What was that," I ask?

"Now you know what I see."

"You mean that was actually taking place?"

"Yes, but look at it this way. Now we know what the enemy is about to do."

"You're kidding! One against 6 gunships and a 180 seasoned troops. I don't need to know odds like that."

"But you'll have a lot of backup."

"Yeah? Who?

"The elephants."

CHAPTER 14
The Elephant Class

The night before I leave, I organize all my clothes
and travel gear on my bed and double-check my list. This is
not to be a trip with creature comforts, and I am to take
only the bare necessities. I roll up my sleeping bag and stow
it in the bottom compartment of my backpack. I assemble
each day's clothes in separate bundles and stow them in the
backpack in reverse order of use. Now I will not have to
disturb everything in my pack to find a pair of socks. Rain
gear has its own compartment in the pack. My detachable
daypack attaches to the top of the backpack. In it I carry
my first-aid kit, ten essentials, and my maps and compass in
the top pouch. Two empty water bottles go into their
compartments on each side. Three wide webbing straps
with side-release-buckles go into a small compartment on
the front. I will wrap these around the pack and bind all
the straps together for baggage check in on the airlines.

In my small personal bag, I put my contact
information, itinerary, tickets, passport, billfold, electronic
tablet and all my travel gear. This fastens to the front
shoulder straps when I am wearing the backpack and has its
own over the head strap for when I'm carrying just the
personal bag. I make one last check of the list. I am ready.

On the fifth day, I start the first leg of my journey.
As I step off the bus and collect my backpack, I ask the
'Great I Am', "When do I change into Hayah?"

"Not until you arrive in Chad. You only have a
passport for Hoss."

"Of course! I'm only hoping for a younger body to
do the travelling. To say that travelling is difficult and

exhausting would be an understatement."

"I hear that all the time, but you will do very well."

As I check-in and go to the gate, I smile and greet all those I meet. Most people don't know how to deal with this anymore; but a few go from a frown or pensive stare to a smile. Now, I can actually feel that their whole day is about to change.

I meditate and engage in my favorite pastime of people watching during the flight to Paris. I often try to identify the people that are connecting with the 'Great I Am' within. This is very difficult to do. Some people think they are connecting and aren't. While others are connecting and don't know who is talking to them. I only wish that it could be more people, especially for Him, because He wants it to be everybody.

As I wait for my connecting flight in Paris, I connect with my eternal present to rekindle all the joyful experiences I had in this city. It is a special city, with a special culture and special people. These people can really connect with the true meaning of Love; this is it. People of Paris please pay attention. The Author of Love is calling you now.

I board the flight to Addis Ababa, Ethiopia, Africa on Ethiopia Airlines. This turns out to be a very interesting flight. The woman sitting next to me is a Professor of Biological Sciences at the University of Cambridge, UK, and her areas of expertise are the African elephant and other African spices. She is coming back to study the migration of the elephants and revisit the silverback gorillas. (Of course, you know this is not a chance meeting.) Phyllis likes to talk about elephants, so I shut up and listen. She gives me a wealth of information. My attraction to her makes this easy. During that eight-hour flight, I learn more about elephants and silverback gorillas than all my research for the last month. Phyllis is an incredible teacher and instinctively is able to fill in all the gaps in my understanding of these animals. The only question I'm able to answer for her is, "Why are the elephants doing this unusual migration?"

The answer comes in the form of two questions, "Will you consider that instinct is a connection with the Essence of Being in all things; and that most all animals still connect with it, but humans don't? Can it be possible that the planet is about to go through a new reversal; and the animals know it and we don't?"

She ponders these questions as the plane lands. We are both changing planes to go to N'Djamena, Chad. During this time, I see her studying me carefully and then looking away. She catches me doing the same. When we board the connecting flight, she is sitting in the front and I am sitting in the back. I can't help but think, "Well that's that."

The cabin settles down, and I begin to focus on my meeting with Dan and Nan in N'Djamena. I look out the window and start to meditate on a beautiful tree no more than 15 meters high, but whose branches spread out 12 meters from its trunk. Immediately, I connect with the 'Great I Am' within. It is peaceful. Now, I feel a disturbance next to me and start to come out of my meditation. The very large man sitting next to me is struggling out of his seat with some difficulty and moving toward the front of the plane. To my surprise, Phyllis emerges from the galley and slips into his seat.

She smiles broadly and says, "I've been pondering your questions."

I return the smile and look down the aisle at the

large man.

She reads the question on my face, "He was desperately in need of the extra room in the front seats."

I smile radiantly, "Welcome." I have to remind myself that this woman is at least fifteen years younger than I am. And I am on a mission. "If you have the answers then you're a lot smarter than most of the people I know."

"To even ask those questions, you are a lot smarter than you're letting on!"

"Oh, I am just a bear of very little brain, and strange things just pop into my gray fluff all the time."

"You're a Pooh fan? Well, that moves you up three notches higher. It means that you already know the answers and the rest of the scientific community isn't even close."

I take off my glasses to clean them. "I don't 'know' answers. They seem to come to me. But you are right about the scientific community."

"Will you share the answers with me?"

"I can't. You must find them within yourself."

"My mind doesn't have a clue as to where to look."

"That is exactly correct. To see that is the first step. Now put your mind aside and what is left?"

"My gray fluff?"

"Precisely, and what is your gray fluff?"

"My stuffing."

"And the other name for your stuffing is…?"

"My body. The answers are in my body?" She is having a revelation.

An announcement interrupts this banter, that we can see the migration of the elephants out our windows. Phyllis leans over me and we look out. There are thousands of elephants on the move. It is spectacular!

Phyllis says, "This is strange. A month ago, the

elephant count in this area totaled only 457. The poachers nearly wiped them out and they stopped breeding. I hope they're safe."

"They're safe now and for…" I'm about to say 'for all time', but I catch myself and quickly cover, "for now anyway." Fortunately, she doesn't react.

Suddenly, I see two white flatbed trucks, with UN letters on the front, racing parallel with the elephant herd. They are about two kilometers from the elephants. In a flash, a nightmare becomes a reality and reminds me of the real danger that lies ahead. I quickly pull back from the window and press my head against the headrest.

Everyone on the plane is looking out their windows and watching the spectacle for several minutes. They don't have a clue as to what is going down. I utter under my breath to the 'Great I Am', "You never do anything in a small way."

He quickly replies, "That's not true. Sometimes, I help a 12 year old with his Halloween pranks." His laughter rings inside me, helping to prepare me for what's ahead and relieves the tension of the moment.

I look at the back of Phyllis' head. The smell of her hair fills my nostrils. I really like this woman. Oh, to be younger, that I might expose my heart to Cupid's arrow. The fact is, I am smitten, but in a very different way. Phyllis looks up into my face and pauses for a second. Her eyes are clear and full of compassion. (Yes, that's the right word, not passion but compassion.) At least that is how I read it. If I let my imagination loose, I'm sure it will create the other in a heartbeat. I blush and hope Phyllis doesn't see my thoughts.

Phyllis leans back in her seat.

The captain comes on and announces that we are

about to land.

Phyllis turns to me, "I hope we meet again."

"I hope so too, but I have a big meeting here. Our time together has been joyous. Thanks for the crash course. With any luck, we'll connect again."

"I look forward to that," she says.

As we walk off the plane, I stop to let another man and woman go in front of me. In the next five steps, I change into Hayah. When Phyllis steps onto the tarmac, she turns to look back, but the man she is looking for is gone. I feel sorry for her, but have to avoid eye contact.

CHAPTER 15
The Elephant Meeting

After I retrieve my backpack and go through the Chad version of customs, I spot Dan and Nan and head toward them. They are studying the passengers from the plane, but don't notice me.

I walk up and introduce myself, "Hi, I'm Hayah."

He responds in a friendly tone shaking my hand, "Nice to meet you." He looks over a list on a clipboard and checks off my name. "Great, put your backpack on the wagon over there and we'll head for the plane in a couple of minutes." He then turns to study the other passengers.

I follow his directions and stand by the wagon waiting patiently and studying the situation. My ego seizes the opportunity to work on me, 'You're the VIP here. They have no right to push you off to the side like this.' I center myself immediately, bending over to touch the ground, stretch, stand up one vertebra at a time, stretch my hands up to the sky, stretch again and breathe.

My ego retreats and I hear His voice, "Keep a low profile. Remember, this is not about you. It is about the mission."

A few others check in and Dan and Nan warmly receive them. Finally, Phyllis checks in. Of course, she is going to the same place. She engages Nan in a concern.

She explains, "The elderly gentleman sitting next to me on the plane is not getting off. Can you see if something is wrong with him?"

Nan walks over to the crew and returns after a brief discussion. "The crew says the plane is clear and all passengers are off."

"That's strange. I wonder where he is. I wanted to

ask for his name."

I smile and chuckle to myself. The words that ring in my ear are, 'Who is that masked man?'

Now I hear His voice again. This time I can tell that He is very serious, "LOW PROFILE!"

I focus on the mission as Dan herds everybody over to the MAF plane. Dan stows the luggage, everybody buckles up and we take off for Zakouma National Park.

As soon as the plane levels off and the course is set in, Dan addresses the passengers, "I want to welcome you onboard Mission Aviation Fellowship. I am Dan and this is my wife Nan. If you need anything during the flight, she is happy to help you. Since most of you are first time fliers to Zakouma, I want you to know that the airstrip is grass and can be a little bumpy. After we land you will have about a twenty minute hike to your brand new lodge, (There is a groan among the other passengers.) which comes with the Zakouma ambiance. I thank you for flying MAF and remind you that we are a non-profit mission, and encourage you to visit our website at www.maf.org and make a personal or institutional donation to our African Mission. Enjoy the flight and the beauty that surrounds you and is within you."

Bingo! They are connected to the 'Great I Am', I assume.

"Not quite yet," He chimes in. "They are ready, and you are going to bring them home."

I study Dan and Nan and can see their radiance flickering on and off in them. Now I shift my gaze to the others. The inner energy in them is a dull gray in all but one. Phyllis has a slight glow. As I listen to their chatter, I learn that they are all VIP science experts from all over the world. They are swapping ego stories about publications and research projects. The only reason they are here is to study the elephant migration. I think; well at least their energy is not black. I have enough to deal with, meaning the pending attack, without having to deal with these well-meaning intellectuals.

I look out the window to enjoy as Dan put it, "The beauty that surrounds me." Everything that my eyes can see is awesome! There are not only thousand of elephants; there are thousands of water buffalo, thousands of antelopes, thousands of Lelwel's hartebeests, hundreds of kob (*Kobus kob*, a fawn colored antelope) and many lions. Then there are the birds. Oh, the colors of the birds! We are not so high so a saddle-billed stork flies along with the plane for a while. The Fan-tailed widowbirds give a completely new meaning to the red-winged blackbird species. The Scarlet-chested Sunbird redefines red. The Egyptian Vultures, majestic in flight, but drab in color, circle in the sky over new lion kill. I can't help but think that I am seeing a little piece of paradise.

Dan circles the new lodge before banking and lining up with the landing strip. The other passengers are white knuckled in their seats. I sit back and relax, knowing the landing is going to be a lot softer than tarmac, and the run out will be as bouncy as a snowmobile.

Everyone climbs out of the plane and most of them congregate to figure out if there is a way to have a lift to the lodge. I thank Dan and Nan for a great flight as they are pulling out the bags and supplies. I ask if they are staying or flying back and am very pleased to learn that they are staying. I invite them to my meeting with Reid, the park manager and the park rangers and ask if we can meet afterward. I am grateful for their positive response.

I grab my backpack, undo the binding bands, stow

them, throw the pack on my back and start up the trail to the lodge. I notice Phyllis watching me as I head up the trail and give her a broad smile. She smiles in return.

It takes me only fifteen minutes to hike to the lodge.

Our host greets me warmly, "Welcome, Mr. Hayah. Mr. Reid says you shall have our best room. Follow me."

"Wait a minute. This is very kind of you, but I will take your smallest room. The one nobody else wants. There are many VIPs on their way and they will want nice rooms. I may not even sleep in my room tonight. I will probably sleep with the elephants."

"Mr. Hayah, you don't need to do that. We don't have any small room, but you can have a bunk in the bunkroom."

"I think it will be more fun with the elephants. Do you have a safe place for my backpack?"

"Yes, Mr. Hayah. I can have it in the office, which is my room."

"Thank you so much." I take off my backpack and give it to her. "Where can I find Reid?"

"He's down at the horse barn, about thirty meters to the right." She points out the front door.

As I step off the front porch, I meet Phyllis, who is about fifty meters ahead of the others. I tip my hat, smile and buzz past her. She returns my smile, and her eyes follow me as I walk down to the horse barn. I turn around, walking backward now, and catch the eye of the host as Phyllis climes the steps. I give her an OK signal and point to Phyllis. The host smiles broadly and knows exactly what I mean.

In the horse barn, I find Reid tossing the last couple of forks full of horse manure in a wheelbarrow. I grab an extra fork and start to pull down fresh straw for the stall.

Reid wheels the load out of the barn, dumps it and returns with an empty wheelbarrow. He watches in silence for a few seconds while I finish.

He holds out his hand. "Thank you for the help. You must be Hayah. I see you know your way around horses."

"For all the work, they are still less maintenance and more reliable than a car."

"Isn't that the truth!" We both laugh and shake hands.

Reid takes my fork and racks it with his. "Thanks for coming down. I need to talk to you before we meet with the team." He leads me into the tack room and we sit down. "Look, when I read your letter, I thought to myself, 'He is just another nut case.' Then after your phone call, all this starts really happening. The elephants not only start migrating, they come strait here and are congregating at the exact spot you said. In fact, most are already here. I'm not going to ask how you know all this, but I sense that you are connected to a higher power than I am."

I smile and look him in the eye, "Not higher Reid, but within you, just like He is within every one of the creatures out there in the park. Over the next twenty-four hours, the elephants are going to turn everything we know upside down. What is important right now is that you follow my instructions exactly, so no one is hurt or killed."

"Whatever you say goes. I will back you a hundred percent. But what do you know that I don't know?"

"There will be an attack on the elephants tomorrow morning at sunup, bigger than any attack you have ever seen or can imagine."

"Oh, no! There is no way my team can deal with that. What are we going to do?"

"You and your team are going to do nothing. Take all weapons and lock them up. I need you and your team to be my witnesses along with the VIPs. Can you do that?"

"Who's going to stop them?!"

"The elephants and I."

"I hope you know what you are doing."

"We're just doing what He tells us. The rest is up to Him."

"You have more guts than I do, my friend." Reid shakes his head and stands up. "Come on, let's go talk to the team." I follow him to the meeting room in the lodge.

Everyone is assembling including Phyllis, Dan, Nan and the VIPs. The rangers are in their camouflage dress uniforms and very military looking. They are all in their late forties to early fifties. The gathering of the elephants is creating an extremely positive mood and electric excitement among the group. Reid settles everyone down, "I welcome you all here on this very special occasion of the gathering of the elephants. In a few moments, we are going to hear from the man that brought the elephants here. After his talk, we're going to have a fine dinner done by our new staff. You are in for a real treat. After dinner, we will go down to the elephants and celebrate. Now I give you Ja Hayah Im."

"Thank you Reid. First of all, I'm not the one responsible for bringing the elephants here. The 'Great I Am' deserves that credit. And from now on all endangered species are under His protection, just as you can be. The elephants are going to teach you how. All you have to do is connect to Him as they are connected to Him with only Love in their hearts and you can have the same protection. Tomorrow at daybreak, you will witness the new curtain open. Tonight, we will walk and talk with the elephants and you can take all the pictures you want.

"For tomorrow, I have very specific instructions. You are to witness the event from the roof of the lodge only. From that vantage point, you will be perfectly safe and be able to see everything. Do Not, I repeat, DO NOT come down to the elephants! It will only result in your death. If you have weapons of any kind, leave them in your room. You will not need them to defend yourself. Are we perfectly clear with this?"

A man stands up in the back, bubbling with anger, "Look Mr. ...Whatever, I didn't get my reputation by playing it safe. No one is going to tell me NOT to be in the thick of the action. I'll shoot where I bloody well please!"

I calmly focus on his fiery eyes, "I know who you are Dick, and I know your work. Please try to work with me on this. Otherwise, you will be a casualty before breakfast, and you won't leave behind one shot worth printing."

Reid stands up and addresses Dick in a commanding tone, "Dick, you either agree to work with him on this or you're out of here tonight."

I see Dick's ego about to explode and jump in, "Dick, Dick! Answer your phone! Your wife, Abby is calling." His cell phone starts to ring. Reid looks at me, shakes his head and sits down. Dick picks up. The whole room is on hold waiting for him to complete his call. Dick disconnects and looks up with a puzzled look on his face. I calmly ask, "Dick can I meet you out on the porch for a minute."

Dick replies softly, "Sure."

I conclude, "Any other problems?" The room is silent. I start to laugh, "Then let's have some great food and a little fun. The elephants are calling us!"

Everyone stands up and goes into dinner and Dick

and I slip out on to the porch. I can see Reid out of the corner of my eye standing discreetly in the window.

Dick is full of concern now, asking me, "You know what that was all about don't you?"

"Yes, I do. Everything is going to be just fine, and what was in her dream will not happen. Do you see that tall tree over there, a little over twice the size of the lodge?"

Dick nods, "Yes."

"Figure out a way to climb that tree and you will find at the top a natural platform. (Don't ask me how I know. I just do.) Up there you can set up your tripod and use a telephoto lens to take the best award winning photos of your life. Now Dick, can you promise me you won't do anything dumb tomorrow morning?"

Dick meekly responds, "Thank you. I promise."

We walk into dinner, but Reid pulls me off to the side.

Reid asks me, "Who the hell are you anyway?"

I respond with a smile, "I feel that you know the answer to that already."

"Well you are sure making a believer out of me!"

We walk into dinner together. Reid sits with his team and I sit with Dan and Nan.

CHAPTER 16
The Elephant Dance

Both, Dan and Nan, are about to jump out of their skin with excitement.

Nan starts asking her questions before I can take a breath, "Who is this 'Great I Am' you're talking about?"

I breathe out, "I takes the name from Moses' story of the burning bush. Moses asks the Creator, 'What shall I call you?' The correct translation of the answer is, 'I am the Essence of your Being I am.' Which tells us not only Who or What He is, but where He is. The 'Great I Am' is within us and all things. I can see Him right there within you. You are just not looking for Him yet."

Both of them sit there with their mouths open. Now they both start to speak at the same time, "We both are…" They look at each other and laugh.

Dan continues, "We have been talking about this for the last three months. We both feel something inside but can't connect."

Nan jumps in, "We pray to Him for hours. We talk to Him all day long. We both are sensing something, but can't define it."

Again, both of them chime in at the same time, "How can we reach Him?"

We all laugh and I notice that the rest of the dining room is focusing on our table.

I speak loud enough so those that are listening can hear, "It is the greatest secret in the universe, which has been hiding in plain view for all to find. It is so simple, but so hard to do. Are you ready? Stop talking; stop thinking; turn off your ego. Now breathe. Listen in silence and stillness!"

The room becomes totally still and silent. I watch Dan and Nan focus on their breathing. Each of them begins to glow with an inner radiance. Tears stream down their cheeks. Slowly one of Nan's hands moves toward one of Dan's and they touch. Light beams dance on their heads like fire. A total peacefulness fills their bodies and expands throughout the room.

Nan whispers to Dan, "Is He talking to you?"

"Yes! Do you feel His Love?"

Together they both say, "Yes. Yes. Yes!" And they slowly open their eyes.

I reach across the table and put my hand on theirs, "Now you are baptized with the fire of the Holy Spirit." I look deep into their eyes, "Now the hard work begins. Your mind and ego will try to take charge. You will need to learn how to quit them down."

The staff, who was watching all this, quickly brings out the plates and sets them in front of us.

The host asks me, "Hayah, will you offer the blessing?"

"Surely!" I respond without hesitation and add, "But let's do this a different way. Let's do it together. Meditate on your plate. Be aware of the essence of being in the vegetables. It is not dead, and it is about to become part of you. Be aware of the essence of being in the venison, who offers herself for you. She shall live on within you. Rejoice and be aware that your essence of being is one with them, and they are one within you. Oh, Yes."

We eat. The room buzzes with excitement. I notice that Phyllis is watching me. The Rangers are laughing and in high spirits for the first time in years. The VIP scholars are deep in debate about the migration. As I finish my meal, I clear my place and take my dirty dishes to the kitchen. I thank the staff and congratulate the cooks. Now, I reenter the hall only to end up face to face with Phyllis.

She says, "I met an elderly gentleman on the plane, who has similar views to yours about the essence of being in animals and things."

Feigning interest, I respond, "Really? Is he here?"

"No, I lost him in N'Djamena. Can we talk about your ideas?"

"Great, walk with me down to the elephants."

"OK."

We walk down the front steps and head toward the meeting place of the elephants.

The scientist in Phyllis is looking for documentation, "From where do you come by your ideas?"

"It is not an idea. It is an experience."

"So you don't have any proof, any evidence."

I laugh and smile at Phyllis, "Forgive me Phyllis, but I am about to turn your scientific world upside-down. An idea is a thought. Any proof is also thought. Any evidence is a thought interpretation of a perception. Now Phyllis, can you tell me if you actually see, hear, smell, taste or touch thoughts?"

"OK, but how do you experience the essence of being?"

"By shutting down your mind and ego and connecting with your body through your breath, you will see, hear and feel your essence of being. You will find the 'Great I Am' within you."

"It sounds so simple."

I know that Nan and Dan are following us along with many others.

Nan startles Phyllis, "It is simple, but very difficult. We felt Him very strongly, but now He is gone."

I comfort them, "You're mind and ego will not give up without a fight. They will draw on all that doctrine and dogma which is part of your thinking, all the laws religion uses to control you, and they will beat you down with them. Don't be angry. Don't be worried. Just shut them down with each breath you take. Tonight and tomorrow you have a valuable ally to help you, the elephants."

Dan is struggling. "I feel that, but what do they have that we don't?"

"Dan, can you see that that question is a mind and ego question? Phyllis knows the answer. Phyllis, tell them what WE have that the elephants don't have."

Phyllis smiles like the star pupil with the right answer, "A rational mind and ego."

"There is nothing to block the 'Great I Am' within them. All day, the incredible energy all around us grows stronger and stronger. Breathe and let your mind and ego go. Connect with the elephants and He will be there. Now I have to prepare them for tomorrow."

I walk closer to the elephants. Dan and Nan follow, but keep a safe distance. Phyllis holds her position and watches from there.

The elephants are growing more eager with my presence. A large family bunches together in front of me. I raise both hands over my head. Immediately the elephants lift their trunks and trumpet. I slowly move into the midst of the family. There is a young calf. When I open my arms in love, the calf comes running. He slides to a stop just centimeters away. He raps his trunk around my waste; as I hug his head. I put my forehead to his forehead and together we connect to the 'Great I Am'. Now I look up and there are twenty-five huge heads hanging over us. As I walk out of the group with my hands outstretched and palms up, each elephant swipes the palm of my hand with the tip of their trunk.

I run up the long column of elephants greeting each family, hugging their young calves and connecting with them. The elephants are so loving and responsive; I form an instant bond with them and them with me. They trust me; I trust them. This is the way it should be between all humans and animals. This is the way it CAN be when humans connect!

As I reach the end of the column, I look back down the column and cannot see the beginning. We need to be more together tomorrow morning. I motion to the last family; they already anticipate my move. Slowly the end of the column bends out and follows me next to the first column. After about fifty meters, l turn and walk backwards a few meters. The column is bending in perfect order, one family after another.

According to Phyllis, this kind of family interaction is very rare if not impossible. She must be having a field day watching this behavior.

We are making great progress, a hundred meters without a hitch. As I come on two-hundred meters, I can now see the beginning of the column. Uh oh! We are about six-hundred meters from the beginning. That means we will be four hundred meters long when these two columns are together. I keep the column moving.

I can't resist the joke with the 'Great I Am', "How many children are you inviting to this party?"

"Do you want more? I can fly some in."

I don't know if you can hear an elephant laugh, but hearing ten-thousand laughing all at once is enough positive energy to wake Red Buttons from the dead.

I am really starting to like these elephants. They are

such gentle and friendly creatures. And a lot more intelligent than humans are ready to admit. It's a heavenly love affair. Now I can hear the 'Great I Am' laughing, which starts the elephants going again.

We are making great progress, only about two-hundred meters to go. I can see the rangers checking the elephants out. Nan and Dan are playing with the young calf in the first family. Phyllis watches me and starts to walk closer to the elephants. Reid is studying the military formation of the elephants.

As l reach the head of the column, Reid shouts out, "A three column defense will be stronger."

I signal him with an OK sign.

Phyllis reaches out and pets one of the females, and asks, "How do you know so much about elephants?"

As I turn to head back to the end of the formation, l shout back, "l had a great teacher."

In a full run, l head for the end of the columns. I shout to the 'Great I Am', "l need your help. We don't want to split up any families. Tell me when to stop." After l reach about three-hundred meters, I slow to a fast walk. I hear his command, "Three, two, one, stop. Now hold your hands together and motion for them to separate."

I do this and one-hundred and fifty meters of elephants move at the same time. Even I am in awe. I motion for them to follow and again they anticipate my wishes. Slowly the third column moves in front of the first two.

Suddenly, I see the two white flatbed trucks pull into view about a kilometer away. Now a young bull elephant breaks ranks and charges toward the trucks. I whistle in a shrill piercing tone. The bull elephant skids to a stop and paws the ground with his ears wide spread. I run over and stand directly in front of him. He lowers his head. I step forward and put my arms around his head and my forehead to his forehead. He reconnects to the 'Great I Am' and I feel him breathe deeply. When I step back, I raise my hand over my head. He raises his trunk and trumpets. Together we walk back to the formation. He takes his place with his family, with a few very distinct gestures from the lead bull elephant.

In short order, the third column is in position. Reid comes out to join me in front of the formation. He scans the formation from left to right and back again.

Now without looking at me, he says quietly, "Wow, it looks so intimidating. It looks like an ancient Roman attack formation. Now, I know what it is like to face such a force. I can imagine coming face-to-face with this in battle; if I ever do, I will probably freeze with fright. By the way, what are the UN guys doing here?"

"They're not UN. They're doing reconnaissance."

"Do you want us to take them out?"

"No, I have plans for them."

"No surprise there!"

In the distance, I can hear country western line dance music. I turn to be sure, and confirm that it is coming from the white trucks. They see me looking at them and start to turn it up. I give them thumbs up, and they crank it as loud as they can.

I turn and motion for Phyllis, Dan and Nan to join us. Now, I notice Dick coming out from among the elephants.

I shout to him, "You may want to shoot this on video." Dick changes settings on his camera, as I line everybody up.

No explanation is necessary. The five of us start

doing a line dance and laughing boisterously. Within a few seconds, the elephants join in, and Dick goes nuts. Over ten-thousand elephants doing a line dance, and without the footage no one would believe it. Quickly the rangers, the staff and the VIPs all join in. The joy and positive energy is over the moon. All of us are near hysterics when Dick points towards the trucks. Our lines turn to face them, and the trucks are bouncing up and down about a half a meter off the ground. Only then do we realize that our bouncing step is due to the elephants moving the earth.

We turn around to face the elephants again and clap our hands, raise them over our head, shouting and singing. The elephants raise their trunks and trumpet. The sound and energy of that moment was just what we all needed to end the day.

The sun sets slowly behind the elephants.

CHAPTER 17
The Boomerang Effect

Reid pulls me aside, "Where will you be tonight?"

I put my arm around his shoulders so he can feel my calm resolve, "Sleeping with the elephants to keep them calm. At sun up, we are forming a battle circle. I am counting on you to keep everyone else in line. Remember, no weapons of any kind, regardless of what they see, and don't panic. After 04:00, no one comes down to the field. When it is over, use your own judgment about coming down. Those that do come down must do so in the spirit of loving reverence, not victory."

"Affirmative! I want you to know that you're making a believer out of me, and I never thought those words could cross my lips." Reid shakes my hand and heads up to the lodge with the rangers.

Phyllis comes up and takes my hand and holding on to it says, "Thanks for the best dance of my life." She rounds up the rest of the VIPs and heads up to the lodge.

Dan and Nan come up to me and study my eyes for a moment. Dan says, "We want to be with you through this and help you and the 'Great I Am'."

Nan adds, "We don't care what the sacrifice is; we are ready."

"I can feel your commitment, but listen to what He is telling you. Your connection is still fragile, and your mind and ego can trip you up very easily. He wants you to build up your armor, by controlling your mind and ego, because He has plans for you. Go back to the lodge, be my witnesses tomorrow and tonight read in THE MESSAGE, the Gospel of John, chapter 6 along with the 8th chapter of Paul's letter to the Romans. With the 'Great I Am' within you, it will be like reading them for the first time. You will surely wonder why others can't see it. Is that OK with you?"

They both answer, "Yes."

Dan adds, "Can you teach us to meditate?"

Nan jumps in, "You make it look so easy. But you're right; we can't hold the connection very long. We need your help."

"You can count on it. Let's make a plan for tomorrow afternoon. Don't let it be a surprise if others want to join us. For now, just exhale and relax. Let the breath flow in and out. Shut down your mind and ego and focus on your breathing. We'll work on the details tomorrow. Have a restful night."

They turn and head back to the lodge with an arm around each other. I head into the center of the elephants. They know why I am there. What they do next is a total contradiction to their normal family behavior. All of the calves come to the center around me and their mothers surround them. Normally each individual family does this, but this massive group is going to function in unison tomorrow morning. For the first time a massive family bond is present throughout the herd.

I lie down and go to sleep, as do they.

It is a peaceful night and a gentle wakeup call at 04:00. I slowly pick my way from the center to the outer perimeter through the sleeping elephants, waking them as I go. The wakeup moves through the herd like a slowly rolling wave. I peer through the darkness to the east and notice that the white trucks are facing us about five-hundred meters out. By the time I look back, the elephants are on their feet including the calves who remain in the center. The 'Great I Am' puts the circle picture in all our heads, and I make a sign with my hands in the air.

For a moment, everything looks like it is in complete chaos. All the alpha elephants, male and female, are moving to the outer perimeter. The families are mixing with the males in protection of each other. Now a powerful feeling begins to move through all of us. It is the desire for wholeness. In the next moments what was once chaos, now clicks into place, and there is total order and harmony. Finally, an overwhelming feeling emerges within us. We are whole! We are one!

I raise my hands in joy and enthusiasm as the elephants raise their trunks. There is no trumpeting, but a powerful light is surrounding us. We all know at once that something very different is happening. We are ready!

The 'Great I Am' says to me, "You are about to redefine Newton's third law of motion, 'every action has an equal and opposite reaction'. Let's do it."

I look up to the lodge. Everyone is on the roof. They are safe. Dick is in his tree perch.

As the sun breaks over the horizon, for a moment I see the 6 Mi-17 choppers like black specks on the sunglow. Within seconds, the blinding light of the rising sun seems to swallow up the specks and make them invisible to our sight. I cross my arms over my chest and cherish the feeling of Love and wholeness within us. I feel the elephants curling up their trunks and tilting their heads back. I then open my arms in a gesture to embrace our enemy. The elephants lower their heads and trunks, with only a curl on the end. The sound of the choppers is now banging in our ears.

From deep within me comes a powerful voice, which booms out to the approaching choppers, "Do not fire upon us! Your action will only result in your own destruction. Please return home in peace." They can hear these words on their sound system and in their earphones. I then repeat the same message in the three different languages of those coming. But they keep coming.

For a second time the voice fills my mouth, "Do not fire upon us! Your action will only result in your own destruction. Please return home in peace." I repeat it in all the languages. They keep coming.

For a third time, the voice booms out, "Do not fire upon us! Your action will only result in your own destruction. From now on there will be consequences." They ignore it.

I can now see their laughing vicious faces as they swoop in for the kill. A deep sadness fills my heart.

The choppers face us, a hundred meters out on three sides. Hovering about a meter off the ground, they each insert 30 heavily armed soldiers. The choppers pull up hovering above the troops as they move in to about thirty or forty meters.

We do not move or make any change in our gesture. I can feel our steady rhythmic breathing that is now in unison. There is no fear. There is no anxiety. There is only a deep anticipated sadness for the loss of so many lives.

As it always does with human perception during crisis moments, time goes into slow-motion perception. The soldiers begin to fire. Their bullets are like tracer bullets, tiny red balls of fire. The air is full of them coming from all three sides. There is no mistaking that their course is deadly accurate. The looks on the faces of our attackers is one of humor. They see us as sitting ducks. Their joy in the kill is mindless madness. They are completely insane and incapable of any human compassion for the elephants or me. Their rational minds and egos turn them into hideous monsters. They all fire again and again and again. All the tiny red balls race toward us.

Our unison breathing seems oblivious to any danger. There is no reflex reaction. We simply watch the incoming bullets.

All the bullets come within half a meter of us and boomerang back along the same path from which they come. If the shooter took aim, his bullet was now heading straight for his head. If the shooter was spraying the herd or me with bullets from an automatic weapon, all the bullets were now heading straight back toward his body. I look into the eyes of one shooter. All this is happening faster than he can blink.

The bullets reach their source. Heads explode. Bodies rip apart. Body parts fly through the air. A wall of gushing bodily fluids now surrounds us, filling the air.

The choppers open up with their gunpods and rockets. These create larger and fiercer looking fireballs speeding toward us. The three-man crew of each chopper watches with excitement. They are much like the soldiers on the ground only now there is fear in their eyes along with a big question mark. How can we have taken out all their ground troops so quickly? Suddenly they realize and fear turns to terror in the face of impending doom.

We watch and wait. The waiting to see another human being die needlessly is agonizing. There is no victory in it. There is only hopeless senselessness. We all feel a deep sense of remorse.

The second wave of fireballs boomerangs off us and speeds back toward the choppers. The pilot of the chopper to my far right anticipates what is happening before the others and leans over on his stick. The chopper starts to respond. The fireballs return home and five choppers explode in a white flash and flying debris of twisted metal and burning flesh.

The returning bullets strafe the chopper to my far right, but it is still flying. I see that it still has its rockets. The pilot repositions the chopper, but... not... on... US...!

I scream out, "NOOO!"

The pilot lines up on the lodge.

The 'Great I Am' calmly says to me, "Take a breath. This is covered."

On the roof of the lodge, Dan, Nan, Reid and two rangers step in front of the others. They breathe out and focus on their breath. They cross their arms over their chests and then open them in an embrace to the three men in the chopper. I can feel their Love and connection. I can see the Light surround them, as they become one.

The pilot fires his rockets. They race mindlessly toward the lodge and the shield protecting the five newly enlightened spirits. There is no magic in what we do. I cannot divert the rockets or cast a spell to protect the people and the lodge. All the elephants and I can do is to unify the five on the roof with us and let the 'Great I Am' protect them. In a breath, we are all one.

The huge fireballs reach their shield and boomerang back toward the chopper. The crew struggles to be free of their seatbelts. The co-pilot shakes his fist at the five loving gestures in front of him with a twisted demonic expression on his face. In seconds, the rockets return home and the chopper bursts into flames and hovers for seconds in the air before falling to the ground and breaking into bits. It is over and my slow-motion perception of time returns to normal. All this happens in less than twelve minutes.

Almost 200 souls are dead along with their rational minds and egos twisted by greed and hatred. Now their spirits are condemned to an eternity in darkness with no possibility of connecting with the 'Great I Am' within them. I weep and notice that the elephants are weeping.

While everyone at the lodge freezes in silence and wonder, I dispatch fifty elephants to surround the white trucks. As I walk toward them, I can see that the drivers are terrified and frozen with fright. The elephants form a half circle around them, leaving only a narrow opening for them to drive forward. The drivers don't understand. They fling open their doors and throw out their weapons. Now, they slowly and meekly climb down with their hands in the air. They fall on their knees and beg for their lives.

I call out, "Climb back in your trucks and drive toward me. No harm will come to you. We mean no harm to anyone."

The drivers climb back into their trucks and drive toward me; the elephants escort them. I walk back to within twenty meters of the dead bodies and direct the trucks to park about a hundred meters apart on both sides.

I call out to the drivers, "Turn off your engines. Remove the tarpaulins and tie-downs from the flatbed and put them under the truck. Then climb back in your trucks."

The drivers do as I ask and are very happy to climb back into the safety of their cabs.

The elephants already know what to do. With tears running down their faces, they come forward. There is one for each body, one for each body part. They gently pick up a body and form four lines, one on each side of the two trucks. They carefully place each body on the flatbed, move the legs together, and cross the arms over the chest. When the flatbed is full, they start a new layer with the bodies lying in the opposite direction. They do all this with a great deal of loving respect. We all feel the enormous sadness of the 'Great I Am' for the loss of so many lives.

Reid and the rangers come down to the field with fire extinguishers. They put out the fires in the choppers. Three elephants stand around them waiting at each chopper. The rangers notice their tears and are deeply moved. When the fires are out the rangers realize that the elephants are there to remove the bodies. They step back as soon as it is safe.

The elephants pull apart the twisted metal to expose the charred bodies. When they can easily remove the bodies, the first elephant gently lifts out a body and carries it to the closest truck. The other two elephants do the same.

In the same manner, the elephants liberate the dead from each chopper and respectfully place the bodies on the trucks. They soon finish the job.

I ask Reid, "Can you have your men cover the bodies and tie them down for transport?"

"Affirmative," says Reid and then puts his men to the task.

I walk to each driver and have the same conversation. I ask, "Describe your experience here?"

They respond, "Our men fire on you and the elephants and our bullets bounce off you and the elephants only to fly back to kill the man or chopper that fires them."

I ask, "Is that the story you will tell?"

They respond, "Yes, Sir."

The second driver has a little twist to his story, "You have powerful magic."

To which I respond, "It is not me. It is not magic. It is the elephants, who have the power. Anyone who tries to harm them will suffer the consequences. Is that clear?"

"Yes, Sir. Yes, Sir. Thank you Sir."

As soon as the trucks are ready, I bring them together for final directions, "Take these bodies back to al-Egsiro and tell him that the elephants are returning them. Any further violence and hatred will have the same consequences. Then tell your story."

I stand in the bloody field with Reid watching the trucks drive east. We then turn to the elephants and watch the individual families come back together. When they are ready, Reid and I cross our arms over our chests embracing the Love and wholeness within us. The elephants curl up their trunks and tilt their heads back. We then open our arms to embrace them all. The elephants lower their heads and trunks, with a curl on the end. We can hear the 'Great I Am' blessing them and sending them home.

Slowly the elephants depart in all directions for their home ranges.

CHAPTER 18
Many Questions

Reid turns to me and says, "I don't know if I should get on my knees to you or what. You waltz in here…"

Not wanting or needing any praise, I interrupt, "Whatever you do, don't kneel. I'm just another slob like you, who finds the 'Great I Am' within. We all can live in His praises now."

"You do know that this is a major game changer!"

"Yes, I do Reid. It is the end of an old way of life and the beginning of a completely new way to live. It is an incredible feeling and a wonderful commitment, but it does have a down side. We can't convert anyone. Everyone has to find Him within himself or herself. All we can do is help them a little and point them in the right direction."

Reid reminds me, "Speaking of help, there are some people up at the lodge that need you. We will all be talking about last night for years to come." He motions to the other rangers and we head up to the lodge.

Nan and Dan are sitting in the large hall, trying to answer questions from everyone, when we walk in. Dick is standing in the back of the room. I spot an empty chair and sit down. The rangers sit comfortably on the floor. Reid is the only one left standing, with no seats left.

He stands still as though he is listening to the silence. Out of nowhere, he begins to laugh, and says, "He is asking me to tell you about Dan, Nan, two of my rangers and me last night."

I laugh boisterously, "That's the way He works."

"Before I begin, let me just say that I am not a religious person and never have been. Yet I have a strong

Spiritual curiosity. Yesterday, when Hayah flies in here talking about the 'Great I Am' within us, I think he's a kook. Then when he says the elephants are connected and humans aren't, I start to listen. I feel that is true, but don't know what it is. To me it is the only explanation, which makes any sense as to why they are here. Just watching him with them and seeing them in such perfect harmony with him, starts to make me a believer. You'll have to agree, that was one hell of a party last night.

"When I came back to the lodge, I found Dan and Nan reading over two Bible chapters. They can't believe what they are reading. It was like reading it for the first time. They shared the passages with me, and I was flabbergasted. I couldn't understand how humans could be so stupid. The truth has been right there in front of us for millennia, and we blinded ourselves and let others control us for power and greed.

"We then did what Hayah said. Stop talking; stop thinking; focus on our breathing; shut down the mind and ego; and listen in silence. After a while, He started talking to us. The fun part was that He has something different to say to each of us. He knew what each of us needed to hear. The only thing that we all experienced in common was His Love. I can honestly say I didn't know what Love was until last night.

"This morning, when we saw what the elephants were doing, the five of us knew we could do it too. He says, 'As long as you have no hatred in your mind and heart, I can protect you.' I had no idea what that meant until it happened. With Him inside us calling the shots, we all become one. We even become one with the elephants and Hayah. I still have a lot to learn, but nothing has ever felt so right to me. With that let me turn this over to Hayah.

I'm sure you have lots of questions for him."

I stand up and offer my seat to Reid. As I cross to the front of the room, a deep silence fills the space. Some of the faces are ready to connect with the 'Great I Am' right now. Other faces show confusion and uncertainty. While, still others are angry, because this is a challenge to their entire belief system and requires change. Any second now, the silence will explode into a heated confrontation.

I quickly say, "I want everyone to blow out as much air as you can. Then just relax and let your body do what it wants to do." I watch their breathing take over, "focus on your breathing and count them out loud. When you reach seven, use your thinking mind to tell the body to stop breathing. For those who find that impossible, just keep counting." By the time everyone reaches twenty-one, they are all breathing together. The tension in the room is gone.

"OK, now let's take some of your questions," I say calmly.

Phyllis stands and asks, "Can you tell us exactly what was happening out there this morning?" She sits back down.

"You are witnessing the beginning of a new era. (I leave it to you to define the old era.) From now on, anyone who connects to the 'Great I Am' is protected. The animals' connection to Him goes back to the great flood and His rainbow promise. As for humans, the list is short, but this event is going to change that, as you can see with the five today.

"This is how it works. The 'Great I Am' is redefining Newton's third law of motion, 'For every action there is an equal and opposite reaction.' If someone tries to shoot a person, an elephant or any protected animal, the bullet will bounce off the person or animal and boomerang back at the person who shot the bullet, with equal deadly force. If the shooter is using an automatic weapon, the shooter will be spraying himself or herself with bullets. If someone slaps you on your right cheek, the slap will boomerang back on the cheek of the person who slaps you. If you turn the other cheek, then the slapper will be hit twice. If a person tries to stab you, the wound will appear on their body not yours. Because of the shield, an animal or person feels none of the pain and receives no wound, but the attacker feels all the pain and may even die from the wound. The 'Great I Am' calls this the 'boomerang effect'. This one little thing is going to end the world, as you know it and open a new curtain on a new world. Today you are witnesses to that event!"

A young ranger stands, "I feel naked out there without my gun. I hate those people and despise what they want to do to the elephants. It must have given you a feeling of great power to wipe them out like that. How do I signup?"

Reid rolls his eyes, as I smile, "First, you must destroy all your weapons. You will never need them again. Secondly, you must tattoo this American Indian proverb on the back of your right hand, 'Hatred is the poison you take and expect your enemy to die.' Thirdly, at the moment of crisis, prepare yourself to feel completely powerless and a deep sadness for the loss of lives you cannot save. Do these three things and you will know how to sign up."

Dr. James from Harvard, leans back in his chair and asks, "Are you trying to create some kind of new age religion? What is your theological foundation? And what are your credentials?"

My ego wants me to put this haughty professor in his place, but I take a breath and listen.

The 'Great I Am' says, "I have been trying to connect with James for years, but you might be able to tip the scale toward me with your response. Be as loving as I am."

I begin, "Dr. James, these are very important questions. Thank you for asking them. But allow me to answer them simply, so everyone can understand.

"The last thing this world needs is another religion. Every religion throughout history, from Zoroastrianism to Baha'i, became an institution to control its followers and their beliefs through doctrine and dogma. This often happens in direct defiance of their founder's whishes and the intention of the 'Great I Am' within. All sacred texts contain the 'Great I Am' within message, but you have to know that to find it. It is the central theme for Mohamed. He says we do not have to go through the Roman Catholic Church to reach Allah. Allah is within and we have a direct connection. Does this mean that we have to confront all these institutions and their clerics? No! The 'Great I Am' failed with that approach two thousand years ago. If religious people or clerics find enlightenment somehow, that's wonderful. If not, they will simply die or destroy themselves. It is the joy of each individually enlightened person to find the 'Great I Am' within and let Him and only Him run your life. Do that and you will find your real purpose in life and real freedom.

"As for theology, that word is an oxymoron. The 'Great I Am' is not an idea but an experience. Not one word of theology is from the 'Great I Am'. Why? Because He does not and will not deal with what does not or will not exist, the knowledge of Him. Have you ever seen an idea or thought? Of course not! They're only smoke and mirrors created by the mind and ego, and they have convinced you that they are real. On the other hand, the 'Great I Am' is as real as the breath in our body. Ask the five people in this room who can testify to that fact. And most importantly, you are witnesses to the connection of more than ten-thousand elephants out there.

"As for my credentials, I probably have what you are looking for. I have eleven years of higher education. I also have twelve centimeters of alphabet soup after my name. However, all that knowledge is useless and an exercise in apple eating. Which leaves me with only one credential; I am connected to the 'Great I Am' within me and that is the mother lode.

"Dr. James, by disproving Descartes' proof of existence, 'I think therefore I am', through our breathing exercise, you are taking the first step. Your thoughts could not stop you from breathing, so you kept counting. Stick around if you want to take the second step."

Dr. James stands, "Mr. Hayah, or should I say Dr. Hayah?"

"Just Hayah will be fine. I also answer to Hay You."

Everyone laughs including Dr. James, who says, "I thank you for your clarity and understanding. You bet I want to take the second step!" He sits down full of enthusiasm.

One of the lodge staff, stands, "Is there a list of those chosen?"

"Yes there is a list, but it is more like a list of those choosing. One of the biggest theological debates of the last two millenniums is why did Joshua choose to save one thief crucified with Him and not the other? The answer is He didn't choose. Only one thief chose to connect with Him. The same is true today. Anyone choosing to connect with the 'Great I Am' within will be putting themselves on the list."

I look over the group and most are bubbling with joy and excitement. When my eye stops on Dan and Nan, I can see a deep question trying to come to the surface. I say to them, "OK, out with it before it eats a hole in your bellies."

Dan blurts out, "What about forgiveness?"

Nan tacks on, "Do we have to face a Last Judgment?" Their fear and panic is over the top.

I smile, holding back my laughter and ask in a caring way, "Aren't you glad that that fear wasn't distracting you this morning? These people are here to have this conversation, because of your connection." I look at the group and ask, "Do you see what religion does to people, turning God into some kind of boogeyman. Here are two wonderful people with a new connection with the 'Great I Am' and their mind and ego is beating them up with trivia."

I take Dan and Nan's hands, and I say to them for all to hear, "Blow all the bad air out and relax and breathe. Just focus on your breathing. There is no need to worry. Yes, there is a Last Judgment, but it is not what you think. Your mind and ego are lying to you. When you're ready, the 'Great I Am' is going to ask you 'Do you forgive yourself for all the times you missed the mark.' (He likes to use the Johannine term for sin, ἁμαρτία/hamartia.) That's it. He has been within you your whole life. He witnessed everything you did. There is no need for confession. He has already forgiven you. Now you must forgive yourself. For some that will be easy. You can't erase an action, but you can acknowledge it, regret having done it and forgive yourself. For others it will be extremely difficult, because they are rationalizing and justifying an action to the point where they believe they did nothing wrong. Unfortunately, such people will bury themselves under a mountain of wrongdoing and the boogeyman that condemns them is their own rational mind and ego.

"Being connected to the 'Great I Am' does not mean that you will no longer slipup and miss the mark. In fact, I can pretty much guarantee that you will. The wonderful thing is that His Love is unconditional, so when you miss the mark He is right there to help you pick up the pieces and move on."

Nan and Dan look relieved. Nan starts, "Why are we unable to block our mind and ego this time?"

Dan adds, "It's like it comes at us both at the same time."

"The mind and ego will not give up without a fight. The rational mind and ego take an old religious teaching and turn it into a primal fear. Of course, it's not primal, but it makes you think it is. Now the body automatically switches to fight or flight. In this case when facing the 'Great I Am' flight seems like the safer option. Eventually, you will be aware of what the mind and ego are doing, and your consciousness will tell you to breathe and simply set the mind and ego aside. That's how you fight the mind and ego. You give it no power over you. Therefore, meditation is not something you do once or twice a day, but hundreds of one-minute connections all day long."

Dan asks with a feeling of urgency, "Can you please help us with meditation?"

I agree and give the others a chance to leave. To my surprise, only six leave and even Dick stays.

CHAPTER 19
After Meditation

And the elephants will lead them. Everyone can see and feel the elephant's connection to the 'Great I Am', and they want in on the power. During the class, they all listen carefully, struggle through the exercises but fail to quiet their chattering minds and egos.

I can see the five growing stronger by leaps and bounds. They desperately needed these tools. Their connection is becoming complete as they surrender to the 'Great I Am'.

I see that Dick, Phyllis, three more rangers and two lodge staff are close to breaking through. With work and persistence, they will be able to set their minds and egos aside and connect.

The rest are in a fog, including Dr. James, and I don't know why. The more I work with them the harder it becomes for them. I simply can't move them past their initial awakening.

While I am taking a shower, the 'Great I Am' tunes in, "At last! This is tricky." He starts to explain, "During the questioning, no one asked why so many people had to die. In fact, no one even commented on the carnage. I can feel the sadness in you, the five newcomers and the elephants. But the sadness is not in anyone else.

"Why are they anesthetized to such images? Now it occurs to Me; computer games, the media and movies are anesthetizing human feelings. They see and participate in killing and destruction, without attachment, pain or loss. Then the computer game, media or movie glorifies the action without repercussions. The average person may experience twenty-five or more such technological acts of violence every day, but not experience a real one during their whole life. The exception, of course, is the soldier who sees combat. They all return home with emotional and psychological wounds, if not physical wounds. That's why Reid is able to connect.

"In order to experience sadness after seeing death, humans must first experience the joy and beauty in all life. Humans must love life in all its forms.

"What these people are feeling during the meditation is a subconscious fear, not just a fear of judgment, not only a primal fear but a fear that is much deeper. Their fear is that life has no value and they are defenseless victims before the powerful forces of evil. They are desperate to connect with Me and find meaning in their lives. When they can't, their anxiety goes off the charts. Thus, I remain an unknown, a non-entity. And I don't need to tell you what the mind and ego can do with that.

"Here is what we need to do. I will give clear dreams of the new life on the new earth to all those who began to awaken. At first, the dreams will be in bits and pieces and will become more and more complete as they come closer to Me. This will put a positive image in their subconscious in contrast with the negative imagery in technology. This gives them a choice and a vision what they are working.

"Your job is to let them know that as long as they are *actively* working toward a connection with Me under the guidance of five others who are connected, they will be protected. This should minimize their desperation and anxiety so they can overcome fear and find newness of life. You already have the first five with whom they can work."

I hesitate for a moment before responding, "That's a

great plan." I pause, "Can I towel off and dress now? Or should I stand here and drip-dry?"

He laughs with great relief. We really do enjoy each other. He adds, "You better towel off and dress. You have a plane to catch."

I hang up my towel and start to dress.

He continues, "By the way, My decision about the person or persons who orchestrate these atrocities is that they shall all experience the consequences. The boomerang shall go right up the chain all the way to the top. This is effective immediately."

I finish dressing, "That's a good thing. Accountability can slow down the madness a little." I start to put my backpack together.

He assures me, "I feel your concern. But the next three legs of your journey will be a lot easier. If anything starts to develop, I'll let you know. I'm right here if you need Me."

I grab my backpack and head up stairs to meet Dan and Nan. To my surprise, Reid and his two rangers are there as well.

Reid says, "The 'Great I Am' says that you have something to tell us."

"Well that's quick. He says that any person that the five of you take charge of will be protected as long as they are actively trying to reach Him. There is no need for them to be afraid, and they can look forward to a newness of life. I will add to that that joy and laughter will also help a lot."

Reid is beaming, "My rangers will be very happy to hear that. Of course He knows what is bothering them before they know it themselves."

"Soon you will feel like you are in the palm of His

hand."

"I already do," says Reid. "Thanks for everything. You are always welcome here." He heads back toward the barn with his rangers.

Dan says, "He is not big on goodbyes. But you have no clue as to how deeply you are touching us all."

Nan adds, "We will follow you to the ends of the earth."

"Just follow Him. That is all that is required." Turning to business, "How many are going with us to Rwanda?"

Nan checks the manifest, "Dick, Phyllis, Dr. James and I believe one other VIP. Hayah, Dan and I want to be with you, at least for the African part of your journey."

"You honor me. You will be a big help, and you are welcome. I thank you very much."

Dan is out the door and heading down to the airstrip to prep the plane.

Nan starts to gather people together to head down.

Dick and I connect and head out the door together.

I ask Dick, "You've been awfully quiet. How's your wife, Abby?"

Dick has trouble written all over his face, and says, "When I called Abby after we returned to the lodge, she was reacting strangely. She was glad to hear that I was safe. Then I told her the details, and I know I'm pumped and still running on adrenalin from everything. But she couldn't believe a word I said and accused me of being drunk. She said it's like some "Matrix" sci-fi movie. That stopped me cold. I am an eyewitness. I can feel the incredible energy coming from you and the elephants. We all feel it. We all want to be part of what is starting here. I saw the military/poachers destroyed by their own hatred and greed. And I have incredible video footage to prove it. The elephants weeping and loading the dead on the trucks with respect and dignity brought me to tears and gave me some of the best shots of my life. It is more humane than anything I've ever seen a human do. My life will never be the same after this event. It is truly a 'Hinge in History'.

"But will the world believe it? Will NGM (National Geographic Magazine) accept the story? I am at a total loss as to what to do. Here I am with the biggest story of my life and no one will believe it."

I am very sympathetic with the problem. Now the 'Great I Am' starts to feed me a solution. I relay the message, "Once you connect you will receive these answers yourself. It seems that everyone here has the same problem. If you all want your own by-line, your credibility is limited to your own circle of friends and colleagues. And just as you discover with Abby, many of them will be a hard sell. However, if you team up with say, Phyllis from the UK, Dr. James from Harvard and Dan and Nan on the local scene, you will have a story with maximum credibility and an interesting mixture of personal and professional observations. And don't forget Dan and Nan are now connecting to the 'Great I Am'. I will add to that, that the collaborative effort will make it easier for the rest of you to connect to Him and once you do you all will be speaking with strength and conviction."

"That's a brilliant idea," Dick blurts out! Then he adds quickly, "Of course it's a brilliant idea. It's His idea! Do I have to apologize?"

"No, He's actually laughing."

"Tell me, Hayah. What's it like walking around with Him inside you like that? It must be pretty special."

"Special is not the word I use. It's mostly fantastic, for all the obvious reasons. Then there are the moments when.... How shall I put it? Do you know the expression, 'It's easier to ask forgiveness than to ask permission?' Well with Him that isn't true."

Now both Dick and the 'Great I Am' are having a big laugh.

Suddenly Dick stops and looks me in the eye, "I hear Him laughing. Holy shit!"

I can't resist. "Where? I have to see that," Now all three of us are laughing.

CHAPTER 20
Flight to Rwanda

Form the air, the beautiful panorama of the African landscape slips beneath us. Pristine lakes, spectacular waterfalls, wonderfully varied vegetation and a rich abundance of wildlife slides past. Flying at low attitude is a delightful experience. It creates a feeling of being part of everything, a oneness, a wholeness that is difficult to experience on the ground. From up-here, there are no borders or boundaries. There is only one race, the human race. There is only one country and human kind is its citizens. A feeling deep inside me comes to the surface. This once united indigenous people lived in peace with the land and at peace with their inner beings. Then under the perverted views of the Belgian and German colonists, they were divided to control and breed like racehorses based on superficial genetic traits and measurements. This innocent people bought into the perverted views along with the ethnic hatred. When the Belgians and Germans were gone, their perversion and hatred was still killing senselessly. Racists ignore the black African DNA chain that runs through all human's veins. I see an image of the 'Great I Am' within me and shake my head. The words slip out without thinking, "They don't have a clue."

When I look out the window again, I see the elephants returning to their home in Dzanga Bai (a natural clearing in the middle of the jungle in the Central African Republics). Later, over the Congo, I see huge refugee camps, mass grave sites from the genocide and the movement of rebel forces. The insanity of our planet is deeply entrenched even in this African paradise. I sense that all of this information is preparing me for something. I wonder what.

I look over at Dick, and he is already deep in a conversation with Dr. James and Phyllis. Their eyes light up as he shares with them some of his footage. When he pops the question about a collaborative effort to get the news out, they quickly accept the offer. After that, the tablets come out and they all start writing down their experiences.

I turn to Nan, who is tugging on my arm.

Nan asks, "Who doesn't have a clue?"

I ponder my answer for a moment, then say, "I am thinking about the Tutsi and Hutu ethnic groups, but in actuality it is humanity in general. The animals know it, but people don't. But now there is a new beginning."

"Dan and I are wondering what we should do about MAF. Should we introduce our revelation to them?"

"In a word, No! I know how you feel. You want to shout it from the mountaintops. The good news is too wonderful to hide under a bushel. But reforming religious institutions does not work. Joshua proved that. Consider there is a lot that you need to know before you try to tame the beast. I am willing to help you start, but He is the one who will tell you when to do it and how to do it. You're already learning to listen to Him and doing a great job. Now the next thing you need to learn is how to act upon His instructions. Note that I use the words 'act upon' and not 'obey'; this is not about obedience; you always have a choice; it's about wanting to do as He asks. He may even want your feedback."

Dan chimes in, "This sounds like a Joshua to the 'Great I Am' conversation. Not that I'm saying that Nan and I are like Joshua."

"Forget the apology. It is not necessary. You know the humility with which you say it; so He knows it. It is exactly like the conversations between Joshua and the 'Great I Am'. My favorite is the Garden of Gethsemane conversation."

"I know that and accept His will in all things," Dan says without reservation. "But why not change the MAF into an organization that is working for the 'Great I Am'?"

"There are two important points in your question," I respond with compassion. "On the one hand, the 'Great I Am' does not exist and cannot exist in the MAF, meaning that an organization has no essence of being. On the other hand, the 'Great I Am' is within all its members and those members are doing His work weather they know it or not. To quote the 'Great I Am', 'It is not what you do that counts, but why you do it.' A person can help the poor, the sick and wounded, the spiritually downtrodden and the socially rejected only for self-gratification and to stroke their own ego. Or like the people in the MAF, they can do all those things to pass on the Love of the Holy Spirit within them."

Nan is bubbling over with excitement, "I see what you mean. We are not converting the institution. We are converting the people in it!"

Her enthusiasm makes me smile, "You're almost there. Just drop the idea that you are converting anything or anyone. To convert implies that you are controlling a person's choice. That's what religious leaders think they can do. Yet, not even Joshua did it with the thief on His left as He was crucified. See yourself as a lighthouse. Let the Light of the 'Great I Am' within you be a beacon to all that are out there on the sea of life. Let them choose to

144

come to you. Then show them the way into the harbor of Love. And the 'Great I Am' will do the rest."

"Wow, I like that," says Dan. "We just need to be ourselves and let the Light shine, and they will come. There will be no confrontations, no theological debates. That is the best soft sell ever. How long will it take for everybody to be on board?"

"Only the 'Great I Am' knows that. All I can tell you is that His hope to connect with everybody seems to be gone. Right now, to connect with most people will give Him great joy."

Nan's light is absolutely radiant, "I hope people will be able to see my Light."

"Nan, if your Light is any brighter, people will have to wear sunglasses to look at you!"

Everyone on the plane brakes into laughter.

Dick says, "Ain't that the truth!"

The energy on the plane is electrifying. Now, I notice that Phyllis is studying me carefully. I return her gaze with a warm smile. She does not look away, but smiles back. I have no idea how long we hold this gaze, but Dan interrupts it with the announcement that we are approaching the Virunga Volcanoes. He is heading straight for the saddle between Sabyinyo and Bisoke. The change in vista captures everyone's attention.

As we approach, the hilly farmland quickly gives way to a dense equatorial rain forest, which races up the steep slopes of the mountain and thins out into a meadow surrounding the crater with low shrubs and a few palm-like trees. When the plane pops over the ridge of the saddle, we can instantly see Volcanoes National Park, the Kinigi farmlands eating deep into the Park Range and a few kilometers beyond the Ruhengeri airstrip in Musanze.

The approach to the airstrip is a straight shot with the wind in the right direction. Dan sets us down gently and taxies up to a number of waiting vehicles and a large crowd of people, who are mostly women.

CHAPTER 21
Welcome to Kinigi

I am the first to hop off the plane and go around to help Dan pull out the bags. He is all business now, and we work harmoniously without words. I sense a wonderful connection between us. Suddenly, cheers from the crowd go up.

When I look up, I can see that Phyllis is stepping off the plane. She barely takes three steps before she is surrounded with women hugging her and greeting her. Her excitement and theirs fills the air with rays of joy and happy sounds of homecoming. I see that Dr. Kathrin, one of the co-directors of Gorilla Doctors, is among them. Of course, I realize; Phyllis must have done some of her primatologist research here. I can't help but wonder; did she know Dian Fossey. Sometimes, I wish that the 'Great I Am' could be less private about other people and what they're thinking. It all boils down to what I need to know for safety reasons, and what I can find out for myself. Considering the opposite, would I want others to be able to read me through their connection to the 'Great I Am'? I feel happy for Phyllis. She deserves this.

Dan and I pull off the last bags, and I spot Phyllis' bags. I quickly grab them, take them over and set them down behind the group of women. I make gestures to one of the women, so she knows whose bags they are. I return with the other passengers to the neatly arranged bags, grab my backpack and start putting it on.

An official looking man walks up to Dan and introduces himself as Jasper, the Chef Park Warden. He asks, "Hi Dan, Can you point out Ja Hayah Im? I'm supposed to pick him up." Dan points to me with his thumb over his shoulder. Jasper sheepishly says, "Oops! I thought he was the hired help."

Dan laughs and turns to me. "Hay you, your ride is here." I walk up. "Jasper, I want you to meet Hayah. Hayah, this is Jasper, our Warden at the Park. Jasper, you have no idea! Can you wait for Nan and me? We need a ride to Kinigi Guest House too?"

"Of course," Jasper says and looks at me.

Dan grabs my arm, "Just give the help and me a chance to tie the plane down."

We grab hold of the plane and start pushing. Nan moves the women out of the way, and we role the plane over to one of the docking spots. Dan throws me a rope, and he ties down one side as I tie down the other. He then checks all the switches in the cockpit, sets the brakes and locks the plane. Dan grabs his and Nan's bag and we head for the Park Land Rover.

Jasper is leaning up against the car, with the back hatch open. We carefully load our bags, and Dan motions for Nan to hurry up. I ask Jasper, "Have you put together the meeting for this evening?"

Jasper smiles, "The women of the WSOFERWA are taking care of that. I'm getting off easy. They're having a dinner/reception for Dr. Phyllis, after which Dr. Phyllis will give a talk. You can make your announcements after that." Dan takes a step toward Jasper and looks at me. I shake my head no and look back to Jasper. Jasper adds, "Aline is the woman in charge. Do you want to meet her now?" I shake my head no. "It's going to be at the Guest House, and I suspect that most of Kinigi will be there along with many Rwanda VIPs."

"Sounds great Jasper. Will you mind introducing me to Aline when we arrive at the Guest House?" Oddly, my ego is totally disengaged through all this.

My only concern is that the warning message gets out before people start being hurt. The protection of the Gorillas is already in force. The 'Great I Am' is giving me a very uneasy feeling. He or I can do nothing to change the circumstances. He assures me that any attempt to alter the program will result in hostility on the part of the women. However, He wants me to stay on alert, because something is not right here.

Dan, Nan and I settle into our seats in the Land Rover. It seems that everyone else has places in other vehicles. I can see that Dan is deeply concerned about coming events. Soon Nan notices it as well. The two of them are stewing in silence with fiery glances back and forth. I can tell that the 'Great I Am' is bringing them up to speed and trying to keep them calm.

In a cordial tone, I ask Jasper, "Can you tell me about the WSOFERWA?"

Jasper speaks in a proud manner, as a husband who is proud of his wife. He says, "They are a non-profit women's organization. The Kinigi Guest House is just one of their projects. I can give you the website spiel about helping the poor and abandoned children. But the real accomplishment of these women was the ending of the genocide. Their efforts brought about the peace, and they are keeping the peace. Dr. Phyllis is raising them huge sums of money in the UK and the United States. She is their hero." He pauses, and then adds, "That's the short version."

"Wow," I say! "It sounds like the right group of woman to have on your side." I look at Dan and Nan and raise my eyebrows. "I look forward to mingling with them to night. Can you be our guide and introduce us around?

Are the women spiritual?"

Jasper smiles, "Good choice of words. They are all spiritual seekers, fed up with the Church. And yes, I'd be happy to make the introductions."

"By the way Jasper, are the women aware of my warning letter describing the protection of endangered species and the consequences?"

"Yes they are." His tone is less than enthusiastic.

"And the reaction is...?"

Jasper hesitates then says, "To be frank, they thought it was a hoax."

"And have you spoken to Reid at Zakouma lately?"

"Not in the last couple of weeks."

"I suggest that you call him before dinner and ask him what happened at Zakouma this morning."

Jasper pulls up in front of the Guest House. Dan, Nan and I climb out and collect our luggage. Jasper shouts back to us before we close the hatch, "I'll be back shortly to do those introductions."

We acknowledge his message and close the back hatch. He pulls off and the other cars pull up. We wave and smile as friendly as we can.

I turn to Dan and Nan, "Let's powwow some place up in the Guest House and let them check in first."

We grab our stuff and head up and into the Guest House. We ask the greeter at the door, "Is there a place we can talk for few minutes," and she points out a small room in the back. We quickly go to the room and shut the door. In unison, we all take a deep breath.

There is a long silence, while we are listening to the 'Great I Am'. Nan is the first to speak, "That's strange. He is as baffled as we are. I always think of Him as knowing everything."

I explain, "He does, but only when it is about to happen. Because of our Free Will, what we are going to do is an educated guess until we make our choice to act. For example, right now we don't have a clue as to what we are going to do."

Dan comments, "Maybe something will come out of Jasper's conversation with Reid."

I say, "I feel that it is going to wake him up, but he is going to be afraid to ask the women to change their plans. I wonder why."

Nan chimes in, "Wait just a minute; I need to ask Him a question. Lord, what does Jasper mean when he says 'They are Spiritual seekers, fed up with the church.'?"

His voice comes to all of us, "Good catch Nan. Most of the women are seeking a deeper spiritual connection, but a few are into black-magic, voodoo."

"That's what I'm feeling," Nan blurts out. "They are using Phyllis to upset the apple cart and block our warning. They have her under some kind of spell."

I ask the 'Great I Am', "What should we do?"

His voice is clear to all again, "You let things unfold as they have planned. I will create a spell breaker for all the women. Just be ready to act and be as loving and caring as you can to everyone. Thank you Nan, we are going to do great things together."

Dan turns to me, "This is incredible. I have goose bumps all over my body."

Nan adds, "Me too!"

"OK we have our orders. Let's go in there and meet and great everyone and turn on the charm. Remember to relax because He has it under control."

After we check in and go to our rooms to freshen

up, we meet back in the reception area where a large table is set with many hors d'oeuvres and a selection of African wines, beers and non-alcoholic drinks.

A crowd begins to gather. I take a couple of minutes to study the people in the group. When I spot one of the women fussing with the hors d'oeuvre table, I approach her and complement her on the beautiful spread. At first, she is a little shy; so I ask which things are typically Rwandan. This opens her up, and she begins to tell me what is in them and how the women make them. I find the details fascinating and ask where she was able to buy such exotic ingredients. She laughs and proudly proclaims that she grows them in her own garden. This leads to an exchange of gardening stories and the swapping of gardening secrets. We are so engrossed in our joyful conversation that I fail to see Jasper enter. I have no idea how long he was standing there trying to catch my attention. I excuse myself and go over to meet him.

Jasper's face has panic written all over it and his hands are trembling. "Hayah, I'm sorry. I'm so deeply sorry. I don't know what to say! Reid described to me this morning's events and your protection of the elephants. His description was beyond anything I have ever experienced. Then he concludes by saying, 'And this, my friend, isn't a tenth of what actually happened.' Please tell me that this isn't going to happen here. I don't know what to do. The people need to hear the warning. But the women are single minded in their program to celebrate Phyllis. They will hand me my head if I try to interfere. This is going to be a disaster isn't it. I can see it on your face."

"Just relax Jasper. We're working on a solution to warn the people. If there is any immediate danger from outside sources, I don't know about it. However, you can do something. Call all your staff and have them meet us at the Park office in about one and a half hours. Just tell them it is an emergency."

"OK, but what do I tell my wife?"

"Nothing, absolutely nothing." I add quickly, "Let your wife have her special occasion. Make the calls, come back and introduce Dan and Nan around. Thanks for your help Jasper." I smile confidently and return to the hors d'oeuvres table.

The problem here is I don't have a clue as to what is going down or when. All I know is that He is working on something that will interrupt the program, capture everyone's undivided attention and break the spell on Phyllis. If I know Him, it will be all the warning they will need. Now all I need to do is practice my own medicine and relax.

CHAPTER 22
Black Magic

Dan and Nan arrive at the reception at the same time that Jasper returns. He gives me an OK sign and then starts making the rounds with Dan and Nan. Dan turns out to be a real chowhound and seems tethered to the hors d'oeuvres table. Nan can't maneuver him more than an arm's length away.

Across the room, I see two women escorting Phyllis into the Party. They are chattering and laughing, but there is no brightness in Phyllis' eyes. Some women toast her and others approach and chat with her. Her responses are cold and stiff. I am sure that no one else sees this, but after spending twelve hours on two flights with her, I can see this is a different woman. Unexpectedly, Nan walks up and takes her hand warmly in both of hers. She leans forward and whispers in her ear. The two women on either side become alarmed, but before they make a move, Nan pulls back. Phyllis' face is expressionless, but I can see tears in her eyes as she briefly glances at me. I feel her trapped feeling of desperation. I make a broad gesture with my body and begin to breathe deeply. She starts to do the same.

Our host invites everyone to sit in the dining room. I slip over next to Nan and ask, "Can you tell me what you said?"

Nan whispers in my ear, "The 'Great I Am' is within you. We will help you."

I look into Nan's eyes, and say quietly "You are one incredible woman, and you did it without a gram of fear."

We all take our assigned places in the dining room. Phyllis is still flanked by the two watchdogs escorting her. Dan and Nan are across the room. Dick is at a corner table.

No sooner does he sit down than he pops up again and starts shooting pictures. Jasper and Aline are sitting right across from me. Jasper introduces us. After a polite exchange, Aline leans across the table and motions for me to do the same.

She says quietly, "I am sorry about the warning. I am afraid Assouma and Uwase are misleading us. She gestures with her head toward the two women with Phyllis. They say it is important to make it all about Phyllis' visit. But Phyllis doesn't seem to be herself. They say that your announcements (their word) are not important. Is there anything we can do?"

I respond, "Not now, it's in the hands of the 'Great I Am'. Just be prepared for anything, because He loves a sense of the dramatic. He'll get His warning across one way or another. Until then, smile and have a good time. Jasper and I are ready." I lean back and nod to Jasper, who nods back. We are set.

I look over to check on Phyllis. She is doing a good job with her breathing meditation, but it is difficult for her. There is panic in her eyes. She sees me watching her and pushes her hair behind one ear. I see a string around her neck. In an instant, I know what it is and nod affirmatively. There is a sumu (in Swahili the word is often synonymous with "black magic", here it refers to a small pouch containing "black magic" charms,) around her neck. Just its presence can interrupt her concentration. I say to the 'Great I Am', "We need to take that thing off her."

"OK, I'll have Dan and Nan take care of it. You have Dick set up a diversion."

I look for Dick and catch his attention and motion for him to meet me.

I step outside the dining room and Dick joins me. I

tell him, "Laugh as though I'm telling you a joke."

Dick laughs, "Something's wrong. I can feel it. You need to warn these people and you're being blocked."

I make large ridicules and meaningless gestures, laughing, "They're using voodoo (black magic). They are hijacking the evening program."

Dick makes all kinds of humorous gestures, "That's it! They're all over Phyllis aren't they? She's as cold as ice since our arrival. Is it the two women next to her?"

"Yep, but the 'Great I Am' is working on this and putting the warning back on track. A minute ago, I noticed a cord around Phyllis' neck, which is probably a sumu. We need you to create a diversion in front of them, so Dan and Nan can walk behind her and pluck it off without the two women seeing it. They will time their pass to your actions."

"Consider it done! By the way, I'll bet anything that Jasper has a sumu on too. He is not the same man I remember. He's much more laid back."

"I'll let you deal with that sumu after we snip this one off Phyllis."

We both walk back into the dining room. Dan and Nan are looking at me. I smile and node my head yes. They return the sign. I silently say as I sit down, "This is better than communication devices!" The 'Great I Am' laughs, and so does Dan and Nan. He lets them hear my thoughts.

Dick starts to make a tour through the tables, chatting up the guests. It's no wonder why he snaps such great shots of people. Dan slips his Swiss army knife out of his pocket and opens it under the table, while making small talk with the people at his table. He palms it in his hand to conceal it. I can see that Dick is working the table next to Phyllis' table. Nan feigns a cramp in her leg and excuses herself to stand up and walk it off. Dan rises to help her. They time their pass to coincide with Dick's picture taking performance. Dick leans into the two women on either side of Phyllis, rearranging things on the table, commenting about their clothes and jewelry and asking if they made them. For those things they make, he invents poses to show them off in the pictures. With all this going on, Dan briskly walk past Phyllis' chair with only a half-second pause to cut the string and Nan pulls off the sumu a half-second later. A moment later, they are passing my seat and Nan leans over and says loudly, "Are we having fun yet?" I feel the sumu slipping safely into my pocket. Everyone at the table laughs, as Nan and Dan return to their seats. Not even Phyllis notices what is going on until she is almost through with her dinner. Mission accomplished

Dick sits down to eat. The food is so good that the chatter in the room drops about 3 decibels. There are lots of exotic fruits and vegetables and fish from a nearby lake. They serve the fish with a special sauce, which is tangy and sweet. Perhaps the most outstanding part of the meal for me are the homemade breads. There are three different kinds all traditional Rwanda loafs; one is similar to a dark rye; another is a wheat bread made with dark malted syrup; and the third is a light bread made with a barley grain. One thing is for certain, these people know how to cook and bake.

Toward the end of the meal, Uwase, one of the women with Phyllis, stands up and leaves the room. Phyllis is breathing easily now, but pretends to be in a daze as she eats. I seize the opportunity to whisper in her ear. I quickly walk behind her and bend down over her shoulder. I whisper, "Play along with them now. Why don't you deliver your 'DNA out of Africa' lecture? You're probably going to be rudely interrupted in about twenty minutes. At that point, their spell will be completely broken, but you may want to play along until we neutralize the threat. We are here to help you."

Her eyes sparkle and the artery on her neck stands out as she forces herself to hold a deadpan look on her face. I squeeze her shoulder gently and look at Assouma, the woman still sitting next to her.

I smile broadly, "Phyllis seems to be focusing on her talk. I apologize for the interruption." Then changing the subject, "You ladies sure know how to throw a party for a friend! Thank you very much. I miss the welcoming dance though." Assouma nods to me then looks away. I go back to my seat and continue my conversation with Jasper and Aline. I am reliant on the 'Great I Am' as to whom we can trust. He says that Dick is right about Jasper, but Aline is blocking Him, which can be because of a spell on him or a completely dominant mind and ego like most people today. The one message that I am receiving clearly is that His trap is about to spring. What that is I don't know.

Uwase returns and announces that everything is ready for Phyllis' talk. She invites us to move into the main hall. Oddly, I am hearing Uwase's thoughts. The 'Great I Am' must be doing this. She is planning to use her black magic to control Phyllis' thoughts. The subject is to be on the power of black magic and the need to control the minds of weaker people. All this will come out of the mouth of Phyllis and carry all her credibility.

The 'Great I Am' says, "You have done well. We will see how this plays out. I need a connection between Phyllis and me; then there could be a lot more certainty in this. Right now, she is close, but not there yet. I feel that she is looking to you for help. Maybe you can find out why she is hesitating."

I shake my head as I walk into the main hall, "Don't I have enough to do? You know how hard it is for me to multitask, especially when it comes to women."

He smiles, "I have a feeling that you will enjoy this assignment."

"OK, OK, I forget that you can read me like a book."

Everyone is settling down in the main hall. I make a quick trip to my room to grab my daypack and return to my seat in the back on the outside isle, which Dan and Nan are saving for me. Dick is posing Jasper and Aline for a picture. He fusses with Jasper's uniform, smoothing it out in some places and blousing it in others. Then he discovers some leaves in his hair. He has him bend over and close his eyes, while he shakes the leaves out of his hair. He then arranges his hair in that unkempt stand up look that is so popular. Finally, he takes the picture of them talking together.

As Dick passes me, he nonchalantly drops something in my lap and continues to walk to the front of the room. He is now in a perfect position to take some great shots of Phyllis' lecture and the people's reaction.

I look down in my lap and see another sumu. I quickly cover it with my hand and slide it into my pocket with the other one from Phyllis. That's when it dawns on me what Dick was doing when he was prepping Jasper for the picture.

Uwase escorts Phyllis to the podium and then takes her seat in the front row. I can only imagine the expression on her face when Phyllis begins to speak.

CHAPTER 23
The Warning

She starts with a warm smile, "Friends, I want to talk to you about racism and ethnic genocide which is refuted so clearly in the DNA coming out of Africa. Our misguided colonists blew family characteristics into racial distinctions and ethnic superiority. Their rhetoric fooled you, and they gave you the names Tutsis and Hutu. Are those your tribal names? No! Look around the room. Can't you see how ridiculous that is? Of course, you can! Yet we continue to delude ourselves by factions in our society. Poor Michel Jackson struggled to become white. Now, women want nose jobs, breast implants, Botox treatment and liposuction. Soon when they hold the Miss Universe pageant, the award will not go to the woman, but the best plastic surgeon.

"Well, here is some breaking news for all those white racists and ethnically superior individuals. Your DNA comes out of Africa! We all have black roots!" Everyone laughs, and Phyllis has her audience sitting on the edge of their seats. She continues, "In fact Mitochondrial Eve lived only a few hundred kilometers from here. She is the mother of us all." Phyllis continues to bring all the scientific information alive. She introduces Y-chromosomal Adam and explains Haplogroups and their migration. It is obvious that she is now weaving her own spell over the people.

Suddenly, a fourteen-year-old boy comes running and hobbling into the room screaming at the top of his lungs. He runs directly up to Assouma, his mother.

He screams, "Mama, Mama my leg is being torn

off."

Assouma says, "Let me see Bosco." He holds up his leg and screams in pain.

There is a serious red abrasion around his ankle. Dan, Nan and Dr. Kathrin come to his aid. She has seen this before. She looks at Assouma with her mouth open, but no words come out.

Bosco screams, "Mama make it stop." His screech is bone chilling.

Right before our eyes, the abrasion cuts deeper into the boy's leg and breaks the skin. The wound starts to bleed. We all feel his agonizing cries.

Assouma shouts at Dr. Kathrin, "Do something Dr., please! What is happening?"

Dr. Kathrin finds her words and speaks with panic in her voice, "I need my kit!"

Nan says the obvious, "It looks like his foot is caught in a snare."

Dr. Kathrin wraps a rag around the wound and shouts, "Can someone go for my kit?!" Everyone is paralyzed.

I calmly step forward and hand her the first aid kit from my daypack. She looks in my eyes and mutters, "Oh no!"

Bosco's cries are even louder now, and people are trying to cover their ears. The wound cuts deeper into his leg, which is now pulled taut by some invisible force.

Assouma looks at me and screams, "You are doing this!"

"No, I am not! He has done it to himself. That is the warning you don't want to hear. Now your little game has consequences, and your son may lose his leg. And soon, the traps of others will begin to snare their owners. They will have you to thank for their troubles." The room goes dead silent, except for the whimpers of Bosco.

Assouma's eyes fix on mine as tears roll down her cheeks. She asks in a desperate pleading tone, "Mr. is there anything you can do?"

"Yes, but we have to act fast. Nothing that I ask is open for discussion, and you must do exactly as I say. That goes for everyone here. Does everyone agree?" There is a resounding YES.

Dr. Kathrin looks up to me, "What do I do? I'm a veterinarian."

"Tie a tourniquet a little above the wound and wrap the wound with the sterile gauze bandage." I turn to Bosco, "You need to show us where your snares are." Bosco hesitates. "Look son, this is your only chance to save your leg. That gorilla out there is caught in your snare and feeling no pain. The pain and damage is all yours, because you set the trap. It is all a big game to him. He's having fun pulling on the string. I know he doesn't want to hurt you, but you are suffering because you are trying to hurt him." Bosco shakes his head no. "Alright everyone, Bosco is willing to give up his leg. The rest of you still have time. If you have any family or friends that laid snares, they need to go out and collect them immediately. Call and tell them to meet us at the park office in five minutes. Warden Jasper has a team waiting to go out and help you collect the snares. Remember, do not leave one behind, because that can be the snare that ends up around a gorilla's neck and strangles you."

Bosco cries out from a new wave of pain, "Mama, do something! Kill this man!"

Assouma hisses at him, "Hold your tongue boy and show the man where you laid your snares or I'll chop that leg off myself."

Bosco whimpers, "OK, OK, but I can't walk."

I motion to Dan and Nan and show them how to carry him in a chair carry. I motion for Jasper and Dr. Kathrin to come with us. Bosco directs us to a bamboo section just above the farms that have eaten into the Park boundary. We can hear the cry of the gorilla in the snare and head toward it. His cry is more one of fear than pain. Bosco's cry of pain causes the gorilla to stop moving. It senses what is happening. As we reach the snare, we can see a two-year-old baby in the snare. The whole gorilla family is there to protect the baby. The baby gorilla makes eye contact with Bosco, and Bosco makes eye contact with the baby. There is a miraculous communication taking place between them. The baby gorilla senses Bosco's pain and holds very still. Bosco sighs in relief.

He says to me, "Please Mr. set him free."

Dr. Kathrin says, "We need to dart the mother and baby so we can take off the snare. I have to go for my gear." She looks at me as I reach into my daypack and she adds, "Don't tell me you have a dart gun in there too!"

"No, just my facemask, don't worry this will be fine." I take out a facemask, which looks like a gorilla's snot. I slip on the mask with smiles from everyone including Dick, who is snapping away.

Slowly I walk toward the baby. The silverback comes at me pounding his chest and making that frightening popping sound. Using my tongue and open mouth, I return the popping sounds and open my arms to him. He stops and turns away. Next, the mother charges me. I make some comforting sounds and open my arms to her. She stops and I motion for her to come to me while I continue the soothing sounds. Slowly she comes closer and closer. When I hold out my hand, she takes it, and we walk over to the baby together. The baby is still very still watching Bosco. As I reach down to lift him up the baby looks in my eyes. All his fear disappears, and his mother strokes the hair on my arm. I carefully slip the snare off his leg and show his mother that there is no wound. She makes the sweetest sound ever to fill my ears, and I hand him to his mother. The silverback comes up to me and sits down right in front of me. I return the compliment and sit down facing him. We have a nice stare at each other before I rise slowly and return to the others.

Bosco asks me, "Mr., can you teach me to be their friend like that?"

"Maybe one day, Bosco, but right now, to be their friend, you need to show us where the rest of your snares are."

He does just that along with the rest of Kinigi. At the end of the day, Jasper reports that we cleared out 288 snares. His team was extremely proud, as they should be.

Jasper is more excited and joyful than I have seen him before. He asks, "What do we do if there are still some out there? Is the perpetrator going to suffer the consequences?"

"Do the same thing as with Bosco. Only take Dr. Kathrin along to rescue the gorilla. If you rescue the gorilla, you rescue the perpetrator. Hopefully, everyone will get the point and stop laying snares. Then you can teach them how to hunt. I understand you are an excellent hunter."

Jasper shakes my hand with a smile, "Have everyone meet us at the park office for the climb up Bisoke at 07:00. We will depart promptly at 7:30. And I can't wait to see what tomorrow brings. Now my job has become the best job in the whole world!"

Dr. Kathrin taps me on the shoulder and says, "Mr. I don't know who you really are, but seeing this I can tell you're very very special. I'll see you tomorrow morning."

"You might want to bring Dr. Spike," I suggest.

"Don't worry; I won't let him miss it."

Dick walks back to the guesthouse with me. After a long silence, he finally says, "This has to be one of the most spectacular days of my life. Can you help me connect to your 'Great I Am'?"

"He's not my 'Great I Am'. He is the 'Great I Am' in everything. But yes, I can help you connect with the 'Great I Am' within you."

"I look forward to it," Dick says. Then he adds, "This is the world's game changer, isn't it?"

"Yes it is!"

CHAPTER 24
The Summit Meeting

I arrive at the Volcanoes National Park office at 07:00 sharp and immediately check the gear that Jasper and his team are carrying. They are in good spirits and ready for an exciting day. I ask them not to carry guns, because there is no need. They put them away without questions or comments. I then ask Jasper if I can tack on a few words after he gives everyone their climbing instructions. Jasper agrees. Then he asks with a slight twinge of caution, "Are you expecting any bad stuff today?"

"Not on the climb, this is all good stuff. However, we have no control over human stupidity." My confidence sets him at ease.

Jasper chuckles, "Isn't that the truth."

The others start to arrive. Dick, Phyllis and Dr. James are in a huddle. The other VIPs are studying papers and talking with Dr. Kathrin and Dr. Spike, the co-directors of GorillaDoctors, the new name for 'Mountain Gorilla Veterinary Project'. Dan and Nan are mingling with many of the women from yesterday who are there with their families, and the main topic of their conversation is that the gorillas are now protected. Assouma and Uwase are conspicuously absent. However, I notice Bosco watching us from a distance and sporting a very impressive bandage on his leg. I wave for him to come closer. To my surprise, he runs up without even a limp. His Auntie grabs him by the arm and looks at me.

I walk over, "Hi Bosco how's your leg?"

"Ah, that's nothin. I hurt myself worse than that all the time," he says. "But I won't do it ever again. I feel the love of that little gorilla, and he stopped movin so I'm not hurting worse."

"Do you want to come with us Bosco?"

"Can I?" He looks up to his Auntie.

She looks at me, and smiles warmly, "That's mighty kind of you Mr. Hayah. Bosco promise me that you will stay close to us and do as I tell you."

"Yes Auntie, I promise."

Warden Jasper calls for everybody's attention. "I want to welcome everyone to Volcanoes National Park. Today we will be climbing to the summit of Bisoke. It is the only summit totally in the boundaries of the park. Some of you are return climbers with us, but I ask that you listen carefully to your guides instructions at all times, because the trail may be different from your last visit. Now your guides will pass among you to check your daypack to make sure that you have enough food and water and enough clothes to keep you warm at altitude.

"Remember, that this is the home of the Mountain Gorillas and you are their visitors. We are giving you a facemask to wear if we encounter any gorillas. Most of the gorilla families are habituated and accustomed to human presence. However, you must mimic their sounds; move slowly at all times in both walking and gestures; and use your common sense.

"If you are in reasonably good condition, you should be able to do this climb. To accommodate everyone in a group this size, it may be necessary to divide the group into fast, medium and slow climbers. There are enough guides to lead each group. Also, we have an extra guide to bring people back who find it too difficult. We will take regular breaks to drink water and take a short rest.

"Now I want to turn this over to Hayah who will say a few words."

My enthusiasm is bubbling over, "The 'Great I Am' is asking me to make this climb to celebrate the protection of all endangered species. In this case, it is the mountain-gorillas. For many millenniums, they have been connected to Him, while we as humans have lost our connection. What you witness here today can be yours. And don't be surprised when you walk down today, that you no longer feel like the higher species on this mountain.

"As you make the climb, don't be alarmed when you don't see any gorilla families. They are all waiting for me at the top. If there are any stragglers, please do not interact with them, because they are late for the meeting. I guarantee those of you who reach the top that you will see a wonder beyond all your imaginings. Now let's have fun! Lead away Warden Jasper."

The road to Bisoke, oh the road
Where potholes are craters
And bumps small hills.
It's only a few kilometers
Of wicked butt bouncing
And kidney shaking thrills.
They have yet to invent
The vehicle undercarriage
To make this road flat.
No matter how high the purpose
To climb to the summit
And fulfill this or that,
You must take precautions
A rubber mouth guard
And two pain pills.
Consider a laugh a minute
With a friend you like

And have a good chat.
Then you will arrive there
No worse for the wear.

Nothing more and nothing less can I say about the road to the Bisoke Volcano trailhead.

The trail starts just outside the bamboo zone. Like all bamboo stands it is very tight, but the diameter of this bamboo is the largest and tallest I have ever seen. Fortunately for us, the path is clear and easy to navigate. There are gorilla signs everywhere, but no mountain-gorillas.

The next zone is the equatorial rain forest. Here the forest is so dense that we are constantly pushing our way through the fast growing undergrowth. Without a guide, it could be very easy to wander off the path. The variety of birds in this zone is plentiful and tempting. I am frequently making myself focus on the summit. I am not here on a bird watching tour. As the rainforest canopy begins to thin out, we are able to pick up the pace. So far, we haven't seen any straggling gorilla families.

Then Mother Nature seems to draw a line. The tall trees stop and we cross into the alpine meadows zone. A few plants are waste high, but most of the vegetation is below my knee. Occasionally, I see a tall plant that looks like a palm tree, but not as tall or with as broad a leaf. After about thirty minutes in this zone, we pop over a ridge and stop dead in our tracks.

There, covering the summit, are hundreds of mountain-gorillas. They look like a crowd of people attending a summit meeting instead of many family groups of mountain-gorillas. On the rim of the volcano, forming a huge circle, are all the silverbacks sitting in total peace and harmony with each other.

Jasper turns to me, "I have never seen anything like this in my life. They must have come up from the Congo side as well. Whom am I standing in the presence of?" He bows his head.

I reach out and lift his chin, "Just another man like you. In the future, this can be you Jasper." I put a hand on each of his shoulders, "Now I must lead us up through the crowd. When I stop and set down my daypack that is where you stop and sit down. The rest of the group can join you there, standing, kneeling or sitting. Remember, everyone should use habituation sounds and movements. Dan and Nan will be attracting many gorillas to you. Follow their lead. I will end up near that spot, so everyone can watch the procession. Right now, I will climb to and then circle the rim to greet all the silverbacks. That should give everyone a chance to come up here." I take out my water bottle and have a long drink. Then I put on my gorilla facemask.

I put my daypack on and start toward the crowd of mountain-gorillas. When I reach the edge of the crowd, I slow my pace and begin to make my gorilla sounds. The gorillas open a wide path for us. Many of the others are clearing the ridge now and standing with their eyes and mouths wide open in awe. Slowly they move down to follow our group.

Suddenly a female comes rushing toward me with her baby. When she is about ten meters away, I recognize her. It is the mother and baby from yesterday evening. I open my arms making comforting sounds. She rushes up, takes me by the hand and leads me up through the crowd. Soon, I reach a good spot that will give everyone a good vantage point. I take off my daypack, remove my full water bottle and put it in my belt pouch. I set the pack down and continue up to the rim and the silverbacks. I am not surprised to see that the mother is bringing me to her silverback first. As I approach him, he stands erect, but with no chest beating.

I feel an incredible surge of love swelling up from the 'Great I Am' and I open my arms with my hands up to pour it out to the silverback. To my surprise, the silverback mimics the gesture, which I think is new to him and claps his hands against mine with a deep guttural grunt ending in a hum. As I move to the next silverback, I see all the babies rushing toward the human gathering. In seconds, they are all over Nan and Dan. Bosco now stands watching them.

I circle the rim sharing the love from the 'Great I Am' with each silverback and with the same gesture. They all repeat the same movement and sound as with the first silverback. Gradually, He helps me realize that this movement is an ancient ritual between them and the creator. It is in their genes. Their joy fills me until my cup runs over.

Back to where I start, I sit down, facing downhill, a few meters from the human group. The procession begins. The youngest, who are sick or with injury, come first. The 'Great I Am' carefully instructs me as to what to do with each one. Some have small wounds, which I simply put my hand over, and the 'Great I Am' heals the wound. When I take my hand away, there is no sign of any wound.

Dr. Spike and Dr. Kathrin move next to Dan and Nan. Spike asks, "What is he doing?"

Nan whispers, "He is healing them."

Dr. Spike and Dr. Kathrin look at each other dumfounded. Phyllis and Dr. James join them.

Some of these children have old wounds and scars

from snares. All of these are serious with permanent damage or deformity. He has me do the same thing with them. Again, when I take my hand away all traces of the wound are gone. He senses a question rising within me and says, "Their connection to me is healing them."

Many of the children are suffering from respiratory problems. I put a hand on their chest, front and back, and take deep breaths. They take deep breaths as well. In less than a minute, they are healed.

The next group is the older children and the mothers. Their illnesses and injuries are much the same. The only difference is that their wounds are generally much more severe. Then a mother steps in front of me. She is supporting herself on her front arms and her left hind foot. The 'Great I Am' says to me, "don't worry, she has the connection." I take her hands and help her to sit down in front of me. My tears are rolling down my cheeks as He gives me clear and specific instructions. I pull up all the vegetation growing between my legs, tear it into bits and set it aside. My tears are dripping on the top soil now. I take out my water bottle and add a little water to my tears. With both hands, I knead the soil into a mud pile. He has me add some of the vegetation bits a little at a time. When it is the right consistency, I gesture to the mother to put the stump of her right leg into the mud pile. She quickly does this. He quickly guides my hands to mold the mud into an ankle and foot. My tears are streaming heavily now and falling on the molded foot. My hands stroke the molded foot, smoothing it out. Then beneath my hands, the mud becomes flesh and grows warm. My hands continue to stroke the ankle and hair grows on it. I lift her leg and foot out of the mud and flex it at the ankle. She curls and uncurls her new toes. When she stands, she makes the same sweet sound my ears embraced from the other mother yesterday. I bow my head in thanksgiving, unable to comprehend this event completely. The mother reaches out and strokes my hair. It takes me a few minutes to recover, but the mother is prancing around, showing everybody her new leg and foot.

The last group is the elderly silverbacks. I stand and again I feel the incredible surge of love welling up within me. All the silverbacks on the rim are now standing. As I open my arms and raise my hands, they all make the guttural grunt and hum together and repeat it continuously. Each elderly silverback, one by one, steps in front of me, smacks my hands and joins the grunting-humming chorus.

When the procession is over, the family members rush about reassembling into their family groups. When they are all together, the grunting-humming chorus stops and they wait in silence for me to leave the mountain.

I grab my daypack and head down the trail with Jasper leading and Dr. Spike and Dr. Kathrin following. We hike in silence for several minutes, which gives me time to recover. When we stop for water, everyone starts talking at once. I hold up my hand for them to stop.

Dr. Spike asks, "Please, please, what happened up there? I saw you mold a new leg out of mud on one that was amputated."

I blow out all my air and take a deep breath. "I'll give you the short version. First of all, I do nothing; the 'Great I Am' within me and the mother do everything as an act of Love. He does the healing and the mother has the image of her leg whole. Secondly, the scientific explanation He is asking me to give you will mean more to you than it does to me. The mud and plants and the leg are all matter, with cells, molecules, and many atoms with neutrons and protons in their nucleus and electrons attached to it, which forms the different elements. All He does is swap a few electrons here and there to create the atoms he needs to create the molecules and cells. Then He arranges the cells in the proper form according to the mother's image. Her body does the rest, because she is connected to the 'Great I Am'. Thirdly, it takes three to do the healing: the 'Great I Am', a connected person to be His hands (that is me), and a connected patient who can see themselves whole again (that is the mother). You cannot heal yourself. Finally, if you and Dr. Kathrin connect to the 'Great I Am' you, too, can help Him heal these animals who are connected. You will never have to amputate another leg." They are speechless. "I'll let you chew on that while we take these people off the mountain."

Oh, how nice it would be to find a secluded spot and hole up for a few hours. But this situation has a life of its own. Most of the people coming down the trail are reflecting on images from moments ago. In many ways, they don't know what to make of it yet. Is it a miracle? Is it magic and sorcery? Is there something new happening on the planet? How can the mountain-gorillas do this and humans can't? Who is this 'Great I Am' that Hayah is always talking about? And on, and on.

As we are approaching the trailhead, the 'Great I Am' is preparing me for a new problem that is about to emerge. I ask Jasper to find Phyllis so I can prepare him and her for what is coming up. I grab Dan and Nan and pull them aside. They know what I am about to ask. The 'Great I Am' already has them prepping to lead a discussion about the miracle on the mountain. I am grateful that they are here.

CHAPTER 25
Justice Prevails

Dick returns to the trailhead and walks over to me just as Jasper appears with Phyllis.

I say to Dick, "I want you to listen in on this."

Phyllis approaches bubbling with enthusiasm and takes my hand, "Hayah, I want to be part of this new awakening; I'll do whatever you say; just show me how."

Jasper quickly adds, "Ditto to that!"

I open my arms and huddle them together putting a hand on one of their shoulders. "After tonight we will go to work on your connection. But right now, we need to prepare you both for a very difficult event. In a few minutes, a black Land Rover is going to pull up to take you back into Kinigi. They will assume that both of you are still under the spell of your sumu. Play along and do as the driver asks without question. If you do so, you have nothing to fear. No matter what you see, do not react or try to do anything. Pretend to be in a blind stupor. Do that, and we will succeed."

No sooner are these words out of my mouth than the black car pulls up. The driver hops out and calls to Jasper and Phyllis in Swahili. They both assume their trance-like states and move toward the car.

Dick is puzzled, "What is going down?"

"There is no time to explain. I am going to walk over and talk to Dan and Nan. You're going to take your gear and go down behind that bush, as if you're going to take a leak. A pickup truck will pull up and two guys will jump out and walk up toward me. Climb in the back of the truck, hide under the tarp and brace yourself for the bumpy road. As soon as they unload me, hop out, because they will be pealing out within minutes."

"Yes, sir!" Dick says without hesitation.

I turn and head up to Dan and Nan. No sooner does Dick reach the bush than the pickup truck pulls up. The two burly men pile out of the truck. And before anyone can react, I am bound, blindfolded and manhandled into the cab of the truck between the two men. They start the slow drive down the bumpy road. There is only silence and the sound of bouncing objects in the bed of the truck. Poor Dick!

Soon we are off the road to Bisoke, and we pick up speed. We are only driving for what feels like ten minutes; when the truck pulls into a rutted driveway and stops. The men manhandle me into a building, untie and remove my blindfold. The two men salute and leave at once. I am standing in a large working area of a barn. At the far end, I can hear livestock kicking their stalls in protest to what is going on. A large hayloft nearly full of hay is above the animal stalls. About four meters to either side of me sit Phyllis and Jasper on milking stools. They are holding their trance-like gaze, but breathing rhythmically. In front of us to the left are standing Uwase and Assouma, each holding a large dog. On the right is a gray-haired woman, dressed in very expensive clothes with a mink stole and a stylish hat. She is weaving together a straw doll. In the middle is a potbellied old man with gray-hair. He too is dressed in an expensive suit, with a white shirt and silk tie. He is holding a machete.

The older man in the center steps toward me, slapping the flat of the machete in the palm of his hand. "Well, Mr. Dogooder, do you know why you are here?"

Under normal circumstances, I will treat an enemy with more respect, but this man commands or deserves none, nor at this moment does the 'Great I Am' require me to give him any. I laugh and say, "You want me to teach you and your sister how to milk the cows?"

There is a flash of anger in his face as he looks at the others on either side of him, "I'm going to enjoy doing this one!"

Still chuckling, "I'm required to warn you that any action you take against me or my friends will boomerang back on you. You do know what a boomerang is don't you?"

He snaps back smugly, "It's a toy!"

I become very serious, "Not in this case, unless you consider that machete a toy. Whatever action you take against us will happen to you not us." I look him in the eye. "Just like what is happening with the mountain-gorillas." I look over to Assouma, and her eyes become big as saucers and fear fills her face.

The old man becomes very haughty, "You talk big for a man who is about to die. Do you know who I am?

"Yes I do. You are Monsieur Zed and that old woman is you sister Agathe. But both of you better take seriously what I'm telling you."

Zed's ego is puffing him up beyond common sense. "You forget who this is!" He smacks the machete in the palm of his hand. "This is Mr. Cleave. He's the one I used to split Dian Fossey's head in two. And he's itching to do you."

"Monsieur Zed, I implore you to shut down your irrational mind and runaway ego and back off from what you intend to do, before you destroy yourself."

"And how are you going to destroy me, Mr. Bigshot?"

"I'm not! You are going to destroy yourself!"

"Don't be ridiculous!" He laughs manically.

Agathe steps in, "I need a piece of him, brother." She walks over to me to take a pinch of my hair. When she pulls, the hair that comes out is her hair from her own head. She winces and rubs her head under her hat. When she looks between her fingers, she sees the hair and assumes it is from my head. She turns to her brother, "Give me another minute and I'll have this ready."

Agathe walks back to her place and starts to weave the hair into the head of the doll with bits of straw. All of the others in front of us are watching what she is doing with evil grins on their faces.

I glance up and see that Dick is camouflaged in the hayloft and shooting away at the action on the main floor. I thank the inventor of digital cameras and no shutter sound.

When Agathe finishes putting the doll together, she holds it up and starts to say a ritual prayer in Latin. The prayer drones on for over a minute, and she concludes by making the sign of the cross.

I quickly ask the 'Great I Am', "What's that all about?"

He explains, "Voodoo and the Roman Catholic rituals and signs are totally entwined, so many of the people practicing it think they are serving Joshua. Don't worry! It can't be further from the truth."

Agathe pulls a pin from her hat and looks back at her brother. "OK, let's kill the bastard. He'll wish he never set foot in Rwanda."

Zed starts to do some kind of chant and weaving dance. He waves the machete around in broad gestures. The sharp edge of the dark blade flashes in the air. I can understand why this could be extremely intimidating. I use this time to strengthen my connection with the 'Great I

Am' and go into slow-motion perception.

Finally, Zed spins in a circle, with the blade outstretched. As he comes around the blade is at my neck height. I can see it coming, closer and closer. When it is within a few centimeters of my neck it bends backward with his wrist, slides past under my chin and appears to come out the opposite side. During the follow-through, Zed's arm crosses over his chest and the machete goes flying, nearly taking out Agathe who jumps out of the way.

Zed is frozen in his final position. His eyes are huge and bulging out. His mouth is open. His face is full of surprise and terror. There is only a thin red line around his neck.

Agathe rushes over to him and pulls her arm back to slap him; she screams, "Snap out of it, and kill the son-of-a-bitch;" her hand connects with the side of his face; and Zed's head goes flying toward Uwase and Assouma. His body topples over on his potbelly and bounces twice. Agathe screams with an evil screech spinning toward me. She raises the doll shouting, "You have no power here!" She stabs the needle into the chest of the doll; she doubles in pain still screeching; she stabs the doll several more time; she drops the doll as she grabs her chest. She screams, "NOOO!" and falls to the floor dead of a massive heart attack.

The dogs go crazy over the bouncing rolling head, pulling loose from their masters. They chase the head and attack it. The chase turns into a fight over position of the head.

The women are frantic, shouting at the dogs trying to control them. It is futile. Assouma turns and rushes toward Jasper, shouting commands. Uwase runs to Phyllis doing the same. Jasper and Phyllis do not respond. The women start to search around their necks for the sumu.

I take the sumu out of my pocket and hold them up. "Are you looking for these?" As the women turn to face me, I quickly put both sumu around my neck.

Uwase and Assouma scream in agony, covering their eyes.

Uwase screams, "The light, make it stop."

Assouma screams, "It's too bright, turn it off."

I take off the two sumu and crush them under my foot. The two women no longer feel any pain. They stand up and open their eyes. They rub them with their hands and then open them again. They both say at the same time, "I'm blind!"

I say in a comforting tone, "So you are. Are you ready to listen to me now?"

The two women crumple to the floor weeping, but no tears can be shed. I come back to normal perception.

I walk over and help Phyllis to her feet. She throws her arms around me in a strong hug. She is full of joy and enthusiasm saying, "I thank you; I thank you; I thank you! I am breathing as you tell us to, and all of a sudden, I am in that empty space and free from everything around me. Then I see His Light and He speaks to me. I feel such incredible Love. I give myself to Him, and He shows me my purpose. Now, His will be done! As I watch you, I can see Him at work and I know we are safe."

I take her hand and we walk over to Jasper, who is watching everything with his eyes open. We stand in front of him and are both amazed at the radiance that is surrounding him. Jasper is saying, "Yes, yes, yes!" repeatedly. He looks up at us. "That is spectacular! I am hearing the most incredible running commentary. Finally, justice prevails. It's funny, I don't feel any sadness for their deaths but I know He does. Is He always going to be inside me like this?"

"He always has been and always will be, and as long as you choose to maintain the connection to Him you will receive the running commentary, even when you're making love to your wife."

We all laugh.

I turn to the two dogs and start a very quiet whistle in a high pitch almost outside the human hearing range. The dogs look up and come to me. I take them to their masters and put their leashes in Assouma and Uwase's hand. Jasper and Phyllis help them to their feet.

I give the women their instructions, "You will be blind for three days. During that time, you must do three things. You must remove all hatred from your heart and mind. Next, you must find the love in yourself by focusing on your breath and only your breath, setting all other thoughts aside. Finally, you will have the chance to connect with the 'Great I Am' within you. If you make that choice, your dog will lead you to Jasper. Jasper will lay his hands on your eyes, and if you can see yourself whole again, the 'Great I Am' will restore your sight. The choice is yours. If you choose to live in darkness, as you have been for most of your life, then you will remain blind for the rest of your life. And the 'Great I Am' wants you to know that He has a higher purpose for both of you."

Dick comes down out of the hayloft. He takes my hand and says, "Hayah, you know that I have been flirting with this connection for three days now. Well, while I am being bounced about in the back of that truck, I start to meditate. The next thing I know I am floating on a cushion of air (and I don't mean an air cushion). When the truck stops I remember your instructions, and I roll over to gain my footing. The next thing I know, I'm standing in the hayloft totally concealed. The rest is much like what they're telling you. I guess I am part of the new awakening."

"And your purpose is as important to us as the young scribe's purpose is to Joshua."

CHAPTER 26
Soul Searching

It is late by the time the police leave. Jasper calls one of his rangers to come and pick us up. We drop off the two women and their dogs at their homes. Jasper drops Phyllis, Dick and I off at the guesthouse.

Nan, Dan, Dr. James, Dr. Spike and Dr. Kathrin are sitting in the lounge in a deep debate, when we walk in. Everyone is happy to see us and wants to know what happened. We are not in the mood to go over the gory details again, but Phyllis and Dick are eager to share their new connection experience. This turns out to be the perfect injection into their debate. James, Spike and Kathrin really want to make the connection with the 'Great I Am', but they can't break through. Phyllis and Dick's stories help the others to be more optimistic.

Nan turns to me. "Hayah, we are trying everything we know, but nothing seems to work. And it seems like the 'Great I Am' wants them to connect, but all He says is that they are close. What can we do?"

I say to James, Spike and Kathrin, "Understand that He wants you to make the effort and choose to find Him. It is all about your Free Will. These are the kind of problems I am very happy to deal with." I continue with a broad smile, "Everybody should settle back and relax. The tension and frustration are far too high to be productive." I pause and give everyone a chance to recover. "I'm going to ask the three of you some questions and the rest of you can throw in your experiences if they might be helpful."

Nan interrupts, "You all haven't eaten dinner. I'll find something in the kitchen, and we can all use some green tea." She leaves the room through a sea of "Yeses!"

"OK, first question. Why do you want to connect to the 'Great I Am'?"

James is on the edge of his seat and starts. "My whole life, I have tried to learn as much as I can. Intelligence has always been important to me. I consider myself an intellectual leader in the Age of Reason. Now, I want to take the next step and achieve enlightenment."

Phyllis jumps in. "That's what I thought too, but then I discovered that it was my rational mind and ego that were making intelligence so important."

James ponders this comment.

Kathrin is full of enthusiasm. "I love animals and believe them to be more faithful than humans. As a little girl, I dreamt of being a healer of animals. After yesterday and today's miracles all I can think of is that I want to be able to do this too!"

Spike speaks calmly and sincerely. "I am filled with doubts and questions. None of what I witnessed today makes any sense. Yet I have always felt a hole inside me, a void that needs filling. I am hoping that this is what I need to find."

Dick responds, "I know that hole, man. Been there, done that. And believe me this is what you need to find. It's worth the effort. By the way, does anyone mind if I shoot some pictures?" There are only positive responses.

I continue, "Second question. What do you consider to be your greatest obstacle?"

James leans back in his seat. "I don't know. But I need to know!" He pauses. I jump in.

"I think you nailed it James. Leave it there."

Kathrin stands up and starts walking about the room. Everyone watches her. She stops as though she is about to say something, then she continues to walk.

Finally, she says, "Maybe my scientific training is blocking me!"

Spike is very thoughtful now. There is a long silence. He says, "I guess I need answers."

Dan says, "Don't we all." He pauses. "The problem is there are no answers. And those things we consider answers aren't answers at all."

Nan returns with a tray of food and snacks and a large pot of herbal tea, which serves to relax the group and make everyone much more compassionate. As we return to the discussion, the tone is less desperate and urgent.

I turn to Spike. "Spike let me start with you. You say that you have many doubts and questions and the questions are your obstacle. I will venture a guess that you experience the same problem in your study and work as a Veterinarian. Is that true?"

"Yes, it is." He reacts to my ability to see this.

"The fact is that your doubts and questions are what help you to excel in your profession. They are also, why you feel there is a hole or void inside you. Let me show you. Picture a model of any complex cell and its molecular structure. What is the cell, and what is the most predominant part of the model?"

"The cell is from a silverback gorilla sperm, and the most predominant part of the model is space."

"How much space?"

"Roughly 95%."

"Compare that with all other cells."

"It is an average somewhere between 95-99%."

"So everything on the planet that we perceive as real is only 1-5% real and the rest is no-thing. And how long is the life-cycle of this sperm cell?"

"A few hours under the right conditions."

"That means that what we call real is not only minuscule in content, but fleeting in life duration. Can that be why you feel a hole or void inside you?"

Spike looks at Dan, "Oh, now I understand what you mean."

I continue, "But here is the punch line. That space is not empty! When you meditate, go into that space and stay there as long as you can, a few seconds or a few minutes. Then in that no-thingness, you will..."

Nan, Dan, Dick and Phyllis complete my sentence in unison, "find Him."

I turn to Kathrin. "Kathrin, it is not your scientific training that is blocking you. It is your ego. You want the healing power. You want to heal the animals that you love so much. Your ego is hiding in that well-meaning phrase, 'I want to be able to do this too!' Do you remember what my part is in this healing back on the trail when Spike asked me what I was doing?"

"Yes, you said, 'I do nothing; the love of the 'Great I Am' and the mother do it.' But then you said the 'Great I Am' is using your hands. I see! There is absolutely no ego in that, where I want something for myself."

"Go to the head of the class. In your meditation, shut down your chattering ego, and when you reach your inner space you will find Him. Then you can give yourself over to His will. And you will become His healing hands with the mountain-gorillas."

Kathrin looks over at Dick, "You're right Dick. This is worth the effort."

I continue, "James, in one way your situation is the simplest, but at the same time it is the most complicated. It is the simplest because you say 'I don't know. But I need to know.' All you have to do is change one little thing and you will be in the inner space. What you need to be able to say is, 'I don't know. And I don't need to know.' Unfortunately, it is complicated because you know so much and intelligence is important to you. Now you have the same struggle as Phyllis. There are two stories I want you to recall, Plato's story about Socrates' search for wisdom and Joshua's story about the Rich Young Man."

James is quick to respond, "I know them both. Plato writes, 'He is wise, who knows as Socrates knows that his wisdom is nothing.' In the Joshua parable, Joshua tells the Rich Young Man to give all his money to the poor and come and follow Him. But the Rich Young Man can't because his wealth is too great."

"Great, those are the punch lines. But let's look at the meat of the story. The Oracle tells Socrates that he is the wisest man in the world. However, Socrates can't accept this and he goes on a quest to find the wisest man. He interviews one wise man after another, all of whom think they are wise, but Socrates always finds the flaw in their wisdom. Now look at the logical syllogism: Many men are known to be the wisest of men; But Socrates knows the flaw in their wisdom; Therefore, Socrates is the wisest of men because he knows what they do not know. Then Socrates extends the syllogism, 'But I know that all my knowledge amounts to nothing.' That is how Plato comes up with his hypothesis. James, can you say the same about all your knowledge and intelligence?"

James is thinking and slightly nodding yes. "I see my flaw Socrates, but how do I fix it?"

"Use the Joshua parable by switching wealth for knowledge. The Wise Young Man comes to Joshua and says, 'I want to be part of enlightenment.' Joshua asks, 'Do you love me and your neighbor, and can you remove all hatred from your heart and mind?' The Wise Young Man answers, 'I did that.' Joshua says, 'Then **give** all your knowledge to your pupils and come and follow me.' The Wise Young Man responds, 'But I have done that!' Joshua makes an important distinction, 'You have **shared** your knowledge so your pupils can rise to your level of intelligence. However, you must **give** your knowledge to them; let it go to nurture them so they can grow beyond what you know.' When the Wise Young Man herd this he..."

There is complete silence in the room. There are tears streaming down Phyllis' face.

James is leaning forward, with his head down staring into an empty cup. He speaks softly, "I have never had anybody look into the depths of my soul before."

I respond lovingly, "Don't forget, I have help."

Phyllis looks at James compassionately. "James, Socrates wants me to ask you a question." James looks up. "Of which do you feel I am the most proud: my own accomplishment, or the accomplishments of my pupils, Plato and Aristotle?"

I can see a judgmental thought come into James' face, and I speak before he can, "Don't judge yourself James; no one here is; there is only love in this room. Just focus on your choice. It will take however long it takes. It is enough for us to see that you're not walking away. Why don't we all meditate together before we go to bed?"

Nan jumps in, "Dan and I are wondering. If the 'Great I Am' is within us, can He still be considered a transcendent being?"

"What a fantastic theme for meditation. Transcendent is a Latin word from the 15ᵗʰ Century. In your meditation when your rational thoughts and ego are bombarding you consider, 'Is my mental comprehension, thoughts and reason real? Can I experience them through any of my senses? Then when you reach your inner space let these questions emerge. What am I experiencing or feeling? Do I perceive this with my senses? Is this experience real? Now when you come out of your meditation you will see the heart of the Kantian debate, and then you can decide which is real and which is transcendent."

We begin to meditate.

I meditate for a few minutes. Then I open my eyes to study each person in the room. I see on Kathrin's face that she is seeing the light. Her eyebrows pull together in a curious wonder. Now they relax as she connects to the 'Great I Am'. The energy that is welling up in her almost has her floating out of her chair.

Spike looks like he is floating peacefully in his inner space. Suddenly, he becomes startled. His head cocks and turns slightly, as if someone is speaking to him. As he listens, he smiles and nods his head yes. Then his face fills with wonder as though someone is revealing the secrets of the universe to him.

James is struggling. I can see that he is being bombarded with thoughts and a chattering ego. At one point, his right shoulder starts to twitch, as if he is trying to shake something off it. Then for a few seconds he slides slowly into his inner space, only to be jerked out by another thought. But he is persistent and eventually overcomes his annoyance and brushes his thoughts aside as if they are nothing. Soon, he is sliding into his inner space for several minutes at a time. Then it happens. He actually stops breathing for a minute and begins again with a very slow exhale. Tears are rolling down his cheeks. His whole face is glowing. As he comes out of his meditation, he looks at me and says, "I can't believe how small I feel in the presence of His knowledge."

The energy in the room, as people come out of their meditation, is extremely powerful. We all can feel the connection. We all can feel that this is going to make a difference in this community.

The unanimous opinion about transcendent being is that our inner space, consciousness, the 'Great I Am', and Love are the experience of reality and non-transcendent. And what lies beyond the ordinary limits of our experience, is comprehension, knowledge, and the ego which are only phantoms and transcendent to our inner experience. Immanuel Kant would be proud. Everyone is enlightened and emerging from his or her self-imposed immaturity.

CHAPTER 27
The Flight to Kenya

The next morning, we all gather for breakfast together. I invite Dr. Spike, Dr Kathrin and Jasper to join us. I enjoy listening to the buzz about their new purposes in life. I realize that I am really growing fond of enlightened people, and they are all growing fond of each other. Dan and Nan begin to talk about the incredible Love connection they are feeling with everyone. It turns out that everyone shares this feeling. Dan then opens up and tells us that his love for Nan is taking on a new dimension. He says, "Our understanding of each other is incredible. Our tolerance of each other is unimaginable. The bond between us is growing beyond what any poet has ever captured. The lovemaking..."

Nan clears her thought loudly, and everyone laughs. She then blows Dan a kiss and grins. She then turns to me, "Did the Disciples feel this bond, this Love, this connection."

"In some ways maybe, but for the most part they are clueless. Mary Magdalene, John, Bartholomew and Paul probably feel it more than the others do. But remember that their connection with Joshua is different. He is there with them. As hard as He tries, He cannot help them to connect with the 'Great I Am' within.

Dr. James looks around at the group and exclaims, "All this makes me feel like we are turning the world upside down." There are many heads nodding, yes.

I reverse the image, "I prefer to give it a different twist. Since the fall, humans have been turning the world upside down. Now, the 'Great I Am' is asking us to help turn it right-side-up."

Everyone laughs, and James adds, "Wow, He really likes that image!" He turns to Nan, "Is this what it is like to hear Him laugh and talk in your head all the time?"

Nan says, "It becomes better and better. But, it is as Hayah says. Now, you have to make that choice every minute of every day."

Dan stands and announces that he and Nan need to prep the plane.

I catch Jasper, Spike, Kathrin and Phyllis before they scoot out. "We need to have a short powwow about Uwase, Assouma and Bosco." We find a quiet place in the guesthouse lounge.

Jasper opens up, "I'm glad you called us together, because I'm not sure what I'm supposed to do. I've never done anything like this before."

"Sometime over the next two days, the 'Great I Am' will give you very specific instructions. The reason He can't do that now is their Free Will. They can change their minds a dozen times between now and then. Right now, Assouma has connected, but she still has many issues to overcome. Bosco is 100% on board, but can't tell you why. He may need to talk to one of you before this happens. Don't be surprised that he will make the connection quicker and easier than you did. As for Uwase, she is so full of anger and hatred that it may take her a long time. You will discover with the 'Great I Am' that deadlines and promises are often extended to 'today'. Since it is always 'today' some extensions can go on indefinitely, like his extensions with His Hebrew children to this day."

Jasper asks, "What about the healing part? That's scary to me. Can Spike or Kathrin help me? That's more their thing."

"Do as He asks. Follow His instructions explicitly. Remember you are His hands. He and the other person or animal are doing the healing. Jasper, you may end up being the greatest healer of us all, simply because you are so humble about it. Spike and Kathrin are here to back you up if that is what He wants."

Spike is supportive, "We're in this together Jasper."

Kathrin agrees, "Right now, I feel that with Him we can do anything!"

Phyllis reassures him, "Jasper, we are all new at this. If we can survive that nightmare last night, we can do anything. Simply by giving myself over to His will, I feel real purpose for the first time in my life."

"Well put all of you." Then I add, "There is one last thing of which I am sure you're aware. The community is in an uproar over the two women being blinded, because of their own anger and hatred through voodoo. Only a few see the justice of it. Most are feeling confusion and fear. And a minority is not ready to give up the all-consuming power of their hatred. Remember, you are connected like the mountain-gorillas, and as long as you stay connected, they cannot harm you. Confront their hatred firmly and lovingly, always giving the warning that any violent action they take will boomerang back on them. He will be within you, helping you and protecting you. In Him you are safe."

There is a great group hug.

Jasper tells us he will meet us outside to take us to the plane, and Phyllis and I hurry to grab our things.

Once we are airborne, I look around and realize that everyone on board has a connection with the 'Great I Am'. I say to Him, "This must make you feel very good."

He says, "It sure does, Hayah. Thank you. I feel so

good, I can show you how this plane can fly itself."

Sometimes, He says things that I haven't a clue as to what they mean.

Everyone is full of positive energy. Dick, Phyllis and James are going over notes about their article. When Dick reviews with them the shots and video footage from the barn James is shocked. He looks up at me and sees that I am watching him.

James is trying to sort out his experience and interpret the images he is looking at. "Hayah how can you be so calm in the face of such hatred and violence? I'm not sure that I can do that."

Phyllis sympathizes, "I'm not so sure either."

"I have been with Him a long time and have a total trust in Him. He is always trying to break through to us humans, and we keep walking away from Him. So when He came up with this boomerang idea, I said why not. It is quite simple. If you are connected, you are protected. If you live by the sword, you will die by the sword. And evil will destroy itself. T. S. Eliot nailed it on the head in *The Hollow Men*, 'This is the way the world ends: This is the way the world ends: This is the way the world ends: Not with a bang but a whimper.' The main point here is trust Him, and you can do it."

Nan adds, "At first, Dan and I have our doubts. Our minds and egos are working on us extra hard. Then when the time comes and He asks us to stand up and protect everyone, we just do it without thinking, and our minds and egos run and hide. The other thing is that everything goes into slow-motion perception, so you have plenty of time to react. Granted it is a weird sensation to see a rocket coming right at you and then turn around and fly right back to where it came from."

James and Phyllis turn back to their discussion with Dick. I look out the window and see that we are flying over Lake Victoria, the source of the Nile, which is much bigger than I imagined. It truly is in the same class as the North American Great Lakes. Out of the windows on the other side of the plane, I see that the elephants of Tanzania are in their bais (a natural open clearing in a tropical forest where the wildlife comes to water, eat minerals and graze). Only a few elephants are still making their return migration to Kenya and Zimbabwe. After a half hour, I begin to see the migration of the rhinos. There are a few moving to the east, but most of them are coming up from the south. They are all heading to the Ngulia Rhino Sanctuary in Tsavo West National Park in southern Kenya, our next destination.

I catch Phyllis' attention and point out the window. When she sees the Rhino migration, she becomes just as excited as I am. She exclaims, "Another once in a lifetime phenomena!" The next thing I know Dick and James are also in the South windows of the plane and Nan and I have to make a quick shift to the other side of the plane to trim her.

The two of us are laughing at the whole scene of musical seats, as she shouts to Dan, "Honey, you must play the music!" This starts Dan laughing too. Oddly enough, the other three don't notice a thing. Dick as usual is experiencing everything through the lens of his camera.

As I settle into my new seat, I see the flight log lying next to Dan, with a flag in the upper left corner. I ask, "Is that the Kenya flag?"

Dan smiles, "Yes, it is one of my favorites for its symbolism. The top bar is black for its people. The middle bar is red for the blood shed for freedom. The bottom bar is green for their land. And the two white dividing bars are for peace and honesty. The Massai shield and spears are for the defense of their ethnic equality."

"That's incredible!" I then notice a Swahili word written under the flag. "What does 'Harambee' mean?"

"Let's all pull together."

"Wow, I believe I'm going to like these people!"

Nan taps me on the shoulder and points out the window. "Dan you better put on the music."

Dan turns on some music. Nan and I stand up and poise ourselves. Dan comes over the speakers with a very official tone, "Ladies and gentlemen, this is your captain speaking. On the North side of the plane, you can see the famous Mt. Kilimanjaro. When I turn off the music, you may move about the cabin." He turns off the music and the other three scramble for the North side of the cabin. Dan, Nan and I are in hysterics. Dan comes back on with his official tone. "The tall mountain to the North is Kirinyaga. Since the British can't pronounce it, they call it Mt. Kenya. I prefer the Swahili."

Phyllis looks at me and asks, "What's so funny?"

"We are enjoying watching you folks play musical seats."

Phyllis giggles and shakes her head.

Suddenly, a call from the ground interrupts our laughter. Dan quickly switches the speakers over to his earphones only. The cabin becomes very quite. Dan is writing down instructions, with an occasional "Yes, sir." In the silence, the rest of us are connecting with the 'Great I Am' within us.

To me, He starts to explain the details of what people are intending to do on the ground. This is going to be a very different kind of reception. It is almost like listening to a news broadcast on the radio before it happens. The only person He can't read is a rancher from a farm bordering the Park. The rancher's name is Tobias, and I have to keep a close eye on him, because he is extremely unpredictable and carrying a concealed weapon.

I look around the cabin. The others are sitting with their eyes closed and listening very intently. I am sure that they are receiving their specific instructions as well. One by one, they open their eyes and look at me. I simply nod with an "I know" look on my face.

Finally, Dan comes on the speakers, "There has been a change in our landing instructions. We will be setting down at Kilaguni airport. It is a better airport, but a little longer ride to Ngulia Safari Lodge. There seems to be some VIPs that want to meet Hayah."

Nan interrupts, "We have the message, Dan." She looks around, "I assume the rest of you have your instructions too."

Everyone nods yes.

I add, "Do what He is asking you to do. There is no need to compare notes because we are all on the same page, even though our specific instructions may be different. Goodness, I feel like I have a team!"

We all chuckle with confidence.

Dan banks the plane and lines up for an approach to the new airport. Within minutes, we are taxiing up to many vehicles and a crowd of people.

CHAPTER 28
Who's Who in Kenya

As Dan turns off the engine, he comments, "Holy mackerel, this looks like a who's who in Kenya!"

We all climb out of the plane. Dan goes directly over to a small group, with Zahur, the President of Kenya, Willis, the Director of the Kenya Wildlife Service (KWS), Frank, the Assistant Director of Tsavo Conservation Area and Damon, formerly from the Australian Special Forces now training Rangers to fight against poaching. Phyllis and James head directly for the press, who are gathering on the side of the landing strip. Dick is going crazy taking shots everywhere. Within seconds of our feet touching the ground, the police officials surround Nan and me. Adam, the Warden of Tsavo West National Park greets us and tries to hold the others at bay. These include Joseph, Inspector General of Police in Kenya, Jackson, the Senior Warden of KWS, Aurelius, the Chief of Police Intelligence in the coastal area and Odis, Inspector General of Police in Tanzania. Joseph and Odis are having a heated debate over custody.

Odis shouts in Joseph's face, "This man is responsible for over 340 deaths over the last two days in Tanzania. That gives me every right to have custody of him first."

Joseph is very calm, "Odis, you have no jurisdiction here. You are on Kenya soil."

"I don't give a damn whose soil I'm on. Ever since those fraking Rhinos started migrating through Tanzania, my people have been dropping like flies."

Nan asks him, "Is that the letter of warning about poaching endangered species there in your pocket?"

Odis flips, "Yes, what does that have to do with anything?"

Nan presses him. "And you sent the word out to warn your people of the boomerang consequences, right?"

Odis is in a tirade, "Look, bitch, I don't have to answer to the likes of you!"

Nan leans into his face and says quietly, "And what does the Qur'an say about the treatment of the Warner?"

Odis goes silent. Nan turns to Joseph and whispers in his ear. "Tell him that he can have Hayah, if he can cuff him."

Odis is back in Joseph's face, but before he can say anything Joseph looks away saying, "Look my friend, in order to keep the peace between us, if you can cuff him you can have him."

Odis grins and walks over to me. I am studying the crowd looking for the rancher, Tobias. Without thinking or looking at Odis, I hold out my wrists toward him and continue my visual search of the crowd. Odis slaps the cuffs on me, but turns away wearing the cuffs himself.

Without realizing what is happening he says, "Come with me asshole. You're all mine!" His telephone starts to ring, and he reaches for it only to discover he is in the handcuffs and can't reach the phone.

Everyone is watching this fiasco and the laughter is building.

Odis has his partner take the cuffs off him. He grabs them and slaps them on my still extended wrists. He quickly reaches for his phone, which is still ringing only to find that he is in cuffs again. He shouts at his partner, "Take out my damn phone and put it on speaker."

The phone announces to everyone present, "Inspector, I have the forensic results of those alleged murders. Their own bullets killed all of them. I'm afraid I have to classify their deaths as suicides."

Odis screams, "Shut that damn thing off!" He starts to make wild gestures with his handcuffed arms. He knocks the phone to the ground and starts to jump up and down on it. Everyone but me is rolling with laughter.

I spot the man who can be Tobias. He is expensively dressed like a Western Dude Rancher, which looks totally out of place in this environment. He is standing by a horse trailer. I ask Adam, "Who is that man over there by the horse trailer?"

Adam glances in that direction, "That's a local rancher, Tobias, with a big spread adjacent to the Park. We have a lot of trouble with him and his family. I think they are behind a lot of the poaching in the Rhino sanctuary."

I turn to Joseph and the other Police Officials. "Heads up, there is about to be an incident, and I don't want anyone to be hurt. Please step behind Nan and don't try to be heroic." Warden Adam herds them together. I ask the 'Great I Am' to alert Dan and note that Dan is already huddling the President and everybody behind him. Damon wants to go on the offensive.

Dan firmly insists that he comply, "Watch and learn, because you can be doing this with us. If you don't believe me, step back there and call your friend Reid in Chad." He does as Dan asks.

I look over at Phyllis and James. They are already prepping the press. Dick is setting up to capture this.

I turn and slowly start to walk toward Tobias. His movements are jerky and uncontrolled. He may be high on something. He starts pacing back and forth beside the trailer. When I am within thirty meters, he stops pacing and shouts, "Are you the one who is trying to put me out of the Rhino business?"

"I guess so, if your business is to cause them harm."

"Mister, nobody comes here and tells me how to run my business."

"I'm not telling you how to run your business. I'm warning you that if you try to do harm to any of these protected animals, your violent actions will boomerang back on you with equal and instant consequences."

"Blah, blah, blah. I will do what I want with what is mine."

"Tobias, you can do what you want with what is yours, but that Rhino you have in that trailer is not yours." Tobias freezes in his tracks.

This revelation causes a ripple reaction to run through the crowd. I can feel the itch of the wildlife people wanting to do something for the Rhino. I can feel Dick changing his position to catch a better camera angle on the trailer. I take a few more steps toward Tobias.

"Tobias, why don't we sit down and talk about this? There are lots of ways to put your ranch back in the black, without destroying yourself." Tobias is off balance because of what I know.

Tobias snaps, "What do you know?!! For three generations my family has a very lucrative living off these damn Rhinos. Now I am the master of this domain and you are not welcome here!"

"Tobias, your family and families like yours have reduced the Rhinos in this Park alone from 10,000 strong down to only 40. Can't you see that you have depleted your own resource? It is time to change the business plan, raise cattle. They'll thrive on this land."

"Too much work for to little money!"

"So this is not about you being the master of your

domain, Tobias? It is about your greed. Well Tobias, I'm here to tell you that this vain of gold has petered out. You **can not** harm another Rhino."

Tobias screams, "I can't? I can't?!! Just watch me!" He pulls a 44 magnum from under the back of his shirt. The crowd is shocked by this threat and near panicking. My leaders with each group calm them quickly and assure them that they are protected.

Tobias throws open the latches on the tailgate of the trailer and lets it fall to the ground. A black Rhino moves forward slowly on hobbled legs.

Tobias is fanatical, "Well Mister, this damn Rhino is mine, and I can do with him as I please." He points the gun at the Rhino's forehead.

"Don't do it Tobias. You cannot kill him. You will only kill yourself. The animal is protected. You are not. Do you understand what I am telling you?"

"You're telling me that this stupid beast is bullet proof, but I'm not buying it! I'm going to kill it, and then I'm going to kill you."

I go into slow-motion perception shouting, "Please don't…"

The gun fires with a bright flash, a deafening bang and a very loud report.

I see the bullet boomerang off the forehead of the Rhino and speed back to hit Tobias between the eyes. It is enough to say that the damage to his head is extensive.

All of us are feeling a deep sadness as I ask the 'Great I Am', "Does this ever become any easier?"

He responds, "Unfortunately not, not for you and not for me."

With tears in my eyes, I come back to normal

motion perception. I walk back to Odis and offer him my hand and say, "Are we good here?"

He shakes my hand with a hardy, "Yes Sir!"

I ask him, "Will you mind cutting the hobbles off that Rhino? He is from Tanzania. He'll stay here for the gathering tomorrow, and then he'll start home."

With a lump in his throat, he says, "Me?!!"

I smile, take out my Swiss army knife, and walk back and cut the Rhino loose. He paws the ground and then takes off in a flash, brushing right past me. I walk back past the police, collecting Warden Adam on the way, to meet President Zahur and the other officials. Zahur is a real sharp man for a politician. He thanks me for sending him the warning letter, and tells me how it took some convincing to have the radio and TV people put the word out there. Director Willis of KWS confirms what Zahur tells me and adds that his department has signs up in every Park. He also explains that their efforts have paid off, because unlike other African nations, Kenya is only experiencing double-digit losses of human life. Assistant Director Frank of the Tsavo Conservation Area makes an important point; since the protection announcement, they have not lost one ranger. He then asks a very good question, "Hayah, is it wrong of us to back off when we see poachers and let them kill themselves?"

"No, it is not wrong! They receive the warning, and there is nothing else that you can safely do."

Damon extends the question, "Then why do you and your team try to talk them out of it?"

"Damon, I see that you already know the answer to that question, and you are right, it must be clarified. My team and I are protected. The same as the endangered species are protected. Any hostile or violent action taken against us will boomerang back on the perpetrator."

A voice shouts from the back of the group, "Like some dumb cop trying to put cuffs on you!" Everyone looks back and sees Odis making fun of himself. Only now, he is able to join the laughter.

Damon continues, "What do I have to do to sign up for your team?"

There is an energy that races through the group like an electric current, with Adam and then one person after another saying boldly, "Me too! Me too! Me too!"

I look at them all and smile, "Remove all anger and hatred from your heart and mind and connect with the 'Great I Am' within you. We will talk more about this later on. I hope everyone will stay through tomorrow and the gathering of the Rhinos. I am sure there is plenty of room at the Ngulia Safari Lodge. Right now we need to meet the press."

CHAPTER 29
From Questions to Connections

Phyllis and James turn the press loose. Everyone in our group turns around to face the surge of press people approaching.

I raise my hands to attract their attention. "I ask that everyone remain orderly. We will make every attempt to answer all your questions. I know that many of you are not from Kenya, so we will have to bring you up to date first. I will introduce everybody so you can direct your questions to the right person. I am Hayah. This is Kenya's President Zahur. This is Willis, KWS' Director. This is Warden Adam from the Park." I continue down the list and introduce everybody including the police officials. When I finish, I recognize a woman waving her hand.

"Mr. Hayah, when you sent out your original warning, did it explain this boomerang effect?"

"Yes, it did. But the consensus is that people don't believe it or choose to ignore the warning. President al-Egsiro of Sudan thinks he can just up the caliber of the weapons. But the elephants repelled even the attack helicopter's rockets. As a result, he lost almost 200 of his best soldiers and 6 M:-17 choppers. Their bodies should be arriving back in Khartoum as we speak."

I point to an older person.

"Hayah, can you tell us, are the Rhinos and other animals really bullet proof?"

"No, it is more like an inner force setting up a shield around them. I'm sure if you want to kiss a Rhino on the nose, you'll be kissing flesh." The crowd chuckles.

I call on another reporter.

"President Zahur, what made you so confident in

the warning, to take such positive action?"

"There are two things that jumped out at me when I read it. First, it was sincere. I could tell it was not the hand of some quack or lunatic, but a person or being who really cares about this planet, its people and its animals. Secondly, I could feel that something has to give with the insanity in this world. If the animals can do this, why can't humans? I could see a new world of enlightened people, a new earth."

The reporter counters, "Mr. President is that practical thinking for a political leader?"

"Well, let me ask you a question. You have two choices. You can choose to do whatever it takes to be one of these people protected from violence. Or you can choose to take your chances and try to survive in a world where 'might is right', 'greed succeeds' and 'he who lies best wins.' Which of these choices is the right practical choice?"

"That's a no brainer, the one where the people are protected."

"Precisely, and that is where I want to lead the people of Kenya."

Another reporter speaks out.

"Warden Adam, with your training with the special forces in Australia, do you think that those skills are still needed in this 'New World'?"

"One of the basics in my training is to adapt and survive. I intend to do just that. And until everyone is protected, someone has to protect those that are not. And that includes animals and people."

A young reporter is dancing out of his skin for me to recognize him.

"Director Willis, what new challenges do you see now and in the future for KWS?"

"It's funny you should mention that. I believe my

greatest challenges will be the reallocation of recourses and talents, and the preparation for the tourist escalation. These are problems that every Director loves to have."

There is a very timid reporter from Zimbabwe, who barely raises her hand to shoulder height and close to her body. I recognize her.

"Mr. Hayah, I sense that I can ask you this. We have had a terrible time in Zimbabwe. With the Rhinos migrating north to Kenya, people just go crazy. People who never thought of poaching go out and try to bag a Rhino. The death toll is over 470. I didn't even know that there was a warning, until I come here. It may be stupid of me to think that you will know. But can you tell me what happened with the warning in Zimbabwe? Who forgot us?"

I take a deep breath, and answer gently, "Your people got the warning letter. The officials who received the warning were only moderately moved by it, but they passed it on. The warning then stopped on the desk of your news producer and went no further. There is your real story, if you have the courage to write it. At this point the international media is broadcasting the warning."

She smiles, with a delighted look on her face. I hear an inner voice, "That should break the logjam."

I can see that the reporters want to mingle and talk to my team and the other officials one-on-one. And I am sure that I am not the only one who needs the use of a toilet. I turn to Joseph and ask, "Can we take this back to the Ngulia Safari Lodge?"

He responds quickly, "I'll make it happen."

That evening Nan, Dan, Phyllis, James and Dick are answering the questions about being protected and connecting to the 'Great I Am' within. It may be the first and only who's who class, but I enjoy taking a back seat. To my surprise, they are able to handle all the basic questions, with some very interesting insights of their own. They cover, the purpose of life, Free Will, religion, anger and hatred, judgment, meditation, controlling the mind and ego, breathing and mantras, making the connection and affirming your choice constantly. Phyllis and James, of course, are excellent teachers and it is pure joy to see them working together.

I ask the 'Great I Am' if He is coaching them. He answers, "Only a word here and there. You have taught them well."

"It's not my doing. I feel that they are finding their niche. It's a beautiful thing."

Then out of the clear blue comes a very simple question, "Where do I signup?"

All five of my team turn and look at me.

I stand up and ponder the question, "That's a very interesting question. It is not as simple as it sounds. This is not an organization or institution, nor will it ever be. There are no dues or membership. The closest thing to a list is putting your name in the Book of Life. And contrary to popular opinion, the 'Great I Am' does not create that list. You do! When you connect with Him within you and surrender to His Will, you put your name in the Book of Life. I suppose you can call that signing up, but that was not what you wanted to hear. Is signing up important to you?"

Wanjiku, the young woman who is asking the question is beaming with joy, "Absolutely not! I will be much happier to be in the Book of Life."

A young man, who is a dead ringer for the young Bill Gates asks, "Do I have to convert? You know all that yelling, praying and conked on the forehead stuff."

I look at my team. They all shrug their shoulders, with big question marks on their faces.

"I guess this one is mine too. The simple answer is No. You're not changing from one belief to another. The fun answer is you are finding your true self. The 'Great I Am' is within you and has always been. When you connect, it is like finding three '000' in your computer programming that you discover for the first time. When you activate those three '000' everything changes on your computer, just as the 'Great I Am' will change everything in your life."

Warden Adam asks, "Why can't we just profess our faith and believe?"

"This is one of my favorite questions. When I asked the 'Great I Am' this one, He asked me, 'I have been trying this approach for the last 7000 years, would you say it was working?' What do you say Adam?"

"Not by a long shot!"

"Even Joshua can't convince the people to connect. He says it repeatedly, 'I am in you. You are in me.' 'The Kingdom of Heaven is within you.' 'I am in the Father, as the Father is in you.' But everyone turns their backs on Him, and they have been turning their backs ever since. Now the 'Great I Am' is trying this connect and protect plan. If it works for the animals, it can work for you."

President Zahur stands and asks me, "I sense that faith and belief are quite different in what you are describing. You are no longer asking us to believe in an unseen God somewhere up there. So how do faith and belief work with the 'Great I Am' within us?"

"It is interesting that you ask that question, Mr. President, because many spiritual guides create confusion with the use of the words 'awakening', 'enlightenment' and 'pure consciousness' which seem very abstract. More clearly put, your **faith** is the realization that the 'Great I Am' is within you and you're working to connect with Him. This is awakening. Once you make the connection with Him, you must **believe** in Him enough to surrender to His Will and purpose for you. This is enlightenment. After you surrender to His Will, you must have **faith** to renew your choice constantly to follow His Will in all you do. This is how you find pure consciousness. This is how you become protected and remain in His protection.

Aurelius, the Chief of police intelligence in the coastal area around Mombasa says, "This is too complicated, I don't have time to meditate all day."

James jumps in on this one, "I used to think that. But then I discovered that time is irrelevant. The only moment we have is right now. On top of that, I realize that this is only my mind and ego talking, and it doesn't want me to connect because it will lose control over me. And believe me; I am under the thumb of my mind and ego frequently. Granted, it is not easy, but every time I break through, I connect. Now I have all the time in the world."

Director Willis asks me, "I understand that we must remove all hatred from our minds and hearts, but where is Love in all this?"

"The 'Great I Am' is Love. By becoming one with Him, you become part of His Love as well."

Nan quickly adds, "When I experienced His Love for the first time, I realized that what I knew as love was not Love at all. In Him, my love for my husband became something completely different. In His Love, it becomes the bonding of two Spirits, two Beings. Believe me that changed everything in our relationship for the better."

Odis is deeply troubled, but he asks, "What happens

to those who kill themselves?"

"Odis, that is a question, with which all religions struggle. If Heaven is somewhere out there and Allah is somewhere out there, then we can imagine that Heaven is some kind of paradise and Hell is the opposite. But if the 'Great I Am' is within us, Heaven is within us, so when a person commits an act of self-destruction, that person is destroying the presence of the 'Great I Am' and Heaven within. That person's spirit will then live the rest of eternity without the 'Great I Am' or any possibility of connecting with Him; while at the same time knowing that He once was right there within, and that person chose to ignore His presence. You can call that whatever you want, but I can't imagine a blacker more hopeless place to be for all eternity."

Odis's eyes are as big as saucers. He realizes how close he is to that precipice.

There are no more questions, so I suggest that we have a short break after which we can have a meditation together with those who want to stay.

Only ten people in this group decide to stay for the meditation. The rest retire to the TV lounge or the bar.

In the group meditation there is a powerful energy growing. A few connect with the 'Great I Am' and the rest are very close. I have a very good meditation and become aware that something is bothering the 'Great I Am'.

The 'Great I Am' is a bit apprehensive about tomorrow's gathering. I question Him if there is going to be another attack. He doesn't say. He seems to be very preoccupied. Usually when this happens, it means big trouble. But I have faith in Him.

In my meditation, the light is bright and powerful. I bask in His glory and bathe in His Love.

CHAPTER 30
The Rhino Gathering

The Ngulia Safari Lodge in Tsavo West National Park is adjacent to Ngulia Rhino Sanctuary. This means when I wake up just before daybreak, I can walk out on my balcony and see the Rhinos gathering at the waterholes. There are several thousand, which is quite impressive considering that the population of this sanctuary was only 40 Rhinos before this migration. In another way, it is very sad, because this sanctuary was once the home to over 10,000 Rhinos.

I shower and dress for the day. I grab my Columbia ventilated hat and check out the balcony view one more time before breakfast. Now there are many guests out admiring the large herd. There is still no warning from the 'Great I Am'. When I ask Him what's up, he says, "Be prepared for anything."

When I ask what that means; I receive no answer. Although I have complete faith in Him, I decide to play it safe. I go back to my room and collect my daypack. Then I head to the dining room for a buffet breakfast. My team is already there. They are deep in conversation and very serious. I put together a healthy plate of food and join them.

As soon as I sit down, Phyllis asks, "What is going on? None of us is receiving anything from the 'Great I Am'. The Light and Love are there, but He is not saying anything."

I report to them, "I know. All I hear from Him is 'Be prepared for anything.' That can mean anything. Something big is going down somewhere else; an attack on the Rhinos is in the making; someone is waffling about doing something; or none of the above. Your guess is as good as mine."

Nan speaks up, "So what do we do?"

"The same as we always do. Only now, we need to play it safe. I recommend that you lead our guests to the Rhino lookout and narrate to everyone what is going on. Dick, you can be with me out among the Rhinos, but keep a safe distance. But stay on your toes and be aware of what is going on around you."

"You guys aren't going out there among those Rhinos without protection are you? That doesn't sound too safe to me," says James.

"Don't worry! He is protecting all of us, even though He may be otherwise occupied. He is still right here. (I put my hand over my heart.) I feel His presence and so should you. Close your eyes and check." I watch each one as they check and break into a broad smile. "It is like Phyllis says, 'His Light and Love are always there'. I remember during the last tsunami, His distraction was like this for days, both before and after."

We finish our breakfast just as the others are starting through the buffet line. Dick and I put our things together and start for the door waving to the newly arrived guests.

Adam meets us at the door and asks what the plan is. I take the time to explain that we need to take everyone out to the Rhino lookout. He agrees to ferry groups out there in his Land Rover as they finish breakfast. Of course, he is concerned about any attacks like the one in Chad, and I assure him that we have no knowledge of anything like that happening here. He is greatly relieved. However, I caution him that it is best not to have any weapons. And I tell him that if anything does happen, we will protect them. Given his Special Forces training, this takes a little bit of friendly persuasion and plenty of reassurances. He offers to drive us out to the lookout, but we decline. We are very eager to be among the Rhinos.

Our hike to the Rhino Lookout would normally be a short one, but with this large number of Rhinos, hiking there is going to take some time, which will give the others a chance to arrive at the lookout before us. I greet the Rhinos with my open arms gesture; a transformation begins to take place within me; and I find myself walking right into the midst of them. I can feel their connection growing as they make room for me to pass through. To my surprise, I am able to touch them, rubbing my hand along their bodies. Some even try to walk along with me, but the density of the herd does not make this possible for more than a few meters.

Dick plays it safe and works around the edge of the herd dodging in and out behind bushes. It is always amazing to watch him work. He is on his knees taking a head on shot of a female Rhino. He is lying down under a bush catching shots as the Rhinos walk past him. Now that he is protected, he is bolder than usual. With the camera he is using, he can switch back and forth between still shots and video. These are going to be great shots and footage.

By the time, we are within fifty meters of the lookout all of the guests and Adam are safely up on top. My team is working with different groups of the guests.

From deep inside me, I feel a powerful connection filling me with Love for these animals. This is more than normal. I can feel Him taking over my... No, it is not Him. It is Joshua taking over my body. His Love pours through my body and out to the animals. I relax and let Him take control. Everything that follows from now on is Him not me. I raise my hands and call out in a Rhino call.

All the Rhinos turn to face me. I call again and all the females with calves start to move toward me for the blessing of their children. With my arms down and slightly forward, I turn my hands out palms open and hold them only twenty centimeters apart. Each calf approaches and places his head in my hands. I bend down holding their head, put my forehead to their forehead and kiss each one. Each mother prances past with pride and joy. Every now and then, a calf will turn back and want Him to do it again. He always obliges them; before their mothers can call them to her side. Although this takes almost an hour, He deeply regrets that there are not ten times as many calves. This dampens His joy. Shortly after the last mother and calf move off a commotion starts about 50 meters away.

Two bull Rhinos square off on each other, snorting and pawing the ground. They charge and crash heads, jabbing each other with their horns.

He shakes my head like a disappointed father preparing to scold his naughty children gently.

The two bulls back off a few meters and repeat the snorting and pawing of the ground.

The next thing I know my feet are walking toward them. My back is straight; my head is up; and His Love is pouring out of every centimeter of my body.

They charge again and crash as before. They jab and thrust with their horns.

He can feel the pain in both of them, but the Love grows even stronger. The pace of my walk quickens.

The two Rhinos back off again, scratching the earth, snorting and shaking their heads. Every muscle in their body flexes for another attack. Suddenly, I hear their muscles twang like the string on an archers bow. These huge bests are now racing toward each other at incredible speed. Their heads are down. Hot bursts of air gush from their nostrils. The earthquakes and rumbles under their pounding feet.

He has me only a few meters away now, but my feet keep walking toward the point of their meeting. The Love pours out of me with compassion and understanding. I can feel the heat of their bodies coming from the right and left. Everything goes into slow-motion perception. Their heads crash together. I can see the repercussion of the crash ripple down through their bodies. The shockwave smashes into my body moving me back a half meter. He automatically extends my hands and puts one on each of their heads. It feels like I have done this a thousand times before. All motion stops for a few seconds. I feel their muscles relax and all the tension and anger drains out of them. They each take a deep breath and release a hot stream of air in a big sigh. Very slowly, they roll their eyes up to look into His/mine. His Love fills them, and they both fall onto their front knees. He bends down and kisses each one on the forehead. Time returns to normal speed. He reaches down putting a hand under each of their chins and raises them to their feet. As I look up, I see that all the other Rhinos are getting up off their front knees, but one. A large cow in the back of the herd is standing and looking at me.

Up in the Rhino lookout, the 'Great I Am' is giving a message to all of my team. "Until now, Joshua is the only one who can do that."

Joshua returns the control of my body and normal motion perception to me, but His Light and Love fills me.

Every member of the team turns and looks at each other. Dick stops shooting and stares at me. Those in the lookout turn and start to stare at me. Everyone else is in wide-eyed amazement. I look up, see their reaction and

humbly dismiss the moment with a shrug of my shoulders.
I start to walk back toward the lookout.

After only a few steps, I can feel a commotion
among the Rhinos behind me. I turn and see the large cow
charging towards me. She is a hundred meters out and
closing on me fast. Suddenly, I hear the 'Great I Am'
calling out within me, "Run Hayah, RUN!"

Without hesitation, I take off in a mad dash for the
Rhino Lookout. It is now a little over 200 meters away.
Every time I look back over my shoulder, I see that this one-
ton sweetheart is closing the gap.

I am at my fastest pace, which never beaks any
records and all I hear is "RUN HAYAH, RUN!" I focus on
the goal and don't look back. I reach down inside myself
for every ounce of speed I can find. Unfortunately, it is not
enough. I can feel the thunder of her charge behind me. I
can smell the anger on her panting breath. I am still over
50 meters out.

I spot a section of dense brush and make a sharp
turn behind it. Fortunately, our fat lady is not so agile, and
she has to slow down to turn on me. As she comes around
the thicket, I take off again at top speed. He shouts again,
"RUN HAYAH, RUN!" I make some zigzags to slow her
down. I sense the reason for her anger and throw my hat up
in the air. Five strides later, I dive into the stone bunker
under the Rhino Lookout. I roll on the floor in
uncontrollable laughter.

The Rhino is stomping on my hat, first with her
front feet, then with her hind feet. She scoops it up with
her horns and throws it in the air, then chases it down again
and tramples it into the dust. Dick is having a field day
clicking shots of this. The guests don't know what is going
on.

My team comes rushing down into the bunker. My sides are aching from all the laughter.

Phyllis asks, "What was happening out there!"

I gasp for breath and can't stop laughing. I can't spit the words out.

Nan presses me, "What happened out there?"

I try to gain control of myself. "She…" My laughter cuts me off, "She… She…"

James shouts, "She what?"

"She… She… She doesn't like my HAT!" Now, everyone else is laughing.

CHAPTER 31
"A New Heaven; a New Earth"

By that afternoon, the 'Great I Am' is talking to all of us again. He explains that keeping the Rhinos under control was a major ordeal. There were six at a time, which He found completely unpredictable. For example, He had four of them in line and then went to work on the other two. As He had those two under control, six more lost it altogether. Then He went to work on the new rebels and brought them back in line, only to lose three or four others. At no point did he ever have all of them under control. It is only thanks to Joshua that we were able to accomplish this. He concludes, "They are almost as bad as humans."

The good news is that seven of our new recruits are connected to the 'Great I Am': Adam, Damon, Willis, Joseph, Zahur, Wanjiku and surprisingly Odis. I smile as He gives me the list. Titles mean nothing to Him. He is ecstatic and wants them all included in the debriefing.

As we all settle down in the meeting room with the chairs arranged in a circle, Zahur thanks me for inviting him. Dan smiles and leans forward toward Zahur and says, "It is the 'Great I Am' who invites us all. Now we are part of the New Earth, and I, for one, am glad to have everyone on board."

Wanjiku shifts in her seat and asks, "I don't know; why am I here? I'm just a freelance reporter nobody. I'm not in the same class as the rest of you."

"Well put, Wanjiku." I confirm her importance to everyone, "But in this room we are all equals. We are all nobodies. The only way we can be in here is to let go of our egos, the same as you."

I look around at the others. "Before we begin to

talk about our experience this morning, I want to hear from all those who are now connecting to the 'Great I Am' within. Can you tell us your connection story? Wanjiku, you can go first."

"There isn't much to tell. I have always been a meditator, but rarely do I reach my inner space or experience the sensation of pain and suffering. I'm always looking for a higher intelligence and self-awareness. Then yesterday after witnessing the meaning behind the warning, you say the 'Great I Am' is within me. All of a sudden, I have something to look for in my inner space. And sure enough, there He is with open arms and a boat full of Love. When I surrender to Him, a whole new life opens up to me and I see the grand plans He has for me. I can't express the joy that fills me now." Wanjiku is radiant.

Odis is eager to tell his story, "I don't know how Nan knew that I was a student of the Qur'an, but when she whispered in my ear about the Warner, she got my attention. After that, everything starts to point me in a different direction, from the handcuffs to Tobias blowing his head off. In the evening, I'm blown away. And I'm sure you know this, it is like attending a course on the hidden secrets of the Qur'an and Torah. When Hayah tells me that Paradise is to live in the presence of the 'Great I Am' and He is in me right now, and Hell is to live through eternity, knowing you had a chance and blew it, because you will never have a chance to connect again. For me all the cards were on the table, so I tried the meditation. Getting past my rational mind is a simple proposition for me. Getting past my ego is another story. I am a bully and have the foulest mouth on the planet. When I see this little ego gremlin on my shoulder, I squash the little booger like a bug, and there I am seeing nothing. At first, I think it's all a joke, and then I see His Light. He is coming to me or I am going to Him. I don't know which. I brace myself for the beating of my life. Instead, He takes me in his arms and His Love washes all my sins away. Now, I need to cleanup my act, so I can serve him well." There is a profound transformation in him.

Damon wants to go next. "I'm a no nonsense kind-a guy, so when I sees this warning, I think it's a pile of BS. I come up here to expose you as spiritual frauds and to take charge of the Rhino's defense. When Dan tells me to chill-out and call my friend Reid in Chad, my confusion explodes. How does he know that Reid is my friend and working in Chad? When Reid tells me about his experience at Zakouma NP; I becomes extremely excited. I know in that moment, this is an answer to my prayers. I'm not a meditator, but I gave it a shot yesterday evening, with very little luck. I keep at it all night; until I finally break through. All I can say is that this is the mother lode of all experiences, and for the first time in my life I am ready for action." Damon has a real fire in his belly to serve the 'Great I Am' within him.

Willis is leaning forward in his chair with his face in his hands. Slowly he sits up and speaks softly. "I am an atheist, because God isn't doing something about what is happening on this planet and especially to the animals. When I received the warning, I thought it was too good to be true. When I discovered it was true, and the 'Great I Am' was within me, I felt like I had a new lease on life and a whole new purpose. I will do whatever it takes to help this New Earth emerge from the ashes of human greed and destruction." Willis's determination is written all over his face and in his body language.

Joseph leans back in his chair and puts his hands

behind his head. "I am a lifelong cop. I come from a family of peacekeepers. Looking at the underbelly of society is my daily vista. Then this man comes along and tells me he is going to turn the world upside down to see if any good can fall out of it. Well, I say why not. Nothing else is working. Now this 'Great I Am' is my commanding officer and we're going to kick ass together, lovingly of course." Joseph chuckles.

Adam takes a deep breath. "A few weeks ago my heart and mind were so full of anger and hatred of the damn poachers, I wanted to kill them all without mercy. Then I had this dream about a Messenger, who was going to come and turn everything around. He was going to put a shield of Love around the Rhinos and me. In the end, those with anger and hatred will have destroyed themselves. Now, all this is unfolding within us and around us, and I am deeply humbled to be part of the New Heaven within me." Adam looks at me and nods.

Zahur focuses on a green stone in his hand. "As a child, I connected to the 'Great I Am' within me. Then because of the ways of the world and fear of being called insane, I lost the connection. Now, these last two days are the most important days of my life. I am one with Him again and the real purpose of my life is clear. Just as the first humans are out of Africa, so the first city of the 'Great I Am' will arise from this blessed land. The New Earth begins here and now." He kisses the stone and puts it back in his pocket.

Listening to all these stories is very moving, and tears well up in my eyes. The joy of the 'Great I Am' is beyond description. From the animals and a few connected souls, the numbers are now blossoming. I say to Him,

"This is going to work."

Phyllis breaks in, "Hayah, you need to tell us what was going on out there with you and the Rhinos. It is beyond our experience or comprehension. Even the 'Great I Am' says, 'Until now, Joshua was the only one who could do that.' And He has more trouble with them than you did. What were you doing? Can you tell us?"

"Yes, I can tell you, but don't jump to conclusions and listen very carefully to what I am saying. I know that I say this so much it must sound like a mantra, but it is the simple truth. I-do-nothing.

"When there is healing, I am not doing the healing. It may be my hands, but the healing is from the 'Great I Am' within me, the 'Great I Am' within the other person and their vision of wholeness. The parts of the healing that are me, are my hands, my connection with Him and the love that is in me. As Joshua says, 'Without my Father, I can do nothing.'

"To understand today's events; you need a little background and some basic cautions. The primary caution is not to discuss this with anyone who is not connected with the 'Great I Am', no matter how well you think you know them or how intimate your relationship.

"Remember, your connection to the 'Great I Am' is in the eternal present, the point at which all the past and all the future come together right now. Put another way, when we connect to the 'Great I Am' within us, we are standing in the stream of eternity. For us eternity is Now. Our Living Spirit is now timeless.

"Now that you are connected to the 'Great I Am' and for as long as you choose to remain connected there is an open **portal** between you and Him. (This portal is not a way for you to burden Him with wants and wishes. To do so, is the first sign that your connection is gone. Remember, if you have a need or wish, He knows it before your mind has a chance to register it.)

"Through the portal you will hear Him, see Him, feel His Love and talk to Him. This is more real than any other experience that your senses can communicate to your brain. (The human thought that He is 'an invisible God' is laughable.) Through this portal, you will receive your instructions and receive His guidance. Through this portal, you will have access to His knowledge. And most importantly, through this portal you will have access to all those who are connected to Him or have been connected to Him. This brings me to the main point.

"Every Living Spirit has access to the portal. Many come to me regularly: Adam and Eve, Zarathustra, many Prophets, several Apostles, Zacchaeus, the Young Man, Muhammad, Krishna, Buddha and Joshua. (Do not confuse this with some parlor trick to communicate with the dead. That cannot be done!) These are Living Spirits, living in the eternal Now. Unfortunately, we can't decide to whom we want to talk. They decide with whom and when they want to make a connection. When they do, don't be surprised and listen carefully to their story. They have a reason for coming to you.

"Here comes the new one; what were you seeing this morning? What does the 'Great I Am' mean when He says, 'Until now, Joshua was the only one who could do that'? Remember, I am doing nothing.

"As soon as I walk among the Rhinos, I feel Joshua enter my body. (He is not talking to me. He is in my body!) I relax and let Him take it over. The whole morning unfolds like some after creation ritual, beginning with the blessing of the calves. Then the fight starts. He immediately walks over like a parent about to teach them how to turn anger into love. When He puts a hand on their heads, their eyes roll up and connect with His. That is when they realize who is with them and they all go down on their knees. He then raises them to their feet. After that moment, He leaves my body, and I start to walk to the lookout. Unfortunately, the fat lady didn't want to sing and decided to charge me instead. The 'Great I Am' cannot control her and tells me to run. The rest you know. She doesn't like my hat. In a flash, I have just gone from the sublime to the ridiculous."

Nan looks at the surprised faces around the circle. "Wow, this is one incredible journey. I assume this can happen to any of us."

"That's right, just like Socrates came to Phyllis in Rwanda. You are in His hands now."

CHAPTER 32
Goodbyes and Travel

The next morning, we are all up early for our buffet breakfast on the exterior dining terrace. The lingering Rhinos are omnipresent to everything else. Dan and Nan will be flying Phyllis, James, Dick and me to Addis Ababa, Ethiopia, where we will all go our separate ways. The others will all be heading back to their respective lives, but as different people. The morning is full of emotional goodbyes and well wishes. There is also a busy exchange of contact information. It is no surprise to hear this group start talking about their new assignments from the 'Great I Am'. Dan and Nan will be working with the refugee camps between Chad and Sudan. Dick, James and Phyllis will be putting together an entire issue of NATIONAL GEOGRAPHIC MAGAZINE on the *Protection of Endangered Species.* The newly connected from yesterday divide into three groups, each with a separate mission. Zahur, Willis and Joseph are going to work on Political Change in Africa. Adam, Damon and Reid will work on new protection defenses for the rangers. Wanjiku and Odis will develop a communications network for connected Africans. The changes in Africa will be monumental. Zahur may truly realize his vision.

I pull Dick aside after finding out that he has a flight to New Delhi, India and invite him to join me on the tiger piece of my journey. I explain that it will be quite different and more dangerous, because we need to train a new special group of Beat Officers to deal with the armed extremists in the forest interior.

Nick's eyes light up. "Boy, you just don't quit. I've been wondering why the 'Great I Am' is talking tigers with me. When and where?"

"Can you meet me at Srisaila Devasthanam in Srisailam tomorrow afternoon?"

"No problem, I can make a connection to Hyderabad tomorrow morning."

"Great, I feel a lot more comfortable having you with me."

Dick smiles, "I feel like I can follow you around for the rest of my life and never have a dull moment."

"I apologize for taking you away from your NGM story."

"How do you know about that? I only heard about it this morning." Dick reflects for a moment, "Never mind, you probably knew before I did. This is always hard to fathom. I have to spring it on Phyllis and James now." He goes back to James and Phyllis.

I cruise around the room talking with the different groups and answering questions. Finally, the inevitable parting takes place.

After takeoff, Dan and Nan are deep in a discussion on how to approach the Sudan refugees.

James is sitting with Dick and they are trying to figure out the best approach for the articles.

Phyllis is sitting with me. To my surprise, she starts to ask many personal questions. At first, the questions are about when I first realized that the 'Great I Am' was within me, and when I first connected with Him. I enjoy telling these stories. Then she shifts to my academic history. This requires a great deal of focus, because I have to leave off date and time related details. I'm grateful for the 'Great I Am's' assistance with all of this. When she exhausts this part of the interview, she starts to ask about my romantic relationships. For the first time, I realize that she is flirting with me and has been all along.

Like a romantic klutz, I ask, "Are you flirting with me?" Instantly realizing it was a dumb question.

"Of course," she answers without hesitation. "I've been flirting with you for days. Not that I expect you to return the advances, considering the age difference between us."

"You flatter me," I say sincerely. Then I remember she thinks I am thirty-five. Recovering, I say, "You don't look that much older."

"Oh, to be twenty years younger."

I think to myself, "I wonder how she will feel when it is the other way around."

She continues, "I've always been attracted to younger men."

I think, there goes that opportunity, and politely ask, "Why's that?"

"Better chemistry!" She says with flair.

Oops! I'm thinking, that's the modern code word for a woman looking for sex and not a meaningful love relationship. I debate for a fraction of a second; should I engage her on the subject? I reject the idea. Then I reconsider; I am attracted to her. But then I realize; I've had enough of those relationships. Then while my mind is lost in the debate, my heart asks, "How do you feel about meaningful Love relationships?"

"What's that, one of those New Age soul mate relationships? They don't exist. I've never seen one!" Her words are a lot more flip than her body language. She is still flirting with me. I am not so sure she isn't toying with me.

Still responding sincerely, "I'm inclined to agree

with you, if you mean one of those split souls that become human and try to find each other in order to be whole again, or if you mean two spirits that know each other from heaven up there and meet down here on earth. On the other hand, what if two people meet who are connected to the Love of the 'Great I Am' and out of or through that Love they find a Love for each other that is eternal."

Still playing with me, she asks, "Do you have any experience of such a Love?"

"No, but they have." I point to Dan and Nan.

Phyllis stops flirting and reflects. Then with deep emotional feeling, "I wonder what that is like."

"I don't know. But I do know; it was not present in the most passionate of my sexual relationships. Yet to hear them talk now, their sexual relationship has moved to a whole different level. What about you?"

"Not even close. I wonder if He will talk to me about it."

"Who, Dan?"

She smiles, "No, the 'Great I Am'."

"I feel that you have a better chance of talking to Him than you do of prying anything out of Dan and Nan."

"Isn't that the truth!? You can see it radiating out of them. Their faces are latterly shinning and bubbling with Love. Yet every time they start to reveal something, they stop short and calm up. It is like they are guarding the greatest secret in the Universe."

My words slip out, "That's what I want to find."

Phyllis looks at me in a different way. "So do I!"

We look into each other's eyes for the longest time. I want to touch her. I want to hold her. I want to kiss her. I sense that she feels the same. But...

Dan announces that we are on approach to Bole

Airport, Addis Ababa. Phyllis looks at her watch. She and James will have only 45 minutes to check in and make their flight. Dan arranges for a passenger shuttle to pick them up and take them to check-in. She panics. "How can I reach you? Am I ever going to see you again? What if something happens to you?"

I calm her down, and make her take a deep breath. I say, "In an emergency, you can always reach me through Him. I can also send you my Skype address. Please don't worry; nothing bad can happen to me. As for seeing each other again, we'll have to make it happen somehow."

I help Dan pull out the bags, give her a warm hug and send her and James on their way.

Phyllis looks back and blows me a kiss.

I blow one back.

Dan and Nan fly out strait away to return to Chad.

Dick has a couple of hours before his flight and I have all afternoon. After seeing Dick off at check-in, the 'Great I Am' tells me to go to the restroom. When I come out, I am Hoss again. After so many days as Hayah, it is hard to be back in my old body again. As fit as I am, the arthritis is still a handicap.

I say to Him, "You know, traveling as a senior is not a fun thing."

I check in my bag and walk around the airport. For the first time in days, I stop to look at the news on TV. It is full of all the warnings and footage released by Dick. The general buzz in the airport is that it is about time that the animals are being protected. A few are critical that human life is a lot more important than any animal; however the resulting debate usually concludes that poachers are the lowest of the low. In an interview with al-Egsiro, he denies any knowledge of any actions of the government troops. In an interview with Zahur, Willis and Joseph the Kenyan government will be doubling their efforts to stop poachers from killing themselves, and they will be addressing the insurance problem of suicide coverage. They are also calling for a United Africa in protection of all animals.

My flight leaves at 21:20. I put on my blindfold and earplugs and sleep soundly through the flight. We land in Mumbai about 04:40 the next day. I have a 2 hour 40 minute layover to people watch. To my surprise, the architecture of this terminal is stunning. It is a very space age design with a high lofted ceiling to carry off the human body heat. As I walk from the international terminal to the domestic terminal, I can't help but notice that men are stopping to urinate against any wall that is handy, even when a toilet is only ten steps away. By an entrance, where I see one of these men relieving himself, I see a sign over his shoulder which reads, "No Dogs Allowed!" Standing next to him is his wife complaining to their children and texting that the place smells like a urinal. I can't help but laugh. I buy a cup chai tea from a cart that an old man is wheeling through the airport. It is actually quite good.

By the time I reach my gate, I am acutely aware of how angry travelers are these days. They complain about everything from the security checkpoints to the air conditioning. One guy is complaining to the person at the ticket counter that the lofted ceilings are a waist of space. I look around smiling at people and let the Light and Love within me shine. When I sit down, the ten-year-old child with the woman next to me says, "Look Mommy, he's one of those idiots."

She turns and quickly glances at me and says to her son, "Yes, Dear."

I guess I must be projecting my sentiment, because the 'Great I Am' asks, "What's the matter Hoss?"

"I am having a hard time forgiving myself for my anger toward human stupidity and poor behavior. "

"Well, if it is any consolation, I often have that problem too."

"Are you sure you want to even bother with them?"

"Hummm," He hums in the deep hum of the mountain-gorillas. "I've seen Love turn some pretty nasty people around. This reminds me. Jasper's Love is helping Assouma and Bosco connect with me in a very powerful way. Not only can she see again, but she and the boy are awakening the village. Unfortunately, Uwase has slipped deeper and deeper into the darkness. That is what anger that leads to hatred can do."

"Point taken," I humbly respond. He always amazes me at how He can slip these little lessons in here and there.

I look at the little boy and stick my tongue out at him, following with a hearty laugh. Now, I have his attention. I show him that both hands are empty, while I am actually palming a walnut. I point to his hat. He takes it off and hands it to me. I reach inside it, take out the walnut and give it to him along with his hat. He puts his hat on and plays with the walnut, tapping it on this and that. He cannot open it. He asks his Mom, but she can't open it. He comes back to me. I show him how to lace his fingers tightly together. Then I place the walnut between them, with the seam running up and down his palms. By this time, his mother is watching carefully. Next, I motion for him to squeeze hard. He does and the walnut cracks open. He is delighted. All this I do without saying a word. I finally say, "Every shell has a lot of Love in it!" This stuns him and the mother blushes. I stand and board my flight.

The flight departs at 07:20. I remember the flight with Phyllis from London to Chad. The next thing I know we are on approach to the airport in Hyderabad. We should be at the gate by 08:45. There is a strange thing about me and arrival airports, I rarely see much. All I see are the signs to 'baggage claim', 'customs' and 'bus stop' in whatever language. The rest is a blur.

I hop on the shuttle to the Jubilee Bus Station to catch the 10:15 bus to Srisailam. The buses are considerably better than ten years ago and far exceed my expectations. I climb on board and settle into my seat for the seven-hour adventure. Fortunately, for me, the bus driver is the chatty type with an excellent knowledge of everything along the route. His name is, Siraj, and he becomes our personal tour guide. It doesn't take long until everyone on the bus, tourists and locals alike, are chatting, joking and asking questions. It is so much fun that practically everybody turns off his or her cell phone. The time literally flies by.

The next thing I know we are pulling into Srisailam. I give Siraj a big hug and thank him for the wonderful trip. After collecting my backpack, I walk over to Srisaila Devasthanam. As I arrive there, I become Hayah again and check in. There is a message waiting for me from Rohan. I call him and let him know I am here.

CHAPTER 33
The Tiger Plan

I am sitting in the lounge waiting to go in for dinner, when Dick arrives with his wife Abby. Dick goes to check in so we can all go in to dinner together. Abby smiles and holds out her hand.

I take her hand and shake it vigorously. "What a wonderful surprise! I'm so happy to meet you, Abby. And you are interested in doing the training class with us. That will be fantastic!"

"I am?" She asks timidly and adds, "I am. How do you know?"

"Oh, a little birdie told me," I say sheepishly.

"I know all about your little birdie. He talks about nothing else. That's why I came to surprise him in New Delhi last night. I don't know where you put my old husband, but you can keep him. I like this one much better." We both laugh.

Dick returns with a smile, "I see the two of you are hitting it off already."

"Honey, he already knew that I wanted to join the class."

"And it's OK?" Dick asks.

"Of course! It is His idea; you know. How can I say no? But I feel that Abby will add a healthy dimension to the group. He is also hoping that Rohan will want to join the group."

"Who is Rohan?" Abby asks.

"Rohan is the Conservator of Forest & Field Director of Nagarjunsagar-Srisailam Tiger Reserve (NSTR). He was the one that put this together."

They call us to go into the dining room.

As soon as we are in our seats Abby asks me, "Are you going to play with the tigers too? I want to see that!"

Dick jumps in, "Abby cut the guy some slack!"

"It's OK Dick. I think I am going to like this woman. Thanks for bringing her to the party. To answer your question, which I know you ask in jest. Yes, I would enjoy playing and cuddling with the tigers, and they would enjoy it too. Unfortunately, with the way things are with people these days, it is not a good idea for the tigers to be too trusting of humans. My contact can give them the wrong signals, so there will not be a gathering of the tigers." I switch to a lighter tone, "The day is almost here when we will all be able to lie down with the tigers."

Abby turns to Dick and takes his hand. "I can see why you like this guy." She looks into my eyes. "Am I going to be able to connect with the 'Great I Am'?"

"He says you are closer than you know. Your dreams are telling you the truth."

She reacts blushing, "You can see my dreams?"

"No, but He can." I smile broadly, "Although, I'm sure they are interesting."

Abby giggles shyly.

After we order, Dick turns to business. "So what's the plan here? And how long do you think we'll be here?"

"I hope it won't take longer than four or five days. He has me on a tight schedule. The plan at the moment is to meet with Rohan at 18:30 to discuss the training class and the candidates he has screened." (I turn to Abby and interject, "As Dick knows, all plans with people are never set in concrete, because people can change their minds.") "I want you both to be part of that meeting.

"Tomorrow morning at 07:30 sharp we will start the class. The first thing we need to do is thin out the group of candidates. I understand that there are eight selected. We need to end up with three emotionally strong and centered people. Dick, you have been through this, so you know the rocks and ruts on the path. Abby, He and I are hoping that your efforts will be a catalyst for the candidates' and Rohan's development. It will be a very long day and may go until 22:00. If we don't have our three Special Beat Officers by then, we will have to continue the next morning.

"The next step is to go into the interior of the forest and confront the armed extremists, who are logging, setting snares and killing tigers. They all need to be warned as to what happens when they do this, as well as the results of their destroying the tiger's habitat and the game they depend on. For, if the tigers starve, then the extremists will starve. In two days, we hope to give the Officers a good foot hold and build their confidence. The goal is to have three Officers to manage this operation indefinitely.

"Finally on the third day, we need to visit the traders in tiger skins and body parts. They will be presented the letter of warning, which basically says they have 30 days to burn their tainted stuff or die a painful death like that of the animal. That's the plan."

Dick responds, "I've seen that letter. You gave them no wiggle room. Can I have a copy of that letter for publication?"

"Rohan has a copy and will be printing them for posting and distribution. By the way, I can't take credit for the letter. I only took His dictation."

The food is delicious and we shift to lighter conversations. That is if you can consider the trials and tribulations of being a photographer's stay at home wife, lighter conversation. Abby admires Dick's adventurous life and wants to share in part of it. This is their first real opportunity to do so.

Abby hesitantly asks, "Can I go into the interior with you guys?"

"As long as He says you are ready, you can."

"Why does he get to say I'm ready?" She motions to Dick with her head.

Dick laughs heartily, "He means the 'Great I Am' not me, dear."

"Oh." Abby replies with wide shifting eyes and a sheepish grin.

About 18:00, we all decide it would be a good idea to go to our rooms and freshen up before our meeting. This would also give Abby and Dick a chance to unpack.

I am down in the lobby by 18:25 and ready to great Rohan. Dick, Abby and Rohan show up punctually. I make the introductions and hope that Dick and his wife Abby will not be a problem for Rohan's plan.

To my surprise, the first words out of Rohan's mouth are, "Dick! You are my favorite photographer! This is really exciting. If I bring in one of my National Geographic Magazines, will you autograph it for me? My kids will flip when they see it."

Abby and I exchange glances and smile.

Dick responds, "I will be delighted."

Rohan turns to Abby and me. "Excuse me; you have just made my day. Come, we can meet in a small lounge here. How do you know Dick?"

Abby and I are enjoying this. Abby says with a smile, "I'm his wife."

"Oh, yes, yes, yes."

I add as we walk to the lounge, "We connected in

Chad. Dick will have another full issue on the saving of protected species. Maybe he will be able to include the tigers in it and what you're trying to do here."

Rohan turns to Dick. "Wow, this is fantastic. It's so exciting. You'll have to autograph that one too." Dick nods yes. "Yes, yes, yes. Sit, sit be comfortable. Water, drinks anyone?" He goes to the small bar and takes out bottled water, soft drinks, wine, beer and some liquor. Dick and Rohan have a brandy; Abby has a white wine; and I have water.

When Rohan settles down, I ask if there are any changes in the plan.

There are none, but Rohan asks me, "Can you go over the high points of the class, so I can see if my choices of candidates are correct?"

"After the introduction on the mind and ego, the first part will cover body awareness; learning to listen to the body; learning to trust the body (it will never lie to you); learning to separate the mind and ego from the body; and learning to center the body. The second part will be on breathing; finding the natural source of breath in the body; connecting the breath with the body center; and shutting down the mind and ego with natural breathing. The third part is meditation training; learning to eliminate all but one thought, using the breath, a mantra, or focus on one object. The fourth part is seeing and connecting with the 'Great I Am' within you. The fifth part is surrendering to the 'Great I Am' and His purpose for you."

Rohan says, "Most of these things I do already. Why can't I connect with Him?"

"I know you are a meditator, but you have never completely broken free of your mind and ego."

"This is spooky. How could you possibly know

that? I have never talked about this, not with anyone."

"The 'Great I Am' within you is the same 'Great I Am' in me. He tells me what I need to know to help you. Would you consider taking the class with the candidates?"

"Will that be appropriate?"

"Once you are connected to the 'Great I Am' there is no social/political status. Everyone is equal. I feel that you and Abby taking the class will be an inspiration to the candidates. You both have similar problems and are close to connecting, so if they see you connect it will encourage them. The end result is a connection with them that you would never have otherwise."

Rohan turns to Dick, "What do you think?"

Dick responds warmly, "I don't think; I know. It's the best thing you will ever do.

"Ok, Ok, I'll do it."

I ask, "Rohan, tell me a little about the candidates."

"They all meditate to one degree or another. They are all spiritual seekers. Two are trained in the martial arts, two in Yoga and one in Tai Chi. One was a monk at one point. All of them, including me, see this as the only sensible solution to a very difficult problem. I am glad I am not the one to choose between them."

"Actually they will do the choosing up until they surrender to Him. Then His purpose for them will determine the outcome. He wants nothing more than to see your project succeed. Do you have the list for me?"

Rohan hands me the list.

Abby is full of excitement, "I want this more than anything. Will that work against me?"

"Only if that is your mind and ego talking; otherwise you will have an edge. From what he's telling me; you have the edge."

Abby breathes a sigh of relief.

Rohan asks, "Is He going to talk to us like that too?"

"Absolutely! You will know what your enemy is thinking before he or she does anything."

Rohan is blown away, "Whoa, that's a major game changer!"

Dick throws a great one into the pot, "My favorite is that I always do what he tells me, so I know that I'm always doing the right thing. Since doing that I never have any regrets."

I interject, "He is telling me that we all need some rest for our busy day tomorrow, so I think we should call it a night."

Rohan thanks us all and says, "See you at 07:30 sharp, here in the meeting hall."

CHAPTER 34
An Explosive Class

The class starts bang on the dot of 07:30. Those present are: Dudekula, Karry, Nune, Shaik T, Uddatla, Vallupusetty and Yanamala. Unfortunately, Shaik C is a no show. As usual, the 'Great I Am' gives me an inner sense of who each person is. The only one he is having a problem reading is Yanamala, a young man in his mid twenties, with a father from India and a mother from Iraq.

I jump into the hidden secrets of the Hindu Creation Story, which everyone in the class knows. I point out that I call the Supreme One in the story the 'Great I Am'. My second point is that Patanjali tells us the syllable ॐ (OM) is the unutterable syllable, and therefore has no sound (Aum), as in most accounts of the creation story. It has all the other characteristics mentioned in the story, but these must be seen as representations of the infinite present, where all the past and all the future come together. In the story, Brahma struggles with how to make His created beings of Man and Woman aware of and responsible for the rest of creation. The syllable ॐ is the key to His solution. I tell everyone, he or she will discover its true importance when we come to the breathing section of the class. Finally, Shiva, the destroyer in the story, who repeatedly causes the destruction of creation and starts the endless cycle of recreation and more destruction, is none other than the rational human mind and ego. These elements are the same in every creation story known to us.

"Now, we are going to unravel this puzzle in reverse. You will learn to disconnect your rational mind and ego and reconnect to your body, which never lies to you. You will learn to breathe from your essence of being. You will find the 'Great I Am' (Supreme One) within you. You will have the choice to surrender to Him, and find your purpose in life. You will be one of those, who will end the destructive cycle of Shiva (your rational mind and ego) forever. And forever change the planet.

Suddenly the door bursts open, and Shaik C flies in disheveled. "I am so..."

I cut her off, "Don't bother Miss Shaik. You may leave. You are interrupting this class."

She looks at Rohan, "Uncle?" He shrugs his shoulders at her, with a disappointed look on his face.

I walk toward her. "Miss Shaik, you had to watch the end of your Soap Opera instead of being here on time." I turn her around and escort her out the door.

She calls back, "How can you possibly know that?" I close the door without answering her.

"OK, everybody stow your note pads. We are done with the academic part of this class. Your body is talking to you all the time. So is your rational mind and ego. The purpose of this exercise is to shut down the rational mind and ego. Now it is time to learn to listen to your body."

I guide them through their bodies from their feet to the top of their heads, becoming aware of every part, every ache or pain, rubbing it, moving and adjusting it. "What is your body telling you? Enjoy the feeling."

Next, I help them explore some movements that are part of their DNA: the position of their thumbs when the hands are folded, the way they cross their legs, the position of the little finger when the palm of their hand is resting above the knee. I walk around, change the position and ask what their body is telling them. It is as if the whole class is discovering their bodies for the first time. Dudekula says, "Unbelievable, my body is communicating without words."

Now, I ask everybody to sit up in their chairs, with their backs straight and not touching the back of the chair. I have them put their hands in their lap or on their thighs. "Be aware of how your body feels. Tap into your body center. Become aware of the energy moving through your body. There will be an energy flowing up from the earth into your feet and through your body. This is your oneness with the earth. You'll feel another energy flowing up through your body, which flows out the top of your head and then around to re-enter through your navel. It will continue to flow in this circle. It will often have a color, which changes according to your mood. This is your life energy. This is the same energy Vishnu feels in creation. Note that it has no sound, but it has all the properties of sound. As your sensitivity increases, you will feel all kinds of energy around you, from other people, from other organic life, and even some inanimate objects, like a stone or your chair. This is your body's center connecting with the essence of being within all things. Your body center is your essence of being. Note that the ego is quiet, because it is completely outside your body center. Also note that the rational mind has no function here."

I ask everyone to stand and caution them that the ego is going to reappear and try to take control. "The body has developed bad habits and the ego likes it that way, because it is familiar and less work. However, your body will not lie to you. Now I am going to help you to rediscover your natural body structure."

I have them stand as straight as they can. I move among them and adjust their feet to the right position, then their knees, their pelvis and backs.

As I am doing this, I notice that Yanamala is sweating profusely. I work on him to relax, and he does.

(The 'Great I Am' breaks in, "You're doing it. I can finally read him. He has a bomb! And he plans to destroy you and everyone here." Dick immediately picks up on this message. I look down at Yanamala's backpack. It is slightly open. I see the bomb peaking out beneath his note pad.) I circle around behind him and massage his trapezius muscles. He relaxes even more. (I look at Dick and nod my head yes. Then I nod toward the backpack. Dick goes into high gear, grabs his camera and starts shooting pictures. He positions himself a couple of meters behind Yanamala's chair and backpack.) I ask Yanamala, "Will you help me with a little demonstration?" He nods yes, and I lead him to the front of the classroom. (Dick uses this opportunity to grab the backpack and take it out of the room.)

I ask Yanamala, "Close your eyes and turn around to face the class. Everybody, we are going to take a little break here, to do a demonstration of the power of complete relaxation. Mr. Yanamala has volunteered to help me. Mr. Yanamala, continue to relax, feel the energy moving up your back and out through the top of your head. Now, keeping your eyes closed, I want you to follow the energy with your mind's eye and describe what you see."

Yanamala studies what is happening, "The energy is like a white thread. No, it is a narrow stream of smoke. It is circling me and lifting me up. It is carrying me through the darkness. I see the blackened shapes of trees sliding beneath me. Now the trees disappear. The smoke stream carries me on. I pass over black waters and into the mountains. Then we go down, down, down into a deep valley. It is so dark now. The smoke sets me down upon what feels like a rock. I hold up my hand in front of my face. I can barely see it. Slowly, I become aware of a light far above me. I look up. The very top of the mountain is bathed in a brilliant light, but it casts no shadows in the blackness around me. In the light, I can see Vishnu and Brahma. They are laughing with the One. All the animals, birds, fish and insects swarm around them. Now, I see the family of man join them. There is great joy and the Supreme One embraces them all. Now, this wonderful vision becomes farther and farther away as I slide back into the darkness, until I realize that I am still sitting on the rock. I sense there is someone sitting next to me. I turn and look, but I can't make out his features. Slowly, very slowly my eyes adjust a little until I can see who it is. My heart is pounding faster. It is my idol. It is Osama Bin Laden. He is saying something to me. I lean closer to hear him. He is saying, 'This is paradise. This is paradise.' He says it over and over and over again. Strangely, the rock I am sitting on moves. I look down, and I see that I'm sitting on the back of Shiva. I look up at the Supreme One on the mountain and realize..." Yanamala screams, "THIS IS HELL!" He snaps out of his vision and is surprised to see where he is.

I put my arms around him and hold him lovingly until Abby brings him a chair, and I sit him down. He weeps on my shoulder. I can see the police in the doorway. I say to him, "At least now you know the truth, because your vision is true. Only now, you can make a different choice. Just know that the 'Great I Am' is not giving up on you, Yanamala." I help him up and walk him to the door. I say to the police, "Please be gentle with him. He is no threat now."

I walk back in the classroom with Dick, and resume, "Everyone back in your places. We will pick up right where we left off. We will use this opportunity to test your concentration and ability to bring your mind and ego back under control. Rebalance your pelvis and continue straightening your backs." I move among them to check their progress and making minor adjustment on the candidates. Rohan and Abby are perfect.

I now help them to find the correct position of the shoulders by rolling them forward, up, back and slowly down until the trapezius muscles are relaxed, noting that the middle finger is falling on the side seam of their trousers. Then we focus on the neck and head, moving the chin up or down, in or out to complete the perfect alignment of the human skeleton. "Feel an invisible string pulling you up. Feel the energy moving up through your body. Every muscle in your body is using a minimum of effort to stay erect. This is giving you a sensation of having an incredible lightness of being. What is your body telling you?"

Uddatla says, "For the first time, I feel whole as a woman."

Vallupusetty says, "It wants to fly."

Nune says, "I feel it lifting my inner being."

Shaik T says, "It is healed, and now it wants to heal my inner being."

Dudekula says, "It wants to stay like this all the time."

Karry says, "It feels beautiful."

Rohan says, "It feels ten years younger."

Abby says, "It's telling me it's about time."

Dick is taking pictures of everybody in full-length profile.

"While you enjoy this for a moment longer, I am going to prepare you for what is about to happen. I am going to ask you to take one-step and all this is going to collapse. Let the negative reaction go, ignore the ego, and focus on regaining the natural body position. When you are comfortably in your center again, take another step. Keep doing this routine, making the ego back off, until you can walk across the room, walk up stairs and run. Note that you are walking lighter. When you start to run, you will feel like you are flying. Now take a step."

I watch them and make adjustments as needed. I pull out three exercise steps and put them in three different positions around the room. Abby is the first to lock it in, and Rohan is only a few minutes behind her. Soon they are running around the room flying over the steps like gazelles. Dick is having a field day catching this on film and giving Abby a lot of attention and verbal support. The candidates double their efforts and one by one, they start to break through. The joy of everyone is electrifying as I bring them to a stop, while maintaining a centered stance.

I look them over, with a broad grin on my face. "Great job everyone! Your body is now your temple. Let's have lunch."

CHAPTER 35
The Breath of Life

As we gather in the classroom, Abby asks, "How are you going to top this morning?" The rest of the group reacts with similar excitement.

Dick and I look at each other and chuckle. Dick says, "You ain't seen nothin' yet!"

I ask everyone to take a deep breath. I watch as their chests heave up and down. "I can see that I need to teach you all how to breath." We all laugh. "Let's discover how the body breathes NATURALLY." I ask everyone, "Take out your Yoga mats and lie down on your backs. Become aware of your body as in this morning's exercise. Place your hands on your abdomen just below your ribcage and let them rest there. Slowly bring your awareness to focus on your breathing. This is natural breathing. In this position, your body does it all by itself."

I ask them to note what their hands are doing. They are rising and falling with the natural action of the diaphragm. Now, I ask them to move their hands and place them on the upper part of their chests. "Continue with your natural breathing. Be aware of the effortless ease of each breath. Take note that your hands are not moving. This is a very important note, because your ego is going to tell you that the best way to breathe is with your chest, which is simply not true. The ribcage is not very flexible and can't expand more than 2.7% to take in more air. However, the diaphragm stretches and pulls down expanding your lung capacity considerably.

"Move your hands back to the abdomen position. Now you are going to take a deep breath using the natural body function. This is the exact opposite of what the ego has been telling you for years. On your next exhale, use your hands and push down to force all the air out of your lungs. The more air you force out, the more air you will take in. When you have forced out as much air as you can, do nothing; don't hold your breath, just relax. Your body will take a deep breath all by itself. Your lungs will fill to their natural capacity. Return to your natural breathing."

Now I ask them to sit in their chairs, find their body center again and apply the natural breathing to it. When they do this, I ask them to go through the routine from this morning and apply the natural breathing. Gradually they feel their bodies moving easier and growing stronger. They are now flying about the room at a rapid pace.

I call out "STOP!" They all stop. "I want you to note three things: none of you is out of breath, you are all experiencing an incredible lightness of being and the rational mind and ego are completely shut down."

There is a unified "Wow!" as they look at each other.

I add, "The goal is to be able to maintain this centered state as you move through your daily life. Your body will emerge confident and in charge of your physical being. It will become your greatest ally."

Spontaneously, they all break into conversation at the same time. Do you feel this? Do you feel that? And they make several exclamatory comments! Uddatla cries out, "This is a whole new life!" Abby gives Dick a big kiss. Rohan is mingling as one with the candidates.

I have to shout for them to hear over the uproar, "Let's take a ten minute break."

After the break, I lead the group in a series of stretches to loosen up and center the body. The breathing should now be an integral part of the body as a whole. I ask everyone to sit on their chairs or on their mat for meditation. I walk around to make sure their backs are straight and neck and head elongated. While I do this, I prepare them for what is to come. "Under ideal circumstances you may be meditating in silence and stillness at least once or twice a day for about twenty minutes. Now our goal is to be connected with the 'Great I Am' and stay connected all day long. This can be done with many short meditations of only a few seconds throughout every hour of every day, or one long meditation that lasts the whole day, but allows you to function in heightened consciousness."

I can see them settling into a very relaxed breathing pattern. As an introduction and outline of our spiritual journey, I recite a passage from the UPANISHADS (The sacred scriptures of India).

"Inside your body is a shrine.
Inside the shrine is a lotus flower.
Inside the lotus is a tiny space.
Inside that tiny space lives the creator.
Inside the creator is the Universe.
Find it, and you will be one with the
creator and all things.
Be there, and all things and the creator
will be one with you."

"Now, I want you to shut out all thoughts and set your ego aside. Focus only on your breathing, which your body is doing without thought. Breathe in and breathe out." I watch and wait for their breathing to click together, with everyone breathing in unison.

When this happens, I add one little detail, "Breathe in with your mouth open. Breathe out with your mouth closed." Now I watch and wait. Several minutes pass.

Starting with Abby and Rohan I see a smile appear on their faces. There is a joy building within them. There is an intense excitement swelling up in Rohan; he is literally vibrating in his seat.

"OK, Rohan, you better share it before you explode," I say with a smile.

He says enthusiastically, "I see it! I see the unutterable syllable ॐ! I feel it in every part of my body! I hear it so loud that it fills my head! Yet there is no sound! All these years I thought it was only a myth."

Karry wants to share her experience, "The ॐ (OM) is just naturally flowing through and out of my body. It is like the two are one."

"How can we have gotten something so wrong for so long," asks Dudekula?

"That's what our mind and ego are doing to us," says Vallupusetty. "Mine keeps telling me, no, this cannot be but the ॐ (OM) sound joyfully plays on as though the mind and ego don't exist."

Nune observes, "Now, even when I am not meditating it is still there. Will it always be there?"

"It always has been and always will be, because it is always now," I respond.

Uddatla blurts out, "How can anything be so joyful and peaceful at the same time?"

Shaik T exclaims, "I don't want to stop! I want to go on!"

Abby adds, "It is so powerful, that it is drawing us deeper into our essence of being."

"With that, let us all continue our breathing and see if you can find your inner center, the vast darkness within you, your inner space, the place of stillness, the place of perfect peace. This is where many meditators stop, because they see this as 'nirvana' or absolute nothingness. But the darkness (yin) is only half of the 'yin-yang'. ☯ (The Tao symbol 'yin-yang' represents the wholeness within us and each half contains the seed of the other half.) The light (yang) is also within you. When you find the darkness (yin) be aware of the tiny speck of light that will be floating in it. Move toward the light as it moves toward you and soon you will find that you are in the light (yang). The moment you meet the 'Great I Am', you have a choice to surrender completely to Him and discover your true purpose. Our consciousness begins when we surrender to the Will of the 'Great I Am'. Have faith in His Will and believe that He will fulfill His promise to help you fulfill your purpose. You will be making this choice constantly for the rest of your life. The rational mind and ego will always be ready to take over, if you let them."

Now, I wait.

Remaining connected to the 'Great I Am', I listen to His running report on their inner progress. I notice that Dick is doing the same.

Abby is the first to connect with the 'Great I Am' within her. Her face is glowing. Slowly she reaches out a hand and takes Dick's hand. Now they both light up with a dancing light. I can feel the radiance of the Love within them, and can only imagine what it must feel like for them. They are now united in a way they have never been united before. My heart fills with joy for them.

Uddatla is the next to connect to the 'Great I Am' within her. There is a lot of personal and privet pain being washed away. She is weak and vulnerable. When He embraces her, she fills with an incredible power of spirit as a woman. His Love transforms her from the inside out. In an instant, she becomes strong and confident. As He reveals her purpose to her, her whole body begins to radiate a powerful light. She becomes literally a beacon in the room, as I am sure she will be to the world.

Now, Rohan connects. At first, he pauses, while standing in awe not knowing what to do. He starts to humble his spirit, but the 'Great I Am' scoops him up in His arms. Instantly there is oneness between them, a bond forged by His Love between them. Rohan fills with the feeling that he is home; at last, he is whole.

Dudekula reaches the Light within him. The Light surrounds him in a warm Loving cocoon, but he cannot surrender to the Will of the 'Great I Am'. His ego has him convinced he will lose his freedom. He returns to his breathing, and as the ॐ (OM) reappears, his ego fades away. In a joyful action, he throws himself on to the Will of the 'Great I Am'. In an instant, his caterpillar like spirit transforms into a beautiful butterfly, and he flexes his wings in the warmth of His Loving Light.

Nune reaches the black peacefulness of his inner space. He is experiencing it for the first time. He bathes himself in it to wash off all the pain and insanity of this world. He discovers the seed of Light almost by accident. Then he jumps upon it and surfs on a black wave right into the Light of the 'Great I Am' who is waiting for him on the beach. The 'Great I Am' puts his arm over his shoulder and says, "We will ride the rest of the waves together."

Vallupusetty is struggling with some relentless mental war images. This is his third attempt to set them aside. The first two times, he tried to command them to get lost, but they would not obey him. Now the marching cadence of his breathing slides into a slow steady pattern.

Karry's connection is after a methodical meditation. She is in control at every moment. Her mind and ego don't have a chance. However, when she finally reaches the 'Great I Am', she goes to pieces. She weeps uncontrollably. He cradles her in His arms and comforts her. A lifetime of bad stuff comes up, which He washes away and she emerges as a strong and sensitive person.

Vallupusetty relaxes and before he knows it, he is standing in front of the 'Great I Am'. He raises his arm to salute, but the 'Great I Am' takes his hand and shakes it. When He is done shaking it; He doesn't let go. He sits him down and explains his purpose. Then He helps him to his feet and holds him in an embrace. He does not let go. He holds him until Vallupusetty's love is equal to His own Love. Vallupusetty emerges a different kind of warrior.

Finally, I am allowed to see Shaik T's connection with the 'Great I Am'. The opening encounter is past. The two of them are now deep in a discussion. Shaik T is being lead through one vision after another. With each vision, Shaik T becomes more and more excited. I understand in an instant that He has something very special planned for this young man.

I ask everyone to come out of his or her meditation. Slowly they look around the room at each other. It is like seeing each other for the first time. In different ways, they are new people. But now, they all have one very important thing in common. They are all connected to the 'Great I Am' within them. I can see on their glowing faces that they all see me differently. Now there is equality between us.

I turn to Rohan, "Are you glad you are part of this?"

"Without a doubt, this is the most important thing I have ever done. I am ecstatic to be on the same page as everyone else. This is beyond words."

I ask, "Are you ready for the results?"

"Yes!" Rohan is full of enthusiasm.

"Everyone here has a solid connection with the 'Great I Am', and they are all protected. However, there are two here that the 'Great I Am' has other plans for." All but Uddatla and Shaik T look around the room.

"Uddatla, please tell the group what your new purpose is."

Uddatla speaks from a position of great strength, "I am to be the leader to free all women from family, social, political and judicial injustice in India. I will train them so they will be protected too."

The entire group applauds and cheers. Abby is nodding her head.

"There is more great news from the youngest member of our group, Shaik T. Tell us about your new purpose."

"This is a little bit strange; I'm thinking to myself, how am I going to apologize for backing out of the program?" Shaik T says frankly. "The 'Great I Am' is asking me to train and recruit 1% of the population of India to be the enlightened residents of His crystal city. Rohan, we will need your help to find the best location."

There is another round of applause and cheers.

I turn to Rohan, "That leaves us with only one small problem. We have four people and only three vacancies. Is it possible to stretch your budget so you will always have an extra relief officer?"

"I can do that. I will make it happen."

I conclude, "Then we can take the evening off and start our field work tomorrow."

CHAPTER 36
Tiger, Tiger in the Wood

The next morning Dick, Abby and I meet for breakfast. The new joy in which this couple is immersed is a beautiful thing. Both of them are literally glowing with love.

Abby asks, "Can I go with you in the field? I know it is dangerous, but I want to experience what Dick is doing, so I don't have to be afraid all the time."

I reflect for a moment. This is a very good reason, and I can imagine what it is like for her. However, Dick is all over the place when he is shooting. I say, "I'll agree under one condition, that you stick close to me for extra protection, because Dick is a wild man when he's working."

Dick says to Abby, "You see. It's true."

Abby responds, "OK, but I thought I am protected."

"You are, but this is your first time out. You and I have no idea how you will react under fire. And I mean that literally."

We meet everyone else at the Director's Office in Sundipenta. The Special Beat Officers (SBO) are sporting their new uniforms and are duly sworn in. During the next three days, for training purposes, all four will be accompanying us.

Rohan briefs us on the background of the people with whom we will be dealing. They are a hostile group that NSTR suspects are behind poaching the tigers throughout the reserve. They are so heavily armed that the regular Beat Officers are rightly afraid to go into the area.

From the office, we have a scenic but rugged ride to

a tiny village on the edge of the Forest. It turns out that
Dudekula is very knowledgeable of the flora and fauna. He
makes an excellent guide and enjoys talking about the
forest. He has Dick so fired up it feels like we are stopping
every fifteen minutes to take special shots. In actuality, it
makes the trip go faster. It takes a little over three hours to
reach the village. As we approach the village, I am painfully
aware that we have not seen one tiger.

In the village center, a large crowd is gathered. We
park the NSTR Land Rover, and cautiously emerge from
the vehicle. Dick immediately goes into high gear. I work
my way through the crowd with Abby at my shoulder. In
the center of the crowd, there are three dead bodies. I check
them out carefully. One has a deep gash around his neck
and obviously, his cause of death was strangulation. The
second has a bullet between his eyes. The third has several
serious blunt force trauma marks all over his head and
upper body. Through all this the 'Great I Am' is telling me
the real attack scenario and the false report that a witness
told the crowd. I can feel the tension and festering rage of
the crowed. On a nearby tree, I see the tiger warning
posted.

I raise my hands for everyone to be silent. Slowly
they quiet down. I ask, "Will the witness to this atrocity
please come forward? You will not be harmed." A young
boy, no more than fifteen, steps forward. I motion for him
to stand by my side. Without asking his name, I say for all
to hear, "Siva, these people need the truth and not some
fantasy. Will you tell them or should I?" Siva hangs his
head and timidly points to me. "Siva, if I say anything that
is not completely true, I want you to stop me."

I point to the poster on the tree. "Look at that
warning poster. It is deadly serious as you can now see by

these three deaths. These three men and Siva have set
snares in the forest for the tigers. One snare caught a large
male tiger around the neck." Siva's eyes are as big as saucers
in wonder as to how I can possibly know this.

I point to the strangled man, "This is the man who
set that snare." I look at Siva. He slowly nods yes. I stand
over the man shot in the head, "This man found the tiger in
the snare and tried to shoot the tiger in the head. But the
bullet boomeranged back and killed him instead." I stand
over the man beaten to death. "This man took up a large
stick and began to beat the tiger in a blind rage. Every blow
he struck on the tiger appeared on his body instead, while
the tiger was unharmed and growling. He beat the tiger all
over its body and head screaming in pain with each blow.
Then with all his strength, he came down with one last
violent and powerful blow on the back of the tiger's neck.
This blow killed this man instantly." Siva is weeping and
nodding his head, yes.

"But that's not all, is it Siva? There is another snare,
with a young cub in it." I walk back to Siva and hold up his
right arm. There is a red mark above his wrist, which is
becoming deeper and deeper. "If we don't free this cub,
Siva will lose his hand. Siva, can you show us where the
snare is set?"

Siva nods, "Yes, mister! Are you a god? Can you
tell the Supreme One that I am sorry?"

"You can tell Him yourself, Siva." I put my hand
on his chest. "He is right in here."

Siva leads us into the forest about thirty minutes
from the village. To my surprise, everyone in the village
follows. Before we reach the site, Siva is screaming in pain;
I have to stop and give him first aid; the wound is bleeding
now.

At the site, we quickly find the tiger and cub. The female is pacing up and down in front of the cub. Everyone stands back, sensing the danger of the situation.

The SBOs, Karry, Dudekula, Nune, Vallupusetty, instinctively step between the tigers and the people.

Abby can see Dick moving in closer without any fear. She turns to me and asks, "Now what?"

"You stay here and stay alert!"

I slowly approach the female cat and hold out my open arms. She comes bounding toward me. I can feel the power of His presence filling my body as I keep walking toward her. I can hear the crowd gasp in anticipation of the attack. When we meet, she slows to a walk and brushes past my body and around behind me. I stroke her body and let her tail trail through my hand. She comes back and licks my other hand. Together, we walk up to the cub. The cub starts to struggle against the snare, and Siva screams in pain. The female starts to purr and lick the cub, who calms down. It only takes a few seconds to slip the snare off his paw. Both the cub and Siva feel the relief. The cub has no injury and quickly moves off with his mother.

I turn now to the male tiger and slowly walk toward him. I look into his sad eyes and can see that he is hungry and thirsty. He does not move. To my surprise, he is not wearing a tracking collar. I sit down next to his head to see if I can slip the snare off. He puts his head in my lap to make my job easier. But try as I might, I cannot slide the snare over his head. It is made of a steel cable about 4mm thick and five meters long. The other end is fastened around a long log, which the tiger is pulling into the saplings on the forest floor, where it is lodged tightly and holding the cable taut. My Swiss army knife is useless with this cable. The log is too thick to break and unmovable.

My only choice is to move the cat. When I say it like that, it doesn't sound like much. Only this little man is about 3 meters long, which will make him almost 300 kilos. That is a lot more than I can ever dream of lifting. The only option left is to help him up on his feet and convince him to take a couple of steps in the one direction he does not want to go. Before I start, I meditate with the cat while stroking his head. The 'Great I Am' is aligning our spirits. Like it or not, he has to trust me. I open my eyes and he opens his. There is only love between us. We both have the same image as to what we are going to do. I stand up. He stands up with some difficulty, even with me trying to relieve the tension on the cable. I motion for him to come toward me. I am only a meter away. He hesitates. I'm not sure how much longer I can hold back the cable. I beckon with all the Love in my heart. Slowly, he takes one-step, then two and his nose is in my belly. With my free left hand, I am able to slide off the snare. I let go of the cable and it snaps back through the trees, with a twang.

The tiger jumps back and runs to the female and the cub. When he reaches them, he turns back to look at me, with a thank you in his eyes. I shoo him with the back of my hand. He and his family disappear into the underbrush.

I start to walk back to the others, when the 'Great I Am' gives me an alert. Siva's older brother is now in the crowd with a loaded weapon and intends to attack us. I see that all the SBOs, Abby and Dick are receiving the alert and taking positions. Abby is trying to protect Siva. Dick is setting up for the best possible angle. I can only see the top of the young man's head and the muzzle of his gun coming through the crowd. The people from the village are attempting to conceal him, without realizing that we are already alerted. I am still 50 meters from the crowd and too far to engage them in a warning.

Suddenly, Siva sees his brother and the gun. He shouts, "NO! DON'T SHOOT! You will only kill yourself!" Abby steps in front of Siva as time goes into slow-motion perception.

Siva's brother pays no attention to the warning. He is carrying a twelve gage, pump action shotgun. His face reveals an evil grin. The villagers start to laugh and cheer him on. He lowers the shotgun to his hip and begins pumping off rounds until the chamber is empty. The air is full of lead-shot. Most of the rounds are headed for Karry, Dudekula, Nune and Vallupusetty. Two rounds are headed for Abby, who is shielding Siva. I am too far way to be of any assistance.

The shot reaches the SBOs first and boomerangs back. The shot reaches Abby, who quickly moves her arms to block some pellets that might whizz past her, all the pellets boomerang back. Because, the shot is so spread out, some of the pellets are going to fly past Siva's brother and into the crowd. The majority of the shot hits Siva's brother and his body is literally torn to bits. Six members of the crowd experience serious hits, but not life threatening.

As usual, the time comes back to normal, and I am standing in front of the crowd. I quickly check the wounded, and do what I can for them.

The next thing I know, Siva is shouting at the villagers, "I hate you all! You should have stopped him! I hope you all die! Read the sign, and take warning, or just put a gun to your own head and blow out your own pea brains!" The villagers are dumb struck.

I grab Siva's arm as he turns to run and hug him. When he calms down I say, "Siva, the hatred stops here. If you ever want to be on this side of the disaster, you have to let the hate go. We come here in Love and we leave here in Love. All the death you see around you is caused by their own hatred. Help them to see that Siva."

I turn to the SBOs and motion for them to start back. I am right behind them.

Abby collects Siva and Dick joins them. Siva asks them, "Who is that man? Is he who I think he is?"

Abby smiles, "No, but he knows Him real well. You can know Him real well too. He is right here." She puts her hand on his chest.

"That's what he said. How do I find him in there?"

Dick answers, "Ask any one of those four Special Beat Officers. They will show you."

The first part of the ride back to the office is in silence. Dick is reviewing his shots. Everyone else is trying to digest the events of the day. I am having an intense discussion with the 'Great I Am' about peoples' difficulty to accept the warning; and why it is so hard for them to realize how easy it is to connect with Him. The warning problem is difficult for both of us to figure out. The consequences are clear. They know what will happen, but they do it anyway. I then suggest that their rational minds and egos are manipulating them. To which He adds that the rational mind and ego are the playground of the Dragon Lady. She can be the one misdirecting them. To which I add that we must bring her back as soon as possible. Yes, there is the dilemma; she is misdirecting them; only the people can bring her back to the 'Great I Am'; we need 1% of the people to make it happen; therefore through misdirection, she prevents it from happening and stays in control of them.

We then turn to the connection acceptance problem in hopes to find a solution. The meditation process is producing very positive results, those in the Rover for example. He now goes off on a tangent about how pleased He is with all those that are now on board because of the protection of the endangered animals. Each of these seeds is going to make a difference. I bring him back to the problem by suggesting that with salvation as the tool, tens of thousands were converted in one morning or afternoon. He of course knows this and is quick to point out that less than one tenth of a percent of those converted end up with a connection to Him. He then goes on to explain that our efforts over the past two weeks produced more truly connected people than a life time of crusades done by Billy Graham, Billy Sunday and Jerry Falwell combined. The big difference is that our people are highly motivated. The question then is why is it so difficult to motivate people to connect. We kick that one around for a while, but cannot come up with the reason.

Out of the clear blue, Abby breaks the silence, "Because they think they're already connected!"

Without thinking, I respond, "How?"

Everyone else in the Rover says at the same time, "By mobile phone!"

There is a hearty laughter among us all including the 'Great I Am'. I suddenly realize that everyone was listening in on our discussion.

CHAPTER 37
Habitat Protection

The briefing the next morning is about a logging company that indiscriminately goes into the forest reserve and strips out huge sections, thus threatening the habitat of the tigers. The company uses heavily armed men to scare off any interference by the NSTR. Rohan says that their spotter helicopter is reporting activity in a remote area. The plan is to fly us within 50 kilometers of the location and then take us in by elephant to the site. We are to warn the loggers and through them the company.

I ask Rohan, "Are you debriefing the SBOs?"

"There is no need. I receive a blow-by-blow description from Him while it is happening. And by the way, I have the approval for the extra person. This team is more effective than an entire military regiment and a lot less expensive. We can't thank you and Dick enough."

The chopper ride is breathtaking. This time it is Karry's chance to shine. She is a geographical expert. She knows every mountain, valley, cave and crevice by name. She even points out all of the hidden temples from antiquity. This tour is much too short for Dick, Abby and me. At one point, Vallupusetty holds on to Dick's belt as he leans dangerously out of the chopper to take shots. If I hear the words "Great shot!" once, I hear them a thousand times. Of course, I know that Rohan will love everything he shoots.

When we touchdown, I can't resist greeting the two Indian elephants. I start with the salute with one hand in the air and they raise their trunks. I then approach with open arms and they lower their heads so I can put my forehead to theirs.

One of their trainers asks me, "Do you know a lot about elephants?"

Dick says, while taking pictures, "You might say." He then turns to me, "That's OK Hayah, you will soon be famous." Turning back to the trainer, he says, "This is the protector of the 20,000 elephants in Chad, Africa."

"Dick, knock it off, it was only about 10,000."

"May be," says Dick. "But by this time next year it will be 500,000." He enjoys laughing at his own joke.

Abby says in an aside to me, "He's a nut, but loveable."

Soon we are on the elephants heading into the dense forest. Dick, Abby and I are on one, and the SBOs are on the other. We are only out for a short while, when I receive a message from the 'Great I Am' that the elephant trainers are taking us in a round-a-bout way. I motion to Karry, but she already has the message.

We order the elephant trainers to stop and everyone climbs down. Nune and Vallupusetty place the two men under arrest and handcuff them together. They instruct them to report to the helicopter officer and wait in the station hut nearby. Vallupusetty takes their cell phones. Dudekula reads them their rights and tells us we will decide on the charges when we come back, and if they decide to run, he says, "We will chase you into Hell if we have to, but we will find you." The two men bow obediently.

Karry and I plan to switch places, but first I teach her how to communicate to the elephants. I tell her to create a clear picture in her mind as to where we are going. When the picture is there, she is to put her forehead to the forehead of the elephant. The 'Great I Am' will tell you when she has it. Karry follows the instructions to the letter with both elephants. As she comes back to me she says, "That's the coolest thing ever!"

Karry joins Dick and Abby on the lead elephant, and I join Dudekula, Nune and Vallupusetty on their elephant. I note that the two trainers are amazed as to how easily we communicate with the elephants, and timidly start back up the trail. The elephants turn and head in a different direction. The elephants move through the forest with a lot more confidence now. They know where they are going, and they know whom they are serving. Their course is direct except for minor changes to navigate the terrain. In less than two hours, the elephants stop abruptly. We listen. We can hear the voices of several men a short distance away, but we cannot see them. We silently dismount. Communicating through the 'Great I Am' we formulate a plan to take them by surprise. Dick is the only one on his own.

Three of us go in one direction and three in the other. Along the way, we disburse until we surround the men and their camp. Through their minds eye we can all see exactly what the camp looks like. We can see the cook pot on the fire with their lunch. We can see their weapons leaning up against a rock or tree here or a log there. There are six of them; each one of us is no more than two meters from their guns and we are totally concealed by the underbrush. In a few moments there is going to be a hiss and pop in the fire. On the hiss, we are to move in next to their weapons, turn them barrel down and shove them into the soil, making them dangerous to fire.

We go into slow-motion perception. The hiss starts and we all move. I can see everyone taking their positions next to the weapons. The men are looking at the fire.

Before the pop, all weapons are turned and in the sod, and we are standing calmly. Dick is shooting away. After the pop, the men look up and each reaches for their weapon. They are so startled that two of them pea their pants and one shits himself. Another backs into the fire and sets his pants ablaze. The other two fall to their knees in prayer.

Suddenly, we all receive a message that a woman is coming from the trailer with a gun. All eyes turn on the trailer. Karry steps forward to meet her with her arms outstretched. The woman is holding a 45 automatic. She pulls off three rounds, which boomerang off Karry and throws the woman back into the trailer.

In less than ten seconds, all the men are reduced to a quivering pleading state. We return to a normal motion perception.

Vallupusetty looks at me silently asking for permission to take the lead. I nod my head. He tells the men to sit back down and eat their lunch. They are quickly obedient. He then asks, "Which one of you is the leader of this crew?" One of the men timidly lifts his hand. Speaking directly to him now, "It is obvious what your intentions are with all these chainsaws and gas cans. You know the law. By all rights, I should arrest you and haul you in. But this time we are not here to harm you; we're here to warn you. How many of you have seen the warning letter." The crew leader is the only one who puts up his hand. "OK, listen up! In a nutshell, the letter says that all endangered species (which includes the tigers) are now protected and any hostile action against them will boomerang back on the perpetrator with equal force. This also includes the tiger's habitat. To make it clear, the tigers depend on the forest and its creatures for food and shelter. That means that if one tiger or cub dies of starvation, then you or one of your children will die of starvation. There are no exceptions. Do you understand?" The men all nod.

"As you can see, we carry no arms. We don't need to. We are protected as well and any hostile action against us will boomerang back on you with equal force (as it did with the woman in the trailer). Make no mistake, if any of you come into any forest reserve we will reappear and you will be arrested and sent to prison."

I notice that the man in front of Dudekula is moving his hand toward his chainsaw. I look at Dudekula and can see that the 'Great I Am' is already talking to him. I watch him go into slow-motion perception. (This is the first time I see it from an observer's point of view.) Dudekula's actions are barely a blur. He opens his arms in the Love gesture.

The man pulls the cord and starts the chainsaw. In one quick motion, the man brings the chainsaw up under Dudekula's left arm. It slides around, but cuts off the left arm of the man. The chainsaw falls to the ground and stalls out in the dirt. The man's hand on the severed arm is still gripping the chainsaw. The man is standing over the chainsaw looking down at his twitching arm in horror. It takes several seconds before the impact, of this sight and the pain, to reach his brain. He begins to scream hysterically. Dudekula goes into action to perform first aid on the man (which is only a blur to us).

When normal motion perception resumes, the man's shirt is off; the right sleeve is tied around his left arm as a tourniquet and the rest of the shirt is around the stub of his arm. Dudekula says to the other men, "Take your buddy and his arm to a hospital immediately!" The men are on their feet in an instant. Dudekula runs over to their cooler dumps out all the beer and food and puts the arm in on the ice. He hands the cooler to one of the men. The men help their buddy toward their half track tuck.

Vallupusetty stops the group leader. "They can load him in the truck. Before I let you go, call your boss and tell him what went down here." The leader takes out his cell phone and dials.

When the boss picks up, the leader tells him everything that happened. We can all hear the boss on the other end screaming uncontrollably, "Hand the damn phone to the ass hole."

Vallupusetty takes the phone and holds it at his waist while he speaks to the leader, "Take your man to the hospital as soon as you can. They might be able to save his arm." He watches the leader climb in behind the wheel of the half-track and pull out. He slowly puts the phone to his ear and says, "Vallupusetty here."

The boss on the other end screams into his phone, "Look moron, I have friends in high places. You are dead meat. I'll make you suffer beyond your wildest imaginings. You will not only lose your job you will never find another one for the rest of your pathetic life." Vallupusetty is listening coolly and calmly and starting a big long yawn. "Are you listening to me, moron?" The boss pauses to take a breath.

"Mister, unless you are connected to a higher source then the Supreme One, you are in deep trouble. I know everything you are doing; you are rolling that souvenir shell casing between your fingers right now. Now, you drop it on your desk and use the same hand to adjust your balls." There is a vocal reaction on the other end. One of the cell phones Vallupusetty has from the elephant trainers starts to ring. He answers and continues, "Yes, I have all of your cell phones, Afzal, and as we speak a warrant for your arrest is being written. Consider yourself out of business. This time you will not escape the death penalty. We will leave the body of your daughter in the trailer. You might want to pick her up and give her a proper Islamic burial." He hangs up the phone and puts it in his pocket.

I walk over to Vallupusetty and put my arm around his shoulder. I compliment him, "Perfect job, well done!" I turn to the rest of the team, "I am very impressed with each of you. You learn quickly and are a credit to your uniform."

Nune says, "I don't know how the rest of you feel, but this job is the best in the whole world. Thank you."

Everyone repeats, "Thank you." Which we all know is directed to the 'Great I Am'.

"Now let's call the elephants and head home." I let out a call like the elephant trumpet. Everyone including Abby tries the call with different degrees of success.

Dudekula ask me, "Can you teach me how to talk to the elephants?"

"Actually, Karry can teach you that as well as I can."

The elephants walk into camp. Karry takes Dudekula aside and explains how to talk to the elephants. Dudekula gives one the picture and Karry the other. When done, they give each other high-five. They are both surprised when the elephants put up their trunks to do high-five too.

When we arrive back at the choppers, Vallupusetty lets the two elephant trainers go, with a warning. They are overjoyed and relieved. The officer/pilot of the helicopter explains that they have been sweating bullets all day long.

CHAPTER 38
Black-market Tiger Trade

The next morning I have breakfast with Dick and Abby. Abby is full of joy over her experiences of the last two days and feels that her life is now forever changed. She says, "The 'Great I Am' is revealing a purpose for me, which is better than anything I ever dreamed possible. And it is not just schlepping camera gear for Dick. Aside from all that, our relationship is absolutely incredible and rock solid." She reaches out and takes his hand, with a warm and tender smile.

Dick responds warmly to her and then uses the pause to ask a pressing question. "Hayah, is there any way that I can tag along for the rest of your trip? I assume you are going to be pressing the warning about using the body parts of endangered species."

"Your assumption is correct, but you're going to take some footage on that today. As you already know from Him, your job is to publish that issue of NGM as quickly as possible and put pictures and footage in circulation with all the media. Let me reinforce what He is telling you. The success of this entire mission is hanging on your putting the word out there in a believable way, so people will follow the instructions of the warning to the letter. You have no idea how many obstacles the Dragon Lady is going to put in your path. She would like nothing better than to see people ignore the warning. Think about it for a minute. How many people around the world have trinkets, jewelry, artwork, decorations, trophies, cloths, makeup, medicines, potions and elixirs, made of protected animal's body parts? The warning includes everyone, not just traders, artisans and merchants. Now if people don't heed the warning the death toll will make the bubonic plague look like a common cold. That will make the 'Great I Am' and all of us connected with Him a target of public outrage. I don't want to imagine how many more souls will be lost, because they will try to kill us."

"Wow, you really know how to put on the pressure!" Dick says.

Abby says, "It is not pressure, my love. We just do what He tells us and stay focused. I feel so little stress now, my whole life is different."

I add, "Dick, I know He is asking you to go and take some shots this afternoon of the hidden temples from yesterday. It sounds like a holiday to you (and it will be), but I'll guarantee you that He has a purpose for it. We just don't know what it is yet."

Abby asks, "That reminds me, why doesn't He clue us in on His master plan?"

"It all has to do with the Free Will, which He gives us. Picture this, the life of each person on the planet is like a chess game; He is playing all of us at the same time; He doesn't know our move until we make the choice; since every choice can change the outcome, that means that any outcome can flip in a second. Once I calculated that mathematically with an average of three choices per person; the number was so big it was beyond my comprehension; so I'm perfectly willing to let Him deal with the master plan."

Dick says, "I think that was a good idea. I got lost in the middle of that example let alone the calculation. But then, I'm no chess player." We all laugh.

At the briefing, Rohan hands out copies of the warning letter in three different languages. He tells us that they have been distributed all over the country, but the media has yet to notice it. He says, "Hopefully your actions today will change all that. The warning says that the illness and death of the human perpetrator will be equal to the death of the animal. To make that point clear, the 'Great I Am' put me in touch with an artistic printer, who printed up these pictures which Dick has loaned me." He hands three pictures to each of us. "You are to show them to whomever you meet and evaluate their reaction. If the reaction is strong enough, then we will print and distribute them all over the world."

I look at the picture on the top. It is a dead tiger cub hanging on a poll being carried by two men out of the Forest. The emotion I feel is pure disgust. As I move the picture to change to the next one, the first picture changes. The scene is the same only now it is a dead human baby hanging on the poll. My emotions immediately switch from disgust to total horror.

The second picture is a close-up shot of a dead Rhino with the two horns cut off. When I tilt this picture, it reveals a beautiful woman in tears with two Rhino horns growing out of her face. This is so horrifying to Abby and Karry that they can't look at it.

The third picture shows a dead elephant carcass collapsed, empty of all flesh and its tusks hacked off with a chainsaw. I tilt the picture, it is now a human male, whose lower face, chest and abdomen are completely eaten away by a black fungus. I find this one extremely difficult to look at; It is far worse, than anything Stephen King could dream up.

I look up at Rohan, "If these don't catch their attention nothing will. Good job! (I don't know if 'good' is the right word choice.)"

Rohan continues, "Your assignment today is in Doranala south of here. I have an alert from The

Environmental Investigation Agency (EIA) that there may be a trader collecting tiger parts to move up to New Delhi. You are to investigate and press the warning upon them, if the information is correct. You are not to make any arrests." There are question marks written all over the SBOs' faces. "Instead (and you may quote me on this), 'there will be no further arrest for this offense, because the Conservator of Forest & Field Director believes fully in the warning letter and the whole problem will be resolved in 30 days, making any costly legal action unnecessary. I sincerely wish that all perpetrators would burn what they have, so there will be no needless loss of human life. The warning says that poaching and trading of animal body parts ends here and now and for all time!'

"An hour after you arrive at your destination in Doranala the media will arrive. There is a leak that you will be conducting a raid at that time. Use that time wisely to sell the importance of the warning letter. Reluctantly, give your picture packets to each of the lead reporters. That's it! Listen to Him as you always do. Now let's make a difference."

Everyone heads for the Land Rover, but I hang back. I say to Rohan, "You are a changed man, my friend."

"I don't understand. Everyone says that, my bosses, my family, everyone."

I assure him, "This man has always been in you, only now the 'Great I Am' is bringing this man out of you. Do you like who you are now?"

"Absolutely! I feel fantastic. My mind is clear. And I enjoy every minute of every day." Then Rohan asks, "By the way, you can take the chopper up to the airport after lunch. He tells me it will be better than waiting until tomorrow."

I am overjoyed, "That will be great! You're not concerned about the expense?"

"Nonsense, I will do anything for you and Him."

We pull up to our destination in Doranala. It is a small rundown farm, with junk piled everywhere, a broken-down and rusty ancient tractor, other rusted farm equipment and stacks of gray weathered lumber. The house is small and in need of repair. The barn is leaning on its foundation and has not seen a coat of paint in thirty years. Standing on either side of the door to the barn are two burly security guards. They obviously look out of place.

We all pile out of the Rover. Dick starts taking pictures immediately. I put my hand on Abby's shoulder to hold her back. "Let's watch and see how they do by themselves."

Karry and Dudekula approach the guard on the left. Nune and Vallupusetty approach the guard on the right. Karry says to the guard, "We are here to inspect the barn."

The guard flippantly replies, "Hey dolly, you can inspect me anytime." He makes an obscene gesture.

Nune orders the guard on the right, "Open the door."

The guard steps forward, "No can do, sonny! Come back when you're old enough to shave."

The two guards are about to become hostile. The team instantly goes into slow-motion perception. They are moving so fast, everything they do is a blur. The guards reach for their side arms, but their guns are already flying out on either side into a junk pile. The guard on the right takes a swing at Nune, who moves out of the way and lets the man's follow-through, pull him off balance. Nune then pushes him over with one finger. His face crashes into the gravel, and Vallupusetty puts him in handcuffs. The guard on the left reaches out to grab Karry, who moves quickly behind and taps him on his shoulder. Before he can turn around Dudekula has him in handcuffs. After the guard turns, Dudekula bumps him behind the knees and Karry sets him down.

Suddenly the backdoor to the house swings open and a young man appears with an automatic weapon. Before he can clear the bottom step, Dudekula and Nune are on him. Dudekula grabs the barrel of the gun and pulls him down the last step yanking the gun from his hands and throwing it in the junk pile. The young man starts to fall forward and puts out his hands to catch himself. Before he hits the ground, Nune has his handcuffs on him. The team comes back to normal motion perception.

The two guards and the young man are now sitting in the gravel. Vallupusetty is standing over them. Karry opens the door to the barn. Inside is a large bundle of tiger skins and two large canvas bags with bones in them. Dick is documenting everything.

I walk forward and hand a copy of the warning letter to the guards and young man. The young man starts to protest, but I cut him off, "I suggest you read!"

I motion for the team to come over. "Congratulations, you have perfected the slow-motion perception. You can consider yourselves graduated." No sooner are the words out of my mouth, than the media shows up early. Abby quickly hands the team their picture packets and warning letters. I hastily add, "Remember, be charming and sell the warning. They need to see the seriousness of what is going down."

The media are all over us in a minute. Abby and Dick team up. The SBOs divide up and talk to the individual stations one on one. I drift into the background and watch what is going on.

The warning letter is not a hit until Nune takes the newsperson interviewing him over to the young man, who now finishes reading his warning letter and is staring off into blank space. Nune asks him, "What is the worst thing you can imagine happening to you, if you don't burn all this stuff?"

The young man is trembling, "I will be very sick and all the skin will fall off my body. I will watch my flesh boil and fall off my bones. And no matter how painful it is, I will not be able to die until I see my eyes fall out of my skull and feel my brain explode." Every network camera is on the young man.

Nune presses him, "And what will happen if you sell the tiger skins and bones?"

The young man turns white as a sheet, "Then all that buy them will suffer the horrific death, and I will start to suffer my death immediately."

Nune continues, "So what are you going to do?"

"I'm going to burn the whole lot before lunch. And then I'm going to call my Uncle Shabbir and tell him that he better burn everything he has and notify every person he ever sold to."

Nune turns to the reporters after unlocking the cuffs on the three suspects. "There will be no further arrest for this offense, because the Conservator of Forest & Field Director believes fully in the warning letter and the whole problem will be resolved in 30 days, making any costly legal action unnecessary. The Director will make himself available for comments."

At this point, I can see that the media is only 60% sold. Dudekula takes out his photo packet and starts to look at the three pictures. His facial reaction is so strong one of the cameramen picks up on it and signals the reporter. The reporter takes one look at the pictures and almost faints. She holds it up for the cameraman. He says, "I can't make it work here. We need to take it back to the studio." All the networks are now tuning in on Dudekula and asking him to part with his picture packet.

Karry jumps into the fracas and says, "Who will promise to run this as the lead story tonight?" Everyone holds up their hands, some are jumping up and down. Some minor pushing and shoving begins, before the SBOs pull out the photo packets and award them to each reporter. Karry shouts, "Don't forget! A promise is a promise!"

The 'Great I Am' is ecstatic over the outcome.

CHAPTER 39
Journey into Hell

I start this part of the journey with a foreboding feeling. The 'Great I Am' wants me to do this leg of the journey alone. He is telling me that the people I will encounter are unpredictable and a long way from being connected to him. Here in India and in Africa I can walk through the landscape and feel the connected presence of the animals. From the animal's connection with Him, there is growing a solid connection of many people. This is wonderful for Him and me. All these seeds can now grow and produce much fruit. Thus, we move from things being bleak to there being hope.

Where I am going, the connected animals I come to protect are near extinction. The greed and misguided appetites of the people are manufacturing most of the finished products for worldwide distribution. The places I am going to visit are only the tip of the iceberg in the 'blood trade' epidemic. The delivery of the warning in these areas is critical, if anyone is to survive the 'blood trade plague', which will soon be upon us.

My first stop is Manila in the Philippines. I fly from here to Hyderabad by helicopter, from Hyderabad to Hong Kong and Hong Kong to Manila. It is a total travel time of about 13 hours. I arrive at 16:45 (19:45 Srisailam time). That makes for a very long day (over 20 hours) from my early rise this morning until I can go to bed tonight in Manila. This is nothing for the seasoned traveler, but for me it's a bit much. Add to this that I have to travel as the senior citizen, Hoss Proxetter, and you have one weary traveler by the end of the day. I just have to make sure that I sleep on the plane.

Upon arrival, I take the subway into metro Manila and check-in at my inexpensive hotel, Malate Pensionne. I pay for two nights in advance and grab a quick bite to eat. Afterward, I take a walk to try to stay awake until 21:00 Manila time. I still have at least 2 hours of sunlight.

The area in which the hotel is situated has a charming old Manila feeling. I pass many nice eating-places and other hotels. There is even a 7-Eleven. Within a block, I discover Remedios Circle, a huge traffic circle with a beautiful park in the middle. Turning downhill, I come upon another beautiful park in only two blocks, Rajah Sulayman Park. Rounding some high-rise buildings and continuing downhill, within another block, I am standing looking at a freeway and the Bay. I see a sign to 'Baywalk' pointing under the freeway and decide to follow it. Sure enough, I come out on a fantastic walkway along the Bay. I look to my right, then left and decide to take the path to my right. This walk feels good. Now I can stretch my legs and pick up the pace. I really like to walk.

After a while, the walkway ends. And there in front of me is the new three-story US Embassy, with extremely tight security. The opulence of the Embassy blends right in with the modern high-rises across from it. Beyond the Embassy I can see the grand Manila Ocean Park, another display of wealth and grander.

I turn and walk up the hill again through the glistening high-rises. I now become aware that what I am looking at is wealthy and mega-wealthy. Most of the cars that pass me on the street are luxury brands. Most of the people coming and going from the buildings are wearing white pressed linen. From experience, I know that is high maintenance apparel.

As I top the hill, I pause to look up and down the

long street of high-rises, which seem to have gotten higher. Here a shopper would be in paradise. Not being a shopper and not knowing where I am, I decide to walk down the other side of the hill.

After only a few blocks, I emerge from the canyons of the high-rises. I stop, not quite sure what I am looking at. Are these demolished building? No, it can't be the rubble left from WW II. Then I realized, this was what others have described to me as "makeshift settlements" or "squatter towns" or "shanty towns" obviously trying to avoid the word slum.

The 'Great I Am' says to me, "These are my poor. I want you to visit them."

"Then why not bring me here in the first place?"

"You need to have the right perspective. Now you can understand what you are about to see. I recommend that you look beyond the poverty."

I follow some children down a narrow walkway. They are naked from the waist up and have no shoes. They laugh and play while kicking a plastic bottle down the alleyway. To my surprise, when they reach their home, they pick up the bottle and take it in with them. I stop to look closely at the house they call home.

Yes, it is a shack that you and I might reject as a place to live. The electric wiring is hanging dangerously on the side of the buildings. One building is no more than two spans of my arms outstretched. Then I look closer. This homeowner has built his house entirely from discarded materials, using only a knife. There are no nails or screws. He or she lashed the boards to posts with bits of black plastic twisted into rope. The builder wedged the windows and doors in with bits of cedar shingles. Makeshift bits and pieces of PVC slipped together makes up what plumbing exists. It doesn't take long to see that this home is built with skill and pride. A lazy person looking for a box in which to live does not build this way. This person will survive when the "civilized world" destroys itself.

I continue down the alley, marveling in the creative living. A young man approaches. He's in his mid-twenties, with a goatee and casual clothes. I smile as we pass.

He says, "Ass hole!"

The 'Great I Am' responds instantly, "He is full of anger and hatred, but means no harm."

I turn and walk up another street that is only a little wider than the alley. Every dwelling is different; let's call the design style 'early recyclable'. The design works itself out depending on what you are able to find. A few meters ahead, I see a young woman in her late teens drawing water in two 20-liter plastic containers.

I stop and ask if I can have a drink. The 'Great I Am' says, "This is Maan. Her family lives close by. She is close to connecting with me. She is studying in the community school to become a Project Director of Projects like this one."

She says, "I'll hold the hose for you."

I cup both hands and drink and drink. I had no idea how thirsty I was. When I quench my thirst, I say, "Thank you Maan. How are your studies going at the community school? I'm sure you will receive your Project Directors job."

"I graduate this year. How do you know so much about me?"

"The 'Great I Am' within you is telling me."

"I know He's there. How do I find him?"

"I'll show you, if you like?"

She responds quickly, "Yes, please!"

I tell her about her mind and ego. Then I show her how to breath in through the mouth and out through the nose. She goes into a perfect breathing pattern almost at once. She struggles with the darkness for a few minutes. After that, I see the light come into her face.

She smiles broadly, "Your name is Hayah." She gives me a big hug.

We are now connected through Him. I already feel better about what lies ahead.

I help Maan with one of the two jugs back to where she lives. She is such a sweet caring person, and yet a complete contradiction given the circumstances under which she lives. We say good-by, and I continue my walk back to the hotel.

I say to Him, "I know you're cooking something up. Let me know when you have a plan."

CHAPTER 40
Blowing Smoke

The next morning, my first appointment is with Director Mandie, a Doctor of Veterinary Medicine, at the Bureau of Protected Areas and Wildlife (BPAW), a division of the Department of Environment and Natural Resources (DENR), in Quezon City outside Manila. (Please note the bureaucratic layers that I am up against.) I take the subway and arrive early; however, Director Mandie is twenty minutes late. When she arrives, she has me follow her into her office. She is flustered and struggling to find something. I offer to leave for a moment so she can collect herself. She says that is not necessary, but the next five minutes are extremely painful for her, because she cannot find what she is looking for. Finally, she turns to me and asks, "What is this meeting about?"

"The warning letter regarding ivory possession and other animal body parts," I say calmly.

Still flustered, "It's not about the ivory trade?"

"Indirectly, yes." I add, "I have another copy of the letter, if you want?" I hand it to her without waiting for an answer. She reads it, and I wait until she finishes.

She puts on a composed demeanor now. "I vaguely remember reading this, but I don't think we are taking any action on this. (Note the highlighted smoke words in the following.) I can **assure you** that we are **encouraging** the leaders in the church to **avoid** purchasing blood ivory icons. We are doing **everything we can** to fulfill the terms of the CITES treaty. And we are **looking into** the **allegations** concerning Monsignor Cristobal Garcia (one of the best known ivory collectors in the Philippines) from Talisay city in Cebu province." She says this with such smoothness that a robot could not have done better.

"Director Mandie, I will give you a few minutes to read the letter again? While you're at it, write today's date at the top." She writes the date and reads.

When she finishes, she looks at me with a blank expression on her face.

I ask, "What is the letter telling you?"

She sputters through the main points. "It says that anyone possessing non-antiquated ivory must burn it within 30 days of the date I wrote on top or they will become ill and die the same death the animals suffered."

"Please note it does not say 'non-antiquated' ivory. It includes all body parts taken by poaching and no treaty or local laws will apply."

She looks at the letter again and turns pale. "How does one know that the animal was killed by poaching?"

"If you don't know, I suggest you burn it. If you do know, and will stake your life on it, then don't burn it. Have you sent out copies of this letter throughout the Philippines, for example the government officials responsible for the seized contraband being held in storage, like Medel Eduarte? (He is the park superintendent at the Ninoy Aquino Parks and Wildlife Center; and is suspected of pilfering 700 kg of ivory tusks.)"

"No, I have not! And I am not going to!" She slowly tears the letter into four pieces.

"Thank you for your time, Director." I stand up and walk to the door, open it and turn back. The 'Great I Am' wants me to add, "You may want to tape the letter back together and put it in a safe place, because in 30 days people are going to start dying! And that includes you and your own family." I walk out closing the door gently.

My next appointment is with Bishop Jay at the
offices of the Archdioceses on Arzobispo Street in Manila.
It is only a short subway ride, so I am able to be there in
good time.

A priest meets me and ushers me into a waiting area.
During the short walk from the front door to the waiting
area, I see several carved ivory icons. The 'Great I Am' is
becoming agitated. After a short wait, the priest returns and
ushers me into a large office. Bishop Jay is standing in front
of his desk wearing a white linen suit, a purple silk classic
cut clerical dickey with a clerical collar. The room looks
more like an ivory museum than an office, with ivory icons
of every size and Biblical character known to man. The one
of Jonah and the whale is the most ostentatious. He
extends his hand and ring finger to me. The 'Great I Am'
says, "Don't you dare kiss it! Take his hand in both of
yours and I will do the rest." I do as directed, thus covering
his ring with the palm of my left hand and give him a warm
greeting. Only the warm turns into a hot one. The ring is
turning so hot under my hand, he screams and pulls it
away, yanking off the ring as quickly as he can and throwing
it to the floor. The 'Great I Am' says, "I know every animal
in this room and all of them died a horrible death. I am
itching to set them all ablaze right now, including him.
Joshua says this man makes the moneychangers look like
candy salesmen. He's more furious than I am."

Bishop Jay says to me, "What is that all about?"

"Bishop, you are quoted as saying, 'If all of this stuff
is plain stupid, then God, put a stop to this.' Guess what
Bishop, now you have your message!"

The Bishop reaches across his desk to push a button
under the front.

I continue, "Push that button and this whole room,

all your precious treasures and you will go up in a white hot blaze. Right now, He wants nothing better than for you to push that button and make it happen, so turn around and sit down on the floor next to your ring."

Bishop Jay does as he is told. I see the warning letter on his desk and pick it up along with a pen. Handing it to him, "Write today's date on the top of the letter."

He writes the date, but asks, "Can we negotiate this? Many of these artifacts are priceless antiques."

"There is nothing to negotiate. According To Him, every one of these is from an elephant that suffers a horrific death at the hands of poachers. He knows them all! I think He is being generous in giving you a chance to destroy them and save your own life and immortal soul.

"Now let's get down to business. Have you sent a copy of this warning letter to your Muslim friends on Mindanao?"

He responds meekly, "No."

"You will do so and tell them their devotion is not accepted by their creator."

He responds, "Yes sir!"

"Have you sent it to the traders and carvers in the Philippines, especially to the two families in Tayuman?"

He responds, "No, but I will."

"Now, you will tell Archbishop Jose Palma, what is happening here and tell him that he is responsible for sending the warning letter out to all the churches in the Philippines and everyone in the Vatican. Is that clear?"

He responds, "Yes sir." He stares at the floor.

"Starting tonight, you will have dreams of the deaths of every elephant from which your ivory trinkets come. They will continue until all your ivory is burned or the day you die. What you see in the dreams will also be your death."

I go into slow-motion perception and leave the building unnoticed.

I stay in slow-motion perception and walk to my next appointment on Taft Avenue (normally a 19-minute walk, but it only takes 3 minutes). When I am within a block, I come back to normal motion perception. My 14:00 meeting is with Sjuto at the National Bureau of Investigation (NBI). The old Manila architecture is very inviting although security is tight with the use of a guard dog, which becomes very friendly with me on first contact. I ask if I can talk to her and touch her. The guard responds, "I have never seen her behave like that with anyone, including me. Knock yourself out!"

I take the dog's head in my hands and put my forehead to hers. We have a short reunion and I let her go. She sits down at attention, and I say, "high-five." The dog, JoJo (pronounced HoHo), and I do perfect high-five. I turn to the guard and tell him to try it. He does and is blown away with joy.

The guard checks his list and logs me in.

Sjuto is on the dot punctual and comes out to meet me. He is a sharp looking man with a warm manner about him and dressed in shirtsleeves and slacks. He walks me into his office and we both sit in comfortable chairs in front of his desk. He gets right down to business.

He picks up the warning letter from his desk and says, "I have a couple of questions about your letter."

I say, "Before we start write today's date on the top."

He writes down the date. "That takes care of question number one."

I cut in again, "The CITES treaty and local statutes have no power over this directive. And as to your third question, less than 1% of all ivory is taken without the senseless slaughter of the elephants. The owners of that 1% know who they are, because they either take it themselves or know who has. But keep that last part to yourself."

He asks, "Are you some kind of clairvoyant?"

"No, I'm just a person connected to the 'Great I Am' within you."

"So what do you want me to do," He asks.

"Send the warning out and burn everything. If someone comes to you who knows how the ivory is taken and it is not blood ivory, you can tell them they have nothing to fear from Him. However, the value of their ivory will go through the roof and it should be securely protected."

"OK, how do I know you are who you say you are whatever that is?"

I check with Him, "Do you know Joseph in Kenya or Odis in Tanzania?"

He laughs, "I know them both. Is Odis still coming off the walls?"

I smile, "Not any longer, he is on His path." Sjuto is already dialing a number into the telephone.

There is a connection and he says, "Howdy buddy, this is Sjuto. I have a chap her by the name of Hayah. What do you know about him?" He listens. He stands up and walks around the room. He looks out the window. He comes back and sits down. "Thanks Joseph. I'll tell him you send your best." He hangs up and looks me in the eye. "I hope someday I can receive a reference like that. Look, I'll do what you ask, but it is not going to be easy."

"We know, but all we are trying to do here is save

lives and turn back the tide. In the end, which is 30 days from today, if they don't burn their blood ivory, they will die a horrible death. You might set the example by starting with your confiscated stockpile." The telephone rings.

Sjuto picks up, "Hello, Sjuto." He listens. "Yes, He's right here, and I checked him out. They don't have connections any higher than him." He listens. "I'll ask him." He turns to me with his hand over the receiver. "This is Fred with the Metro Police; He wants to know if you will meet with him and Bishop Jay at 22:00 tonight after the 21:00 mass at Saint Anthony church in Forbes Park. He wants to go over his plans to expedite your warning letter." I nod yes. "He says yes. Very good. Goodbye Fred."

I start to leave. Sjuto motions for me to wait a minute, but I say, "Don't bother Sjuto, there is no 21:00 mass."

He finishes checking and looks up, "You're right. You shouldn't go."

"I have to go."

"Do you need backup?"

"I have all the backup I need. You can believe Joseph's explanation about the boomerang effect, so do your due diligence with the forensics and clear my name."

We shake hands and I leave.

I now know that Bishop Jay is going to drop the ball. The church and metro police are not going to circulate the warning. I quickly come up with a plan B and head down into the project to Maan's house. She is waiting for me in front of the narrow passageway back into her home.

She says, "He told me you were coming, but not why."

I explain, "We need to get these warning letters out.
You need to write today's date on top of each one. Then
can you find some of the kids in the project to post them at
all the churches, schools and police precincts on all the
islands? Here is almost 500 letters and fifty dollars. I will
send you 500 each week for the next four weeks along with
fifty dollars each week. Share the money with the children
and tell them they are saving lives." She agrees, and I thank
her. We say our goodbyes, and I leave to find a place to eat
and relax before tonight.

I arrive at Saint Anthony's a minute before 22:00. I
push open the large steal gate and gently close it behind me.
I climb the steps to the tall oak doors and enter the church.
Bishop Jay is standing in the chancel at the end of the long
nave. He is dressed in his purple cassock covered with a
white lace over garment and over that he wears a purple
cape. To top it off he wears his Bishop's cap.

I walk down the aisle toward him. I don't see Fred.
When I reach the many steps that go up into the chancel,
Jay shouts, "Come no further, this is holy ground and
beyond the reach of the likes of you." I laugh.

Suddenly, a short man, dressed in a black suit, blue
silk shirt and red silk tie, slips in front of me. He has to
stand on the first step to equal my height. We are almost
nose-to-nose.

I say to him as I go into slow-motion perception
and hold very still, "How nice of you to join us Fred, I feel
so much better having the police here. However, before you
do something you might both regret, I beg you to
reconsider. I am required to warn you that any action you
take against me will boomerang back on you and the
Bishop."

Jay shouts down from his regal height, "Enough of your warnings! Kill the bastard and spare us all!"

I calmly respond, "At least let me hear your confession and give you both your last rights."

Jay shouts, "Impudence, it is you who shall die unblessed. Fred, send him back to hell where he comes from."

Fred seizes me by the throat and squeezes with all his strength, which is incredible. Jay clutches his throat and gasps for air. He cannot scream.

Fred can't see what is happening behind him. He can only see that his grip has no effect on me. He reaches deep inside for more strength and thrashes my head from side to side increasing the pressure of his grip. Jay is being shaken violently. I hear his neck snap, and he falls to the floor in a heap of purple silk and white lace.

Fred is frustrated with his inability to strangle me and lets me go. He quickly draws a knife and passes it under my chin from ear to ear. He steps back and up on the next step proud of himself. He suddenly realizes what happened, grabs his own throat and then holds his hand up in front of him to see the blood. His eyes are bulging out, as he falls backward on the steps.

Coming back to normal motion perception and checking my neck, I look at him kindly and say, "Thank you Fred. That is the best adjustment I have had in years."

As I turn to leave, I call out to Sjuto hiding in the balcony, "Thank you for videoing all that on your phone Sjuto? Good luck my friend."

Sjuto leans over the balcony rail and watches me leave.

CHAPTER 41
Deeper into Hell

I have five hours of sound sleep and am up to head to the airport. I check out by 05:00 and stop at a restaurant close by the subway station to have breakfast. I look around the restaurant and wonder how many of these people are going to live or die. Then I realize the poor will survive and most of the wealthy, clergy and bureaucrats are going to die.

I throw on my backpack and head down into the subway. By the time I reach the platform, I am back in my old body. I protest as usual, but today He says, "You'll be grateful when you arrive at the airport."

As I step onto the escalator at the airport, I look up and see security guards at the top, checking people as they step off. They hold up a picture and compare it to the men as they step off the escalator. I stop and look at the picture over the guard's shoulder. It is a picture of Hayah, taken from a security camera at the Archdioceses. The guard turns and asks, "Have you seen this guy?"

I answer honestly, "Yes, He was at Café Adriatico near Quirino subway station."

The guard says, "Thanks buddy!" And he hurries off talking on his cell phone.

I check-in for my 09:35 flight, go through security and head to the gate to wait. The whole airport is buzzing with security guards checking passengers against Hayah's picture. OK, I am curious and want to know what's happening, and He finally explains that they want me for questioning in regards to the murder of Bishop Jay and Officer Fred of the Metro Police. He advises me not to show any interest and just keep a low profile. He assures me that all will be resolved shortly.

A group of eleven Buddhist monks arrives at the gate in their orange robes and sits down in the seats around me. They are chatting away a mile a minute. I like their enthusiasm and energy. But I sense a deep sadness and confusion within them.

I begin to meditate and almost instantly, I am connecting to the 'Great I Am'. He is quiet, and I can tell that He is studying the group of Buddhist monks. After a few minutes, He starts to talk to me about the monks. They are from the Wat Phra Kaew (The Emerald Buddha Temple) in Bangkok, Thailand. All of them are carrying some kind of an ivory amulet. Some of them are using tiger medicines. Some are using Rhino horn medicines. Four of them have tiger amulets. One of them has a mountain-gorilla tooth amulet. He sums it up by saying, "They are the walking dead, and don't know it."

I ask Him, "But they are Theravada meditators. Aren't any of them connected with you?"

"Not one," He says. "And they are not even close. They don't even know the real meaning of being enlightened or even awakened. They are searching for some higher intellectual power, which is a total perversion to Buddha's teachings. To them being a monk was an easy way of life, which puffs up their egos and makes them look holy and cool to others."

"I don't understand; Buddha is connected."

"Yes He is!" He says emphatically. "These monks are on a false journey. Their leader has left the path many years ago, like his leader before him. They are using objects (Samantha) as points of focus and concentration, which Buddha does to settle the mind and empty it completely. But this group is using it to enhance the mind and reach a higher intelligence within their own minds. The ignorance they are seeking to escape is the exact thing that they are rushing into. The higher intelligence they seek is not in their minds; it is in me. Buddha found the light and Me, but they are not even looking for the light or Me.

"To them, every part of the body must be uprooted and blocked from consciousness. Their minds are telling them that the body is the source of all pain. But the only pain the body communicates to the brain is a warning and bearable. The body can help you breathe through all pain. And the mind will have no memory of it. The rational mind makes it unbearable by magnifying the perception and inhibiting the breathing. The body will never lie to you. The mind lies to you all the time. The ego always lies to you, because the ego is not of Me.

"They are defiling their bodies with potions and amulets from sacred animals. They have no clue that it is Me who makes them sacred within the living creature. If they kill the animals, they kill part of Me; they kill part of Buddha. I am not in the body parts of the dead animals. My Love is a living Spirit. It is the essence of all being. My Love is eternal. The dead body parts shall return to the dust from which they came.

"Now they shall experience the meaning of cause and effect. The root cause is their defilements. The facilitating cause is their ignorance. The only nibbana (the goal to be free from the cycle of birth and death by being completely enlightened) they shall experience is eternal darkness without Me. In that darkness they shall relive in their memory this present life cycle of birth, illness, aging and death over and over again seeing every error, every chance and not being able to change a thing. And that makes Me sad, because I Love even them."

I desperately want to reach them, "There must be at

least one of them that we can reach, so they all might live!"

"OK, the Buddha is about to test them, watch and see what happens."

A moment later, a young woman from the Thai restaurant in the food court arrives at the gate. She is carrying a tray of twelve covered cups, with a paper napkin and chopsticks. She explains that the cups contain pad-Thai noodles in peanut-sauce with bean sprouts. The offering is with the complements of the owner of the restaurant. She bows her head with respect as she presents a cup to each of the monks. Each monk thanks her and the owner profusely with great show and much bowing. Finally, she presents to me the last cup in the same manner.

I stand and place my hand on her head and let the Love of the 'Great I Am' pass through me and into her. Her eyes open wide and her face lights up with a joyous smile. I sit down, open my cup of noodles and start to eat them. They are quite delicious.

That's when I notice that a monk is looking after the young woman and waiting for her to be out of sight. When she is out of sight, he nods to the group. Without a word, the monks stand up in groups of two and three, walk to the trash container and throw away the cup of noodles without opening it. As soon as the last group sits down, they are all abuzz with negative chatter. "The cup is so small; the kitchen must be filthy; why is there nothing to drink; the girl looks so poor; the owner must be stupid." They chatter endlessly.

I finish my noodles before they finish their harangue. I take my empty cup, dirty napkin and used chopsticks to the trash and return to me seat. I loudly hum with deep satisfaction, lick and smack my lips. The monks all take note of this as I go back into my meditation.

Now, I am face to face with Buddha. He shakes his head, "What is happening to my people? They make a mockery of everything I stand for. I ask them to accept gratefully whatever is offered. My example must mean nothing to them. A kind woman offered me food from her pot. I could smell that it was tainted with salmonella. But I ate it anyway because it was generously given, and I died. Did the woman kill me? Not at all! She set me free to continue living eternally with the 'Great I Am' within us all. I thank you Hoss for eating the noodles and blessing the woman. It means a lot to her, her father and me."

As Buddha moves off into the light, the 'Great I Am' says, "He wanted to meet you and thank you himself." I struggle to phrase a question that is growing within me. He says, "Yes, you can try to reach one of them if you can. But don't get your hopes up."

I can never see myself during meditation, so I don't know if what follows is common or extraordinary because of Buddha and the 'Great I Am'. As I come out of my meditation, I sense a silence around me as though the monks are gone. However, I open my eyes and they are all staring at me.

The monk on my right asks, "What were you experiencing in your meditation? Your face was glowing as if you had a brilliant light inside you. I have never seen anything like that before. It was the same when you meditated earlier."

I respond politely, "I go into the Light within me, but of course the noodles help me, because they were a gift from Buddha. When I went back into my meditation, Buddha was there to greet me, and we had a nice chat."

They are shocked. The monk on my left asks, "Can you teach us how to meditate like that?"

I say frankly, "No, you failed the test. Buddha was watching when you threw his gift in the trash." I nod toward the trash bin. "I can offer you something else. It can save your life."

I hand the warning letter to their leader sitting across from me. "Please read this letter to everyone." He reads the letter, with many negative facial expressions and hostile body language.

When he finishes reading, he hands the letter back to me, saying, "What does this have to do with us?"

I smile and cock my head so he can see I know he is lying. "All of you are wearing amulets of ivory, tiger bones and mountain-gorilla teeth. Many of you are using tiger or Rhino potions. You must burn them within 29 days, or you will suffer the same death the animals suffered."

They all clutch different parts of their robes, where the amulets or potions are hidden. Ten of them throw back their heads in defiance, rejecting the warning. One, however, withdraws the amulet and looks at it.

The loud speaker announces our flight, and we all stand. The one holding his amulet leaves it on his seat and queues up with the others. I pick it up and walk over to him. Handing him the amulet, I say, "You better burn this or you will suffer the death anyway. At least if you do burn it, you may one day find the light within you."

A news flash comes on TV. CNN International is covering the Chad story on the elephants, the mountain-gorillas of Rwanda, the Rhinos of Kenya, the tigers of India and the warning letter, which is not a hoax. Hayah's picture is everywhere as the man of Light and Love, who is protected by a higher power. Dick, Phyllis and Dr. James have done an incredible job putting this together. The newscaster interrupts, he says, "This is just in! A video from

an unknown source was posted on Youtube. What we are
looking at is the attempted murder of Hayah by Bishop Jay
in the Philippines and Fred of the Metro Police in Manila.
Note that he does nothing to defend himself, but their
actions boomerang, killing them both." They run the video
of the Saint Anthony meeting.

I look around; the security with Hayah's picture is
gone. Then I see the knot of monks staring at me. I stare
back until they look away.

My flight departs on time, and I settle in to enjoy
my three and a half hour flight to Thailand.

In Bangkok, He changes me back into Hayah; I
check into my hotel and start immediately to make the
rounds of the ivory carvers and traders. Because of
tomorrow's International Conference on Illegal Wildlife
Trade, many of the delegates and government officials from
China are in town doing the rounds. Our hope is to be able
to confront as many of them as possible in these locations.

My first stop is in Phayuha Khiri, north of Bangkok.
The ivory factory is huge, with station after station of
carvers turning out everything from large scenes in one tusk
to small amulets and jewelry pieces. They are so brazen that
the tour is open to the public. I discreetly leave the warning
letter here and there. About midway through the tour, I see
the owner, Mr. Thi, giving a VIP tour to Li from China
and Meng, the top wildlife-trade official who is also the
executive director general of China's CITES. When Meng
sees me, he turns away. Unfortunately, Li sees me leaving a
letter and walks over to confront me.

He reads the warning letter and hands it to Thi,
saying to me, "You have one hell of a nerve coming in here!
You are destroying these peoples livelihood!" All work on

the floor stops.

I respond, "Mr. Li, the root word in 'livelihood' is life. How many elephant's lives did you take to have all this? I'm giving these people a chance at life. They can always find another livelihood. They will never have another life. I am happy you read the letter, because now you too will have to burn all your illegal animal parts or die the same death that the animal suffered…." Before I can say more, security ushers me out of the building.

My next stop is Surin to the East of Bangkok. The ivory factory here is similar to the one in Phayuha Khiri, only with poorer working conditions. Here, I see another of China's wealthy elite, Daxin the owner of Guangzhou's Ivory Carving Factory. He too is trying to blend in by taking the public tour.

I am dropping off warning letters and casually hand one to Daxin. He reads the letter and says, in a phony caring tone, "What a wonderful thing you are doing here. The elephants need protection." I look him in the eye.

I say, "You do realize that I know everything you are thinking?"

"Why, what am I thinking?" He asks coolly.

"You're thinking and I quote, 'This moron is doing me the biggest favor imaginable. He will destroy all that ivory, driving the price right through the roof, and making my ivory worth a fortune.' There are two problems with your logic. You are assuming that someone will be eager to buy it, as in zero demand, and you are assuming you will live past the next 29 days. Now, you are thinking, 'I have to find a way to destroy this bastard.' Daxin, it will be easier to burn your stash."

I call it a day and head back to Bangkok.

CHAPTER 42
The Royal Appeal

"His Royal Highness The Prince of Wales will be speaking at the International Conference on Illegal Wildlife Trade. Also joining us will be Prince William." Thus reads the large placard in the foyer to the conference room. Pictures of Prince Charles and The Duke adorn it.

I pause for a moment to admire its grand design. This is exactly what we need to raise public consciousness worldwide. I ask the 'Great I Am', "Are they connected to you?"

He sees that question coming. "Let's see if your perception is any better. What do you think?"

I consider for a moment, "They're not connected yet. Prince William and Kate are very close. However, Prince Charles is pretty close, but with a little extra baggage to overcome."

He says in the vernacular, "Spot on! Now if they ask, you need to help them."

"I can't think of anything that will give me more pleasure!" I give their pictures on the placard a thumbs up and enter the conference hall.

I'm the first to arrive, so I take a seat in the last row. The stage decorations are spectacular.

The WWF of Thailand is hosting the Conference, and they have gone all out to create a positive and joyful mood. A bold banner stretches across the proscenium arch of the stage. It reads, "Choose Life, Life of the Animals, Life of the Forests, Life of the Planet!" These words trigger many images within me, and I become lost in the collage for several minutes. The next thing I am aware of is a Security Guard trying to get my attention.

"Mister! Mister! Mister!" He smiles when I look at him. "Do you have credentials to be here?"

"No, I don't."

"Well you will have to sign up. There is a long waiting list for the visitor's gallery. Everybody wants to see the Princes. They're setting up the table in the lobby now."

I collect my things and walk back out to the foyer to queue up for the registration desk, which is not open yet. When the desk opens the queue moves very slowly. Everyone has a story as to why they deserve a seat closer, but people with reservations or delegates take all those seats. When I reach the check-in table there is little chance of me having a seat, and as the young woman explains to the person in front of me, "With the royal family being here the odds of any cancellations or no-shows are slim to none!"

I smile and ask, "Do you have anything at all?"

She says, "I have one place at the rail in the third balcony which no one wants."

"What's that, the rail?"

She explains, "Behind the last row of seats in the third balcony there is a wall about chest high dividing the seats from the upper walkway. You can stand on the walkway and lean on the top of the wall. We call it the rail." She smiles and adds, "It's great if you don't have altitude sickness."

"That's perfect! I'll take it!" I sign in and she writes out a pass with my place number, which I pin to my jacket. I spend the next five minutes climbing the stairs to the third balcony and finding my place. Now, I know what she means by altitude sickness. The people on stage are so small I can't read their facial expressions. I ask Him, "Is this going to be productive? Hearing all their speeches may be interesting, but are they going to push the warning letter?"

His response is typical when His information keeps changing, "We have to wait and see. An opportunity may present its self." Whenever He says things like this, I know I have to be on full alert, because anything can happen.

Those sitting on the stage are Prince Charles, Prince William, Prime Minister Youngluck of Thailand, Bellim, CITES' secretary-general, Sebra, TRAFFIC's Director of Advocacy, Wike of WWF-Canon, Bangkok, Thailand, India WWF's, CEO Riffin and Ted, director of The Elephant Trade Information System (ETIS).

Scanning the delegates, I spot Meng and Daxin from yesterday. Wait just a minute, there is Mohd Nor Shahrizam Nasir from Malaysia. The jury found him guilty of illegal possession of Tiger parts and possession of African Elephant ivory. His sentence was supposed to be 60 months, but Judge Mohd Rosli Osman reduced it to serve only 24 months. Then the judge turned around and released him on bail pending an appeal. Now, here he sits 6 months later. The presence of Meng and Daxin makes me question the tone of this Conference. But Nasir's presence creates a much more sinister atmosphere. It is no wonder that the 'Great I Am' is having trouble reading this situation.

The Conference opens with a formal introduction of Prince Charles. You have to love the monarchy of the UK. They take their role as ambassadors of the UK very seriously. From his very first words, Prince Charles is more passionate than I have ever seen him. He is rallying the troops to take up the cause against poaching. It is a battle cry to strike back and end this slaughter. He clearly portrays the poachers and their use of military tactics agents endangered animals as criminal. He calls for an end to the illegal trade in wildlife, which is supporting organized crime and terrorist groups. He closes with this powerful statement, "When the illegal trade in wildlife is coupled with crime involving timber, the illegal trade in *flora* and *fauna*, (it) is ranked as the fourth biggest transnational crime - with a value of $17 billion (£11 billion) - just behind trafficking in weapons, drugs and people."

Next up is Prime Minister Youngluck who pledges to end ivory trade in Thailand. She promises to stop global wildlife trafficking. She says that the call of almost 1.5 million WWF supporters has convinced her to take this action. She says, "As a next step we look forward to amending the national legislation with the goal of putting an end on ivory trade and to be in line with international norms."

The 'Great I Am' says, "She has no intention of doing any of this. She is just using this venue to score international political points. Traders in Thailand will continue to exploit loopholes in domestic legislation to sell ivory which is smuggled in from Africa."

Dan Stiles, from the floor, asks her, "Prime Minister does that mean that you will support a resolution by TRAFFIC to impose sanctions on countries most complicit in the illegal trade in wildlife?"

She responds, "I'll take that under advisement."

Wike, with the WWF in Bangkok, calls for stronger measures to protect wild Tigers in a rousing pep talk. She outlines a new international law enforcement initiative to stop the poaching and illegal trade of Tigers and other Asian big cats. There seems to be a general agreement among the delegates of the Convention.

I say to Him, "I smell a rat in that proposal."

Ted, director of ETIS and the resident statistic expert, is doing a team presentation with Bellim of CITES.

Bellim asks Ted, "Statistically, which country is the least compliant of CITES' regulations?"

Ted responds, "The numbers show that China openly ignores the ivory smuggling regulations. Their government is licensing 35 carving factories and 130 ivory retail outlets. Plus China is sponsoring ivory carving at Beijing University of Technology."

Bellim says, "Mr. Meng and Xueping are you aware of this data we have from ETIS?" He turns to Ted, "Is it safe to say that there is no correlation between decisions at CITES and the illegal trade?"

Ted answers, "Yes, if you mean that CITES' decisions are being ignored. The illegal trade in China has actually increased. While in Japan it was encouraging to note that the illicit trade in ivory progressively declined over the past five years."

Bellim asks, "Is there any correlation between the world wide economic crises and the increase in poaching and illicit trade?"

Ted laughs, "It is funny you should ask that question. It is of great personal interest to me. The decline of bank regulations and the creating of un-backed currencies are directly related to the increase in poaching and trade in wildlife; as the currencies are devalued, the price of animal parts has increased 500% in the past 18 months."

This banter goes on for a few more minutes and many delegates are very uneasy. The pokes and jabs are hitting home.

Finally, everyone receives what they are waiting for, Prince William! Like his father, his speech is passionate and thought provoking. He says, "The poaching crisis and illegal trade is, I believe, a form of 'economic sabotage' of diverse communities in the range states. Tackling illegal wildlife trade will bring about numerous benefits - as we have already heard today - in poverty alleviation, the reduction of organized crime and generally better security.

"I can offer no answers, since the expertise lies with you. Nonetheless, I have asked my Foundation to look at ways in which we might engage young people from all over the world to shape public opinion and to educate about animal parts that are traded illegally.

"Now is the time for young people who believe passionately in protecting these species to speak out before it's too late."

Suddenly, the 'Great I Am' is in my ear.

CHAPTER 43
All Hell Breaks Loose

The 'Great I Am' says, "A man is beginning to execute a decision to assassinate the Princes. The assassin is entering the building now and heading to the projection booth above your head."

I look up. The window to the booth is five meters above my head. I look up and down the wall behind me. There is no door to the projection booth.

He says, "The entrance to the projection booth is from another part of the building. You have to go down to the stage at once."

I go into slow-motion perception and race to the stairs. I take them three steps at a time and hurtle over and around corner posts of the railing. I pass the security guards so fast they cannot see me.

He continues, "The assassin is bribing the security guard to come into that part of the building."

I am only half way down to the main floor. I ask Him, "Can you slow him down?"

"I'm trying, but the security guards either have no compunction or they know the assassin is coming. He is now bribing the security guard at the elevator. He is stepping into the elevator."

I finally reach the main floor. The side aisle is crowded with people there is no way I can squeeze through them in time. I crash through the side door to the outer hallway. The security guard is startled but does not see me. I race down the hallway slinging open the lobby doorway, knocking over the security guard in the process.

The 'Great I Am' says, "He is now bribing the third security guard at the door of the projection booth. He is climbing the ten steps to the projection booth."

I reach the stage door. It is locked. I race back to the side door of the lower main floor. Pulling open the door, I meet a wall of people. I shove people aside until I reach the seats.

He updates me again, "He kills the two technicians in the booth and is opening the window. Now, he is opening his case and starting to assemble his weapon."

I jump up on the armrest of the aisle seat and race down the armrests from row to row occasionally stepping on an arm and causing that person considerable pain. Those people immediately blame the person standing in the aisle next to them, creating a wave of hostility behind me.

"He is attaching the scope!"

As I reach the front row, I leap into the air to clear the crowd of human heads ten people deep. I land on the stage with a loud thud, startling the groupies and the people on the stage. Fortunately, the people can only see a blur and are not sure what is happening.

"He is focusing the scope!"

I am halfway across the stage when I hear the first pop. I look and can see the flash of the muzzle.

Finally, I reach a position in front of Prince William; I stop and face the projection booth. Now, everyone can see me. There is general shock among the crowd. I see the projectile coming in only a meter away. Fortunately, I am in position.

Then I hear a second pop and see another flash. The second projectile is coming in high and to my left. This one is heading for Prince Charles. I have to wait until the first projectile boomerangs off my chest before I can move to the left and reach up to deflect the second projectile. My hand and arm stretch out as the projectile speeds in, with my open hand sliding in front of it at the last split second. It too boomerangs back toward the shooter.

Back in normal motion perception, the projectiles hit the shooter in the face doing considerable damage.

The bodyguards to the Princes are now moving into defensive positions.

Prince William brushes off the bodyguard yelling, "It's him! I'm safe now!"

I turn to face the Prince and start to go down on one knee.

He scoops me up and hugs me, saying, "You are real! They told us you were an illusion, a work of photo trickery. I owe you my life!"

Before I can respond, Prince Charles takes my hand and shakes it heartily, saying, "That was the most remarkable thing I ever saw. You must be a valuable asset in a cricket match."

I respond, "I'm quite ordinary at cricket if there are no bad guys." We all laugh a little.

The bodyguards are trying to encourage the Princes to move off the stage to safety. Prince Charles protests, "Really now, don't you think we are quite safe here with him? I for one want to hear what he has to say."

Prince William adds, "Here, Here!"

Bellim of CITES steps up and asks, "Are you really Hayah?"

"Yes, I am." The people in the audience become very quiet.

Bellim continues, "They told us that you were some illusion cooked up by CNN to disrupt this Convention."

"From your team presentation with Ted, I'm sure you know who is doing the concocting."

"Does that mean the warning letter isn't a Hoax?" Bellim asks.

"It is not only true, but it is a matter of life or death for most of the people here. It is now 28 days and counting."

"I will not blame you if you don't want to save these people, but can you see your way clear to reason with them?"

I respond quickly, "It will be my pleasure; I sincerely want them all to live. Please read the letter to them first?"

"OK," he says. "But I will do you one better, I will put a copy in everyone's hand." He motions to a woman in the wings, and in a flash, there is an army of young people handing out the warning letters in the audience. He reads the warning letter and then introduces me by recapping the CNN news report on all the endangered animals. He closes saying, "Now, I give you Hayah, the Man of Light, here in the flesh."

I start with a respectful bow to the audience. "The countdown on this letter is in progress. You now have 28 days to burn all your wildlife body parts that were taken by poaching. There are no loopholes and the intent of the letter is clear. I say this only because I want you to know that this is dead serious. That is the dark side."

I call on the Light within me, "The light side is simple. We want you to live. Read the banner over my head with me, 'Choose Life, Life of the Animals, Life of the Forests, Life of the Planet!' The 'Great I Am', who is within you, wants you to live. Start your fire as soon as possible. It will be the sweetest fire of your life, and the Spirit of every animal will live in your heart forever. The fire will bring a new light into your inner being and set you free. You will feel a great burden lifted from your shoulders, and you will become one with your planet once more.

"Know this; a wonderful choice is right there within you. The 'Great I Am' wants you to connect with Him, so you can be protected too, so you can become part of His Love, so you can find your real purpose in life. On my journey during the past two weeks, many are now connected to Him, having come through darkness similar to yours. Their lives are now full of joy and newness of life.

"The choice is yours right now. The old earth is fading away; its days are numbered. And a new curtain is opening on a new earth! Do you want to truly live?" I shout with great enthusiasm, "Choose life!"

There is a deep silence and stillness in the conference hall.

To my surprise, Prince William walks up and puts his hand on my shoulder. I turn to face him. He asks, "Can you show me and Kate how to connect? We are both sensing His presence within us."

"Absolutely, let's work on it this afternoon. Right now please step back before all hell breaks loose." I motion to his bodyguard.

With the silence and stillness still holding in the hall, three police officers burst in on the stage. They are heading straight for me. I go immediately into slow-motion perception. They start screaming at me in turn and in unison, "You are responsible for the murder of three people – in the projection boot! And you murdered three security guards – in the other building! Down on your knees! Put your hands behind your back! You're under arrest!"

I fall on my knees and put my hands behind my back. The police start beating me with their batons. Every one of their blows boomerangs back on them. The harder they club me the harder they club themselves. They start cursing and accusing each other of missing me and hit them instead.

The audience and the people on stage begin to chuckle at the antics on stage.

Then, while two of the police officers continue to beat me, and therefore their own bodies, one of the police officer tries to put a nylon cuff band on my wrists, only to end up with it on himself.

Everyone watching this is beginning to laugh. It is like watching a version of the "Three Stooges" vaudeville act.

The second police officer tries to put on a cuff band, while the third one continues to beat me. He just doesn't get it; why every blow boomerangs back on his head or shoulders. The second police officer, of course, ends up in his own cuff band with his hands behind his back.

Everyone is now in hysterics.

The third police officer tries to put a cuff band on my wrists and appears to be successful. Feeling victorious, he puts one around my ankles and appears to be successful. Seconds later the one around my wrists appears on his wrists, and the one around my ankles appears around his ankles. He is now hopping about the stage cursing profusely and bumping into the other police officers.

Everyone watching is experiencing sidesplitting laughter.

I stand up coming back to normal motion perception and wave to the audience. I motion for the stagehand to close the curtain. The curtain closes.

Bellim herds the police officers together in a tight group. He then begins to tell them what really happened,

with many additions from the others on stage. He then
turns to me and asks, "Can I cut them loose now?"

I listen to a message from Him and then respond,
"No, He is telling me that they are part of the conspiracy to
assassinate the Princes. They are not even assigned to this
district right now. Call National Police Chief Priewpan
Damapong and turn them in. You may want to leg cuff the
other two." The three Police officers are in a state of shock.

The Princes' bodyguards drag the three police
officers off stage.

Bellim and Ted approach me and ask if they can be
part of the group this afternoon. I agree as long as it is OK
with the Royals.

Prince Charles steps forward to ask, "May I be part
of the group, questioning? And how important is it that we
all do this together, Hayah?"

"Very important, Your Highness. To Him you are
all equals."

He responds warmly, "Rightly so, rightly so! I
would have it no other way."

I add, "Your Highness, Can I meet with you in
private before we meet with the group? Is that agreeable to
you?"

He responds, "I look forward to it."

That afternoon, we all meet in a secure place.
Prince Charles and I meet first, and I explain about learning
to forgive himself, because that is the only judgment he will
face. At once, he rejoices, but then the complexity of the
process sets in. We are having a very detailed discussion,
which turns out to be very helpful. In closing he asks,
"How do you know so much about me?"

I respond, "I don't, but He does."

The Prince says, "Of course. But this will take a little bit of reflection."

"So it does for us all, Your Highness. Only soon, He will be telling you directly."

With surprise and delight, he says, "Really!?"

In the group gathering, I go through the process with everyone. To my surprise and delight, Charles is the first to connect, and he is absolutely radiant. Bellim is next and the light dances around his head and shoulders. Kate and William connect within seconds of each other, first one ball of light, then another ball of light and finally the two spheres become one large ball of light. Ted has the hardest time calculating a way out of his mathematical head, but when he connects, it is like fireworks going off within him. He blurts out to the group, "He takes all the mystery out of the numbers and now everything makes sense!"

CHAPTER 44
His ABC's of Flying

I have seen corruption before, but nothing on the same scale as Thailand. I am really looking forward to my trip to Israel and Tel Aviv's Ben Gurion International Airport. The 'Great I Am' promised me a few days of R&R before heading home. At this point, that sounds very appealing.

My flight is not until 10:00, so I have a very easy morning. I checkout early and head to the Renaissance Bangkok Ratchaprasong for what is supposed to be the best breakfast buffet in Bangkok. On the way to the restaurant, He changes me back into Hoss. This time I am very grateful, because that means there is no immediate danger lurking right around the corner.

At the restaurant, to my surprise, I meet a group of old friends from Unity Village, Missouri. They are on a group tour of the Far East and Holy Land. They are talking about Beijing, China, where their tour began and Hong Kong where they were before coming to Bangkok. Now they are flying to Tel Aviv, Israel. As it turns out, we are on the same flight.

For the most part, the folks from Unity are connected to the 'Great I Am' within them. I mention this only because most religious people see God and Heaven as being outside themselves, up there, in another metaphysical dimension, a reality beyond what was perceptible to the senses. With this group of friends, we are spiritually connected in the same personal way with the 'Great I Am' within us, and we are part of the same spiritual family.

Contentment is the only difficulty this group has. They
have been connecting for so long, that they are not listening
to Him the way they need to be listening.

One of the discussions they are having about Beijing
is the ivory and tiger trade. From what I gather, many of
them encounter sales people trying to unload the illegal
wildlife at very cheap prices. The hard sell of the merchants
was very aggressive. However, before I can ask if anyone
mistakenly bought any of the wildlife, my friends start
talking about Him being in their ear with the warning.

After a while, the conversation shifts "to this guy
Hayah," "the Man of Light." He was all over the news in
Hong Kong. Some of the things he was doing were so
spectacular that to the average person those things were
beyond their comprehension. My friends could clearly see
His hand in everything that was happening. Then on the
news last night, he saves the Crown Prince in an
assassination attempt. And turns right around and puts the
CITES Wildlife Conference back on track with a global
warning letter. He calls everyone to Choose Life. Through
all of this, I am just listening and taking it all in.

Then out of the clear blue, one of my friends,
Mindy, turns to me and asks, "Hoss, do you think that the
'Great I Am' is choosing the animals as the first step toward
a new world order?"

I respond innocently, "It sure looks that way."
Then I add, "It is no secret that the animals are more
connected than most humans. Our species keeps avoiding
the awakening. Maybe this will wake up the human race."

Frank, the coordinator of the group, interrupts to
announce that the bus is here to take them to the airport.
He then invites me to join them, which I graciously accept.

There is no better way to start a day than with an outstanding breakfast and fantastic friends.

The flight leaves Bangkok on time. It is a nonstop eleven-hour flight to Tel Aviv. For the first five hours of the flight, the Unity group plays musical seats. We enjoy each other's company and the healthy diversity in our points of view. The "new world" theme seems to be one of the most popular topics. My main theme is to get them to renew their listening practices, knowing that if they will do this, then He will be able to answer all their questions about their connection. If I use the word meditation once during these discussions, I use it a hundred times. After five hours of musical seats, I finally insist that I must take the time to meditate. One by one, the Unity group starts to meditate. In this non-stressful environment, my meditation is deeply serene, joyful and like taking a bath in the Love of the 'Great I Am'. As the other members of the Unity group settle down their chattering minds and egos and begin to listen, there is a heightened awareness within each one. There is now a flow of Energy, Light and Love between us all flowing through the 'Great I Am' to each other. Now they all know "the new world" is here and now.

Coming out of my meditation, I feel a renewed sense of oneness not only with Him, but also with all my Unity friends. I lean back and fall into a deep sleep, connected, joyful and enthusiastic.

The next thing I know, He is urgently calling me to wake up. It is three hours later. He starts to fill me in on what is going on, after reminding me that He has no connection to mechanical, electronic or computer devices and relies entirely on the people who run them. "According to the captain and copilot there is something wrong with the jet engines. They are becoming sluggish. The fuel is not igniting properly. They estimate that we will lose complete power in ten minutes and there is no safe place to land between here and Tel Aviv.

"I remember a ground attendant putting in a fuel additive, which was normal. He was doing what he was instructed to do. But there was a chain of contacts between his boss, which I traced back to Daxin, and his ivory carving factory. That is only one chain. There are a dozen more leading back to the Dragon Lady. I am convinced that the additive is contaminating the fuel with the intention to crash this plane and kill you and everyone on board."

I am stunned, "What am I supposed to do? I'm not Superman!" A feeling of hopelessness creeps over me.

"You're going to learn how easy it is to fly a plane," He says casually. "This is what is about to happen. In a moment, the captain will alert the cabin crew, and they are going to prepare passengers for a crash landing. Before that happens, stand up and walk through the galley, so Hayah can take control of the situation. I will guide you through every step along the way."

I have an image of this El Al Israel Airlines, flight 82, a Boeing 767-300, crashing in a country hostile to Israel. I picture its pieces and bodies scattered over several kilometers. There will not be one living survivor.

He urgently says, "Hoss snap out of it. Put those thoughts out of your head. Stand up and go!

I stand up and head through the galley. The head flight attendant is on the phone with the captain. As I step into the starboard isle, I become Hayah. I turn back to look at the head flight attendant. She looks up and sees me. All the fear in her face drains away and she smiles and nods to me. She shouts into the phone, "Captain, Captain, the Man of Light is on the plane! Maybe he can help us!" She motions for me to come over to her. She explains the situation and asks, "Can you help us!"

Answering as He directs me, "Tell the captain not to panic, we will take over the engines and give him power." Looking at the head flight attendant, "I'll keep you informed. Now tell all the passengers to buckle their seatbelts. Those that will not be helping, will fall asleep."

The head flight attendant asks the captain, "Do you hear that?" She listens and then says to me, "Do it!"

While the head flight attendant makes her announcement, I motion for the attention of all the Unity passengers. I then ask the rest of the passengers, "Is there anyone else on board who is connected to the 'Great I Am' within you? Please raise your hand."

Only seven more hands go up. Three of the women are recently connecting through Uddatla's groups. The other four are from Shaik T's groups. Everyone else in the cabin falls asleep, except the flight attendants.

I turn to the head flight attendant, "Have your people check everyone's seatbelt and look for any un-stowed objects."

I then address all of His people in the starboard seats, "Connect with the 'Great I Am' and focus on the rotors in the starboard engine. Through the 'Great I Am' picture the rotors moving faster. Let Him help you. I repeat this message in both the forward and aft cabins.

I check first and business class; there is no one awake.

I address all of His people in the port seats, "Do the same as the other side, only focus on the rotors in the port engine and picture them moving faster and faster. He will help you. I repeat this in both cabins.

Now, I address all of His people in the center section, "Connect with the 'Great I Am' within you. He is going to help you see the landing strip in Tel Aviv. Focus on that picture and see us landing on that tarmac. Picture us pulling up to the gate. Picture everyone here meeting his or her loved ones and friends. Let no other thoughts enter you mind."

All this is accomplished, but the plane is still losing power. The captain tells the head flight attendant that the situation is still critical. I signal that I have the message. I look about the cabins and spot Jimmy, one of the people from Unity, texting on his cell phone.

The plane is losing altitude rapidly.

I run over to him, "Jimmy, you are not connected. You are neither there nor here. You are gumming up the works." I put my hand on his shoulder and he instantly falls asleep.

The plane continues to plummet, faster and faster. He starts to tell me about a woman in the first row of the forward cabin, middle section and middle seat. I race to that location. The woman has her eyes closed and is talking a mile a minute. I ask her, "Hanna what are you doing?"

She replies, "I'm doing Yoga-Meditation. I'm healing this situation."

The 'Great I Am' says to me, "What she's doing is neither Yoga nor Meditation. She's healing nothing. In fact she is blocking most of our positive energy."

I put my hand on her shoulder, and she falls to sleep immediately.

I struggle against the downward dive of the airplane. The flight attendants are already in the crash position. I brace myself by holding onto the overheads and focus on both the port and starboard engines at the same time. Summoning all the energy within me, He pours it into both engines. The breathing of all His people is in unison now. The decent slows and then...

The plane levels off and starts to climb.

The others can now handle it. I step back into my coordinating role.

We are soon at altitude again and resuming our flight plan. The copilot calls in and cancels the 'mayday' call. He then tries to explain what was happening, but to no avail. "Captain, what do I tell them?"

The captain adjusts his mike, "I don't know. We shut off the fuel lines and the engines are operating at 110%. We are at our maximum speed of 898 kilometers per hour and all other systems are working perfectly. If you understand why any of that should be happening, tell them."

The co-pilot opens the line to ground control, "Look, we have the Man of Light on board and he is powering the plane with the help of some of the passengers." He listens. "No, I'm not kidding. In fact our current speed is 907 kilometers per hour." The copilot and the captain look at each other. "Looks like you'll be seeing us early. Need to go. We've another problem to deal with."

The captain reads the air speed at 913, "That's the fastest one of these babies has ever done -- 915, a new record -- 917, maybe we should ask this guy to slow it down before he rips off both wings and rockets us into outer space." He opens a line to the head flight attendant, "Can you ask your guy to slow it down a little? We are already fracturing the speed record."

I signal the head flight attendant that I have the message. "Listen up port and starboard people. You are doing a great job, but we need to slow down a little. Don't stop just slowdown." The speed tops off at 927 and then starts to taper off slowly. When it reaches 913, I say, "That's good; hold it there." I walk over to the head flight attendant. "Ask the captain if that's OK."

She smiles and asks the captain, "He says to hold this speed for an hour and then cut it back to 851 kilometers per hour. As we approach for landing, you can decrease the speed little by little. On the final approach, we should be doing 220 kilometers per hour. Can you do that?"

"Yes, that should be possible. I know you will want reverse engines which might be difficult, so be prepared to break hard."

I spend the next hour and a half coaching His people and encouraging them. Twenty minutes before landing, I explain about the reverse engines. "You want to see the engines stop and on the next breath you want to see them running in reverse full speed. Hold that until I tell you to stop again." I then explain, as per His instructions, how to create a slow speed in the engines to move the plane from the landing strip to the gate.

The landing and taxi to the gate go without a hitch. We are at the gate 35 minutes early. As everyone starts to wake up, I cross through the galley, become Hoss once more without being seen and sit in my seat.

The captain comes out and wants to meet the Man of Light. The head flight attendant looks for Hayah, but he is gone. All His connected people blend in with everyone else, and we all leave knowing fully, that a plane can fly without fuel, but we say nothing.

CHAPTER 45
His Chosen People

After exiting the aircraft at 07:00, I come together with my Unity friends as they assemble outside the gate. (It may seem odd here, but none of my Unity friends needs to talk about their experience on the flight. The fact is we are all connected to the 'Great I Am' and are sharing it constantly, now that we are all listening.) We all avoid the TV cameras, reporters and start walking to baggage claim and customs.

They offer to include me in their tour, but I decline. Guided tours don't interest me. I prefer to explore on my own. However, we do make plans to meet for breakfast before they fly home. We are separated during customs, due to so many checkpoints. I grab my backpack and head out into the airport to find ground transportation.

As I pass a TV monitor, I see a live broadcast interview with the captain, copilot and flight attendants of flight 82. I stop to listen. Aside from their total lack of understanding as to how this is physically possible, they are pretty accurate in the blow-by-blow description of the event. The only passenger, who has any remembrance of the crisis, is Hanna, and she is very happy to share her experience with the reporter, saying, "I healed the engines with my Yoga/Meditation." I laugh, and He laughs.

I turn and head for the ground transportation. After a few steps, I feel a small hand slip into mine and hear, "Hi, old man."

I look down and see Phyllis' face smiling up at me. I stop, still holding her hand, and I'm speechless.

She says, "He told me your secret, Hoss Proxetter, and that you would be on flight 82. Through Him, I heard

everything that happened on the plane. The world doesn't
have a clue as to what we can do with Him helping us."
She gives me a big hug, backpack and all.

After a moment, I find my voice, "I thought you
were only interested in younger men."

"A woman can change her mind. Besides, you look
pretty good for a Methuselah!" She giggles, and adds more
seriously, "After talking to Him, I'm ready to try one of
those meaningful Love relationships you talked about."

I am very excited by this prospect, but hesitate.
"Only now, is He finally filling me in on all this. He says
we should try a 'courtship'. I have no idea what that means
by modern standards. But, being an incurable romantic, I
see the concept as a wonderful way for two people to come
together."

She grins, "So let the courtship begin!"

I take her hand again and ask, "Bus or Train?

"Train," she responds quickly. "They're more
romantic."

Hand in hand, we head for the train.

On the train, I learn that Phyllis is also staying at
the Lutheran Guest House on St. Marks Road in the Old
City. I comment, "I suppose that's no coincidence either."

"Nope, He is very helpful."

Having a sudden realization, I add, "Do you realize
that that means there can never be any secrets between us?"

"What a refreshing thought for a change," she
reflects on the idea. "There will be no more mystery, but
no more lies. There'll be no more surprises, but no more
deception. There'll be no more anticipation, but no more
disappointments."

I share my reflections, "You will know if I love you

and how much. I will know if you love me and how much."

We sit in silence, lulled by the click of the train on the tracks, and connect to Him. We are both bathing in His Love. We each reach out and find the others hand. This is so different from my solo experience with Him. The Light is brighter. The energy is swirling and more powerful. His presence is more whole. I am more whole. Through Him, I begin to feel what she feels. Our feelings are totally in sync. We both feel whole.

Slowly, I move her hand to my lips and kiss it.

She moves my hand to her lips and kisses it.

We sit looking into each other's eyes without a word; yet reading each other's thoughts for the rest of the train ride.

From Malha Railway Station we take a taxi to the Guest House and check into separate rooms, with a shared bath. She confesses that this arrangement is her doing. I suggest we meet in the lobby in 30 minutes, giving me time to shower and freshen up. We can then start exploring the Old City together, with Him as our guide. She says, "It's a date."

Hand in hand, Phyllis and I begin to tour the Old City, with the 'Great I Am' as our guide. He wants us to walk the 4,018 meters around the wall of the city to see a bird's eye view of the city and develop a feeling for its multi ethnical and multi-religious character. The experience is fantastic as He is constantly pointing out details of the new city sprawl on our left and the Old City on our right. He describes each quarter with pride and affection. At first, we pass around the Christian Quarter containing the Church of the Holy Sepulcher. He cautions us to embrace the spirit of what they are trying to represent, because they are not the actual historic sites. Everything here was built on ruins that go back to 300 CE or later. Here, He goes off on a tangent about the early church departing from the simple message of His Son in order to maintain control over the people. He concludes with a deep sigh, saying, "And like all religions they let their minds and egos lead them further and further away from Me. I don't mind the iconic images so much, but the people reach out to touch them; when I am right here within them." We can both feel His sadness.

Next, we pass around the Muslim Quarter, and His spirits lift as He talks about how Muslims, Jews and Christians lived together in this Quarter until 1929. Although racial hatred was always right under the surface, they gave Him great joy, because they were proving that living together was possible. Only 60 Jewish families remain in the Quarter. He then starts talking about the Via Dolorosa (Way to the Cross) reminiscing over Joshua's sacrifice to free us from religious rules. He concludes, "Because of your help Hoss, people are beginning to see His true message. They are beginning to connect like Phyllis here." Phyllis looks up at me and squeezes my hand and smiles.

Soon, we are passing the site of the old temple (now the Temple Mount) and where the Mosque, Dome of the Rock was built over the Temple Mount and the Stone of the Anointing. I initially think that His next comment is another digression. He says, "This temple was a grave misinterpretation of what I said to David. I was perfectly happy with the tent and worship enclosure. It was portable and served their worship needs in the desert and here in Israel. David was choosing to stray from Me so often; I said to him, 'I want to be your Shekhinah!' My meaning was that I wanted to be the 'Divine Presence' within **him**, the 'Great I Am' within **him**, as I am to Abraham and Moses, just as I am present in every natural thing of creation. Instead, he interpreted what I said to mean that I wanted a permanent place to live, a house. But as you know, I don't live in a house, any house. He then told this to his son, Solomon, who first built this temple and paved the way for every religious structure ever since. It is such a waste of money and craftsman ship, to build and maintain. You are my temple. I am within you in a drain pipe, a sky scraper or a rocket to the moon." This is definitely not a digression. It is a symbol of humankind's inability to connect with the 'Great I Am' within.

Phyllis says, "And I hear they are planning on building a third Temple!"

Next, we pass around the Jewish Quarter. From where we are standing the Western Wall, better known as the Wailing Wall, is clearly the most popular attraction for residents as well as tourists. Apart from the archeological digs, there are only a few buildings resembling the old architecture, but they are obviously built using twentieth century construction techniques. Most of the buildings blend in, but are visibly modern. Both of us are noticing that He is strangely silent because these are His chosen people. He responds immediately, "Yes, if ever I had a love affair with any ethnic group; it was with these people, from Abraham to this day. But the pain and heartache they cause Me cannot be measured. During one of many destructions, I say to Jeremiah, 'What fools My people are! They have no idea who I am. They are a company of half-wits, dopes and donkey all! Experts at evil but klutzes at good' (4:22). Yet I tell you here and now, if you search these streets and can find one soul who will connect with Me, I will lead him or her to forgiveness. Thus, is My Love for them."

In silence, we start to pass around the Armenian Quarter. We can easily make out the Monastery of St. James also known as the Armenian Patriarchate of Jerusalem. He says for Phyllis' benefit, "Bartholomew, one of Joshua's apostles, is Hoss' spiritual guide, and he was the apostle who brought Christianity to the Armenian people. Originally, because of Bartholomew, the Armenian people connected to Me with their hearts and not their minds. This changed the whole tone of their early church, unlike the Latin Church, which can never completely accept them. If you are to find any allies for our work, they will be in this Quarter."

Now, we find ourselves back where we started.

During lunch, Phyllis and I start to make plans for what else we want to see in the Old City. When we finish eating, He puts our plans on hold and tells us that He wants us to walk toward Abu Dis. He wants to see the Israeli security barrier through our eyes. Following His directions, we head for the Lions Gate. From there we make a right and left turn, end up on al Shaykh, going over the Mount of Olives. On the way, He invites us to sit with Him in the Garden of Gethsemane.

Here, He is talking to each of us separately. With me, He is outlining His plan for awakening the people. I listen and take it all in. He is hoping to awaken as many people as possible. After the plague and death of all those who do not burn their illegal animal parts, we will have the attention of the people. All those who are now connected with Him are part of the plan. He wants me to return to this spot ten days after the plague. He says, "Make no mistake! The one you call the Dragon Lady will do everything in her power to prevent us from awakening 1%

of the people, the critical number, which will tilt the scale in our favor. You must remember always, that hatred only feeds her power, so don't see her as the enemy. She is after all the Divine Mother, and I want her to return. Your Love and the Love of 1% of the people will bring her back to Me. After all, she is the one who brought Love to Me and produced My Son in the beginning."

As we continue on our way toward Wadi Qadum, Phyllis ponders what He is telling her. Finally, she says, "It looks like we are in this together. It is a lot to take in. But, He says that you can fill me in about the Dragon Lady/Divine Mother person."

"Yes, I can, but that is a very long story. I'll tell you the first chance we have."

We continue to walk hand in hand and talk about us. All these things are bringing us closer together. We each feel His powerful Love. We are both struggling to experience how our feelings fit into that Love.

We stop and look into each other's eyes. We are irresistibly drawn toward each other. I take her in my arms. Our eyes draw us closer, studying every detail of the other's face and mouth. Our lips finally meet. Our bodies press together. Our hearts beat as one. We both feel His Love is part of this. This is more than desire. It is more than passion. It is unity and oneness.

Reluctantly and slowly, we come back to our mission and continue walking in silence, with our arms entwining around each other's waist.

Suddenly, we come upon the security barrier. We both stop and stand there in silence; our mouths open; our eyes tight knit; our foreheads wrinkle. A feeling of shock and horror comes over both of us. He asks, "Can you give it a name?"

We both say at the same time, "AN ABOMINATION!"

He says, "This has to be the most evil thing My People have ever done. It is a monument to their HATRED! It has to go!"

We return to the Old City, via the Herodian road from Shiloah pool to the Western Wall; a long underground tunnel that starts outside the wall and 485 meters below the Temple Mount. As we come up out of the tunnel, He changes me into Hayah and takes over my body. There is a crowd of people at the Wailing Wall. He opens my arms and says in a booming dynamic voice,

> "Listen, My people of Israel.
> Rejoice, My children of Zion.
> I am the 'Great I Am' within,
>   and not a God far off? (Jer. 23:23)
> Pray not to a wall of stones,
>   for you are My dwelling place,
>   you are My Temple.
> Turn now to Me! The time is now!
> A new curtain opens for all.

He gestures to the wall and every paper old and new bursts into flame. All eyes and cell phones turn to the wall. I circle around Phyllis and turn back into Hoss holding her hand and looking at the wall. When the people turn back to Hayah, he is gone.

A dark cloud moves in over us. The temperature drops and the air is ice cold. I remember this feeling and tell Phyllis to go into His Love immediately. I do the same.

Our hands are still entwined. His Light and Love is strong within us.

The Dragon Lady comes roaring into our skulls, like a screeching, swirling black hole, with a fiery rim. She blocks the portals of our eyes. An experience, which kindled terror in me the first time she appeared. She screams in a defining shrill tone, "You are mine! You will not succeed! I shall squash your puny existence like a rotten tomato! You have no power over me!"

I breathe through my body and into Phyllis' hand; while I begin to build the Love within me. I say calmly, "Phyllis meet our Divine Mother, the source of all our Love. Divine Mother meet Phyllis. As for our power, Mother, all we have is the Love that comes from you. Here, take as much as you want."

I raise my hands in Love. Phyllis trembles. I want us to pour out all our Love into Her black whirlpool. She disappears in an instant as Her fires sputter; on my next breath, Love fills me again.

Phyllis is shaken. She looks away, "Is that inside you?"

"No, but our rational mind and ego are her portals to us. And she will do her damndest to stop us."